"I WANT MY HUSBAND BACK!"

Mrs. Vail got her bag and opened it and took out an envelope. "He didn't come home Sunday night, and yesterday this came in the mail."

It was an ordinary off-white envelope. The flap had been cut clean with a knife or opener, no jagged edges. I handed it to Wolfe, and he removed the contents, a folded sheet of cheap bond paper, the kind you get in scratch pads. He held it to his left, so I could read it too. This is what it said:

> We have got your Jimmy safe and sound. We haven't hurt him any and you can have him back all in one piece for $500,000 if you play it right and keep it strictly between you and us. We mean strictly. If you try any tricks, you'll never see him again.

Bantam Books by Rex Stout
Ask your bookseller for the books you have missed

TOO MANY WOMEN
AND BE A VILLAIN
THE SECOND CONFESSION
CURTAINS FOR THREE
IN THE BEST FAMILIES
THREE DOORS TO DEATH
MURDER BY THE BOOK
PRISONER'S BASE
THREE MEN OUT
MIGHT AS WELL BE DEAD
THREE WITNESSES
THREE FOR THE CHAIR
AND FOUR TO GO
CHAMPAGNE FOR ONE
PLOT IT YOURSELF
TOO MANY CLIENTS
THE FINAL DEDUCTION
GAMBIT
A RIGHT TO DIE
TRIO FOR BLUNT INSTRUMENTS
DEATH OF A DOXY
THE FATHER HUNT
DEATH OF A DUDE
FER-DE-LANCE
THE RED BOX

The Final Deduction

by Rex Stout

A Nero Wolfe Mystery

BANTAM BOOKS
TORONTO • NEW YORK • LONDON • SYDNEY • AUCKLAND

*This low-priced Bantam Book
has been completely reset in a type face
designed for easy reading, and was printed
from new plates. It contains the complete
text of the original hard-cover edition.*
NOT ONE WORD HAS BEEN OMITTED

THE FINAL DEDUCTION
*A Bantam Book / published by arrangement with
The Viking Press, Inc.*

*PRINTING HISTORY
Viking edition published October 1961
Dollar Mystery Guild edition published February 1962
Bantam edition published March 1963
2nd printing . . . . . . .August 1963 3rd printing . . . .September 1968
4th printing . . . .September 1969
New Bantam edition published October 1970
2nd printing . . . . . .October 1974 3rd printing . . . . .May 1981
4th printing . . . .November 1985*

ISBN 978-0-553-76310-2

Published simultaneously in the United States and Canada

Bantam Books are published by Bantam Books, Inc. Its trademark, consisting of the words "Bantam Books" and the portrayal of a rooster, is Registered in U.S. Patent and Trademark Office and in other countries. Marca Registrada. Bantam Books, New York, New York.

147028622

1

"Your name, please?"

I asked her only as a matter of form. Having seen her picture in newspapers and magazines at least a dozen times, and having seen her in person at the Flamingo and other spots around town, I had of course recognized her through the one-way glass in the door as I went down the hall to answer the doorbell, though she wasn't prinked up for show. There was nothing dowdy about her brown tailored suit or fur stole or the hundred-dollar pancake on her head, but her round white face, too white there in daylight, which could be quite passable in a restaurant or theater lobby, could have stood some attention. It was actually flabby, and the rims of her eyes were red and swollen. She spoke.

"I don't think . . ." She let it hang a moment, then said, "But you're Archie Goodwin."

I nodded. "And you're Althea Vail. Since you have no appointment, I'll have to tell Mr. Wolfe what you want to see him about."

"I'd rather tell him myself. It's very confidential and very urgent."

I didn't insist. Getting around as I do, and hearing a lot of this and that, both true and false, I had a guess on what was probably biting her, and if that was it I would enjoy watching Wolfe's face as she spilled it, and hearing him turn her down. So I admitted her. The usual routine with a stranger who has no appointment is to leave him or her on the stoop while I go and tell Wolfe, but I can make exceptions, and it was a raw windy day for late April, so I took her to the front room, the first door on your left when you are inside, returned to the hall, and went to the second door on the left, to the office.

Wolfe was on his feet over by the big globe, glaring at

a spot on it. When I had gone to answer the bell he had been glaring at Cuba, but he had shifted to Laos.

"A woman," I said.

He stuck with Laos. "No," he said.

"Probably," I conceded. "But she says it's urgent and confidential, and she could pay a six-figure fee without batting an eye. Her name is Althea Vail. Mrs. Jimmy Vail. You read newspapers thoroughly, so you must know that even the *Times* calls him Jimmy. Her eyes are red, presumably from crying, but she is now under control. I don't think she'll blubber."

"No!"

"I didn't leave her on the stoop because of the weather. She's in the front room. I have heard talk of her, and I understand that she is prompt pay."

He turned. "Confound it," he growled. He took in a bushel of air through his nose, let it out through his mouth, and moved. Behind his desk he stood, a living mountain, beside his oversized chair. He seldom rises to receive a caller, woman or man, but since he was already on his feet it would take no energy to be polite, so why not? I went and opened the connecting door to the front room, told Mrs. Vail to come, presented her, and convoyed her to the red leather chair near the end of Wolfe's desk. Sitting, she gave the stole a backward toss, and it would have slid to the floor if I hadn't caught it. Wolfe had lowered his 285 pounds into his chair and was scowling at her, his normal attitude to anyone, especially a woman, who had the gall to come uninvited to the old brownstone on West 35th Street, his house, expecting him to go to work.

Althea Vail put her brown leather bag on the stand at her elbow. "First," she said, "I'd better tell you how I got here."

"Not material," Wolfe muttered.

"Yes it is," she declared. It came out hoarse, and she cleared her throat. "You'll see why. But first of all it has to be understood that what I'm going to tell you is absolutely in confidence. I know about you, I know your reputation, or I wouldn't be here, but it has to be definite that this is in *complete confidence*. Of course I'm going to give you a check as a retainer, and perhaps I should do that before . . ." She reached to the stand for her bag. "Ten thousand dollars?"

Wolfe grunted. "If you know about me, madam, you should know that that's fatuous. If you want to hire me to do a job, what is it? If I take it, a retainer may or may not be required. As for confidence, nothing that you tell me will be revealed unless it involves a crime which I am obliged, as a citizen and a licensed private detective, to report to authority. I speak also for Mr. Goodwin, who is in my employ and who—"

"It does involve a crime. Kidnaping is a crime."

"It is indeed."

"But it must *not* be reported to authority."

My brows were up. Seated at my desk, my chair swiveled to face her, I crossed off the guess I had made. Apparently I wouldn't get to watch Wolfe's face while a woman asked him to tail her husband, or to hear him turn her down. He was speaking.

"Certainly kidnaping is unique. The obligation not to withhold knowledge of a major crime must sometimes bow to other considerations, for instance saving a life. Is that your concern?"

"Yes."

"Then you may trust our discretion. We make no firm commitment, but we are not fools. I suppose you have been warned to tell no one of your predicament?"

"Yes."

"Then I was wrong. How you got here is material. How did you?"

"I phoned a friend of mine, Helen Blount, who lives in an apartment on Seventy-fifth Street, and arranged it with her. The main entrance to the apartment house is on Seventy-fifth Street, but the service entrance is on Seventy-fourth Street. I phoned her at half past ten. I told my chauffeur to have my car out front at half past eleven. At half past eleven I went out and got in my car and was driven to my friend's address. I didn't look behind to see if I was being followed because I was afraid the chauffeur would notice. I got out and went into the apartment house—the men there know me—and I went to the basement and through to the service entrance on Seventy-fourth Street, and Helen Blount was there in her car, and

I got in, and she drove me here. So I don't think there's the slightest chance that they know I'm seeing Nero Wolfe. Do you?"

Wolfe turned to me. "Archie?"

I nodded. "Good enough. Hundred to one. But if someone's waiting in Seventy-fifth Street to see her home and she never shows, he'll wonder. It would be a good idea to go back before too long and enter on Seventy-fourth and leave on Seventy-fifth. I would advise it."

Her red-rimmed eyes were at me. "Of course. What would be too long?"

"That depends on how patient and careful he is, and I don't know him." I glanced at my wrist. "It's twenty-five after twelve. You got there a little more than half an hour ago. You could reasonably be expected to stay with your friend quite a while, hours maybe. But if he knows you well enough to know that your friend Helen Blount lives there he might call her number and ask for you and be told that you're not there and you haven't been there. I have never known a kidnaper personally, but from what I've read and heard I've got the impression they're very sensitive."

She shook her head. "He won't be told that. Helen told her maid what to say. If anyone asks for me, or her either, he'll be told that we're busy and can't come to the phone."

"Good for you. But there's Helen Blount. She knows you came to see Nero Wolfe."

"She doesn't know what for. That's all right, I can trust her. I *know* I can." Her eyes went back to Wolfe. "So that's how I got here. When I leave I have to go to my bank, and then I'll go back to Seventy-fourth Street." It was coming out hoarse again, and she cleared her throat and coughed. "It's my husband," she said. She got her bag and opened it and took out an envelope. "He didn't come home Sunday night, and yesterday this came in the mail."

Her chair was too far away for her to hand it to Wolfe without getting up, and of course he wouldn't, so I did. It was an ordinary off-white envelope with a typewritten address to Mrs. Jimmy Vail, 994 Fifth Avenue, New York City, no zone number, and was postmarked BRYANT STA

APR 23, 1961 11:30 P.M. Sunday, day before yesterday. The flap had been cut clean with a knife or opener, no jagged edges. I handed it to Wolfe, and after a glance at the address and postmark he removed the contents, a folded sheet of cheap bond paper, also off-white, five by eight unfolded, the kind you get in scratch pads. He held it to his left, so I could read it too. We no longer have it, but from some shots I took of it the next day I can have it reproduced for you to look at. It may tell you what it told Wolfe about the person who typed it. Here it is:

> We have got your Jimmy safe and sound. We haven't hurt him any and you can have him back all in one piece for $500,000 if you play it right and keep it strictly between you and us. We mean strictly. If you try any tricks you'll never see him again. You'll get a phone call from Mr. Knapp and don't miss it.

Wolfe dropped it on the desk pad and turned to Althea Vail. "I can't forgo," he said, "an obvious comment. Surely this is humbug. Kidnaping is a desperate and dangerous operation. It's hard to believe that a man committed to it, a man who has incurred its mortal risks, could be in a mood to make a pun—that in choosing an alias to use on the phone, for himself in his role as kidnaper, he would select 'Knapp.' It must be flummery. If not, if this thing is straightforward"—he tapped the paper with a finger—"the man who wrote it is most extraordinary. Is your husband a practical joker?"

"No." Her chin had jerked up. "Are you saying it's a joke?"

"I suggested the possibility, but I also suggested an alternative, that you have a remarkable man to deal with. Have you heard from Mr. Knapp?"

"Yes. He phoned yesterday afternoon, my listed number. I had told my secretary that I expected the call, and she listened on an extension. I thought she might as well because she opens my mail and she had read that thing."

"What did he say?"

"He told me what to do. I'm not going to tell you. I'm going to do exactly what he said. I don't need you for that. What I need you for, I want my husband back.

Alive. I know they may have killed him already, I know that, but—" Her chin had started to work, and she pressed her lips together to stop it. She went on, "If they have, then I'll want to find them if the police and the FBI don't. But on the phone yesterday that man said he was all right, and I believe him. I *must* believe him!"

She was on the edge of the chair. "But don't kidnapers often kill after they get the money? So they can't be traced or recognized? Don't they?"

"That has happened."

"Yes. That's what I need you for. Doing what he said, getting the money to them, I'll do that myself, there's nothing you can do about that. I've told my banker I'm coming to get the money this afternoon, and I'll do—"

"Half a million dollars?"

"Yes. And I'll do exactly what that man said, but that's all I can do, and I want him back. I want to be sure I'll get him back. That's what I need you for."

Wolfe grunted. "Madam. You can't possibly mean that. You are not a nincompoop. How could I conceivably proceed? The only contact with that punster or an accomplice will be your delivery of the money, and you refuse to tell me anything about it. Pfui. You can't possibly mean it."

"But I do. I do! That's why I came to *you!* Is there anything you can't do? Aren't you a genius? How did you get your reputation?" She took a checkfold from her bag and slipped a pen from a loop. "Will ten thousand do for a retainer?"

She had a touch of genius herself, or it was her lucky day, asking him if there was anything he couldn't do and waving a check at him. He leaned back, closed his eyes, and cupped the ends of the chair arms with his hands. I expected to see his lips start moving in and out, but they didn't; evidently this one was too tough for any help from the lip routine. Mrs. Vail opened the checkfold on the stand at her elbow, wrote, tore the check from the fold, got up and put it on Wolfe's desk, and returned to the chair. She started to say something, and I pushed a palm at her. A minute passed, another, and two or three more, before Wolfe opened his eyes, said, "Your notebook, Archie," and straightened up.

I got my notebook and pen. But instead of starting to dictate he closed his eyes again. In a minute he opened them and turned to Mrs. Vail.

"The wording is important," he said. "It would help to know how *he* uses words. You will tell me exactly what he said on the phone."

"No, I won't." She was emphatic. "You would try to do something, some kind of trick. You'd have Archie Goodwin do something. I know he's clever and you may be a genius, but I'm not going to risk that. I told that man I would do exactly what he told me to, and do it alone, and I'm not going to tell you. What wording is important? Wording of what?"

Wolfe's shoulders went up an eighth of an inch and down again. "Very well. His voice. Did you recognize it?"

She stared. "Recognize it? Of course not!"

"Had you any thought, any suspicion, that you had ever heard it before?"

"No."

"Was he verbose, or concise?"

"Concise. He just told me what to do."

"Rough or smooth?"

She considered. "Neither one. He was just—matter-of-fact."

"No bluster, no bullying?"

"No. He said this would be my one chance and my husband's one chance, but he wasn't bullying. He just said it."

"His grammar? Did he make sentences?"

She flared. "I wasn't thinking of grammar! Of course he made sentences!"

"Few people do. I'll rephrase it: Is he an educated man? 'Educated' in the vulgar sense, as it is commonly used."

She considered again. "I said he wasn't rough. He wasn't vulgar. Yes, I suppose he is educated." She gestured impatiently. "Isn't this wasting time? You're not enough of a genius to guess who he is or where he is from how he talked. Are you?"

Wolfe shook his head. "That would be thaumaturgy, not genius. When and where did you last see your husband?"

"Saturday morning, at our house. He left to drive to the country, to our place near Katonah, to see about things. I didn't go along because I wasn't feeling well. He phoned Sunday morning and said he might not be back until late evening. When he hadn't come at midnight I phoned, and the caretaker told me he had left a little after eight o'clock. I wasn't really worried, not really, because sometimes he takes a notion to drive around at night, just anywhere, but yesterday morning I *was* worried, but I didn't want to start calling people, and then the mail came with that thing."

"Was he alone when he left your place in the country?"

"Yes. I asked the caretaker."

"What is your secretary's name?"

"My secretary? You jump around. Her name is Dinah Utley."

"How long has she been with you?"

"Seven years. Why?"

"I must speak with her. You will please phone and tell her to come here at once."

Her mouth opened in astonishment. It snapped shut. "I will not," she said. "What can she tell you? She doesn't know I've come to you, and I don't want her to. Not even her. I trust her absolutely, but I'm not going to take *any* chances."

"Then there's your check." Wolfe pointed to it, there on his desk. "Take it and go." He made a face. "I must have some evidence of your bona fides, however slight. I do know you are Mrs. Jimmy Vail, since Mr. Goodwin identifies you, but that's all I know. Did that thing come in the mail and did you get a phone call from Mr. Knapp? I have only your unsupported word. I will not be made a party to some shifty hocus-pocus. Archie. Give Mrs. Vail her check."

I got up, but she spoke. "It's no hocus-pocus. My God, hocus-pocus? My husband—they'll kill him! My not wanting anyone to know I've come to you, not even my secretary—isn't that right? If you expect her to tell you what he said on the phone, she won't. I'll tell her not to."

"I won't ask her." Wolfe was curt. "I'll merely ask her how he said it. If you have been candid, and I have no reason to think you haven't, you have no valid objection to my speaking with her. As for her knowing that you have come to me, Mr. Knapp will soon know that himself—or I hope he will."

She gawked. "*He* will know? How?"

"I'll tell him." He turned. "Archie. Can we get an advertisement in the evening papers?"

"Probably, the late editions," I told him. "The *Post* and *World-Telegram,* we can try. The *Gazette,* yes, with Lon Cohen's help." I was back in my chair with notebook and pen. "Classified?"

"No. It must be conspicuous. Two columns wide, or three. Headed in thirty-six-point, boldface, extended, 'To Mr. Knapp.' Then in twelve-point: 'The woman whose property is in your possession has engaged my services (period). She is now in my office (period). She has not told me what you said to her on the phone Monday afternoon (comma), and she will not tell me (period). I know nothing of the instructions you gave her (comma), and I do not expect or care to know (period). She has hired me for a specific job (comma), to make sure that her property is returned to her in good condition (comma), and that is the purpose of this notice (paragraph).

" 'For she has hired me for another job should it become necessary (period). If her property is not returned to her (comma), or if it is damaged beyond repair (comma), I have engaged to devote my time (comma), energy (comma), and talent (comma), for as long as may be required (comma), to ensure just and fitting requital (semicolon); and she has determined to support me to the full extent of her resources (period). If you do not know enough of me to be aware of the significance of this engagement to your future (comma), I advise you to inform yourself regarding my competence and my tenacity (period).' Beneath, in fourteen-point boldface, 'Nero Wolfe.' To be billed to me. Can you do it by phone?"

"To Lon Cohen at the *Gazette,* yes. The others, maybe." I swiveled and reached for the phone, but he stopped me.

"Just a moment." He turned to Mrs. Vail. "You heard that. As you said, your husband may already be dead. If so, I am irrevocably committed by the publication of that notice. Are you? No matter what it costs in time and money?"

"Certainly. If they kill him—certainly. But I don't—Is that *all* you're going to do, just that?"

"I may not do it, madam, and if I don't I shall do nothing. There's nothing else I *could* do. I'll proceed if, and after, you give me another check for fifty thousand dollars and phone your secretary to come here at once." He slapped the chair arm. "Do you realize that I will be staking my repute, whatever credit I have established in all my years? That's what you must pay for; and the commitment. If your husband is already dead, or if Mr. Knapp, not seeing my notice or ignoring it, kills him after he gets the money, I shall have no alternative; and what if you default? I might have to spend much more than sixty thousand dollars. Of course if your husband returns safely there will be no commitment and I'll return some of it to you. How much will be in my discretion. Less if I learn that my notice was a factor; more if it wasn't. I value my reputation, which I am risking in your interest, but I am not rapacious." He looked up at the wall clock. "If what Mr. Knapp told you to do is to be done tonight, the notice must appear today to have any effect. It's nearly one o'clock."

The poor woman—or rather, the rich woman—had her teeth clamped on her lip. She looked at me. People often do that when they are being bumped around by Wolfe, apparently hoping I will come and pat them. Sometimes I wouldn't mind obliging them, but not Althea Vail, Mrs. Jimmy Vail. She just didn't warm me. Meeting her eyes, I let mine be interested but strictly professional, and when she saw that was all I had to offer she left me. She got out her checkfold, put it on the stand, and wrote, her teeth still clamping her lip. When she tore it out I was there to take it and hand it to Wolfe. Fifty grand. Wolfe gave it a glance, dropped it on his desk, and spoke.

"I hope you'll get a large part of it back, madam. I do indeed. You may use Mr. Goodwin's phone to call your secretary. When that's done he'll use it to place that notice, in all three papers if possible."

She fluttered a hand. "Is it really necessary, Mr. Wolfe? My secretary?"

"Yes, if you want me to proceed. You're going to your bank, and it will soon be lunchtime. Tell her to be here at three o'clock."

She got up and went to my chair, sat, and dialed.

2

When Dinah Utley arrived at 3:05, five minutes late, Wolfe was at his desk with a book, *The Lotus and the Robot,* by Arthur Koestler. We had started lunch later than usual because Wolfe had told Fritz not to put the shad roe in the skillet until he was notified, and it was close to half past one when I finally quit trying to persuade the *Post* and *World-Telegram* to get the ad in. Nothing doing. It was all set for the *Gazette,* thanks to Lon Cohen, who knew from experience that he would get a tit for his tat if and when. It was also set for all editions of the morning papers. The bulldogs would be out around eleven, and if Mr. Knapp saw one after he got the money and before he erased Jimmy Vail, he might change the script.

Our client had left, headed for her bank, as soon as it was definite from Lon Cohen that the ad would be in the last two editions. Part of the time while I was phoning, for some minutes at the end, Wolfe was standing at my elbow, but not to listen to me. He had the note Mrs. Vail had got from Mr. Knapp in his hand, and he pulled my typewriter around and studied the keyboard, then looked at the note, then back at the keyboard; and he kept that up, back and forth, until Fritz came to announce lunch. That was no time for me to comment or ask a question, with sautéed shad roe fresh and hot from the skillet, and the sauce, with chives and chervil and shallots, ready to be poured on, and of course nothing relating to business is ever mentioned at the table, so I waited until we had left the dining room and crossed the hall back to the office to say, "That note was typed on an Underwood, but not mine, if that's what you were checking. The 'a' is a little off-line. Also it wasn't written by me. Whoever typed it has a very uneven touch."

Sitting, he picked up *The Lotus and the Robot.* His current book is always on his desk, at the right edge of the pad, in front of the vase of orchids. That day's orchids were a raceme of Miltonia vexillaria, brought by him as usual when he had come down from the plant rooms at eleven o'clock. "Ummmp," he said. "I was merely testing a conjecture."

"Any good?"

"Yes." He opened the book to his place and swiveled, giving me his acre or so of back. If I wanted to test a conjecture I would have to use one of my own. A visitor was due in ten minutes, and since according to him the best digestive is a book because it occupies the mind and leaves the stomach in privacy, he darned well was going to get a few pages in. And when, a quarter of an hour later, I having spent most of it inspecting the note from Mr. Knapp with occasional glances at my typewriter keyboard, the doorbell rang, and I went to the hall and returned with the visitor, and pronounced her name, and put her in the red leather chair, Wolfe stuck with his book until I had gone to my desk and sat. Then he marked his place and put it down, looked at her, and said, "Are you an efficient secretary, Miss Utley?"

Her eyes widened a little, and she smiled. If she had been doing any crying along with her employer it had certainly left no traces. At sight I had guessed her age at thirty, but that might have been a couple of years short.

"I earn my salary, Mr. Wolfe," she said.

She was cool—cool eyes, cool smile, cool voice. With some cool ones the reaction is that it would be interesting to apply a little heat and see what happens, and you wouldn't mind trying, but with others you feel that they are cool clear through, and she was one of them, though there was nothing wrong with her features or figure. You could even call her a looker.

Wolfe was taking her in. "No doubt," he said. "As you know, Mrs. Vail phoned you from here. I heard her tell you not to tell me what Mr. Knapp said to her on the phone yesterday, but you may feel that she is under great strain and your judgment on that point is better than hers. Do you?"

"No." Very cool. "I'm in her employ."

"Then I won't try to cajole you. Do you always open Mrs. Vail's mail?"

"Yes."

"Everything that comes?"

"Yes."

"How many items were there in yesterday morning's mail?"

"I didn't count them. Perhaps twenty."

"The envelope with that note in it, did you open it first or further along in the process?"

Of course that tactic is three thousand years old, maybe more, asking for a detail of a reported action, looking for hesitation or confusion. Dinah Utley smiled. "I always sort it out first, leaving circulars and other obvious stuff until later. Yesterday there were four—no, five—that I opened at once. The envelope with that note was the third one I opened."

"Did you show it to Mrs. Vail at once?"

"Certainly. I took it to her room."

"Were you present Sunday night when she phoned to the country to ask about her husband?"

"No. I was in the house, but I was in bed."

"What time yesterday did the call come from Mr. Knapp?"

"Eight minutes after four. I knew that might be important somehow, and I made a note of it."

"You listened to that conversation?"

"Yes. Mrs. Vail had told me to take it down, and I did."

"Then you know shorthand?"

"Of course."

"Are you a college graduate?"

"Yes."

"Do you type with two fingers, or four?"

She smiled. "All of them. By touch." She turned a hand over. "Really, Mr. Wolfe. Isn't this rather silly? Is it going to get Mr. Vail back alive?"

"No. But it may conceivably serve a purpose. Naturally you want to be with Mrs. Vail, and she wants you; I won't keep you much longer. There's no point now in asking you about that man's voice and diction; even if I got a hint that suggested another wording for the notice it's too late. But you will please let Mr. Goodwin take samples of your fingerprints. Archie?"

That roused her a little. "*My* fingerprints? Why?"

"Not to get Mr. Vail back alive. But they may be useful later on. It's barely possible that Mr. Knapp or an accomplice inadvertently left a print on that note. To your knowledge, has anyone handled it besides Mrs. Vail and you?"

"No."

"And Mr. Goodwin and me. We shall get Mrs. Vail's. Mr. Goodwin is an expert on prints, and even if Mr. Vail returns safely, as I hope he will, we'll want to know if there are any unidentifiable prints on that note. Do you object to having your prints taken?

"Of course not. Why should I?"

"Then Archie?"

I had opened a desk drawer and was getting out the equipment—ink with dauber and surfaced paper. I prefer a dauber to a pad. Knowing now, as I did, what the conjecture was that Wolfe had been testing when he inspected my typewriter keyboard with the note from Mr. Knapp in his hand, and therefore also knowing why I was to take Dinah Utley's prints, it wasn't necessary to write her name on the paper, but I did anyway. She got up and came to my desk and I did her right hand first. She had good hands, firm, smooth, well kept, with long slender fingers. No rings. With her left hand, when I had done the thumb, index, and middle, and started to daub the ring finger, I asked casually, "What's this? Scald it?"

"No. Shut a drawer on it."

"The pinkie too. I'll go easy."

"It's not very tender now. I did it several days ago."

But I went easy, there being no point in making her suffer, since we had no use for the prints. As she cleaned her fingers with solvent and tissues she asked Wolfe, "You don't really think a kidnaper would be fool enough to leave his fingerprint on that note, do you?"

"No," Wolfe said, "not fool enough. But possibly distraught enough. One thing more, Miss Utley. I would like you to know that I'm aware that the primary concern is the safety of Mr. Vail. I have done all I can. Archie, show her a copy of the notice.

I got it from my desk and handed it to her. Wolfe waited until she had finished reading it to say, "That will appear, prominently, in today's *Gazette* and the morning papers. If the kidnaper sees it, it may have an effect; it certainly will if he has some knowledge of me. For I will have publicly committed myself, and if he kills Mr. Vail he will be doomed inevitably. A month, a year, ten years; no matter. It's regrettable that you or I can't reach him, to make that clear to him."

"Yes, it is." Still perfectly cool. She handed me the notice. "Of course he may not have as high an opinion of your abilities as you have." She turned to go, after three steps stopped and turned her head to say, "He might even think the police are more dangerous than you are," and went. There ahead of her, and preceding her to the hall and the front door, I let her out; and, expecting no thanks or good day, got none.

Returning to the office, I stopped in front of Wolfe's desk, stood looking down at him, and said, "So she typed it."

He nodded. "Of course I didn't—"

"Excuse me. I'll do the spiel. When you first looked at it you noticed, as I did, that whoever typed it had an uneven touch. Later, while I was phoning, you looked at it again, got an idea, and came and compared it with the keyboard, and you saw that all the letters that were faint were on the left—not just left of center, but at the left end. W, E, A, S, and D. So you conjectured that the typist had been someone who used all his fingers, not just two or four, and that for some—"

"And probably typed by touch, because—"

"Excuse me, I'm doing the spiel. The touch was merely a probable. And for some reason the ring and little fingers of his left hand had not hit the keys as hard as the other fingers, not nearly as hard. Okay. I caught up with you after lunch, while you were reading, just before she came. You saw me comparing the note with the keyboard."

"No. I was reading."

"Let me not believe that. You miss nothing, though you often pretend to. You saw me all right. Then she came, and you went on ahead of me again, and I admit I ought to be docked. My eyes are as good as yours, and I had been closer to her than you were, but you noticed that the tips of those two fingers on her left hand were discolored and slightly swollen, and I didn't. Of course when you told her we wanted her prints I saw it, and you will ignore what I said about being docked because I found out how and when the fingers got hurt. Any corrections?"

"No. It is still a conjecture, not a conclusion."

"Damn close to it. One will get you fifty. That it is just a coincidence that she, a touch typist, living in that house, hurt just those two fingers, just at that time, just enough to make her go easy with them but not enough to stop using them—nuts. One will get you a hundred. So you had her read that notice and rubbed it in, thinking she'll get in touch with Mr. Knapp. Why did you let her walk out?"

Wolfe nodded. "The alternative was obvious. Go at her. Would she have yielded?"

"No. She's tough."

"And if Mr. Vail is already dead, as he well may be, it would be folly to let her know what we suspect. If he is alive, no better. She would have flouted me. Detain her forcibly, as a hostage, on a mere suspicion, however well grounded, and notify Mr. Knapp that we would exchange her for Mr. Vail? That would have been a coup, but how to reach Mr. Knapp? It's too late to get another notice in the paper. Have you a suggestion?"

"Yes. I go to see Mrs. Vail to ask her something, no matter what, and I manage somehow to get something written on the typewriter Dinah Utley uses. Of course she could have used another machine for the note, but if what I got matched the note, that would settle that."

He shook his head. "No. You have ingenuity and can even be delicate, but Miss Utley would almost certainly get a hint. Besides, to ask a question she asked, would it help to get Mr. Vail back alive? No." He glanced at the clock. In ten minutes he would leave for his four-to-six afternoon session in the plant rooms. Time enough for a few pages. He reached and got his book and opened to his place.

3

It's possible that I have given a wrong impression of Jimmy Vail, and if so I should correct it.

Age, thirty-four; height, five feet ten; weight, 150. Dark eyes, sometimes lazy and dull, sometimes bright and very quick. Smooth dark hair, nearly black, and a neat white face with a wide mouth. I had seen him about as often as I had seen his wife, since they were nearly always together at a restaurant or theater. In 1956 he had made a big splash at the Glory Hole in the Village with a thirty-minute turn of personal chatter, pointed comments on everyone and everything. Althea Tedder, widow of Harold F. Tedder, had seen him there, and in 1957 she had married him, or he had married her, depending on who is talking.

I suppose any woman who marries a man a dozen years younger is sure to get the short end of the stick when her name comes up among friends, let alone enemies, no matter what the facts are. The talk may have been just talk. Women of any age liked Jimmy Vail and liked to be with him, there was no question about that, and undoubtedly he could have two-timed his middle-aged wife any day in the week if he felt like it, but I had never with my own eyes seen him in the act. I'm merely saying that as far as I know, disregarding talk, he was a model husband. I had expected her to ask Wolfe to put a tail on him because I assumed that her friends had seen to it that she knew about the talk.

She also had made a public splash, twenty-five years back—Althea Purcell as the milkmaid in *Meadow Lark*—and she had quit to marry a man somewhat older and a lot richer. They had produced two children, a son and daughter; I had seen them a couple of times at the Flamingo. Tedder had died in 1954, so Althea had waited a decent interval to get a replacement.

Actually, neither Jimmy nor Althea had done anything notorious, or even conspicuous, during the four years of their marriage. They were mentioned frequently in print only because they were expected to do something any minute. She had left Broadway in the middle of a smash hit to marry a middle-aged rich man with a prominent name, and he had left the mike in the middle of *his* smash hit to marry a middle-aged rich woman. With the Tedder house and the Tedder dough taken over by a pair like that, anything might happen and probably would. That was the idea.

Now something *had* happened, something sensational, two days ago, and not a word about it in print. There was nothing in Nero Wolfe's notice to Mr. Knapp to connect it with the Vails. If Helen Blount, Mrs. Vail's friend, saw it, she might make a guess, but not for publication. I saw it not long after Wolfe went up to the plant rooms. Not waiting until five-thirty when a late edition of the *Gazette* is delivered to the old brownstone, I took a walk to the newsstand at 34th and Eighth Avenue. It was on page five, with plenty of margin. No one named Knapp could possibly miss it, but of course that wasn't his name.

I had a date for that evening, dinner with a friend, and a show, and it was just as well. Most of the chores of a working detective, even Nero Wolfe's right hand, not to mention his legs, are routine and pretty damn dull, and the idea of tailing a woman taking half a million bucks to a kidnaper was very tempting. Not only would it have been an interesting way to spend an evening, but there were a dozen possibilities. But since it was Wolfe's case and I was working for him, I couldn't do it without his knowledge and consent, and it would have been a waste of breath to mention it. He would have said pfui and picked up his book. So at six o'clock I went up to my room and changed and went to my date. But off and on that evening I wondered where our client was and how she was making out, and when I got home around one o'clock I had a job keeping myself from dialing her number before I turned in.

The phone rang. Of all the things that I don't want to be wakened by, the one I resent most is the phone. I turned over, forced my eyes open enough to see that it was light and the clock said 7:52, reached for the receiver and got it to my ear, and managed to get it out: "Nero Wolfe's residence, Archie Goodwin speaking."

"Mr. Goodwin?"

"I thought I said so."

"This is Althea Vail. I want to speak to Mr. Wolfe."

"Impossible, Mrs. Vail. Not before breakfast. If it's urgent, tell me. Have you—"

"My husband is back! Safe and sound!"

"Good. Wonderful. Is he there with you?"

"No, he's at our country place. He just phoned, ten minutes ago. He's going to bathe and change and eat and then come to town. He's all right, perfectly all right. Why I'm phoning, he promised them he would say nothing, absolutely nothing, for forty-eight hours, and I'm not to say anything either. I didn't tell him I had gone to Nero Wolfe; I'll wait till he gets here. Of course I don't want Mr. Wolfe to say anything. Or you. That's why I'm phoning. You'll tell him?"

"Yes. With pleasure. You're sure it was your husband on the phone?"

"Certainly I'm sure!"

"Fine. Whether the notice helped or not. Will you give us a ring when your husband arrives?"

She said she would, and we hung up. The radio clicked on, and a voice came: ". . . has five convenient offices in New York, one at the—" I reached and turned it off. When I get to bed after midnight I set it for eight o'clock, the news bulletins on WQXR, but I didn't need any more news at the moment. I had a satisfactory stretch and yawn, said aloud, "What the hell, no matter what Jimmy Vail says we can say Mr. Knapp *must* have seen it," yawned again, and faced the fact that it takes will power to get on your feet.

With nothing pending I took my time, and it was after eight-thirty when I descended the two flights to the ground floor, entered the kitchen, told Fritz good morning, picked up my glass of orange juice, took a healthy sip, and felt my stomach saying thanks. I had considered stopping at Wolfe's room on the way down but had vetoed it. He would have been in the middle of breakfast, since Fritz takes his tray up at eight-fifteen.

"No allspice in the sausage," Fritz said. "It would be an insult. The best Mr. Howie has ever sent us."

"Then double my order." I swallowed juice. "You gave me good news, so I'll give you some. The woman that came yesterday gave us a job, and it's already done. All over. Enough to pay your salary and mine for months."

"*Fort bien.*" He spooned batter on the griddle. "You did it last night?"

"No. He did it sitting down."

"Yes? But he would do nothing without you to *piquer.*"

"How do you spell that?"

He spelled it. I said, "I'll look it up," put my empty glass down, went to the table against the wall where my copy of the *Times* was on the rack, and sat. I kept an eye on my watch, and at 8:57, when I had downed the last bite of my first griddle cake and my second sausage, I reached for the house phone and buzzed Wolfe's room.

His growl came. "Yes?"

"Good morning. Mrs. Vail called an hour ago. Her husband had just phoned from their house in the country. He's at large and intact and will come to town as soon as he cleans up and feeds. He promised someone, presumably Mr. Knapp, that neither he nor his wife will make a peep for forty-eight hours, and she wants us to keep the lid on."

"Satisfactory."

"Yeah. Nice and neat. But I'll be taking a walk, to the bank to deposit her checks, and it's only five more blocks to the *Gazette*. It's bound to break soon, and I could give it to Lon Cohen to hold until we give the word. He'd hold it, you know that, and he would deeply appreciate it."

"No."

"You mean he wouldn't hold it?"

"No. He has shown that he can be trusted. But I haven't seen Mr. Vail, nor have you. It's useful to have Mr. Cohen in our debt, but no. Perhaps later in the day." He hung up. He would be two minutes late getting to the plant rooms on the roof. As Fritz brought my second cake and pair of sausages I said, "For a bent nickel I'd go up and peekay him."

He patted my shoulder and said, "Now, Archie. If you should, you will. If you shouldn't, you won't."

I buttered the cake. "I *think* that's a compliment. It's tricky. I'll study it."

For the next couple of hours, finishing breakfast and the *Times* (the notice was on page twenty-six), opening the mail, dusting our desks, removing yesterday's orchids and putting fresh water in the vase, walking to the bank and back, and doing little miscellaneous office chores, I considered the situation off and on. It seemed pretty damn silly, being hired in connection with something as gaudy as the kidnaping of Jimmy Vail, merely to put a ad in the paper and collect a fee and then call it a day. But what else? I'm more than willing to peekay Wolfe when there's any point or profit to it, but with Jimmy Vail back in one piece the job Wolfe had been hired for was done, so what? As soon as it broke, an army of cops and FBI scientists would be after Mr. Knapp, and they'd probably get him sooner or later. We were done, except for one little detail, to see Jimmy Vail whole. Mrs. Vail had said she would give us a ring when he arrived, and I would go up and ask him if Mr. Knapp had shown him the *Gazette* with the notice in it.

I didn't have to. At 11:25 the doorbell rang. Wolfe had come down from the plant rooms and gone to his desk, put a spray of Oncidium marshallianum in the vase, torn yesterday from his desk calendar, and gone through the mail, and was dictating a long letter to an orchid collector in Guatemala. He hates to be interrupted when he's doing something really important, but Fritz was upstairs, so I went, and there he was on the stoop. I told Wolfe, "Jimmy Vail in person," and went and opened the door, and he said, "Maybe you know me? I know you." He stepped in. "You're a hell of a good dancer."

I told him he was too, which was true, took his coat and hat and put them on the rack, and took him to the office, and he crossed to Wolfe's desk, stood, and said, "I know you don't shake hands. I once offered to fight a man because he called you a panjandrum; of course I knew he was yellow. I'm Jimmy Vail. May I sit down? Preferably in the red leather chair. There it is." He went and sat, rested his elbows on the chair arms, crossed his legs, and said, "If I belch you'll have to pardon me. I had nothing but cold canned beans for two days and three nights, and I overdid it on the bacon and eggs. My wife has told me about hiring you. Never has so much been spent on so little. Naturally I don't like being called my wife's property—who would?—but I realize you had to. I only saw it when my wife showed it to me, and I don't know whether they saw it or not. Is that important?"

You wouldn't have thought, looking at him and listening to him, that he had just spent sixty hours in the clutches of kidnapers, living on cold beans, and maybe not long to live even on beans, but of course he had cleaned up and had a meal, and the talk I had heard had never included any suggestion that he was a softy. His face was dead white, but it always was, and smooth and neat as it always was, and his dark eyes were bright and clear.

"It would be helpful to know," Wolfe said, "but it isn't vital. You came to tell me that? That you don't know?"

"Not actually." Vail lifted a hand to the neighborhood of his right temple and flipped his middle finger off the tip of his thumb. He had made that gesture famous during his career at the Glory Hole. "I just mentioned it because it may be important to us, my wife and me. If one of them saw that thing in the paper they know my wife has told you about it, and that may not be too good. That's why I came and came quick. They told me to keep my trap shut for forty-eight hours, until Friday morning, and to see that my wife did too, or we would regret it. I think they meant it. I got a strong impression that they mean what they say. So my wife and I are going to keep it to ourselves until Friday morning, but what about you? You could put another notice in the paper to Mr. Knapp, saying that since the property has been returned the case is closed as far as you're concerned. That you're no longer interested. What do you think?"

Wolfe had cocked his head and was eying him. "You're making an unwarranted assumption, Mr. Vail—that I too will keep silent until Friday morning. I told your wife that the obligation not to withhold knowledge of a major crime must sometimes bow to other considerations, for instance saving a life, but you are no longer in jeopardy. Now that I've seen you alive and at freedom, I cannot further postpone reporting to authority. A licensed private detective is under constraints that do not apply to the ordinary citizen. I don't want to subject you or your wife—"

The phone rang, and I swiveled to get it. "Nero Wolfe's office, Archie Good—"

"This is Althea Vail. Is my husband there?"

"Yes, he—"

"I want to speak to him."

She sounded urgent. I proceeded as I did not merely out of curiosity. There was obviously going to be a collision between Wolfe and Jimmy Vail about saving it until Friday, and if that was what she was urgent about I wanted to hear it firsthand. So I told her to hold the wire, told him his wife wanted to speak to him, and beat it, to the kitchen and the extension there. As I got the receiver to my ear Mrs. Vail was talking.

". . . terrible has happened. A man just phoned from White Plains, Captain Saunders of the State Police, he said, and he said they found a dead body, a woman, and it's Dinah Utley, they think it is, and they want me to come to White Plains to identify it or send someone. My God, Jimmy, *could* it be Dinah? How could it be Dinah?"

JIMMY: I don't know. Maybe Archie Goodwin will know; he's listening in on an extension. Did he say how she was killed?

ALTHEA: No. He—

JIMMY: Or where the body was found?

ALTHEA: No. He—

JIMMY: Or why they think it's Dinah Utley?

ALTHEA: Yes, things in her bag and in the car. Her car was there. I don't think—I don't want to—can't I send Emil?

JIMMY: Why not? How about it, Goodwin? Emil is the chauffeur. He can certainly tell them whether it's Dinah Utley or not. Must my wife go? Or must I go?

It was no use pretending I wasn't there. "No," I said, "not just for identification. Of course if it's Dinah Utley they'll want to ask both of you some questions, if there's any doubt about how she died, but for that they can come to you. For identification only, even I would do. If you want to ask Mr. Wolfe to send me."

ALTHEA: Yes! Do that, Jimmy!

JIMMY: Well . . . maybe . . . where did he say to come in White Plains?

ME: I know where to go.

ALTHEA: It must be Dinah! She didn't come home last night and now—this is terrible—

JIMMY: Take it easy, Al. I'll be there soon. Just take it easy and . . .

I cradled the phone and went back to the office. Vail was hanging up as I entered. I said to him, "Naturally I want to hear what a client of Mr. Wolfe's has to say on his phone. And naturally you knew I would." I turned to Wolfe. "A state cop called Mrs. Vail from White Plains. They have found a woman's body, he didn't say where, and from articles in her bag and her car they think it's Dinah Utley. Also there must have been something that connected her with Mrs. Vail, maybe just the address. He asked Mrs. Vail to come to White Plains and identify her, and she doesn't want to go, and neither does Mr. Vail. I suggested that she might want to ask you to send me."

Wolfe was scowling at Vail. He switched it to me. "Did she die by violence?"

"Mrs. Vail doesn't know. I've reported in full."

"Look," Vail said, "this is a hell of a thing." He was standing at the corner of my desk. "Good God. This is a real shocker. I suppose I ought to go myself."

"If it's Miss Utley," Wolfe said, "and if she died by violence, they'll ask you where you were last night. That would be routine."

"I'm not telling anyone where I was last night, not until Friday morning. Not even you."

"Then you'll be suspect. You and your wife should confer without delay. And if Mr. Goodwin goes to identify the body and it is Miss Utley, he will be asked about his association with her, when and where he has seen her. You know she was here yesterday?"

"Yes. My wife told me. But my God, he won't tell them about that, why she came here!"

Wolfe leaned back and shut his eyes. Vail started to say something, saw he wouldn't be heard, and stopped.

He went to the red leather chair and sat, then got up again, walked halfway to the door, turned, and came back to Wolfe's desk and stood looking down at him.

Wolfe's eyes opened, and he straightened up. "Archie, get Mrs. Vail."

"I'm here," Vail said. "You can talk to me."

"You're not my client, Mr. Vail. Your wife is."

I was dialing. The number was in my head, where I had filed it when I looked it up Tuesday night. A female voice said, "Mrs. Vail's residence," and I said Nero Wolfe wanted to speak with Mrs. Vail. After a wait our client's voice came, "This is Althea Vail. Mr. Wolfe?" and I nodded to Wolfe and he took his phone. I stayed on, but I had to fight for it. Jimmy Vail came to take it away from me, reaching for it and getting his fingers on it, but I kept it against my ear and didn't hear what he said because I was listening to Wolfe.

"Good morning, madam. I was gratified to see your husband, as of course you were. The telephone call you received from White Plains puts a new problem, and I offer a suggestion. I understand that you prefer not to go to White Plains to see if the dead woman is Miss Utley. Is that correct?"

"Yes. Archie Goodwin said he would go."

Wolfe grunted. "Mr. Goodwin will always go. He is uh—energetic. But there are difficulties. If it is Miss Utley, he will be asked when and where he last saw her, and when he says she came to my office yesterday he will be asked for particulars. If he gives them in full he will have to include the fact that when she left we, he and I, had formed a strong suspicion that she was implicated in the kidnaping of your husband, and then—"

"Dinah? She was implicated? That's ridiculous! Why did you suspect that?"

"I reserve that. I'll explain it later—or I won't. Then they'll demand full information about the kidnaping, not only from Mr. Goodwin and me, but from you and your husband, and they won't want to wait until Friday for it. That's the prob—"

"But why did you suspect *Dinah?*"

"That will have to wait. So I offer a suggestion. You gave me checks for sixty thousand dollars. I told you I would refund a portion of it if your husband came back alive, since it covered the contingency that I might have to meet the commitment I made in that published notice. I would prefer to keep it, but if I do I'll have to earn it. My suggestion is that I send Mr. Goodwin to White Plains to look at the body. If it is Miss Utley, he identifies it, he says that he saw her for the first and last time when she came to my office yesterday in connection with a confidential job you had hired me for, and on instructions from me he refuses to give any further information. Also I engage that neither he nor I will disclose anything whatever regarding your husband's kidnaping before eleven o'clock Friday morning unless you give your consent. That will expose us to inconvenience and possibly serious embarrassment, and I shall not feel obliged to return any money to you. I will owe you nothing, and you will owe me nothing. That's my suggestion. I should add, not to coerce you, merely to inform you, that if it isn't accepted I can no longer withhold my knowledge of a capital crime, kidnaping. I'll have to inform the proper authority immediately."

"That's a threat. That's blackmail."

"Pfui. I've offered to incur a considerable risk for a moderate fee. I withdraw my suggestion. I'll send you a check today. That will end—"

"No! Don't hang up!" Nothing for five seconds. "I want to speak to my husband."

"Very well." Wolfe looked around, then at me, and demanded, "Where is he?"

I covered the transmitter. "Skipped. Right after you said we suspected that Dinah was implicated. Gone. I heard the front door close."

"I didn't." He returned to the phone. "Your husband has left, Mrs. Vail, presumably to go to you. I didn't see him go. I'll send you a check—"

"No!" Another silence, a little longer. "All right, send Archie Goodwin. To White Plains."

"With the understanding that I proposed?"

"Yes. But I want to know why you thought Dinah was implicated. That's incredible!"

"To you, no doubt. It was merely a conjecture, possibly ill-grounded. Another time I may explain it, but not now. I must get Mr. Goodwin off. Permit me."

He hung up, and so did I. I got up and crossed to the hall, went to the front door to see that it was closed, opened the door to the front room and looked in, returned to the office, and told Wolfe, "He's gone. Not that I thought our client's husband would try any tricks, but he might have got confused and shut the door while he was still inside. Instructions?"

"Not necessary. You heard what I said to Mrs. Vail."

"Yeah, that's okay, the worst they can do is toss me in the jug, and what the hell, you're getting paid for it. But are we curious about anything? Do we care what happened to her, and when and where?"

"No. We are not concerned."

I headed for the hall, but at the door I turned. "You know," I said, "some day it may cost you something. You know damned well that we may have to be concerned and you may have to work, and it might be helpful for me to collect a few facts while they're still warm. But will you admit it? No. Why? Because you think I'm so—uh—energetic that I'll get the facts anyhow and have them available if and when you need them. For once I won't. If somebody wants to tell me no matter what, I'll say I'm not concerned."

I went and got my coat from the rack, no hat, let myself out, descended the seven steps to the sidewalk, walked to Tenth Avenue and around the corner to the garage, and got the 1961 Heron sedan which Wolfe owns and I drive.

4

At one-fifteen p.m. Clark Hobart, District Attorney of Westchester County, narrowed his eyes at me and said, "You're dry behind the ears, Goodwin. You know what you're letting yourself in for."

We were in his office at the Court House, a big corner room with four windows. He was seated at his desk, every inch an elected servant of the people. With a strong jaw, a keen eye, and big ears that stuck out. My chair was at an end of the desk. In two chairs in front of it were Captain Saunders of the State Police and a man I had had contacts with before, Ben Dykes, head of the county detectives. Dykes had fattened some in the two years since I had last seen him; what had been a crease was now a gully, giving him two chins, and when he sat his belly lapped over his belt. But the word was that he was still a fairly smart cop.

I met Hobart's eyes, straight but not belligerent. "I'd like to be sure," I said, "that you've got it right. They reported to you before I was brought in. I don't suppose they twisted it deliberately, I know Ben Dykes wouldn't, but let's avoid any misunderstanding. I looked at the corpse and identified it as Dinah Utley. Captain Saunders asked me how well I had known her, and I said I had met her only once, yesterday afternoon, but my identification was positive. Dykes asked where I had met her yesterday afternoon, and I said at Nero Wolfe's office. He asked what she was there for, and I said Mrs. Jimmy Vail had told her to come, at Mr. Wolfe's request, so he could ask her some questions in connection with a confidential matter which Mrs. Vail had hired him to investigate. He asked me what the confidential matter was, and I—"

"And you refused to tell him."

I nodded. "That's the point. My refusal was qualified. I said I was under instructions from Mr. Wolfe. If he would tell me where the body had been found, and how and when and where she had died, with details, I would report to Mr. Wolfe, and if a crime had been committed he would decide whether it was reasonable to suppose that the crime was in any way connected with the matter Mrs. Vail had consulted him about. I hadn't quite finished when Captain Saunders broke in and said Dinah Utley had been murdered and I damned well would tell him then and there exactly what she had said to Mr. Wolfe and what he had said to her. I said I damned well wouldn't, and he said he had heard how tough I thought I was and he would take me where we wouldn't be disturbed and find out. Evidently he's the salt-of-the-earth type. Ben Dykes, who is just a cop, no hero, insisted on bringing me to you. If what I'm letting myself in for is being turned over to Captain Saunders, that would suit me fine. I have been thinking of going to a psychiatrist to find out how tough I am, and that would save me the trouble."

"I'll be glad to do you that favor," Saunders said. He moved his lips the minimum required to get the words out. Someone had probably told him that that showed you had power in reserve, and he had practiced it before a mirror.

"You're not being turned over," Hobart said. "I'm the chief law officer of this county. A crime *has* been committed. Dinah Utley was murdered. She was with you not many hours before she died, and as far as we know now, you were the last person to see her alive. Captain Saunders was fully justified in asking for the details of that interview. So am I."

I shook my head. "He didn't ask, he demanded. As for the crime, where and when? If a car ran over her this—"

"How do you know a car ran over her?" Saunders snapped.

I ignored him. "If a car ran over her this morning here on Main Street, and people who saw the driver say he was a dwarf with whiskers and one eye, I doubt if Mr. Wolfe will think his talk with her yesterday was relevant. Having seen the body, I assume that either a car ran over her or she was hit several times with a sledgehammer though there are other possibilities." I turned a hand over. "What the hell, Mr. Hobart. You know Mr. Wolfe knows the rules."

He nodded. "And I know how he abuses them—and you too. Dinah Utley wasn't killed here on Main Street. Her body was found at ten o'clock this morning by two boys who should have been in school. It was in a ditch by a roadside, where it—"

"What road?"

"Iron Mine Road. Presumably it once led to an iron mine, but now it leads nowhere. It's narrow and rough, and it come to a dead end about two miles from Route One Twenty-three. The body—"

"Where does it leave Route One Twenty-three?"

Saunders growled, in his throat, not parting his lips. He got ignored again.

"About two miles from where Route One Twenty-three

leaves Route Thirty-five," Hobart said. "South of Ridgefield, not far from the state line. The body had been rolled into the ditch after death. The car that had run over her was there, about a hundred feet away up the road, headed into an opening to the woods. The registration for the car was in it, with the name Dinah Utley and the address Nine Ninety-four Fifth Avenue, New York twenty-eight. Also in it was her handbag, containing the usual items, some of them bearing her name. It has been established that it was that car that ran over her. Anything else?"

"When did she die?"

"Oh, of course. The limits are nine o'clock last evening and three o'clock this morning."

"Were there traces of another car?"

"Yes. One and possibly two, but on grass. The road's gravelly, and the grass is thick up to the gravel."

"Anyone who saw Dinah Utley or her car last night, or another car?"

"Not so far. The nearest house is nearly half a mile away, east, toward Route One Twenty-three, and that stretch of road is seldom traveled."

"Have you got any kind of a lead?"

"Yes. You. When a woman is murdered a few hours after she goes to see a private detective it's a fair assumption that the two events were connected and what she said to the detective is material. Were you present when she talked with Wolfe?"

"Yes. It's also a fair assumption that the detective is the best judge as to whether the two events were connected or not. As I said Dinah Utley didn't come to see Mr. Wolfe on her own hook; she came because Mrs. Vail told her to, to give him some information about something Mrs. Vail wanted done." I got up. "Okay, you've told me what I can read in the paper in a couple of hours. I'll report to Mr. Wolfe and give you a ring."

"That's what you think." Saunders was on his feet. "Mr. Hobart, you know how important time is on a thing like this. You realize that if you let him go in twenty minutes he'll be out of your jurisdiction. You realize that he has information that if we get it now it might make all the difference."

I grinned at him. "Can you do twenty pushups? I can."

Ben Dykes told Hobart, "I'd like to ask him something," and Hobart told him to go ahead. Dykes turned to me. "There was an ad in the *Gazette* yesterday headed 'to Mr. Knapp' with Nero Wolfe's name at the bottom. Did that have anything to do with why Mrs. Vail told Dinah Utley to go to see Wolfe?"

The word that Dykes was still a fairly smart cop seemed to be based on facts. The grin I gave him was not the one I had given Saunders. "Sorry," I said, "but I'm under orders from the man I work for." I went to the District Attorney. "You know the score, Mr. Hobart. It would be stretching a point even to hold me for questioning as it stands now, and since I wouldn't answer the questions, and since Mr. Wolfe wouldn't talk on the phone or let anyone in the house until he gets my report, I suppose we'll have to let Captain Saunders go without. But of course it's your murder."

He had his head tilted back to frown at me. "You know the penalty," he said, "for obstructing justice." When I said, "Yes, sir," politely, he abruptly doubled his fists, bounced up out of his chair, and yelled, "Get the hell out of here!" As I turned to obey, Ben Dykes shook his head at me. I passed close enough to Saunders for him to stick out a foot and trip me, but he didn't.

Down on the sidewalk, I looked at my watch: 1:35. I walked three blocks to a place I knew about, called Mary Jane's, where someone makes chicken pie the way my Aunt Anna used to make it in Chillicothe, Ohio, with fluffy little dumplings; and as I went through a dish of it I considered the situation. There was no point in wasting money ringing Wolfe, since he wasn't concerned, and as for our client, there was no rush. I could call her after I reported to Wolfe. So, since I was already halfway there —well, a third of the way—why not take a look at Iron Mine Road? And maybe at the old iron mine if I could find it? If I kidnaped a man and wanted a place to keep him while I collected half a million bucks, I wouldn't ask anything better than an abandoned iron mine. I paid for the chicken and a piece of rhubarb pie, walked to the lot where I had parked the Heron, ransomed it, and headed for Hawthorne Circle. There I took the Saw Mill River

Parkway, and at its end, at Katonah, I took Route 35 east. It was a bright sunny day, and I fully appreciate things like forsythia and trees starting to bud and cows in pastures as long as I have a car that I can depend on to get me back to town. Just short of Connecticut I turned right onto Route 123, glancing at my speedometer. When I had gone a mile and a half I started looking for Iron Mine Road, and in another two-tenths there it was.

After negotiating a mile of that road I wasn't so sure that the Heron would get me back to town. I met five cars in the mile, and for one of them I had to climb a bank and for another I had to back up fifty yards. There was no problem about spotting the scene of the crime when I finally reached it. There were eight cars strung along, blocking the road completely, none of them official. A dozen women and three or four men were standing at the roadside, at the edge of the ditch, and two men at the other side of the road were having a loud argument about who had dented whose fender. I didn't even bother to get out. To the north was thick woods, and to the south a steep rocky slope with a swamp at the bottom. I admit I was a little vague about what an abandoned iron mine should look like, but nothing in sight looked promising. I pushed the reverse button and started backing, with care, and eventually came to a spot with enough room to turn around. On the way to Route 123 I met three cars coming in.

Of the two decisions I made going back to town, I was aware of one of them at the time I made it, which was par. That one was to take my time, with half an eye on the landscape, to see how the country was making out with its spring chores, which was sensible, since I couldn't get to 35th Street before four o'clock and Wolfe would be up in the plant rooms, where he hates to be interrupted, especially when there's nothing stirring that he's concerned about. I made that decision before I reached Route 35.

I don't know when the other decision was made. I became aware of it when I found myself in the middle lane of the Thruway, hitting sixty-five. When I'm bound for New York from Westchester and my destination is on the West Side, I take the Saw Mill all the way; when my destination is on the East Side I leave it at Ardsley and get on the Thruway. And there I was on the Thruway, so obviously I was going somewhere on the East Side. Where? It took me nearly two seconds. I'll be damned, I told myself, I'm headed for our client's house to tell her I identified the body. Okay, that will save a dime, the cost of a phone call. And if her husband is there and they have any questions, I can answer them face to face, which is always more satisfactory. I rolled on, to the Major Deegan Expressway, the East River Drive, and the 96th Street exit.

It was ten minutes past four when, having found a space on 81st Street I could squeeze the Heron into, I entered the vestibule of the four-story stone mansion at 994 Fifth Avenue and pushed the button. The door was opened by a square-faced woman in uniform with a smudge on her cheek. I suppose the Tedder who had had the house built, Harold F.'s father, wouldn't have dreamed of letting that door be opened by a female, so it was just as well he wasn't around. She had a surprise for me, though she didn't know it. When I gave my name and I said I wanted to see Mrs. Vail, she said Mrs. Vail was expecting me, and made room for me to enter. I shouldn't have been surprised to find once again that Wolfe thought he knew me as well as I thought I knew him, but I was. What had happened, of course, was that Mrs. Vail had phoned to ask if I had identified the body, and he had told her that I would stop at her house on the way back from White Plains, though that hadn't been mentioned by him or me. That was how well he thought he knew me. Some day he'll overdo it. As I have said, *I* hadn't known I was going to stop at her house until I found myself on the Thruway.

As the female door-opener took my coat, a tenor voice came from above, "Who is it, Elga?" and Elga answered it, "It's Mr. Goodwin, Mr. Tedder," and the tenor called, "Come on up, Mr. Goodwin." I went and mounted the marble stairs, white, wide, and winding, and at the top there was Noel Tedder. I've mentioned that I had seen him a few times, but I had never met him. From hearsay he was a twenty-three-year-old brat who had had a try at three colleges but couldn't make it, who had been forced by his mother to stop climbing mountains because he had fallen off of one, and who had once landed a helicopter on second base at Yankee Stadium in the fifth inning of a ball game; but from my personal knowledge he was merely a broad-shouldered six-footer who didn't care how he dressed when he went to the theater or the Flamingo and who talked too loud after two drinks. The tenor voice was one of those mistakes that get made when the hands are being dealt.

He took me down a wide hall to an open door and motioned me in. I crossed the sill and stopped, thinking for a second I had crashed a party, but then I saw that only five of the people in the room were alive, the rest were bronze or stone, and I remembered a picture I had seen years ago of Harold F. Tedder's library. This was it. It was a big room, high-ceilinged, but it looked a little crowded with a dozen life-sized statues standing around here and there. If he liked company he sure had it. Mrs. Vail's voice came, "Over here, Mr. Goodwin," and I moved. The five live ones were in a group, more or less, at the far end, where there was a fireplace but no fire. As I approached, Mrs. Vail said, "Well?"

"It was Dinah Utley," I said.

"What—how—"

I glanced around. "I'm not intruding?"

"It's all right," Jimmy Vail said. He was standing with his back to the fireplace. "They know about it. My wife's daughter, Margot Tedder. Her brother, Ralph Purcell. Her attorney, Andrew Frost."

"They know about Nero Wolfe," Mrs. Vail said. "My children and my brother were asking questions, and we thought we had better tell them. Then when this—Dinah—and we'll be asked where we were last night . . . I decided my lawyer ought to know about it and about Nero Wolfe. It was Dinah?"

"Yes."

"She was run over by a car?" From Andrew Frost, the lawyer. He looked a little like the man of bronze who was standing behind his chair, Abraham Lincoln, but he had no beard and his hair was gray; and on his feet probably he wasn't quite as tall. Presumably he had learned how

Dinah had died by phoning White Plains, or from a broadcast.

"She was run over by *her* car," I said.

"Her own car?"

I faced Mrs. Vail, who was sitting on a couch, slumped against cushions. "On behalf of Mr. Wolfe," I told her, "I owe you two pieces of information. One, I looked at the corpse and identified it as Dinah Utley. Two, I told the District Attorney that I saw her yesterday afternoon when she came to Mr. Wolfe's office in connection with a matter you had consulted him about. That's all. I refused to tell him what the matter was or anything about it. That's all I owe you, but if you want to know how and when and where Dinah died I'll throw that in. Do you want it?"

"Yes. First when."

"Between nine o'clock last evening and three o'clock this morning. That may be narrowed down later. It was murder, because her own car ran across her chest and was there, nosed into a roadside opening, when the body was found. There was a bruise on the side of her head; she was probably hit with something and knocked out before the car was run over her. Then the—"

I stopped because she had made a sound, call it a moan, and shut her eyes. "Do you have to be utterly brutal?" Margot Tedder asked. The daughter, a couple of years younger than her brother Noel, was at the other end of the couch. From hearsay, she was a pain in the neck who kept her chin up so she could look down her nose; from my personal knowledge, she was a nice slender specimen with real possibilities if she would round out a little and watch the corners of her mouth, and, seeing her walk or dance, you might have thought her hips were in a cast.

"I didn't do it," I told her. "I'm just telling it."

"You haven't said where," Jimmy Vail said. "Where was it?"

Mrs. Vail's eyes had opened, and I preferred to tell her, since she was the client. "Iron Mine Road. That's a narrow rocky lane off of Route One Twenty-three. Route One Twenty-three goes into Route Thirty-five seven miles east of Katonah, not far from the state line."

Her eyes had widened. "My God," she said, staring at

me. *"They* killed her." She turned to Andrew Frost. "The kidnapers. They killed her." Back to me. "Then you were right, what Mr. Wolfe said about suspecting her. That's where—"

"Wait a minute, Althea," Frost commanded her. "I must speak with you privately. This is dangerous business, extremely dangerous. You should have told me Monday when you got that note. As your counselor, I instruct you to say nothing more to anyone until you have talked with me. And I don't— Where are you going?"

She had left the couch and was heading for the door. She said over her shoulder, "I'll be back," and kept going, on out. Jimmy moved. He went halfway to the door, stopped and stood, his back to us, and then came back to the fireplace. Ralph Purcell, Mrs. Vail's brother, said something to Frost and got no response. I had never seen Purcell and knew next to nothing of him, either hearsay or personal knowledge. Around fifty, take a couple of years either way, with not much hair left and a face as round as his sister's, he had a habit I had noticed: when someone started to say something he looked at someone else. If he was after an effect he got it; it made you want to say something to him and see if you could keep his eye.

Noel Tedder, who was leaning against George Washington, asked me, "What's this about suspecting her? Suspecting her of what?" The lawyer shook his head at him, and Margot said, "What's the difference now? She's dead." Purcell was looking at me, and I was deciding what to say to him and try to hold his eye when Mrs. Vail came in. She had an envelope in her hand. She came back to the couch, sat on the edge, and took papers from the envelope. Frost demanded, "What have you got there? Althea, I absolutely insist—"

"I don't care what you insist," she told him. "You're a good lawyer, Andy, Harold thought so and so do I, and I trust your advice on things you know about, you know I do, but this is different. I told you about it because you could tell me about the legal part of it, but now I don't need just *legal* advice, now that I know Dinah was killed there on Iron Mine Road. I think I need something more than legal advice, I think I need Nero Wolfe." She turned to me. "Would he come here? He wouldn't, would he?"

I shook my head. "He never leaves the house on business. If you want to see him he'll be available at six—"

"No. I don't feel like—no. I can tell you. Can't I?"

"Certainly." I got my notebook and pen from a pocket, went to a chair near the end of the couch, and sat.

She looked around. "I want you to hear it, all of you. You all knew Dinah. I'm sure you all thought of her as highly as I did—I don't mean you all liked her, that's not it, but you thought she was very competent and completely reliable. But apparently she—but wait till you hear it." She fingered in the papers, extracted one, handed it to me, and looked around again. "I've told you about the note I got Monday morning saying they had Jimmy and I would get a phone call from Mr. Knapp. Nero Wolfe has it. And I've told you, haven't I—yes, I did—that when the phone call came Monday afternoon Dinah listened in and took it down. Later she typed it from her notes, and that's it. Read it aloud, Mr. Goodwin."

A glance had shown me that the typing was the same as the note, the same faint letters, but on a better grade of paper and a different size, 8½ by 11. I read it to them:

MRS. VAIL: This is Althea Vail. Are you—

KNAPP: I'm Mr. Knapp. Did you get the note?

MRS. VAIL: Yes. This morning. Yes.

KNAPP: Is anyone else on the wire?

MRS. VAIL: No. Of course not. The note said—

KNAPP: Keep it strictly to yourself. You had better if you want to see your Jimmy again. Have you got the money?

MRS. VAIL: No, how could I? I only got the note—

KNAPP: Get it. You've got until tomorrow. Get it and put it in a suitcase. Five hundred thousand dollars in used bills, nothing bigger than a hundred. You understand that?

MRS. VAIL: Yes, I understand. But where is my husband? Is he—

KNAPP: He's perfectly all right. Safe and sound, not a scratch on him. That's absolutely straight, Mrs. Vail.

If you play it straight, you can count on us. Now listen. I don't want to talk long. Get the money and put it in a suitcase. Tomorrow evening, Tuesday, put the suitcase in the trunk of your blue sedan, and don't forget to make sure the trunk's locked. Take the Merritt Parkway. Leave it at the Westport exit, Route 33. You know Route 33?

MRS. VAIL: Yes.

KNAPP: Do you know where Fowler's Inn is?

MRS. VAIL: Yes.

KNAPP: Go to Fowler's Inn. Get there at ten o'clock tomorrow evening. Don't get there much before ten, and not any later than five after ten. Take a table on the left side and order a drink. You'll get a message. Understand?

MRS. VAIL: Yes. What kind of a message? How will I know—

KNAPP: You'll know. You're sure you understand?

MRS. VAIL: Yes. Fowler's Inn at ten o'clock tomorrow evening. But when—

KNAPP: Just do as you're told. That's all.

I looked up. "That's all."

"But my God, Mom," Noel Tedder blurted, "if you had told me!"

"Or me," Andrew Frost said grimly.

"Well?" Mrs. Vail demanded. "What could you have done? Jimmy's here, isn't he? He's here alive and well. I went to Nero Wolfe, I've told you about that, and what he did may have helped, I don't know and I don't care now."

"I think you were extremely wise," Margot Tedder said, "not to tell either of them. Mr. Frost would have tried to make you wait until he looked it up in the books. Noel would have gone to Fowler's Inn in disguise, probably with a false beard. You went, Mother? To Fowler's Inn?"

Mrs. Vail nodded. "I did exactly what he told me to. Of course Mr. Graham at the bank was suspicious—no, not suspicious, curious—and he wanted me to tell him what the money was for, but I didn't. It was my money. I got to Fowler's Inn too early, and sat in the car until ten o'clock, and then went in. I tried not to show how nervous I was, but I suppose I did; I kept looking at my watch, and at twenty after ten I was called to the phone. It was in a booth. The voice sounded like the other one, Mr. Knapp, but he didn't say. He told me to look in the Manhattan phone book where Z begins, and hung up. I looked in the phone book, and there was a note. I have it." She extracted another sheet of paper and handed it to me. "Read it, Mr. Goodwin."

"Wait a minute." It was Jimmy Vail. He had moved and was standing looking down at his wife. "I think you'd better call a halt, Al. You and I had better have a talk. Telling Goodwin all this, telling Frost—it's not Friday yet."

She lifted a hand to touch his arm. "I have to, Jimmy. I *have* to, now that Dinah—my God, they killed her! Read it, Mr. Goodwin."

It was the same typing, and on the same cheap paper as the note that had come in the mail. I read it aloud.

> Leave immediately. Speak to no one. Go to car. Read the rest of this after you are in the car. Drive to Route 7 and turn right. Beyond Weston leave Route 7 on any byroad and turn off of it in a mile or so onto some other byroad. Do this, taking turns at random, for half an hour, then return to Route 7 and go towards Danbury. A mile beyond Branchville stop at The Fatted Calf, take a table and order a drink. You'll get a message.

"I'll take that," Jimmy Vail said. "And the other one." His hand was there for them. From his tone, it seemed likely that if I tried to argue that I wanted to show them to Wolfe I would lose the debate, so I got the texts in my notebook in shorthand. That wasn't really necessary, since after years of practice I can report long conversations verbatim, but with such documents as those it was desirable. Transferring typed text to shorthand was practically automatic, so my ears could take in what Mrs. Vail was saying:

"I did what the note said. I think a car was following me all the time, but I wasn't sure. I think I didn't want to know, I didn't want to be sure. The same thing happened at The Fatted Calf, the same as Fowler's Inn. At ten minutes after eleven I was called to the phone, and the same voice told me to look in the phone book where U begins, and there was another note." She handed it to me. "Read it."

Same typing, same paper. I read:

> Leave immediately. Speak to no one. Read the rest of this in the car. Continue on Route 7 to the intersection with Route 35. Turn left on Route 35, and continue on 35 through Ridgefield. Two miles beyond Ridgefield turn left onto Route 123. Go 1.7 miles on Route 123 and turn right onto Iron Mine Road. Go slow. When a car behind blinks its lights three times, stop. The car will stop behind you. Get out and open the trunk. A man will approach and say, "It's time for a Knapp," and you will give him the suitcase. He will tell you what to do.

"He did," Mrs. Vail said. "He told me to drive straight back to New York, here, without stopping. He told me not to tell anyone anything until Jimmy came back or he would never come back. He said he would be back within twenty-four hours. And he was! He is! Thank God!" She put out a hand to touch her Jimmy, but had to stretch because he was sticking with me to get the notes. I was getting the last one in my notebook. The Tedder son and daughter were saying something, and so was Andrew Frost. Finishing with my shorthand, I reached around Jimmy to hand the papers to Mrs. Vail. He had a hand there, but I ignored it, and she took them. She spoke to me.

"You see why I had to tell Nero Wolfe. Or you."

"I can guess," I told her. "Mr. Wolfe told you we suspected that Dinah Utley was implicated in the kidnaping. Now I tell you that her body was found on Iron Mine Road, at the spot where you turned over the suitcase, or near there. That complicates your problem when Westchester County comes to ask you about Dinah Utley and why you had her go to see Mr. Wolfe, especially if you and your husband still want to save it until Friday. Haven't they been here yet?"

"No."

"They soon will be. As for Mr. Wolfe and me, we'll stand pat until eleven o'clock Friday morning. He made it eleven o'clock because that's when he comes down from the plant rooms. As for you and your husband, and now also your son and daughter and brother and lawyer, you'll have to decide for yourselves. It's risky to withhold information material to a murder, but if it's for self-protection from a real danger, if you think Mr. Knapp meant business when he told your husband he'd regret it if he or you spilled it before Friday, I doubt if you'll have any serious trouble. Is that what you want from Mr. Wolfe or me?"

"No." She had the papers back in the envelope and was clutching it. "Only partly that. I want to know why you thought Dinah was implicated."

"Naturally." I put the notebook back in my pocket. "You didn't see her there? At Iron Mine Road?"

"No, of course not."

"Not of course not, since she *was* there. Was the man alone in the car behind you?"

"I didn't see anyone else. It was dark. I wasn't—I wasn't caring if there was anyone else."

"What did the man look like?"

"I don't know. He had a coat and a hat pulled down, and his face was covered with something, all but his eyes."

"Who left first, him or you?"

"I did. He told me to. I had to go on up the road to find a place to turn around."

"Was his car still there when you came back past the spot?"

"Yes. He had it up against the bank so I could get by."

"Did you see any other car anywhere on that road?"

"No." She gestured impatiently. "What has this to do with Dinah?"

"Nothing," Noel Tedder said. "He's a detective. It's his nature. He's putting you through the wringer."

"I insist," Andrew Frost said emphatically, "that this is ill-advised. *Very* ill-advised. You're making a mistake, Althea. Don't you agree, Jimmy?"

Jimmy was back at the fireplace. "Yes," he said. "I agree."

"But Jimmy, you must see," she protested. "She was *there!* And they killed her! You must see I want to know why Nero Wolfe suspected her!" To me: "Why did he?"

I shook my head. "I only run errands. But you're welcome to a hint." I stood up. "That phone talk you had with Mr. Knapp Monday afternoon, that Dinah listened to and took down. May I see the machine she typed it on?"

The three men spoke at once. Jimmy Vail and Andrew Frost both said, "No!" and Noel Tedder said, "Didn't I tell you?" Mrs. Vail ignored them and asked, "Why?"

"I'll probably tell you after I see it. And I may have a suggestion to make. Is it here?"

"It's in my study." She arose. "Will you tell me why you suspected Dinah?"

"I'll either tell you or you'll have a healthy idea."

"All right, come with me." She moved, paying no attention to protests from the men. I followed her out and along the hall to a door frame where she pressed a button. The door of a do-it-yourself elevator slid open, and we entered. That elevator was a much newer and neater job than the one in Wolfe's house that took him up to his room or the roof. No noise or jiggle. When it stopped and the door opened, she stepped out and led the way down the hall, some narrower than the one below. The room we entered was much smaller than the Harold F. Tedder library. Inside, I stopped for a glance around—that's habit. Two desks, one large and one small, shelves with books and magazines, filing cabinet, a large wall mirror, a television set on a table, framed photographs. Mrs. Vail had crossed to the small desk. She turned and said, "It's not here! The typewriter."

I went to her. At the end of the desk was a typewriter stand on casters. There was nothing on it. She had turned again and was staring at it. There were only two questions worth asking, and I asked them.

"Is it always kept here, or is it sometimes taken to another room?"

"Never. It is kept here."

"When did you last see it here?"

"I don't—I'd have to think. I haven't been in here today, until just now, when I came to get this envelope. I didn't notice it was gone. Sometime yesterday—I'd have to think. I can't imagine . . ."

"Someone may have borrowed it." I went to the door and turned. "I'll report to Mr. Wolfe. If he has anything to say we'll ring you. The main thing is we'll stay put until Friday unless you—"

"But you're going to tell me why you suspected Dinah!"

"Not now. Find the typewriter, and we'll see." I left. As I went down the hall her voice followed me, but I kept going. I was in no mood for talk. I should never have mentioned the typewriter, since it had nothing to do with the job Wolfe had been paid for, but I had wanted to get a sample from it to take along. Noel Tedder had been right; I was a detective, and it was my nature. Nuts. Skipping the elevator, I took the stairs, three flights down, and when I reached the ground floor the square-faced female appeared through an arch. She got my coat and held it, and went and opened the door; and there entering the vestibule was Ben Dykes, head of the Westchester County detectives.

I said, "Hello there. Get stopped for speeding?"

He said, "I've been in the park feeding pigeons. I didn't want to butt in."

"That's the spirit. I fully appreciate it. May your tribe increase." I circled around him, on out, and headed for 81st Street, where I had left the car.

5

At six o'clock, when the sound came of Wolfe's elevator descending, I was in my chair in the office, my feet up on the desk, my weight on the base of my spine, and my head back.

For twenty minutes I had been playing a guessing game, which was all it amounted to, since we had nothing to do but sit on it, and since I didn't have enough bones to make a skeleton, let alone meat. But some day all the details of the Jimmy Vail kidnaping, including the murder of Dinah Utley, would be uncovered, whether they got Mr. Knapp or not, and if I could dope it here and now with what little I had, and it turned out that I was right, I could pin a medal on myself. So I worked at it.

Question: Was Dinah Utley in on it?

Answer: Certainly. She typed the note that came by mail and those Mrs. Vail found in the phone books.

Q: Who took the typewriter?

A: Dinah Utley. When she learned that Mrs. Vail had gone to Nero Wolfe, and when I took her prints and asked about her fingers, she got leery and ditched the typewriter.

Q: Was she with the man who got the suitcase from Mrs. Vail?

A: No. She was in her car somewhere along Iron Mine Road, and when Mrs. Vail drove back out she drove on in. She wanted to be sure of getting her cut. The man who had got the suitcase, probably Mr. Knapp, didn't care for that and killed her.

Q: Was anyone at the Vail house in on it besides Dinah Utley?

A: Yes. Jimmy Vail. He kidnaped himself. He had another man in it too, because he wasn't Mr. Knapp on the phone; it would have been too risky trying to disguise his voice. But he might have been the man who got the suitcase and therefore the man who killed Dinah Utley. That disagrees with the "probably Mr. Knapp" in the preceding answer, but we're not in court. Items: Jimmy scooted from this office when he heard Wolfe tell Mrs. Vail that we suspected Dinah Utley, he told her she'd better call a halt when she produced the notes she had got from the phone books, and he tried to take the notes from me. Also his reactions in general. Also his insisting on saving it until Friday.

Q: Why did he have Dinah in on it?

A: Pass. No bone. A dozen possible reasons.

Q: Wouldn't he have been a sap to have Dinah type the notes on that typewriter?

A: No. The state of mind Mrs. Vail would be in when she got the note by mail, he knew she wouldn't inspect the typing. When he got back he would destroy the notes. He would say he had promised Mr. Knapp he would and he was afraid not to. She had to use *some* typewriter, and buying or renting or borrowing one might have been riskier. Using that one and destroying the notes, there would be no risk at all. He wanted to take the notes from me.

Q: Could Ralph Purcell or Andrew Frost or Noel Tedder be Mr. Knapp?

A: No. Mrs. Vail knows their voices too well.

Q: Friday, if not sooner, Jimmy will have to open up. Where and how they took him, and kept him, and turned him loose. With the cops and the FBI both at him, won't he be sure to slip?

A: No. He'll say they blindfolded him and he doesn't know where they took him and kept him. Last night, early this morning, they took him somewhere blindfolded and turned him loose.

Q: Then how are they going to uncover it so you can check it with these guesses and get your medal? How would you?

I was working on that one when the sound of the elevator came. Wolfe entered, crossed to his desk, sat, and said, "Report?"

I took my feet down and pulled my spine up. "Yes, sir. It's Dinah Utley. I told District Attorney Clark Hobart that I had seen her yesterday afternoon when she came here in connection with a job Mrs. Vail had hired you to do. When he asked me what the job was it would have been rude just to tell him to go to hell, so I said that if he would tell me when and where and how Dinah Utley had died, and if I relayed it to you, you would decide what to do. Of course there's no point in relaying it, since you said we don't care what happened to her and are not concerned. I have informed Mrs. Vail and told her we'll stand pat until eleven a.m. Friday."

I swiveled, pulled the typewriter around, inserted paper and carbons, got the notebook from my pocket, and hit the keys. Perfect harmony. It helps a lot, with two people as much together as he and I were, if they understand each other. He understood that I was too strong-minded to add another word unless he told me to, and I understood that he was too pigheaded to tell me to. Of course I had to keep busy; I couldn't just sit and be strong-minded. I typed the texts of the two notes and other jottings I had made in my book, then went and opened the safe and got the note Mr. Knapp had sent by mail. It seemed likely that Jimmy Vail would be wanting it, and it was quite possible that developments would make it desirable for us to have something to show someone. I clipped the note to the edge of my desk pad, propped the pad against the back of a chair, got one of the cameras —the Tollens, which I have better luck with—and took half a dozen shots. All this time, of course, Wolfe was at his book, with no glance at me. I had returned the note to the safe and put the camera away, and was putting the film in a drawer, when the doorbell rang. I went to the hall door for a look, turned, and told Wolfe, "Excuse me for interrupting. Ben Dykes, head of the Westchester County detectives. He was there this afternoon. He's a little fatter than when you saw him some years ago at the home of James U. Sperling near Chappaqua."

He finished a sentence before he turned his head. "Confound it," he muttered. "Must I?"

"No. I can tell him we're not concerned. Of course in a week or so they might get desperate and take us to White Plains on a warrant."

"You haven't reported."

"I reported all you said you wanted."

"That's subdolous. Let him in."

As I went to the front I was making a mental note not to look up "subdolous." That trick of his, closing an argument by using a word he knew damn well I had never heard, was probably subdolous. I opened the door, told Dykes he had been expected as I took his coat and hat, which was true, and ushered him to the office. Three steps in, he stopped for a glance around. "Very nice," he said. "Nice work if you can get it. You don't remember me, Mr. Wolfe." Wolfe said he did remember him and told him to be seated, and Dykes went to the red leather chair.

"I didn't think it was necessary to get a local man to come along," he said, "since all I'm after is a little information. Goodwin has told you about Dinah Utley. When he was up there he was the last one who had seen her alive as far as we knew, him and you when she was here yesterday afternoon, but since then I've spoken with two people who had seen her after that. But you know how it is with a murder, you have to start somewhere, and that's what I'm doing, trying to get a start, and maybe you can help. Goodwin said Dinah Utley came here yesterday because Mrs. Vail told her to. Is that right?"

"Yes."

"Well, of course I'm not asking what Mrs. Vail wanted you to do for her, I understand that was confidential, and I'm only asking about Dinah Utley. I'm not even asking what you said to her, I'm only asking what she said to you. That may be important, since she was murdered just eight or nine hours after that. What did she say?"

A corner of Wolfe's mouth was up a little. "Admirable," he declared. "Competent and admirable."

Dykes got his notebook out. "She said that?"

"No. I say it. Your demand couldn't be better organized or better put. Admirable. You have the right to expect a comparable brevity and lucidity from me." He turned a hand over. "Mr. Dykes. I can't tell you what Miss Utley said to me yesterday without divulging what Mrs. Vail has told me in confidence. Of course that wasn't a privileged communication; I'm not a member of the bar, I'm a detective; and if what Mrs. Vail told me is material to your investigation of a murder I withhold it at my peril. The question, is it material, can be answered now only by me; you can't answer it because you don't know what she told me. To my present knowledge, the answer is no."

"You're withholding it?"

"Yes."

"You refuse to tell me what Dinah Utley said to you yesterday?"

"Yes."

"Or anything about what she came here for?"

"Yes."

Dykes stood up. "As you say, at your peril." He glanced around. "Nice place you've got here. Nice to see you again." He turned and headed for the door. I followed him out and down the hall. As I held his coat for him he said, "At your peril too, Goodwin, huh?" I thanked him for warning me as I gave him his hat, and asked him to give Captain Saunders my love.

When I returned to the office Wolfe had his book open again. Always he is part mule, but sometimes he is all mule. He still didn't know when or where or how Dinah Utley had died, and he knew I did know, and he had no idea how much or little risk he was running to earn the rest of that sixty grand, but by gum he wasn't going to budge. He wasn't going to admit that we cared what had happened to her because he had been childish enough to tell me we didn't.

At the dinner table, in between bites of deviled grilled lamb kidneys with a sauce he and Fritz had invented, he explained why it was that all you needed to know about any human society was what they ate. If you knew what they ate you could deduce everything else—culture, philosophy, morals, politics, everything. I enjoyed it because the kidneys were tender and tasty and that sauce is one of Fritz' best, but I wondered how you would make out if you tried to deduce everything about Wolfe by knowing what he had eaten in the past ten years. I decided you would deduce that he was dead.

After dinner I went out. Wednesday was poker night, and that Wednesday Saul Panzer was the host, at his one-man apartment on the top floor of a remodeled house on 38th Street between Lexington and Third. You'll meet Saul further on. If you've already met him you know why I would have liked to have an hour alone with him, to give him the picture and see if he agreed with me about Jimmy Vail. It was just as well I couldn't have the hour, because if Saul had agreed with me I would have had a personal problem; it would no longer have been just my private guess. Jimmy Vail was responsible for our holding it back until Friday, and if he had killed Dinah Utley he was making monkeys of us. Of course that would serve Wolfe right, but how about me? It affected my poker, with Saul right there, but four other men were there also so I couldn't tell him. Saul, who misses nothing, saw that I was off my game and made remarks about it. It didn't affect his game any. He usually wins, and that night he raked it in. When we quit at the usual deadline, two o'clock, he had more than a hundred bucks of my money, and I was in no mood to stay and confide in him as an old and trusted friend.

Thursday, the morning after a late session of hard, tight poker, I don't turn out until nine or nine-thirty unless something important is cooking, but that Thursday I found myself lying on my back with my eyes wide open before eight. It was getting on my nerves. I said aloud, "Goddam Jimmy Vail anyhow," swung my legs around, and got erect.

I like to walk. I liked to walk in woods and pastures when I was a kid in Ohio, and now I like to walk even more on Manhattan sidewalks. If you don't walk much you wouldn't know, but the angle you get on people and things when you're walking is absolutely different from the one you get when you're in a car or in anything else that does the moving for you. So after washing and shaving and dressing and eating breakfast and reading about Dinah Utley in the *Times,* nothing I didn't already know, I buzzed the plant rooms on the house phone to tell Wolfe I was going out on a personal errand and would be back by noon, and went.

Of course you don't learn anything about people in general by walking around taking them in; you only learn things about this one or that one. I learned something that morning about a girl in a gray checked suit who caught her heel in a grating on Second Avenue in the Eighties. No girl I had ever known would have done what she did. Maybe no other girl in the world would. But I shouldn't have got started about walking. I mentioned walking only to explain how it happened that at a quarter past eleven I entered a drugstore at the corner of 54th Street and Eighth Avenue, sat at the counter, and requested a glass of milk. As it was brought and I took a sip, a Broadway type came in and got on the stool next to me and said to the soda jerk, "Cuppa coffee, Sam. You heard about Jimmy Vail?"

"Where would I hear about Jimmy Vail?" Sam demanded, getting a cup. "All I hear is step on it. What about Jimmy Vail?"

"He died. It was on the radio just now. Found him dead on the floor with a statue on top of him. You know I used to know Jimmy before he married a billion. Knew him well."

"I didn't know." Sam brought the coffee. "Too bad." A customer came to a stool down the line, and Sam moved.

I finished the glass of milk before I went to the phone

booth. I may have gulped it some, but by God I finished it. I wasn't arranging my mind; there was nothing in it to arrange; I was just drinking milk. When I went to the phone booth I got out a dime and started my hand to the slot but pulled it back. Not good enough. A voice on a phone is all right up to a point, but I might decide to go beyond that point, and a little more walking might help. I returned the dime to my pocket, departed, walked seven blocks crosstown and ten blocks downtown, entered the marble lobby of a building, and took an elevator.

I gave the receptionist on the twentieth floor a nod and went on by. Lon Cohen's room, with his name on the door but no title, was two doors this side of the *Gazette*'s publisher's. I don't remember a time that I have ever entered it and he wasn't on the phone, and that time was no exception. He darted a glance at me and went on talking, and I took the chair at the end of his desk and noted that he showed no sign of being short on sleep, though he had left Saul's place the same time I had, a little after two. His little dark face was neat and smooth, and his dark brown, deep-set eyes were clear and keen. When he had finished on the phone he turned to me and shook his head.

"Sorry, I've banked it. I guess I could spare a ducat."

He had been the only winner last night besides Saul. "I wouldn't want to strap you," I said. "A dime would see me through the week. But first, what about Jimmy Vail?"

"Oh." He cocked his head. "Is Wolfe looking for a job, or has he got one?"

"Neither one. I'm interested personally. I was taking a walk and heard something. I could wait and buy a paper, but I'm curious. What about him?"

"He's dead."

"So I heard. How?"

"He was found—you know about the Harold F. Tedder library."

"Yeah. Statues."

"He was found there a little after nine o'clock this morning by his stepdaughter, Margot Tedder. On the floor, with Benjamin Franklin on him. Benjamin Franklin in bronze, a copy of the one in Philadelphia by John

Thomas Macklin. That would be a beautiful picture, but I don't know if we got one. I can phone downstairs."

"No, thanks. How did Benjamin Franklin get on him?"

"If we only knew that and knew it first. You got any ideas?"

"No. What do you know?"

"Damn little. Nothing. I can phone downstairs and see if anything more is in, but I doubt it. We've got five men on it, but you know how the cops are, and the DA, when it's people in that bracket. They don't even snarl, they just button their lips."

"You must know *some*thing. Like how long he'd been dead."

"We don't. We will in time for the three-o'clock." The phone buzzed. He got it, said "Yes" twice and "No" four times, and returned to me. "Your turn, Archie. Your fee's showing, or Wolfe's fee is. Yesterday morning the body of Mrs. Vail's secretary is found in a ditch in Westchester. This morning the body of her husband is found in her library, and here you come—not on the phone, in person. So of course Wolfe has been hired by someone. When? Yesterday? About the secretary?"

I eyed him. "I could give you a whole front page."

"I'll settle for half. Don't pin me to the wall with your steely eyes. I'm sensitive. You know who killed the secretary."

"No. I thought I did, but not now. What I've got may break any minute—or it may not. If I give it to you now you'll have to save it until I give the word—unless it breaks, of course. This is personal. Mr. Wolfe doesn't even know I'm here."

"Okay. I'll save it."

"You don't mean maybe."

"No. I'll save it unless it breaks."

"Then get pencil and paper. Jimmy Vail was expected home from the country Sunday night but didn't come. Monday morning Mrs. Vail got a note in the mail saying she could have him back for five hundred grand and she would get a phone call from Mr. Knapp. I have a photograph of the note, taken by me, and I may let you have a print if you'll help me mark a deck of cards so I can win my money back from Saul. How would you like to run a good picture of that note, exclusive?"

"I'd help you mark ten decks of cards. A hundred. Is this straight, Archie?"

"Yes."

"My God. That 'Knapp' is beautiful. How did he spell it?"

I spelled it. "He phoned Monday afternoon and told her to get the money, put it in a suitcase, put the suitcase in the trunk of her blue sedan, and Tuesday evening drive to Fowler's Inn on Route Thirty-three, arriving at ten o'clock. She did so. At Fowler's Inn she was called to the phone and was told, probably the same voice, to look in the phone book where Z begins. There was a note there giving instructions. I haven't—"

"Beautiful," Lon said. His pencil was moving fast.

"Not bad. Don't interrupt, I'm in a hurry. I haven't got a picture of that note, but I have the text, taken from the original by me. The notes were typewritten. Following the instructions, she drove around a while and got to The Fatted Calf around eleven o'clock. There she got another phone call and was told to look in the phone book where U begins. Another note, same typewriting—I have the text. More instructions. Following them, she took Route Seven to Route Thirty-five, Route Thirty-five to Route One Twenty-three, and Route One Twenty-three to Iron Mine Road, which is all rock and a yard wide. She turned into it. When a car—"

"Dinah Utley," Lon said. "The secretary. Her body was found on Iron Mine Road."

"Don't interrupt. When a car behind her blinked its lights she stopped and got out and got the suitcase from the trunk. A man with only his eyes uncovered came from the other car, took the suitcase, and told her to go straight home, stop nowhere, and say nothing, which she did. Around seven-thirty yesterday morning her husband phoned her from their place in the country and said the kidnapers had let him go in one piece and he would come to town as soon as he cleaned up and ate. He also said they had told him to keep the lid on for forty-eight hours or he would regret it, and he was going to and expected her to. I don't know exactly when he arrived at the house on Fifth Avenue, but it must have been around ten o'clock."

I stood up. "Okay, that's it. I've got to go. If your sheet prints even a hint of it before I give the word, I'll write a letter to the editor and feed your eyes to the cat. If and when I give the word, there is to be no mention of Nero Wolfe or me. If it breaks, about the kidnaping, before I give the word, you'll still be out in front with a lot of facts the others won't have. I'll be seeing you."

"Wait a minute!" Lon was up. "You know how hot this is. It could burn my ass to cinders."

"It sure could. Then you couldn't help me mark a deck."

"How solid is it?"

"It isn't. There's an alternative. Either it's good as gold, every word, or Mrs. Jimmy Vail is unquestionably a double-breasted liar and almost certainly a murderer. If the latter, she'll be in no position to burn even your ears, let alone your ass. If she killed Dinah Utley, who killed Jimmy? Benjamin Franklin?" I turned to go.

"Damn it, listen!" He had my arm. "Was Dinah Utley with Mrs. Vail Tuesday night in the blue sedan?"

"No. For either alternative, that's positive. Dinah's own car was there at Iron Mine Road. That's the crop for now, Lon. I just wanted to burn a bridge. You could ask questions for an hour, but I haven't got an hour."

I went. Out to the elevator, down to the lobby, out to the sidewalk; and I started walking again. A taxi wouldn't have been much quicker, and I preferred to be on my feet. Down Lexington Avenue to 35th Street, and crosstown to the old brownstone. I mounted the stoop, let myself in with my key, put my coat on a hanger, and went to the office. Wolfe was at his desk, pouring beer.

"Good afternoon," I said. "Did you turn on the radio for the twelve o'clock news?"

"Yes."

"Did it mention Jimmy Vail?"

"Yes."

I went to my desk and sat. "I dropped in so you could have the satisfaction of firing me face to face. I have disobeyed orders. I am disloyal. I have betrayed your trust. I just told Lon Cohen about the kidnaping of Jimmy

Vail. Not for publication; he won't use it until I say he can. I didn't mention Mrs. Vail's hiring you. I kept you out of it. I'm not quitting, you're firing me, so I'm entitled to two months' severance pay."

He lifted the glass and drank. The idea is to drink when there is still an inch of foam so it will get on his lips and he can lick it off. He licked it off and put the glass down. "Is this flummery?" he demanded.

"No, sir. It's straight. If you want me to tell you why I did it, I will, but not as an excuse, just as information. Do you want it?"

"Yes."

"It was getting too hot. I knew too much that you didn't know. You wouldn't take what I had got at White Plains, and you knew darned well I had seen Mrs. Vail on my way back, and you wouldn't take what I had got there either. From what—"

"I did not refuse to listen to you."

"Nuts. You know as well as I do how it stood. You had said we didn't care what had happened to Dinah Utley and we were not concerned. Will it help to chew at that?"

"No."

"Okay. What I had got had made me decide that Jimmy had probably kidnaped himself, and he had killed Dinah Utley, and he was making monkeys of us. So I was stuck. I had to give in and say, please Mr. Wolfe, put your book down for a while and kindly permit me to tell you what happened yesterday so you can decide what to do. When you came down at eleven o'clock. You know how I liked that. I wasn't going to sit here on my rump all morning looking forward to it, so I went for a walk, and at eighteen minutes past eleven I heard a man tell another man that Jimmy Vail had been found dead on the floor of the library, where I had been yesterday afternoon."

I paused for dramatic effect. "So where was I? If Homicide hadn't already learned that I had been there yesterday in conference with the whole damn family, they soon would. Cramer himself might already be here ringing the bell. When he asked me what I was doing there, if I told him, I would be ditching our commitment to Mrs.

Vail, and if I didn't tell him, I would be in for a picnic and the least I could expect would be losing my license. It wouldn't help any to come and say, please, Mr. Wolfe, even if you're not concerned kindly permit me to tell you what has happened because I'm in a jam. What could you do? I had to handle it myself, and I did. I went and did something you had told me not to do. I told Lon Cohen about the kidnaping. Then I came and saw that Cramer or Stebbins wasn't here, since there was no police car out front, and entered. Now you fire me and I go. Fast. One will get you a thousand that no one will find me before eleven o'clock tomorrow morning, the deadline." I arose.

"Sit down," he growled.

"No. Cramer or Stebbins may be here any minute."

"He won't be admitted."

"They'll cover the house front and back and come back with a warrant." I moved.

"Stop!" he bellowed. "Very well," he said. "You leave me no choice. I concede that we care what happened to Miss Utley and we are concerned. Report in full."

"If I'm fired why should I report?"

"You are not fired. Confound you, report!"

"It's too late. I'd be interrupted. The doorbell might ring any second."

He glared at me, then turned his head to glare at the clock. He made fists of his hands and glared at them, then used them to push his chair back. He got up and headed for the door, and when he reached the hall he roared, "Fritz!" The door to the kitchen swung open, and Fritz appeared. Wolfe was moving to the front, to the rack. He got his coat off the hanger and turned.

"Are the mussels open?"

"No, sir. It's only—"

"Don't open them. Keep them. Archie and I are going out. We'll be back for lunch tomorrow. Keep the door bolted."

Fritz gawked. "But—but—" He was speechless.

"If anyone inquires, you can't tell tell him where we are, since you won't know." He found the armholes of the coat I had taken and was holding. "Lunch at the usual time tomorrow."

"But you must have a bag—"

"I'll manage. Tell Theodore. You know what a search warrant is. If a policeman comes with one admit him, and stay with him. Archie?"

I had my coat on and the door open. He crossed the sill, and as I followed I shut the door. As we descended the stoop I asked, "The car?" and he said no, and at the bottom he turned right, toward Ninth Avenue. But we didn't reach Ninth Avenue. Halfway there he turned right and started up a stoop of a brownstone the same size and color and age as his, but it had a vestibule. He had used his vestibule to enlarge the hall years ago. He pushed the button, and in a moment the door was opened by a dark-haired woman with fine frontage to whom we had sent orchids now and then for the past ten years. She was a little startled at sight of us.

"Why, Mr. Wolfe . . . Mr. Goodwin . . . come in. You want to see the doctor?"

We entered, and she closed the door. "Not professionally," Wolfe said. "And briefly. Here will do."

"Of course. Certainly." She was flustered. I had been there off and on, but Wolfe hadn't; Doc Vollmer had come to him when required. She went down the hall and opened a door and disappeared, and in a minute Vollmer came—a sad-looking little guy with lots of forehead and not much jaw. He had once taken twenty-two stitches in my side where a character with a knife had gone wide enough but not deep enough.

He approached. "Well, well! Come in, come in!"

"We have come to impose on you, Doctor," Wolfe said. "We need a room to sit in the rest of today and beds for tonight. We need enough food to sustain us until tomorrow. Can you oblige us?"

Vollmer wasn't startled; he was merely stunned. "Why —of course—you mean for you? You and Archie?"

"Yes. We expected a troublesome visitor, and we fled. By tomorrow he will be less troublesome. We want seclusion until then. If it would inconvenience you beyond tolerance . . ."

"No, of course not." He smiled. "I'm honored. I'm flattered. I'm afraid the food won't be quite . . . I have no Fritz. Will you need a phone in the room?"

"No, just the room."

"Then, if you'll excuse me—I have a patient in my office—"

He went back to the door and in, and in a couple of minutes the dark-haired woman, whose name was Helen Gillard, came out. She asked us to come with her, trying to sound as if it was perfectly natural for a couple of neighbors to drop in and request board and lodging, and led the way to the stairs. She took us up two flights and down a hall to the rear, and into a room with two windows and a big bed and walls covered with pictures of boats and baseball players and boys and girls. Bill Vollmer, whom I had once showed how to take fingerprints, was away at school. Helen asked, "Will you come down for lunch or shall I bring trays?"

"Later," Wolfe said. "Thank you. Mr. Goodwin will tell you."

"Can I bring you anything?"

Wolfe said no, and she went. She left the door open, and I went and closed it. We removed our coats, and I found hangers in a closet. Wolfe stood and looked around. It was hopeless. There were three chairs. The seats of two of them were about half as wide as his fanny, and the third one had arms and it would be a squeeze. He went to the bed, sat on the edge, took his shoes off, twisted around, stretched out with his head on the pillow, shut his eyes, and spoke.

"Report."

6

At 12:35 P.M. Friday, Inspector Cramer of Homicide West, seated in the red leather chair, took a mangled unlit cigar from his mouth and said, "I still want to know where you and Goodwin have been and what you've done the past twenty-four hours."

The only objection to telling him was that he would have gone or sent someone to check, and Doc Vollmer was a busy man, so it would have been a poor return for his hospitality. As for the hospitality, I had no kick coming, having been given a perfectly good bed in a spare room, but Wolfe had had a few difficulties. Books to read, but no chair upstairs big enough to take him, and he won't read lying down. No pajamas big enough for him, so he had to sleep in his underwear. Grub not bad enough to take credit for facing up to hardship, but not good enough to please the palate; only one brand of beer, and not his. Pillows too soft to use only one and too thick to use two. Towels either too little or too big. Soap that smelled like tuberoses (he said), and he uses geranium. He really bore up well for his first day and night away from home in more than a year; he was glum, of course, as you would be if you were forced to skedaddle, without stopping to take a toothbrush, by circumstances you weren't to blame for.

We had not phoned Fritz to find out if there had been any callers because we didn't know much about modern electronics, and who does? We knew tracing a phone call wasn't as simple as it used to be, but they might have a tame neutron or positron or some other tron that could camp inside Wolfe's number and tell where a call came from. For news there were the papers, Thursday evening and Friday morning. Not a word in the *Gazette* about kidnaping; Lon had kept it; and nothing in the *Times* Friday morning or on the radio at eleven o'clock. There was plenty about Jimmy Vail, but the main fact was still as I had got it from Lon: Margot Tedder had entered the library at 9:05 Thursday morning and found him there on the floor underneath Benjamin Franklin. The bronze statue had flattened his chest.

Five people, not one, had last seen him alive Wednesday evening—his wife; her son and daughter, Noel and Margot Tedder; her brother, Ralph Purcell; and her attorney, Andrew Frost. They had all been in the library after dinner (subject of the family conference not mentioned), and shortly after ten o'clock Jimmy Vail, saying that he hadn't slept much for three days (reason not given), had stretched out on the couch and gone to sleep. He had still been there an hour later, sound asleep, when they broke it up and left. Noel and Margot Tedder and Ralph Purcell had gone up to bed, and Mrs. Vail and Andrew Frost had gone up to her study. Around midnight Frost had left, and Mrs. Vail had gone to bed. Evidently she too had been short on sleep, for she had still been in bed when her son and daughter came to her room Thursday morning to tell her about Jimmy.

Everyone in the house, of course including the servants, had known that Benjamin Franklin was wobbly. The *Gazette* had a piece by an expert about the different methods of fastening the bronze feet of a man to the base he stands on. He hadn't been permitted to examine the statue that had toppled onto Jimmy Vail, but he said the trouble couldn't have been a loose nut; his guess was that the bolt or bolts had had a flaw and had cracked at some time when the statue was being handled. It was quite possible, he said, that Jimmy Vail, half aroused from a deep sleep, on his way across the room to the door, had lost his balance and grabbed at the statue and pulled it down on him. I thought it was darned decent of the *Gazette* to run the piece. A good murder or suspicion of one will sell thousands of extra papers, and here they were promoting the idea that it had been accidental. They had got the picture Lon had said would be beautiful, of Benjamin Franklin on top of Jimmy Vail.

There were no quotes from any members of the family. Mrs. Vail was in bed under a doctor's care, inaccessible. Andrew Frost wasn't seeing reporters, but he had told the police that when he left the house around midnight, unescorted, he had not stopped at the library on his way out.

As I have said, there was nothing new on the radio at eleven o'clock Friday morning. At 11:10 I phoned Homicide West from Doc Vollmer's office downstairs—he was at the hospital—and told the desk man to tell Inspector Cramer that Nero Wolfe had some information for him regarding Jimmy Vail. At 11:13 I called the District Attorney's office at White Plains, got an assistant DA, and told him to tell Hobart that Wolfe had decided to answer any questions he might care to ask. At 11:18 I rang the *Gazette,* got Lon Cohen, and told him it was all his and would probably soon be everybody's, and he could even use our names as the source if he spelled them right. Of course he wanted more, but I hung up. At 11:24 we thanked Helen Gillard and asked her to thank the doctor for us, left the house, walked sixty yards to Wolfe's, found the door was bolted, pushed the button and were admitted by Fritz, and learned that Sergeant Purley Stebbins had come yesterday ten minutes after we left, and Inspector Cramer had come at six o'clock. No search warrant, but Cramer had phoned at 8:43 and again at 10:19. At the office door Wolfe asked about the mussels, and Fritz said they were in perfect condition. Wolfe was at his desk with his eyes closed, in the only chair that will really do, sitting and breathing, and I was at my desk opening the mail, when the doorbell rang and I went. It was Inspector Cramer, his rugged pink face a little pinker than normal and his burly shoulders hunched a little. When I let him in he didn't even give me an eye, but kept going, to the office, and as I followed, after closing the door, I heard him rasping.

"Where have you and Goodwin been since yesterday noon?"

Fifty minutes later, as I have said, at 12:35 P.M., he demanded, "I still want to know where you and Goodwin have been and what you've done the past twenty-four hours."

We had opened the bag. Most of the talking had been done by me because the whole world knows—well, six or eight people—that the only difference between me and a tape recorder is that you can ask me questions. And for some of it—the White Plains part and the session in the Harold F. Tedder library—Wolfe hadn't been present. We had handed over the note that had come in the mail, the original, and my transcriptions, carbons, of the other two notes and the telephone conversation between Mrs. Vail and Mr. Knapp. I did make a few improvements on Wolfe's phrasing, and mine too, by making it emphatic that the main point had been, first, to get Jimmy Vail back alive, and then to protect him and Mrs. Vail by keeping his promise to the kidnapers. Of course Cramer landed on that with both feet. Why had we gone on protecting Vail for twenty-four hours after he was dead? Obviously, so Wolfe could hang onto the money he already had in the bank. Withholding information vital to a murder investigation. Obstructing justice to earn a fee.

Wolfe snorted, and my feelings were hurt. There had still been Mrs. Vail to consider, and we hadn't known that Vail had been murdered. Did he? I had read an article by a statue expert which said that it could have been an accident. Wasn't it? Cramer didn't say, but he didn't have to; his being there was enough to show that it was open, though maybe not open-and-shut. He said we had of course seen the statement of the District Attorney's office in the morning paper that the apparent cause of Vail's death was the statue falling on him, that a final determination would be made when the autopsy had been completed, and that a thorough investigation was being made. Then he took the chewed unlit cigar from his mouth and said he still wanted to know where we had been the past twenty-four hours.

Wolfe would not be riled. He was back in his house, in his chair, the deadline was past, and the mussels would be ready in an hour. "As I told you," he said, "we knew we would be pestered and we decamped. Where is of no consequence. We did nothing and communicated with no one. At eleven this morning, when our obligation to Mrs. Vail had been fulfilled, Mr. Goodwin telephoned your office. You have no valid grievance. Even now you will not say that you're investigating a murder; you're trying to determine if one has been committed. A charge of obstructing justice couldn't possibly hold. Some of the questions you asked Mr. Goodwin indicated that you suspect him of trying to find the typewriter that was missing from Mrs. Vail's study. Nonsense. Since yesterday noon he has been trying to find nothing whatever, and neither have I. Our interest in the matter is ended. We have no further commitment to Mrs. Vail. We have no client. If she herself killed both Miss Utley and Mr. Vail, which seems unlikely but is not inconceivable, I owe her no service."

"She has paid you sixty thousand dollars."

"And by the terms of my employment I have earned it."

Cramer got up, came to my desk, and dropped the cigar in my wastebasket. That wasn't regular; usually he threw the cigar at it and missed. He went back and picked up his hat from the floor where he had dropped it and turned to Wolfe.

"I want a statement with nothing left out signed by you and Goodwin. At my office by four o'clock. The District

Attorney's office will probably want to see Goodwin. It would suit me fine if they want you too."

"Not everything everybody said by four o'clock," I objected. "That would be a six-hour job."

"I want the substance. All details. You can omit White Plains, we've got that from them." He turned and tramped out. By the time I had followed him to the front, shut the door after him, and returned to the office, Wolfe had his book open. I finished opening the mail and put it on his desk and then pulled the typewriter around and got out paper and carbons. That would be a job, and it was water under the bridge, since we had no case and no client. Four carbons: one for Westchester, one for the Manhattan DA, and two for us. As I rolled the paper in Wolfe's voice came at my back.

"Dendrobium chrysotoxum for Miss Gillard and Laelia purpurata for Doctor Vollmer. Tomorrow."

"Right. And Sitassia readia for you and Transcriptum underwoodum for me." I hit the keys.

With time out for lunch and a shave and a clean shirt, it was five minutes past four when I left the house, walked to 34th and Eighth Avenue for a *Gazette,* and flagged a taxi. I had made it barely in time for Wolfe to sign it before he went up to the plant rooms, but there had been interruptions. Sergeant Purley Stebbins had phoned to tell me to take the statement to the DA's office instead of Homicide West. Ben Dykes had phoned and kept me on the wire fifteen minutes and had finally settled for an appointment with Wolfe at eleven-thirty Saturday morning. Reporters from three newspapers had called, two on the phone and one in person, and had been stalled. What had stung them was on the front page of the *Gazette,* which I perused as the taxi took me downtown—the first public notice of the kidnaping of Jimmy Vail and delivery of the ransom money by his wife. Of course it didn't have the big kick of a kidnaping story, the suspense about the fate of the victim, since Jimmy had come back safe and sound, but it had the added attraction of his death by violence in his own home some fifteen hours after he returned. There were pictures of Fowler's Inn and The Fatted Calf and Iron Mine Road. Lon had hung onto it, but he had taken steps. The mention of Wolfe and me was vague and sort of gave the impression that we knew about it because we knew everything, which wouldn't hurt a bit. It was the fattest scoop I had ever given Lon, and that wouldn't hurt either. When I got to 155 Leonard Street and was taken to the room of assistant DA Mandel, he greeted me by tapping the *Gazette* that was there on his desk and demanding, "When did you give them this?" I told him ten minutes after eleven this morning.

It didn't amount to much that time. I have had several conversations in that building that lasted more than six hours, one that lasted fourteen hours, and two that ended by my being locked up as a material witness. That day Mandel and two Homicide Bureau dicks let me go in less than two hours, partly because I had the signed statement with me, partly because they weren't officially interested in the kidnaping since that had been a Westchester job, and partly because they were by no means sure Jimmy Vail's death had been a homicide and if it wasn't that would be okay with them. A dick has enough grief dealing with riffraff, and he would prefer to have no part of Tedders and Vails. So after going through the routine motions for an hour and a half they shooed me out, and at a quarter past six I was paying a hackie in front of the old brownstone and climbing out. As my foot touched the sidewalk, someone grabbed my arm and pronounced my name, and I wheeled.

It was Noel Tedder. "Who the hell does this Nero Wolfe think he is?" he squeaked.

"It depends on his mood." I moved my arm, but he had a grip. "Let go of my arm, I might need it. Why, did he bounce you?"

"I haven't been in. First I was told through a crack to come back after six, and I did. Then I was told Wolfe was busy—'engaged,' he said. I asked for you and was told you were out and he didn't know when you'd be back. I said I'd come in and wait, and he said I wouldn't. What does it take, a passport?"

"Did you give your name?"

"Certainly."

"Did you say what you want to see him about?"

"No. I'll tell him."

"Not unless you tell me first. Not only is that the routine, but also he's had a hard day. There was no homemade blackberry jam for breakfast, he had to skip his morning turn with the orchids, a police inspector came and annoyed him, and he had to read a long statement and sign it. If you tell me what you want, there may be a chance. If you don't, it's hopeless."

"Out here?"

"We can sit on the stoop if you'd rather."

He turned his head to look at a man and woman who were passing. He needed a shave. He also needed either a haircut, a comb and brush, or a hat, and his plaid jacket and striped slacks could have stood a little pressing. When the man and woman were ten paces away his eyes came back to me.

"I've got a chance to make a pot but I can't do it alone. I don't even know how to start. My mother told me that if I can find the money she paid the kidnapers, or any part of it, I can have it. Half a million. I want Wolfe to help me. He can have a fifth of it for his share."

My brows were up. "When did your mother tell you that?"

"Wednesday evening."

"She may feel different about it now."

"No, she doesn't. I asked her this afternoon. She's not very—she's in pretty bad shape—but I didn't think it would hurt to ask her. She said yes. She said she wouldn't want any of that money now anyhow."

My brows were still up. "The police know about the kidnaping. And the FBI."

"I don't know about the FBI. We told the police this morning."

"Dozens of trained men are on the job already. By tomorrow there'll be hundreds. Fat chance you'd have."

"Damn it, I know I wouldn't! That's why I've got to have Nero Wolfe! Isn't he better than they are?"

"That's a point." I was looking at another point. We had never taken a crack at that kind of problem, and if Wolfe could be peekayed into tackling it, it would be interesting to see how he went about it. It would also be interesting to collect his share if there was anything to share.

"I'll tell you," I said. "I doubt very much if Mr. Wolfe will touch it. He's not only eccentric, he hates to work, and he seldom takes a case on a contingent basis. But I'm willing to put it up to him. You may come inside to wait."

"If you can get inside," he squeaked. That tenor didn't fit his make-up at all.

"I can try," I said, and made for the stoop, and he followed me up. The chain-bolt was on, so I had to push the button. If Fritz, letting us in, was surprised to see me bringing a customer who had been turned away twice, he didn't show it. Fritz shows only what he thinks it is proper to show. I took Tedder to the front room and left him, and went to the office by way of the hall instead of the connecting door. Wolfe, at his desk, had the middle drawer open and was fingering in it. Counting caps of beer bottles to see how much he had gained on the week's quota by being away twenty-four hours. I waited to speak until he shut the drawer and looked up.

"Regards from Mandel. I didn't see the DA. They probably won't bother us again unless and until they have to decide that Jimmy Vail didn't die by accident, which they would hate to do. You have seen the *Gazette?*"

"Yes."

"Any comment?"

"No."

"Then I'm still not fired. I'm taking a leave of absence without pay. Say a month, but it may be more."

His lips tightened. He took a deep breath. "Are you bent on vexing me beyond endurance?"

"No, sir. I want to grab an opportunity. When I arrived just now Noel Tedder was there on the sidewalk, vexed beyond endurance because you wouldn't see him. His mother told him Wednesday that he could have the money she paid the kidnaper if he could find it and get it, and he came to offer you a one-fifth share to help him. Of course you wouldn't be interested now that you only take cases where all you have to do is put a notice in the paper, so I'm going to tell him I'll take it on myself. I took the liberty of putting him in the front room. I thought I ought to tell you first. Of course it's long odds, but if I got it, the whole pile, my cut would be a hundred grand and I could quit vexing you and open my own office, maybe with Saul Panzer for a partner, and we could—"

"Shut up."

"Yes, sir. That will be one advantage, you won't have to bellow—"

"Shut up."

"Yes, sir."

He regarded me, not with affection. "So you expect to badger me into this fantastic gamble."

"You might take a minute out to look at it. It would be satisfactory to find something that ten thousand cops and FBI men will be looking for. And each year when you top the eighty-per-cent bracket you relax. I admit it's a big if, but if you raked this in and added it to what you've already collected this year, you could relax until winter, and it's not May yet. If you missed, you would only be out expenses. As for my badgering you, we have nothing in prospect, and if I take a month off Fritz can dust your desk and empty the wastebasket and you can open the mail."

"That's bluster. You wouldn't."

"The hell I wouldn't."

He closed his eyes, probably to contemplate the rosy possibility of months and months with no work to do and no would-be customers admitted. In a minute he opened them and muttered, "Very well, bring him in."

7

As Noel Tedder sat in the red leather chair and crossed his legs, showing blue and yellow socks beneath the striped slacks. Wolfe surveyed him. He had to adjust to the outfit. I have heard him say that men who wear conventional clothes are sheep, but I have also heard him say that men who wear unconventional clothes are popinjays. You can't win.

Tedder asked him if I had told him what he wanted, and Wolfe nodded. He spoke. "The most unpromising enterprise I have ever been asked to undertake, if Mr. Goodwin understood you and I understood him. Mrs.

Vail, your mother, told you that if you recovered the money she paid to ransom her husband, you could keep it; and if I help you, you will pay me one-fifth of what we recover if we're successful, and nothing if we fail. Is that it?"

"That's it. Of course I—"

"If you please. When did your mother tell you that?"

"Wednesday evening. And again this afternoon. With Jimmy gone—my stepfather—I thought I'd better ask her."

"Wednesday evening, did she broach it or did you?"

" 'Broach'?"

"Bring it up. Introduce the idea."

"I don't remember. Does that matter?"

"It may. If you suggested it a conjecture enters. That you knew where the money was and you wanted to get it in a manner that would entitle you—don't interrupt—entitle you to keep it. You come to me for help because you can't very well just go and get it and produce it. You will give me hints, cannily of course, and guided by them Mr. Goodwin, under my direction, will find the money. Even if your hints have made me smell a rat, I'll hold my nose and take my share. So who broached it, your mother or you?"

Tedder tittered. I don't want to give a false impression, especially since I have mentioned his tenor. Men do titter. "Jesus," he said, "that would be pups. That would be sharp. But how would I know where it is?"

"You would know where you put it Tuesday night after you or your confederate took it from your mother on Iron Mine Road."

"Huh?" He was squinting. "You've lost me. Say it again."

Wolfe wiggled a finger. "Mr. Tedder. You have come to me with an extraordinary proposal, and naturally my first question is what about you? Did you kidnap your stepfather?"

"Balls. He might have recognized me."

"Did you have a hand in the kidnaping? Yes or no."

"No. N, O, no." Tedder was still squinting. "Got a Bible?"

"That wouldn't establish it. If I assume your good

faith, where are we? It would be witless to try to compete with the intricate and expert routine of the army of official investigators. If we start at all it must be from a point chosen by us and overlooked by them. Before I accept or decline your proposal I must know if you will agree with me on that point; and first of all I must ask, what if we find the money and your mother repudiates her engagement to let you keep it?"

"She won't."

"She might."

Tedder shook his head. "Four people besides me heard her say it—my sister Margot, her brother Ralph, Frost, the lawyer, and Jimmy. Of course Jimmy's dead."

"She still might. I must tell you that, if she does, my share will be legally collectible and I'll collect it."

"Sure, why not? You won't have to. My mother won't renege. What's the point I have to agree on?"

"It's a series of assumptions, and you may not like them. The first and basic one is that Mr. Vail's death was not an accident. He was murdered."

"Huh?" Tedder uncrossed his legs and sat up. "He pulled that goddam statue over on him."

"No." Wolfe was emphatic. "I concede that that's conceivable; it may even be sufficiently plausible for the police to accept it; but I reject it. There is no implication in the published accounts that he was drunk. Was he?"

"No."

"Had he been drinking?"

"He had had a couple, not more. His usual, bourbon and water. He could handle half a dozen. He wasn't even started. He was just sleepy. He said he couldn't keep his eyes open and went to the couch."

"And later, after you and the others had gone— Did you turn the lights off when you left?"

"All but one. Mother said to leave one on."

"A good light?"

"Fairly good. A floor lamp by the wall."

"And he awoke enough to realize where he was, leave the couch, stand, and walk; and, losing his balance, he caught at the statue, which was insecure, and brought it down on him. It's possible, but I don't believe it. I do not believe that a man awake enough to walk would be so befuddled that he couldn't dodge a falling statue. Was it on a direct line from the couch to the door?"

"Not direct, but not far out." Tedder was squinting again. "You said murder. How? Was he so sound asleep that he didn't wake up when someone dragged him off the couch and over to the statue and pushed it over on him? Do you believe that?"

"No. He was drugged."

"The hell he was."

"He must have been. In one of his drinks. The handiest assumption is chloral hydrate, which is easily procured. In solution in an alcoholic beverage it has almost no taste. A moderate dose induces a deep sleep approaching coma. It decomposes rapidly and will not be detected by an autopsy unless it is performed within three or four hours after death, and even then the only reliable test is identification of urochloralic acid in the urine. That test is made only when chloral hydrate is specifically suspected, and with Mr. Vail I doubt if it was. I am not parading; I had this surmise yesterday and consulted a book."

He hadn't mentioned it to me; it would have been admitting that Jimmy Vail's death might possibly be of interest to us. We had several books on toxicology on the shelves, but he hadn't been here yesterday, so he must have found one when he was going over Doc Vollmer's shelves. I had had personal experience of chloral hydrate, having once been served a Mickey Finn by a woman named Dora Chapin. Two hours after I had swallowed it you could have rowed me out to Bedloe's Island and pushed the Statue of Liberty onto me and I wouldn't have batted an eye.

Wolfe was going on. "So that Mr. Vail was murdered with deliberation may properly be called a deduction, not an assumption. Not a final deduction, but a basic one, for it is the ground for my assumptions. Whether you like it or not, do you concur?"

"I don't know." Tedder's tongue showed between his lips. "Go on with your assumptions."

"They're purely tentative, to establish a starting point. But first another deduction, made three days ago, on Tuesday, by Mr. Goodwin and me. Dinah Utley, your mother's secretary, was implicated in the kidnaping, and not indirectly or passively. She had an active hand in it. Her death—"

"How do you know that?"

"By observed evidence and interpretation of it. I'll reserve it. I'm exposing my position, Mr. Tedder, because I have to if you're going to occupy it with me, but I need not reveal all the steps that have led to it. I'm taking your good faith as a working hypothesis, but there is still that conjecture—that you had a part in the kidnaping and you know where the money is. If so, it was an egregious blunder to come to me. I'll get my share of the money, and you'll get your share of doom. Do you want to withdraw before I commit myself to this mad gamble? Do you want to leave?"

"Hell no. You talk a lot and you talk big."

"I hope to the point—our starting point. I am almost there. Miss Utley was involved in the kidnaping and was murdered. Mr. Vail was the victim of the kidnaping and was murdered. My assumptions are, first, that both murders were consequential to the kidnaping operation; and second, that the person who killed Mr. Vail, with premeditation since he drugged him, being involved in the kidnaping, knows where the money is. He was present at the gathering at that house Wednesday evening. Therefore, if we are to find the money, our starting point is that house and its occupants. If you will proceed from that point with me, I'll accept your proposal."

Tedder was chewing his lips. "Jesus," he said. He chewed some more. "The way you put it . . . I guess I'm in over my head. You're saying one of them killed Jimmy—Uncle Ralph or Frost or my sister."

"Or your mother or you."

"Sure, we were there." He shook his head. "Holy Christ. My mother, that's crazy. Me, I liked Jimmy. He couldn't see me, but I liked him. Uncle Ralph—"

"That's irrelevant, Mr. Tedder. The murder resulted from the kidnaping—my assumption. The kidnaper wished him no harm and rendered him none; he only wanted the money. Logically that excludes your mother, but not you. There are several possibilities. For one, Miss Utley was killed because she demanded too large a share of the loot. For another, Mr. Vail was killed because he had learned that one of those present Wednesday evening was responsible for the kidnaping, and of course that wouldn't do. We ignore the mysterious Mr. Knapp perforce, because we don't know who or where he is. Presumably he was a confederate whose chief function was to make the phone calls, but he may also have got the money from your mother, since he spoke to her, and if he has bolted with it, we're done before we start. We could expose the murderer, to no profit, but that's all. I say 'we.' Is it 'we'? Do we proceed?"

"How?"

"First I would need to speak at length, separately, with those who were present Wednesday evening, beginning with you. You would have to bring them here, or send them, by some pretext—or some inducement, perhaps a share of the money. Then I'll see."

"Great. Just great. I ask them—my sister, for instance—to come and let you grill her to find out if she kidnaped Jimmy and then killed him. Great."

"You might manage to put it more tactfully."

"Yeah, I might." He leaned forward. "Look, Mr. Wolfe. Maybe you've got it right, your deductions and assumptions, and maybe not. If you have and you find the money, okay, I'll get mine and you'll get yours. I don't owe my uncle a damn thing, and God knows I don't owe that lawyer, Andrew Frost, anything. He talked my mother out of letting me have—oh, to hell with it. As for my sister, I'm not her keeper, repeat not—she can look out for herself. You try putting it to her tactfully and see what—"

The phone rang. I swiveled and got it. "Nero Wolfe's residence, Archie Goodwin speaking."

"This is Margot Tedder. I'd like to speak to Mr. Wolfe."

I told her to hold it and turned. "Margot Tedder wants to speak to you."

Noel made a noise. Wolfe frowned at his phone to remind it that he resents being summoned by it, no matter who, then reached for it. "Yes, Miss Tedder?"

"Nero Wolfe?"

"Yes."

"You never go anywhere, do you?"

"No."

"Then I'll have to come there. I'll come now."

"You won't be admitted. I'll be at dinner. Why do you wish to come?"

"I want you to help me do something."

"What?"

"I'd rather— Oh, it doesn't matter. About the money my mother gave the kidnapers. You know about that."

"Yes. What about it?"

"She has told me that if I can find it I can have it, and I want you to help me. We'll have to hurry. I'll come now. Your dinner can wait."

"I can't. More precisely, I won't. You may come at nine o'clock, not before. I'm busy. You will excuse me. I'm hanging up." He cradled the phone and turned. "Your sister says that her mother told her that if she finds the money paid to the kidnaper she can have it, and she is coming at nine o'clock to enlist my help. I'll tell her you have already engaged me. We have twenty minutes until my dinnertime. Where were you from eight o'clock Sunday evening until eight o'clock Wednesday morning?"

8

A man's time-and-place record as given by him may or may not prove anything, even if it doesn't check. There are a lot of people who wouldn't tell you exactly where they had been and what they had done between eight p.m. Sunday and eight a.m. Wednesday even if they hadn't kidnaped or murdered anybody. Wolfe, knowing how easy it is to frame an alibi, has seldom tried to crack one. In all the years I have been with him I haven't checked more than four or five. He has sometimes had Saul Panzer or Fred Durkin or Orrie Cather look into one, but not often. I put what Noel Tedder told him in my notebook, but I knew it wouldn't be checked unless developments nominated Noel for the tag. Besides, only one time and place was essential, either for Noel or for one of the others. It didn't have to be that he himself had snatched Jimmy Vail Sunday evening, or had helped to keep him wherever he had been kept, or had put notes in telephone books Tuesday evening, or had been at Iron Mine Road Tuesday night. The one essential time and place was the Harold F. Tedder library Wednesday evening, and we knew he had been there. They all had. The question had to be asked; if Noel had gone up in a balloon with six United States Senators Sunday morning and hadn't come down until Wednesday noon, he couldn't be expected to know where the money was, and that was the point. But I won't waste my space and your time reporting his whereabouts for those sixty hours.

More interesting was his reaction to the news that Margot was coming to see Wolfe. It fussed him more than anything Wolfe had said to him. When he said he didn't believe his mother had told her that, he had to squeeze it through his teeth. Evidently he had some strong feeling about his sister, and it wasn't brotherly love. Wolfe tried to ask him questions about Dinah Utley and her relations with Purcell and Frost and Margot, but got no usable answers. Noel wanted to be damn sure that Wolfe wasn't going to let Margot talk him into switching to her. He even offered to bring Uncle Ralph that evening and Andrew Frost in the morning. When Fritz announced dinner he followed Wolfe to the dining-room door, and I had to take his arm and start him to the front.

Returning and entering the dining room, I found that Wolfe had pulled his chair out but hadn't sat. "A grotesque venture," he grunted. "Preposterous. Will that woman be punctual?"

"Probably not." I pulled my chair back. "She's not the punctual type."

"But she may be. You'll have to be at the phone with your coffee to get Saul and Fred and Orrie. In my room in the morning at eight, and in the office with you at nine." Fritz was there with the stuffed clams, and he sat and took the spoon and fork. He couldn't have sat before giving me instructions because that would have been talking business during a meal, and by heck a rule is a rule is a rule. As I helped myself to clams I held my breath because if you smell them, mixed with shallots, chives, chervil, mushrooms, bread crumbs, sherry, and dry white wine, you take so many that you don't leave enough room for the duckling roasted in cider with Spanish sauce as revised by Wolfe and Fritz, leaving out the carrot and parsley and putting anchovies in. As I ate the clams I remarked to myself that we darned well had better find at least some leavings of the half a million, since Saul and Fred and Orrie came to twenty-five bucks an hour, plus expenses.

I don't know how Wolfe first got the notion that when I've had one good look at a woman and heard her speak, especially if she's under thirty, I can answer any question he wants to ask about her, but I know he still has it, chiefly on account of little items like my saying that Margot Tedder wouldn't be punctual. She was twenty-five minutes late. Of course if she had been on time I would have commented that she must need some ready cash quick. When you once get a reputation, or it gets you, you're stuck with it for good.

I have said that from hearsay she kept her chin up so she could look down her nose, and her manners when she entered the old brownstone didn't contradict it. Crossing the threshold, she gave me a nod for a butler, though I hadn't seen one at 994 Fifth Avenue, and when I took her to the office she stopped at the edge of the big rug, looked it over from side to side and end to end, and asked Wolfe, "Is that a Kazak?"

"No," he said. "Shirvan."

"You can't possibly appreciate it. Is it yours?"

"I doubt it. It was given to me in nineteen thirty-two, in Cairo, by a man to whom I had rendered a service, and I suspected he had stolen it in Kandahar. If it wasn't rightfully his, it isn't rightfully mine. But of course illegality of ownership does not extend indefinitely. If my possession of that rug were challenged by an heir of the Kandahar prince who once owned it, or by one of his wives or concubines, I would enter a defense. It would be a borderline case. After sufficient time legal ownership is undisputed. Your grandfather was a bandit; some of his forays were almost certainly actionable. But if a descendant of one of his victims tried to claim that fur thing you are wearing, she would be laughed at. I'm pleased that you recognize the quality of the rug, though only an ignoramus could mistake it for a Kazak. Kazaks have a long pile. You are Margot Tedder? I am Nero Wolfe." He pointed to the red leather chair. "Sit down and tell me what you want."

She had opened her mouth a couple of times to cut in on him, but Wolfe in full voice is not easy to interrupt, particularly if his eyes are pinning you. "I told you on the phone what I want," she said.

"You will please sit down, Miss Tedder. I like eyes at a level."

She glanced at me. The poor girl was stuck. She didn't want to sit down because he had ordered her to, but to stay on her feet would be silly. She compromised. One of the yellow chairs was at the end of my desk, and she came and sat on it. As I have said, when she walked you might have thought her hips were in a cast, but sitting she wasn't at all hard to look at.

"I didn't come," she said, "to listen to a lecture about legal ownership by a detective. You know what I came for. My mother paid you sixty thousand dollars for nothing. All you did was put that thing in the paper. For sixty thousand dollars you certainly ought to help me find the money my mother gave the kidnaper. That's more than ten per cent."

Wolfe grunted. "Twelve. That might be thought adequate. How would I go about it? Have you a suggestion?"

"Of course not. You would go about it the way any detective would. That's your business."

"Could I count on your cooperation?"

She frowned at him, her chin up. "How could I cooperate?"

He didn't frown back. Having put her in her place, he didn't mind if she didn't stay put. "That would depend on developments," he said. "Take a hypothesis. Do you know what a hypothesis is?"

"You're being impertinent."

"Not without provocation. You didn't know what a Shirvan is. The hypothesis: If I took the job you offer, I would want to begin by asking you some questions. For example, what were your relations with Dinah Utley?"

She stared. "What on earth has that got to do with finding the money?"

He nodded. "I thought so. You're under a misapprehension. You expected me to pit my wits and Mr. Goodwin's eyes and legs against the horde of official investigators who are combing the countryside and looking under every stone. Pfui. That would be infantile. I would have to approach it differently, and the best way—indeed, the only way—would be through Dinah Utley. You know that Mr. Goodwin and I suspected that she was implicated in the kidnaping; you heard your mother and Mr. Goodwin discuss it Wednesday afternoon. Now we don't suspect it; we know it. Therefore—"

"How do you know it? Because she was there and was killed?"

"Partly that, but there were other factors. She was here Tuesday afternoon. Therefore at least one of the kidnapers was someone with whom she had had contacts, and I would want to learn all I could about her. How well did you know her?"

"Why—she was my mother's secretary. She lived in the house, but she didn't regard herself as a servant. I thought my mother let her take too many liberties."

"What kind of liberties?"

"Different kinds. She ate with us. If we had people in for cocktails, she came in if she felt like it. If I asked her to do something, she might and she might not. You might have thought we were equals. You know, I must say, I think this is clever. Perhaps you *are* clever. I should have thought of this myself, about Dinah, only I really don't know much about her. She was there seven years, and I suppose she had friends of her own class, but I never saw them."

"Would your brother know more about her?"

"He might." She nodded. "Yes, I'm sure he would. He did things with her just to irritate me—like playing cards with her. Gin rummy in the library. You might have thought *they* were equals, and perhaps they should have been. Once he took her to a prizefight."

"That sounds promising. I would want to talk with him. I don't want to shock you, Miss Tedder, but the question should be asked. Is it conceivable that the kidnaping was a joint enterprise of Miss Utley and your brother? That your brother had a hand in it?"

"Good heavens." Her lips parted. She stared. "Of course

it's conceivable. That's the second thing you've thought of that *I* should have thought of."

"Given time, undoubtedly you would have. Your emotions have interfered with your mental processes. We would—"

"But if he—Noel—then he knows where the money is! He *has* the money?"

"Not too fast, Miss Tedder. That's merely a surmise. We would have to consider all possibilities, all those who had frequent opportunity to see Miss Utley. I understand that your mother's brother, Ralph Purcell, lives in that house. Was he on good terms with her?"

She was only half listening. He had darned near lost her with his suggestion about Noel. I wouldn't have been surprised if she had bounced up, granting that a person of her class and with her hips could bounce, and gone to have it out with her brother. Wolfe saw he would have to repeat his question, and did so.

"Oh," she said, "he's on good terms with everybody, or he tries to be. He ran errands for Dinah, but of course he would. He runs errands for me too. He's all right, I like him, I really do, but he's so—oh, well. He just doesn't belong. He certainly wouldn't have anything to do with any kidnaping; he wouldn't have the nerve."

"But he was friendly enough with Miss Utley to make it plausible that he knows the names of her associates not of your class, and possibly has met some of them."

"Yes. No doubt of that. You won't have to talk with my brother. I'll talk with him."

"That would help. That was the sort of thing I had in mind when I asked if I could count on your cooperation. I believe I have named all those who had— No, there's another possibility. I saw in the newspaper the name of your mother's attorney—Frost, I think?"

"Yes. Andrew Frost."

"It might be that an attorney would have frequent contacts with a client's secretary, especially if he is also the client's business adviser. Did Mr. Frost see much of Miss Utley?"

"I suppose he did, but I don't know, after she came to work for my mother. Of course he saw her when she worked for him. She was his secretary. He let my mother take her. It was supposed to be a great favor, but he really did it for my father. My father died not long after that. My father was a true gentleman. I'd like to tell you something, I don't know why, if you'll promise not to repeat it. Do you promise?"

"Yes."

Her eyes came to me. "Do you?"

"Sure."

She went back to Wolfe. "My father told me once that his father was a bandit."

There you are. She was actually human.

Wolfe nodded. "Then I merely corroborated him. I am obliged to you, Miss Tedder. Manifestly, if I took the job you offer, I would need to speak with Mr. Purcell and Mr. Frost. I would also need to be informed about the gathering in the library of your home Wednesday evening. For example, I understand that drinks were served. Who served them?"

She frowned again. "Why? Why do you need to know that?"

"You conceded the possibility that I am clever. Any discussion in which Mr. Purcell and Mr. Frost and your brother took part may be informative. You say that Mr. Purcell likes to do errands. Did he serve the drinks?"

"No. The bar cart was there and we served ourselves, or someone—you know how it is. I think—yes, Uncle Ralph took brandy to Mr. Frost. My mother likes a champagne cobbler after dinner, and she mixes it herself. She poured me some champagne, but I didn't drink much."

"What did your brother have?"

"Champagne. He gulps it."

"And Mr. Vail?"

"I didn't notice, but probably bourbon and water. No matter how clever you are, this can't possibly mean anything. You're just trying to impress me." She glanced at her wristwatch. "Do you want to see my uncle first? He would come tonight if I tell him to."

"Not tonight." Wolfe cocked his head. "I'm not trying to impress you, but I have imposed on you. I must reject your demand, Miss Tedder—I shouldn't have called it an offer, since you have offered nothing. Your brother has.

He was here this afternoon, and I have engaged with him to recover the money. My share will be one-fifth."

She was gawking. Of course a person of her class shouldn't gawk, but you can't blame her. A person of my class would have thrown something at him. "You're lying," she said. "You're trying to make me say you can have part of it. Of course one-fifth would be ridiculous. You already have more than enough from my mother, but I suppose, if you—very well, if you get it I'll give you ten thousand dollars. If you get *all* of it. Of course you'll have to do it, after everything I've told you."

Wolfe was slowly moving his head from side to side. "Amazing," he said. "How old are you?"

"I'm not a minor, if that's what you're thinking. I'm twenty-one."

"Amazing that a creature so obtuse could live so long without meeting disaster. I was at pains to make it clear that we were discussing a hypothesis, and the idea that you were being gulled never entered your mind. I don't know how a brain that is never used passes the time. It will be futile to try to browbeat your brother into deferring to you; I shall hold him to his engagement with me. I was not lying when I said that he anticipated you. He was here when you telephoned."

I suppose her father, Harold F. Tedder, was responsible for the way she took it. Naturally a true gentleman would teach his children never to argue with underlings. Since she couldn't very well order him to leave, his office and his house, there was only one thing to do, and she did it. She got up and walked out, stiff hips and all. She did it all right, too, no hurry and no prolonging it. I got to the hall ahead of her and had the door open when she reached the front, and she said thank you as she passed. Breeding will tell. I shut the door, bolted it for the night, returned to the office, and told Wolfe, "Taking candy from a baby."

He grunted and pushed his chair back. "An insupportable day. I'm going to my bed." He rose.

"What about Saul and Fred and Orrie?"

"The morning will do." He moved.

9

Saturday morning I heard the seven-o'clock news on the radio in my room, and the eight-o'clock news on the radio in the kitchen. Saul and Fred and Orrie had come and had gone up to Wolfe's room. I was listening to the nine-o'clock news on the radio in the office when they came down. Ordinarily two or three times a day is often enough, but ordinarily I am not curious as to whether some dick or state cop or FBI hero has found half a million bucks, with or without a Mr. Knapp in illegal possession of it.

I had also read the morning paper. The DA's office was playing it safe on the death of Jimmy Vail. The cause of death had been Benjamin Franklin, definitely, and there was no evidence or information to indicate that it had not been an accident, but it was still under investigation. I doubted that last. The DA had to say it, to guard against the chance of something popping up, but I doubted if the five people who had last seem him alive were being pestered much.

There was no doubt at all that the kidnaping was being investigated. Since Jimmy had died before telling anyone how or where he had been snatched, or where and by whom he had been kept, or where he had been released, there was no lead at all. The caretaker of the country house near Katonah had been taken apart by a dozen experts, but he had stuck to it that Vail had left in his Thunderbird shortly after eight Sunday evening to drive back to town, and had returned in the Thunderbird about half past seven Wednesday morning, tired, mad, dirty, and hungry. He had told the caretaker nothing whatever. The theory was that the kidnapers had taken the Thunderbird and kept it wherever they had kept him, and, when they turned him loose, had let him have it to drive home in, which was a perfectly good theory, since they certainly wouldn't want to use it. It was being examined by a task force of scientists, for fingerprints, of course, and for where and how far it had been, and who and what had been in it. It was described both in the paper and on the radio, and shown on television, with the request that anyone who had seen it between Sunday evening and Wednesday morning should communicate immediately with the police, the Westchester DA, or the FBI.

Also described, but not shown on television, was the suitcase the money had been in: tan leather, 28 by 16 by 9, old and stained, scuffed a little, three brass clasps, one in the middle and one near each end. Mrs. Vail had taken it to the bank, where the money had been put in it, and the description had been supplied by the bank's vice-president. It was the property of Jimmy Vail—or had been.

The best prospect of some kind of a lead was finding someone who had been at Fowler's Inn or The Fatted Calf Tuesday evening and had seen one of the kidnapers. The man Mrs. Vail had given the suitcase to had had his face covered. It was assumed that a confederate had been present at both places to make sure that Mrs. Vail didn't show anyone the notes she got from the phone books. People at both places remembered seeing Mrs. Vail, and the cashier at Fowler's Inn had seen her go to the phone book and open it, but no one had been found who had seen anybody take a visible interest in her.

Funeral services for Jimmy Vail would be held at the Dunstan Chapel Saturday morning at eleven.

Thanks to Nero Wolfe and Archie Goodwin, though no one but Lon Cohen was thanking us, the murder of Dinah Utley was getting a big play both in print and on the air. Not only had her body been found at or near the spot where Mrs. Vail had delivered the suitcase, but also someone had leaked it, either in White Plains or in Manhattan, that she had been an accomplice in the kidnaping. So Cramer had bought the deduction Wolfe had made from the notes and had passed it on to Westchester, and when Ben Dykes came at eleven-thirty there would be some fancy explaining to do.

As I said, I was in the office listening to the nine-o'clock news when Saul and Fred and Orrie came down from Wolfe's room. The kidnaping and murder items had been covered, so I switched it off and greeted them. If you wanted an operative for a tough job and were offered your pick of those three, never having seen or heard of them before, you would probably take Fred Durkin or Orrie Cather, and you would be wrong. Fred was big and broad, and looked solid and honest and was, but from the neck up he was a little too solid for situations that needed quick reactions. Orrie was tall and handsome and smart, and in any situation his reaction was speedy enough, but it might be the right reaction and it might not. Saul was small and wiry, with a long narrow face and a big nose. He always looked as if he would need a shave in another hour, he wore a cap instead of a hat, and his pants had always been pressed a week ago. But there wasn't an agency in New York that wouldn't have taken him on at the top figure if he hadn't preferred to free lance, and at ten dollars an hour he was a bargain for any job you could name.

"Six hundred three ways," Orrie said. "And I want a picture of Noel Tedder."

"I'll take one of Ralph Purcell," Fred said.

"So you're taking one apiece?" I went to the safe and squatted to twirl the knob. "The very best way to waste time and money. Foolproof. As for pictures, I only have newspaper shots."

"I'll get them from Lon," Saul said. "Mr. Wolfe says your credit's good with him."

"It sure is." I swung the safe door open and got the cash box. "Credit, hell. A truckload of pictures wouldn't make a dent in what he owes us. So you've got Andrew Frost?"

He said he had, and added that Wolfe had said that I would be in the office to receive reports. I had known that was coming. In a tough case it's nice to know that we have three good men on the job, even for chores as chancy as solo tailing, but the catch is that I have to sit there on the back of my lap to answer the phone and go to help if needed. I gave each of them two cees in used fives, tens, and twenties, made entries in the cash book, and supplied a few routine details, and they went. They had arrived at eight and it was then nine-thirty, so we were already out $37.50.

I was behind on the germination and blooming records, which I typed on cards from notes Wolfe brought down from the plant rooms, so after opening the mail I got the drawer from the cabinet and began entering items like "27 flks agar slp no fung sol B autoclaved 18 lbs 4/18/61." I was fully expecting a phone call from either Noel or Margot, or possibly their mother, but none had come by eleven, when Wolfe came down. There would be no calls now, since they would all be at the funeral services.

The session with Ben Dykes, who came at 11:40, ten minutes late, which I had thought would be fairly ticklish, wasn't bad at all. He didn't even hint at any peril to us, as far as he was concerned, though he mentioned that Hobart was considering whether we should be summoned and charged. What he wanted was information. He had seen our signed statement, and he knew what he had told Cramer and I had told Mandel, but he wanted more. So he laid off. Though he didn't say so, for him the point was that a kidnaper had collected half a million dollars right there in his county, and there was a chance that it was still in his county, stashed somewhere, and finding it would give him a lot of pleasure, not to mention profit. If at the same time he got a line on the murderer of Dinah Utley, okay, but that wasn't the main point. So he stayed for more than an hour, trying to find a crumb, some little thing that Mrs. Vail or Dinah Utley or Jimmy had said that might give him a trace of a scrap of a hint. When, going to the hall with him to let him out, I said Westchester was his and he and his men must know their way around, he said yeah, but the problem was to keep from being jostled or tramped on by the swarms of state cops and FBI supermen.

At one o'clock the radio had nothing new, and neither had we. Saul and Fred and Orrie had phoned in. They had all gone to the funeral, which was a big help. That's one of the fine features of tailing; wherever the subject leads you, you will follow. I once spent four hours tagging a guy up and down Fifth and Madison Avenues, using all the tricks and dodges I knew, and learned later that he had been trying to find a pair of gray suspenders with a yellow stripe.

It was one of those days. Shad roe again for lunch, this time larded with pork and baked in cream with an assortment of herbs. Every spring I get so fed up with shad roe that I wish to heaven fish would figure out some other way. Whales have. Around three o'clock, when we were back in the office, there was a development, if you don't care what you call it. The phone rang and it was Orrie Cather. He said his and Fred's subjects were together, so they were. He was in a booth at 54th and Lexington. Noel Tedder and Ralph Purcell had just entered a drugstore across the street. That was all. Ten seconds after I hung up it rang again. Noel Tedder. You couldn't beat that for a thrill to make your spine tingle: Fred and Orrie across the street, eagle-eyed, and the subject talking to me on the phone. He said he had persuaded Purcell to come and talk with Wolfe and he would be here in twenty minutes. I turned and asked Wolfe, and he looked at the clock and said of course not, and I turned back to the phone.

"Sorry, Mr. Tedder, Mr. Wolfe will be—"

"I knew it! My sister!"

"Not your sister. He turned her down, and the arrangement with you stands. But he'll be busy from four to six. Can Mr. Purcell come at six?"

"I'll see. Hold the wire." In half a minute: "Yes, he'll be there at six o'clock."

"Good." I hung up and swiveled. "Six o'clock. Wouldn't it be amusing if he gives us a hot lead and Fred and I hop on it—of course Fred will tail him here and be out front—and we're two hours late getting there and someone already has it? Just a lousy two hours."

Wolfe grunted. "You know quite well that if I permit exceptions to my schedule I soon will have no schedule. You would see to that."

I could have made at least a dozen comments, but what was the use? I turned to the typewriter and the cards. When he left for the plant rooms at 3:59 I turned on the radio. Nothing new. Again at five o'clock. Nothing new. When the *Gazette* came it had pictures of fourteen people who had been at Fowler's Inn or The Fatted Calf Tuesday evening, which showed what a newspaper that's on its toes can do to keep the public informed. I was back at the typewriter when the doorbell rang at 5:55. I went to the hall, saw Ralph Purcell through the one-way glass, and stepped to the door and opened it, and he said apologetically, "I guess I'm a little early," and offered a hand. I took it. What the hell, it wouldn't be the first murderer I had shaken hands with.

As I took his hat the elevator jolted to a stop at the bottom, the door opened, and Wolfe emerged, three minutes ahead of time because he likes to be in his chair when company comes.

Purcell went to him. "I'm Ralph Purcell, Mr. Wolfe." He had a hand out. "I'm a great admirer of yours. I'm Mrs. Jimmy Vail's brother."

Of course Wolfe had to take the hand, and when he does take a hand, which is seldom, he really takes it. As we went to the office Purcell was wiggling his fingers. Wolfe told him to take the red leather chair, went to his, got his bulk arranged, and spoke.

"I assume Mr. Tedder has explained the situation to you?"

Purcell was looking at me. When I gave Wolfe a report I am supposed to include everything, and I usually do, and I had had all the time there was Thursday afternoon at Doc Vollmer's, but I had left out an item about Purcell. I had described him, of course—round face like his sister's, a little pudgy, going bald—but I had neglected to mention that when someone started to say something he looked at someone else. I now learned that he didn't go so far as to look at A when he was speaking to B. His eyes went to Wolfe.

"Yes," he said, "Noel explained it, but I'm not sure—it seems a little—"

"Perhaps I can elucidate it. What did he say?"

"He said you were going to find the money for him—the money my sister paid the kidnaper. He asked me if I remembered that my sister had told him he could have the money if he found it, and of course I did. Then it seemed to be a little confused, but maybe it was just confused in my mind. Something about you wanted to ask me some questions because you thought one of us might know something about it on account of Dinah, Dinah Utley, and I thought he said something about one of us putting something in Jimmy's drink, but when I asked about it he said you would explain that part of it."

So Noel had been fairly tactful after all, at least with Uncle Ralph.

Wolfe nodded. "It's a little complicated. The best— Why do you look at Mr. Goodwin when I speak?"

As Purcell's eyes left me a flush came to his cheeks. "It's a habit," he said, "a very bad habit."

"It is indeed."

"I know. You notice my eyes stick out?"

"Not flagrantly.

"Thank you, but they do. When I was a boy people said I stared. One person especially. She—" He stopped abruptly. In a moment he went on. "That was long ago, but that's why I do it. I only do it when someone starts speaking. After I talk a little I'm all right. I'm all right now."

"Then I'll proceed." Wolfe propped his elbows on the chair arms and joined his fingertips to make a tent. "You know that Miss Utley had a hand in the kidnaping."

"No, sir, I don't. I mean I don't know it, and I guess I don't believe it. I heard what my sister said to Mr. Goodwin and what he said to her, and that's all I know. The reason I don't believe it, kidnaping is so dangerous, if you get caught you don't stand any chance, and Dinah wasn't like that. She wasn't one to take big chances. I know that from how she played cards. Gin. She would hang onto a card she couldn't possibly use if she thought it might fill me. Of course everyone does that if you know it will, but she did it if she only thought it might. You see?"

Wolfe didn't, since he never plays cards, gin or anything else, but he nodded. "But you do take chances?"

"Oh, yes, I'm a born gambler. Three times my sister has staked me to some kind of wild idea I had—no, four—and none of them panned out. I'll bet on anything. When I have anything to bet with."

"Life needs some seasoning," Wolfe conceded. "As for Miss Utley, you are wrong. She was involved in the kidnaping. If I told you how that has been established to my satisfaction you would probably still be skeptical. But having come to indulge Mr. Tedder, now that you're here you might as well indulge me. If Miss Utley was involved, at least one of the kidnapers is someone she knew, and therefore I want information about her friends and acquaintances. I suppose you know them, some of them?"

"Well." Purcell shifted his weight in the chair. "Now, that's funny. Dinah's friends. Of course she had friends, she must have, but I don't really *know* any. She often went out evenings, movies and shows and so on, but I don't know who she went with. That's funny. I thought I knew her pretty well. Of course for acquaintances, she met a lot of people—"

The phone rang. I took it and got a familiar voice. "Archie? Fred. In a booth at the corner. Do I snatch a bite and come back or do I call it a day? I'm supposed to stay on him till he goes home. How long will he be there?"

"Hold it." I turned to Wolfe. "Fred. His subject has entered a building, a tumble-down dump that could be a den of vice. He wants instructions. Should he crash it?"

Wolfe shot me a mean glance. "Tell him to quit for the day and resume in the morning." To Purcell: "You were saying?"

But Uncle Ralph waited until I had relayed the order, hung up, and swiveled. Good manners, even if he didn't belong. "About Dinah's acquaintances," he said, "she met a lot of people there at the house, dinner guests and now and then a party, but that wouldn't be what you want. You want a different type, someone she might use for something dangerous like kidnaping."

"Or someone who might use her."

Purcell shook his head. "No, sir. I don't think Dinah would take a chance at kidnaping, but if she did she would be in charge. She would be the boss." He lifted a hand for a gesture. "I said I'm an admirer of yours, Mr. Wolfe, and I really mean it. A great admirer. I know you're never wrong about anything, and if you're sure Dinah was involved you must have a good reason. I thought I knew her pretty well, and naturally I'm curious, but of course if you're not telling anyone . . ."

"I have told someone." Wolfe regarded him. "I have told the police, and it will probably soon be public knowledge, so I may as well satisfy your curiosity. Miss Utley typed the notes—the one that your sister received in the mail and the two she found in the telephone books. Indubitably."

No perceptible reaction. You might have thought Purcell hadn't heard. The only muscles that moved were the ones that blinked his eyelids as he kept focused on Wolfe Then he said, "Thank you for telling me. That shows I'm not as big a ninny as some people think I am. I suspected something like that when they asked me if I knew who had taken the typewriter from my sister's study."

"The police asked you?"

"Yes. I didn't tell them, because I— Well, I didn't, but I'll tell you. I saw Dinah take it. Tuesday evening. Her car was parked in front, her own car, and I saw her take the typewriter out of the house, so she must have put it in the car."

"What time Tuesday evening?"

"I didn't notice, but it was before nine o'clock. It was about an hour after my sister had left in her car with the suitcase in it."

"How did you know the suitcase was in it?"

"I carried it out for her and put it in the trunk. I saw her with it upstairs and offered to take it. She didn't tell me where she was going, and I didn't ask her. I thought something was wrong, but I didn't know what. I thought she was probably going wherever Jimmy was. He had been gone since Sunday, and I didn't think he was at Katonah, and my sister hadn't told us where he was." Purcell shook his head. "So Dinah typed the notes, and so she took the typewriter. I've got to thank you for telling me. So you're right about her, and I thought I knew her. You know, I was playing gin with her a week ago Thursday—no, Friday—and of course she had it all planned then. That's hard to believe, but I guess I've got to believe it, and I can see why you want to know about her friends. If I could tell you I would. Is it all right to tell my sister about her typing the notes?"

"Your sister has probably already been told by the police." Wolfe palmed the chair arms. "You haven't been much help, Mr. Purcell, but you have been candid, and I appreciate it. Mr. Tedder should thank you, and no doubt he will. I needn't keep you any longer."

"But you were going to explain about someone putting something in Jimmy's drink."

"So I was. Wednesday evening in the library. You were there."

"Yes."

"You served brandy to Mr. Frost."

"Yes, I believe I did. How did— Oh, Noel told you."

"No, his sister told me. I had the idea of trying to get from her who could, and who could not, have drugged Mr. Vail's drink, but abandoned it. Such an inquiry is nearly always futile; memories are too faulty and interests too tangled. The point is simple: Mr. Vail must have been drugged when he was pulled off the couch and across to the statue, therefore someone put something in his drink. That's the explanation."

The reaction to that was perceptible. Purcell stared, not blinking. "Pulled?" he asked. "You said pulled?"

"Yes."

"But he wasn't *pulled*. Unless you mean he pulled himself."

"No. He was unconscious. Someone pulled him across to the statue, to the desired spot, and pushed the statue over on him. I'm not going to elaborate on that, not now, to you; I mentioned it only because I felt I owed you an explanation of Mr. Tedder's remark about Mr. Vail's drink."

"But you're saying Jimmy was murdered."

"Yes."

"But the police don't say he was."

"No?"

"But you didn't tell Noel that."

"But I did."

"You told Noel Jimmy was murdered?"

"Yes."

"You don't know that. You can't."

"The word 'know' has various connotations. I have formed that conclusion."

"Then you didn't really—you don't care about Dinah Utley. You've been taking advantage of me." His cheeks were red. "You've been making a fool of me." He got to his feet. "Noel should have told me. That wasn't fair.

You should have told me too. I guess I *am* a fool." He turned and headed for the door.

I stayed in my chair. There are times when it's better to let a departing guest get his own hat and open the door for himself. When I heard it close I went to the hall to see that he had remembered to cross the sill before he shut it, then went back to my desk. Wolfe had straightened up and was making faces.

"If he's it," I said, "if he's *not* a fool, you might as well cross it off."

He made another face.

10

I have never completely understood Wolfe's attitude on food and eating and probably never will. In some ways it's strictly personal. If Fritz presents a platter of broiled squabs and one of them is a little plumper or a more beautiful brown than the others, Wolfe cops it. If the supply of wild thyme honey from Greece is getting low, I am given to understand, through Fritz, that plain American honey on griddle cakes is quite acceptable. And so on. But it really pains him if I am out on a prolonged errand at mealtime because I may insult my palate with a drugstore sandwich, and, even worse, I may offend my stomach by leaving it empty. If there is reason to believe that a caller is hungry, even if it is someone whom he intends to take apart, he has Fritz bring a tray, and not scraps. As for interruptions at meals, for him there is absolutely nothing doing; when he is once in his chair at the table he leaves it only when the last bite of cheese or dessert is down. That's personal, but he has tried off and on to extend it to me, and he would if I would stand for it. The point is, does he hate to have my meal broken into because it interrupts his, or because it interrupts mine, or just on general principles? Search me.

Anyhow, he does. So when the phone rang while I was helping myself to another beef fillet, and Fritz answered it and came to say that Mrs. Vail wished to speak to Mr. Wolfe, and I pushed back my chair to go, Wolfe growled and glowered. He didn't tell me not to go, because he knew I would go anyway.

When I told our former client that Wolfe was at dinner and said he could call her back in half an hour, she said she wanted to see him. Now. I said okay, if she left in ten minutes he would be available when she arrived, and she said no, she couldn't come, she was worn out, and she sounded like it.

"That narrows it down," I told her, "if it's too private for the phone. Either I come there and get it and bring it back, or let it wait."

"It mustn't wait. Doesn't he *ever* go anywhere?"

"Not on business."

"Can you come now?"

I glanced at my wrist. "I can be there by nine o'clock. Will that do?"

She said she supposed it would have to, and I returned to the dining room and my place and asked Fritz to bring my coffee with my pie. The routine is back to the office for coffee because that's where the one and only chair is, and Wolfe's current book is there if I'm going out. When he had finished his pie and put his fork down, I said I was going to call on Mrs. Vail by request and asked for instructions.

He grunted. "Intelligence guided by experience. You know the situation. We owe her nothing."

I went. Having gone out to the stoop to feel the weather and decided I could survive without a coat, I walked to Eighth Avenue and got an uptown taxi. On the way uptown I looked it over. Wolfe's statement that I knew the situation left out something: I knew it from my angle, but not from his. He might already have made some deduction, not final; for instance, that Noel Tedder was a kidnaper, a murderer, and a liar. Or sister Margot, or Uncle Ralph. It wouldn't be the first time, or even the twentieth, that he had kept a deduction to himself.

Noel must have been waiting in the hall, for two seconds after I pushed the button he opened the door. He did own some regular clothes—a plain dark gray suit, white shirt, and gray tie, but of course he might have bought them for the funeral. He shut the door, turned to me, and demanded, "Why the hell did Wolfe tell Uncle Ralph that Jimmy was murdered?"

"You may have three guesses," I told him. "Mine is that he had to, since you had told Uncle Ralph that someone had put something in Jimmy's drink and Mr. Wolfe would explain it. Did you have to mention Jimmy's drink?"

"No. That slipped out. But what the hell, if Wolfe's so damn smart couldn't he have dodged it?"

"Sure he could. As for why he didn't, sometimes I know why he does a thing while he's doing it, sometimes I know an hour later, sometimes a week later, and sometimes never. Why, did Purcell tell your mother?"

"Certainly he did. There's hell to pay."

"All right, I'm the roving paymaster. Where is she?"

"What are you going to tell her?"

"I'll know when I hear myself. I play by ear. I told her I'd be here by nine o'clock, and it's five after."

He thought he had more to say, decided he hadn't, told me to come along, and led the way to the rear. I was looking forward to seeing the library again, especially if Benjamin Franklin was still there on the floor, but in the elevator he pushed the button marked 3. When it stopped I followed him out, along the hall, and into a room that one glance told me would suit my wife fine if I ever had a wife, which I probably wouldn't because she would probably want that kind of room. It was a big soft room—soft lights, soft grays and pinks, soft rug, soft drapes. I crossed the rug, after Noel, to where Mrs. Vail was flat in a big bed, most of her covered by a soft pink sheet that could have been silk, her head propped against a couple of soft pink pillows.

"You may go, Noel," she said.

She looked terrible. Of course any woman is something quite different if you see her without any make-up, but even allowing for that she still looked terrible. Her face was pasty, her cheeks sagged, and she was puffed up around the eyes. When Noel had gone, closing the door, she told me to sit down, and I moved a chair around.

"I don't know what good it will do, you coming," she said. "I want to ask Nero Wolfe what he means by this

—this outrage. Telling my brother and my son that my husband was murdered. Can you tell me?"

I shook my head. "I can't tell you what he means by telling them. I assume you know why your son came to see him yesterday."

"Yes. To get him to help him find the money. When Noel asked me if he could have the money if he found it, I said yes. The money didn't matter; my husband was back. Now he's dead, and nothing matters. But he wasn't murdered."

So Noel had broached it. "Your son asked you again yesterday," I said, "and you said yes again. Didn't you?"

"I suppose I did. Nothing matters now, certainly that money doesn't— No, I'm wrong, something does matter. If you can't tell me why Nero Wolfe says my husband was murdered, then he will. If I have to go there, I will. I shouldn't, my doctor has ordered me to stay in bed, but I will."

I could see her tottering into the office supported by me, and Wolfe, after one look at her, getting up and marching out. He has done that more than once. "I can't tell you why Mr. Wolfe says it," I said, "but I can tell you why he thinks it." I might as well, since if I didn't Noel could. "Your husband was asleep on the couch when the rest of you left the room, leaving a light on. Right?"

"Yes."

"And the idea is that later he woke up, realized where he was, stood up, started for the door, lost his balance, grabbed at the statue, and pulled it down on him. Right?"

"Yes."

"That's what Mr. Wolfe won't take. He doesn't believe that a man awake enough to walk would be so befuddled that he couldn't dodge a falling statue. He realizes that he couldn't have been merely asleep when someone hauled him off the couch and over to the statue; he must have been unconscious. Since the autopsy found no sign that he had been slugged, he must have been doped. You had all been having drinks in the library, he had bourbon and water, so there had been opportunity to dope him. Therefore Mr. Wolfe deduces that he was murdered."

Her eyes were straight at me through the surrounding puffs. "That's absolutely ridiculous," she said.

I nodded. "Sure it is, to you. If Mr. Wolfe is right, then your daughter or your son or your brother or your lawyer, or you yourself, murdered Jimmy Vail. I think he's right, but I work for him. Granting that it wasn't you, you're up against a tough one. Naturally you would want whoever killed your husband to get what was coming to him, but naturally you wouldn't want your son or daughter or brother to get tagged for murder, and maybe not your lawyer. I admit that's tough, and I don't wonder that you say it's ridiculous. I wasn't trying to convince you of anything; I was just telling you why Mr. Wolfe thinks your husband was murdered. What else would you want to ask him if he was here?"

"I'd tell him he's a fool. A stupid fool."

"I'll deliver the message. What else?"

"I'd tell him that I have told my son that I'm taking back what I told him about the money, that he can have it if he finds it. He can't. I didn't know he would go to Nero Wolfe."

"You went to Nero Wolfe."

"That was different. I would have gone to the devil himself to get my husband back."

I gave my intelligence three seconds to be guided by experience before I spoke. "I'll deliver that message too," I said, "but I can tell you now what his reaction will be. He's stubborn and he's conceited, and he not only likes money, he needs it. Your son came to him and offered a deal, and he accepted it, and he won't let go just because you've changed your mind. If he can find that money he will, and he'll take his share. In my private opinion the chance of his finding it is about one in a million, but he won't stop trying. On the contrary. He's very sensitive. This attitude you're taking will make him try harder, and he might even do something peevish like writing a piece for a newspaper explaning why he has deduced that Jimmy Vail was murdered. That would be just like him. If you want some free advice, I suggest that you have your son in, here and now, and tell him you're *not* taking it back. I'll report it to Mr. Wolfe, and he'll decide if he wants to risk his time and money on a wild-goose chase."

It didn't work. As I spoke her lips kept getting tighter, and when I stopped she snapped, "He wouldn't get any share. Even if he found it. It's my money."

"That would be one for the lawyers. He would claim that his agreement with your son was based on an agreement your son had with you, made before witnesses. It would be the kind of mix-up lawyers love; they can juggle it around for years."

"You may go," she said.

"Sure." I rose. "But you understand—"

"Get out!"

I can take a hint. I walked out, shutting the door behind me, and proceeded to the elevator. When I emerged on the ground floor, there was Noel. He came to me.

"What did she say?" he squeaked.

"This and that." I caught a glimpse of someone through an arch. "She's a little upset. How about a little walk? If there's a bar handy, I could buy you a drink, provided it's not champagne."

He twisted his neck to glance up the stairs, brought his face back to me, said, "That's an idea," and went and opened the door. I passed through and onto the sidewalk, and he joined me. I suggested Barney's, at 78th and Madison, and we turned downtown.

A booth in a bar and grill is not an ideal spot for a private conversation. You can see if there is anyone in the booth in front of you curious enough to listen in, but you have to leave the one behind to luck or keep interrupting to look back. Noel and I got a break at Barney's. As we entered, a couple was leaving the booth at the far end, and we grabbed it, and I had a wall behind me. A white apron came and removed glasses and gave the table a swipe, and we ordered.

"So it's off," Noel said. "You couldn't budge her." I had told him en route how it stood.

"Not an inch." I was regretful, even gloomy. "You know why I wanted to buy you a drink? Because I wanted one myself. That talk with your mother took me back, back years ago, in Ohio. *My* mother. How old are you?"

"Twenty-three."

"I was only seventeen, just out of high school. But of

course the situation was different; it was easier for me than it would be for you. My mother wasn't wealthy like yours. I couldn't hit her for a hundred or a thousand or whatever I happened to need."

"Hell, neither can I. It's not that easy."

"It may not be easy, but the fact remains that she has it, and all you have to do is use the right approach. With me, with my mother, that wasn't the problem. She was a born female tyrant, and that was all there was to it. There wasn't a single goddam thing, big or little, that I could decide on my own. While your mother was talking I couldn't help thinking it was just too bad you couldn't do what I did."

The drinks came and we sampled them. Noel's sample was a gulp. "What did you do?" he asked.

"I told her to go to hell. One nice hot June day, the day after I graduated from high school, I told her to go to hell, and beat it. Of course I don't mean it literally, that it's too bad you can't do what I did. It's a different situation. You wouldn't have to. Now that Jimmy Vail's dead, you're the man of the house. All you'd have to do is just make it clear that you've got two feet of your own. Not in general terms like that, not just tell her to her face, 'Mother, I've got two feet of my own,' that wouldn't get you anywhere. It would have to be on a specific issue, and you couldn't ask for a better one than her taking back a definite promise she made you. That would be a beaut. You could tell her, 'Mother, you said I could have that money if I found it, and on the strength of that I made a deal with Nero Wolfe, and he'll hold me to it, and I'm going to hold you to it.' "

He took a swallow of gin and tonic. "She'd say it's her money."

"But it isn't. Not after what she told you before witnesses. She has given it to you, with only one condition attached, that you find it, and therefore it's a gift and you wouldn't have to pay tax on it. Granting that there's a slim chance of finding it, if we do find it you'll have four hundred thousand dollars in the till after you give Nero Wolfe his cut—no tax, no nothing. And even if we don't find it, you'll have let your mother know that you've got your own two feet, not by telling her so but by standing on them on a specific issue. There's another point, but we'll skip it."

"Why? What is it?"

I took a sip of scotch and soda. "It will be important only if Mr. Wolfe finds the money. If he does, one-fifth will be his, and don't think it won't. If your mother tries to keep him from getting it, or keeping it, the fur will fly, and some of it will be yours. If it gets to a court, you'll testify. For him."

"It wouldn't. It's not the money that's biting my mother, it's Jimmy. It's Wolfe's saying that Jimmy was murdered. Why the hell did he tell Uncle Ralph that?"

"He told you too."

"I had sense enough not to repeat it." He put his empty glass down. "Look, Goodwin, I don't give a damn. If Jimmy was murdered, someone that was there killed him, and I still don't give a damn. Of course it wasn't my mother, but even if it was, I'm not sure I'd give a damn even then. I'm supposed to be old enough to vote, but by God, the way I've had to knuckle under, you'd think I still wet the bed at night. You say I wouldn't have to do what you did, but if I had four hundred thousand dollars that's exactly what I'd do. I'd tell my mother to go to hell. I'm not as dumb as I look. I knew what I was doing Wednesday evening. I knew my mother was so glad her darling Jimmy was back she wouldn't stop to think, and I asked her about the money in front of witnesses, and I intended to go to Nero Wolfe the next morning, but the next morning Jimmy was dead, and that made it different. Now Wolfe has told Uncle Ralph Jimmy was murdered, I don't know why, and he has told my mother, and you tell me to show her I've got my own two feet. Balls. What if I haven't even got one foot?"

I signaled the white apron for refills. "Let's try something," I said and got out my notebook and pen and started writing. I dated a blank page at the top and wrote:

> To Nero Wolfe: I hereby confirm the oral agreement we made yesterday. My mother, Mrs. Althea Vail, told me on Wednesday, April 26, and repeated on Friday, April 28, that if I find the $500,000 she gave a kidnaper

> on Tuesday, April 25, or any part of it, I may keep it for my own. Therefore that money belongs to me if I find it. I have engaged you to help me find it, and I have agreed that if you do find it, or any part of it, you are to keep one-fifth of the amount you find as payment for your services. I hereby confirm that agreement.

The refills had come, and I sampled mine as I read it over. Tearing the sheet out, I handed it to Noel and watched his face. He took his time, then looked up. "So what?"

"So you'd have a foot. I don't really expect you to sign it, I doubt if you have the nerve, you've knuckled under too long, but if you did sign it, you wouldn't have to tell your mother you were going to do so-and-so and stick to it. You could tell her you *had* done so-and-so, you had come here with me and talked it over and confirmed your agreement with Mr. Wolfe in writing. She couldn't send you to bed without any supper because you've already had your supper. Of course legally that thing isn't important, because you're already bound legally. Mr. Wolfe has a witness to his oral agreement with you. Me."

He started to read it over again, quit halfway, put his glass down, and extended his hand. "Give me that pen." I gave it to him, and he signed his name, pushed the paper across to me, picked up his glass, and raised it to eye level. "Excelsior! To freedom!" He put the glass to his mouth and drained it. A piece of ice slipped out and fell to the table, and he picked it up and threw it at the bartender across the room, missing by a yard. He shook his head, tittered, and asked me, "What did your mother do when you told her to go to hell?"

Since I had what I wanted, it would have suited me all right if we had been bounced, but apparently Noel was not a stranger at Barney's. The barkeep took no action beyond occasional glances in our direction to see if more ice was coming. Noel wanted to talk. The idea seemed to be that I had made a hero of him, and he wanted to know who or what had made a hero of me at the early age of seventeen. I was willing to spend another half-hour and another drink on him, but I suspected that he didn't want to go home until it was late enough for him to go to bed without stopping in his mother's room to say good night, and that might mean a couple of hours. So I began looking at my watch and worrying about being late for a date, and at ten o'clock I paid for the drinks and left him.

It was 10:26 when I mounted the stoop of the old brownstone and pushed the button. When Fritz opened the door he aimed a thumb to his rear, toward the office, signifying that there was company. I asked him who, and he told me in what he thinks is a whisper but is actually a kind of smothered croak, "Federal Bureau of Investigation." I told him, "Rub off all fingerprints and burn the papers," and went to the office.

You don't have to believe me, but I would have known after one look at him, even if Fritz hadn't told me. It's mostly the eyes and the jaw. An FBI man spends so much time pretending he's looking somewhere else that his eyes get confused; they're never quite sure it's okay to admit they're focused on you. His jaw is even worse off. It is given to understand that it belongs to a man who is intrepid, daring, dauntless, cool, long-headed, quick-witted, and hard as nails, but it is cautioned that he is also modest, polite, reserved, patient, bland, and never to be noticed in a crowd. No jaw on earth could handle that order. The only question is how often it will twitch, and sideways or up and down.

Wolfe said, "Mr. Goodwin. Mr. Draper."

Mr. Draper, having got to his feet, waited until my hand was unquestionably being offered, then extended his. Modest and reserved. His left hand went to a pocket, and I told him not to bother, but of course he did. An FBI man draws his credentials automatically, the way Paladin draws his gun. I glanced at it, not to hurt his feelings.

"Mr. Draper has been here a full hour," Wolfe said, with the accent on the 'full.' "He has a copy of the statement we signed, and he has asked many questions about details. He has covered the ground thoroughly, but he wanted to see you."

It looked like another full hour. I went to my desk and sat. Draper, back in the red leather chair, had his notebook out. "A few little questions, Mr. Goodwin," he said. "If you don't mind?"

"I like big ones better," I said, "but shoot."

"For the record," he said. "Of course you understand that; you're an experienced investigator. Mr. Wolfe says you left the house around half past six Tuesday evening, but he doesn't know when you returned. When did you?"

I permitted myself a grin, modest, polite, and bland. "Mr. Draper," I said, "I appreciate the compliment. You think I may have tailed Mrs. Vail Tuesday night, against her wishes and with or without Mr. Wolfe's consent, and that I may even have got as far as Iron Mine Road without being spotted by one of the kidnapers. As you know, that would have been one for the books, a real honey, and I thank you for the compliment."

"You're welcome. When did you return?"

I gave it to him complete, from six-thirty until one o'clock, places, names, and times, going slow enough for him to get it down. When I finished he closed the notebook, then opened it again. "You drive a car, don't you?"

"Mr. Wolfe owns it, I drive it. Sixty-one Heron sedan."

"Where is it garaged?"

"Curran, Tenth Avenue between Thirty-fifth and Thirty-sixth."

"Did you use the car Tuesday night?"

"No. I believe I mentioned taxis."

"Yes. You understand, Mr. Goodwin, for the record." He pocketed the notebook, arose, and got his hat from the stand. "You've been very helpful, Mr. Wolfe. Thank you very much. I doubt if we'll bother you again." He turned and went. I didn't get up, because an FBI man moves fast and I would have had to jump to get ahead of him to open the door. When I heard it close I went to the hall for a look, came back, got from my pocket the paper Noel had signed, and handed it to Wolfe.

He read it and put it down. "This was called for?"

"It seemed to be desirable. Would you like a report?"

"Yes."

I sat down and gave it to him—verbatim, all but the last half-hour with Noel, which wasn't material. When I was through he picked up the paper, read it again, nodded, and said, "Satisfactory." He put it down. "When your mother was in New York for a week last year, and dined here twice, and you spent some time taking her around, I saw no trace of the animus you described to Mr. Tedder."

"Neither did I. If we find enough of that five hundred grand to make it worth telling about, and it gets printed and she reads it, she won't mind. She understands that in this job, working for you, the more lies the merrier, even one about her. By the way, in a letter I got last week she mentioned the chestnut croquettes again."

"Did you tell Fritz?"

"Sure. Anything for the morning?"

"No."

"Are Saul and Fred and Orrie still on?"

"Yes." He eyed me. "Archie. Your reply to Mr. Draper's question. Could he have had any other reason for asking it than the chronic suspicion of an inquisitor?"

"Certainly. They might have found the tire prints of your car at Iron Mine Road. I drove it there Wednesday."

"Don't dodge. You have friends who would lie for you without question, and you named some of them in your reply. One particularly. How much of your reply was fact?"

"All of it." I stood. "I'm going to bed. My ears are burning. First the FBI and now you. I wish I *had* tailed her, and Mr. Knapp with the suitcase; then we'd know where the cabbage is."

11

It's always possible that people who invite me to the country for a weekend will get a break; there's a chance that there will be a development that will keep me in town, and they will neither have to put me up nor put up with me. The lucky ones that last weekend in April were a couple in Easthampton who had me booked for Friday evening to Monday morning. I have reported the developments of Friday and Saturday, and Sunday I had to stick around in case a call for reinforcements came from Saul or Fred or Orrie.

Wolfe's routine for Sunday is different. Theodore Horstmann, the orchid nurse, has the day off and goes to visit his married sister in Jersey, so there are no regular two-hour sessions in the plant rooms. Wolfe goes up once or twice to look around and do whatever chores the situation and the weather require, but there is no strict schedule. Usually he is down in the office by ten-thirty, at least the Sundays I am there, to settle down with the review-of-the-week section of the Sunday *Times*, which he goes right through.

From nine o'clock on that Sunday morning I was half expecting a call from Noel Tedder to tell me that he had issued his Declaration of Independence, one hero to another, but it hadn't come by the time I turned on the radio for the ten-o'clock news. Nor had there been any word from any of the tailers, but I was soon to know where Saul Panzer was. As I was turning the radio off the doorbell rang, and I went to the hall and saw Andrew Frost. So Saul was near enough to see the door opening, no matter how Frost had got there. I swung the door wide and said good morning.

It may be cheesy writing to say that Frost's expression and tone were frosty as he said he wanted to see Nero Wolfe, but it's good reporting. They were. It was possible that a factor was the probability that he would have to miss church, since he was dressed for it in a custom-made charcoal-gray top-coat and a forty-dollar homburg to match. I allowed him to enter, took the hat and coat, ushered him to the office, and buzzed the plant rooms on the house phone. When Wolfe's voice came, his usual testy "Yes?" and I told him Mr. Andrew Frost had come and had been admitted, he snapped, "Ten minutes," and hung up. When I told Frost he made a frosty little noise and gave me a frosty look. He didn't seem to look as much like Abraham Lincoln as he had Wednesday afternoon, but that may have been because I had never seen a picture of Lincoln simmering.

It was nearer fifteen minutes than ten when the sound came of the elevator, and Wolfe entered, a spray of Miltonia roezli in his left hand and the Sunday *Times* under his right arm. He takes his copy of the *Times* with him to the plant rooms so he won't have to stop off at his room on the way down to the office. Labor-saving device. He stopped at the corner of his desk to face the caller, said, "Mr. Frost? How do you do. I was expecting you," then put the flowers in the vase and the *Times* on the desk, and circled around to his chair.

Frost said distinctly, "You were not expecting me."

"But I was." Wolfe, seated, regarded him. "I invited you. I told Mr. Purcell that Mr. Vail was murdered, knowing that that would almost certainly bring you. I wished to see everyone who had been at that gathering Wednesday evening. You came, naturally, to remonstrate. Go ahead."

A muscle at the side of the lawyer's neck was twitching. "Are you saying," he demanded, "that you uttered that slander, knowing it was false, merely to coerce me to come here so you could see me?"

A corner of Wolfe's mouth went up a sixteenth of an inch. "That's quite a question. I uttered no slander, because what I said was true. I haven't coerced you; you are under no constraint; if you don't want to be here, go. Has Mr. Purcell told you what led me to the conclusion that Mr. Vail was murdered?"

"Yes. It's pure sophistry. The police and the District Attorney haven't formed that conclusion. It's false, fallacious, and defamatory, and it's actionable."

"Has the District Attorney made his final deduction and closed the inquiry?"

"Formally, no."

"Even if he does, that won't prove me wrong. He needs evidence that will convince a jury; I don't. I merely—"

"You'll need evidence if you persist in this slander and are made to answer for it."

"I doubt if I'll have to meet that contingency. I merely needed a starting point for a job I have undertaken, and I got it—my conclusion that Mr. Vail was murdered. I have no—"

"You have no job. You mean that fantastic scheme with Noel Tedder. That's off."

Wolfe turned his head. "Archie. That paper?"

I hadn't opened the safe, so I had to work the combination. I did so and got the paper from the shelf where I had put it before going up to bed. As I approached with it, Wolfe told me to give it to Frost. He took it, ran his eyes over it, and then read it word by word. When he looked up, Wolfe spoke.

"I'm not a counselor-at-law, Mr. Frost, but I have some knowledge of the validity of contracts. I'm confident that that paper binds Mrs. Vail as well as Mr. Tedder."

"When did he sign it?"

"Yesterday evening."

"It won't stand. He was tricked into signing it."

Wolfe turned. "Archie?"

"No tricks," I told Frost. "Ask him. He's fed up and wants to stand on his own two feet. I bought him three little drinks, but he was perfectly sober. There were witnesses."

"Witnesses where?"

"Barney's bar and grill, Seventy-eighth and Madison." I was still there by him, and I put out a hand. "May I have it, please?"

He took another look at it and handed it over. I went to the safe and put it back on the shelf and swung the door shut.

Wolfe was speaking. "I was about to say, Mr. Frost, that I have no intention of broadcasting my conclusion that Mr. Vail was murdered, or my reasons for it. I had to tell Mr. Tedder in order to explain my approach to our joint problem, and I told Mr. Purcell because I wanted to see you; he would of course tell his sister, and she would tell you. My purposes have been served. As for the murder, I am not—"

"There was no murder."

"That's *your* conclusion—or your delusion. I'm not bent on disturbing it. I am not a nemesis."

"Why did you want to see me?"

"When I know that one of a group of people has committed a murder, and possibly two murders, and I need to know which one, I like to look at them and hear them—"

"Then you *are* persisting in the slander. You're saying that you intend to identify one of the people there Wednesday evening as a murderer."

"Only to my satisfaction, for my private purpose. Perhaps my explanation has lost something on its way to you through Mr. Purcell and Mrs. Vail. No. I'm wrong. I explained fully to Mr. Tedder, but not to Mr. Purcell. Having deduced that Mr. Vail was murdered, I made two assumptions: that the murder was consequent to the kidnaping and therefore the murderer had been involved in the kidnaping, and that he or she knows who has the money and where it is or might be. So I needed to identify him and I had to see all of you. I had seen Mrs. Vail. I intend to find that money."

Frost was shaking his head, his lips compressed. "It's hard to believe. I know your reputation, but this is incredible. You wanted to see me so that, by looking at me and hearing me, you could decide if I was a kidnaper and a murderer? Preposterous!"

"It does seem a little overweening," Wolfe conceded, "but I didn't rely solely on my acumen." He turned. "Archie, bring Saul."

That shows you his opinion of Saul. Not "Archie, see if Saul is around." Frost was Saul's subject, so, since Frost was here, Saul was in the neighborhood. Of course it was my opinion too. I went to the front door and out to the stoop, descended two steps, stood, and beckoned to Manhattan, that part of it north of 35th Street. A passer-by turned his head to see who I was inviting, saw no one, and went on. I was expecting Saul to appear from behind one of the parked cars across the street, and I didn't see him until he was out of an area-way and on the sidewalk, on this side, thirty paces toward Tenth Avenue. He had figured that Frost would head west to get an uptown taxi, and undoubtedly he would. Reaching me, he asked, "Was I spotted?"

"You know damn well you weren't spotted. You're wanted. We need you for four-handed pinochle."

He came on up, and we entered and went to the office, Saul in front. Sticking his cap in his pocket, he crossed to Wolfe's desk with no glance at Frost and said, "Yes, sir?"

Wolfe turned to Frost. "This is Mr. Saul Panzer. He has been making inquiries about you since yesterday morning." Back to Saul: "Have you anything to add to your report on the phone last evening?"

Presumably after I had left to go to Mrs. Vail. Saul said, "Only one item, from a source I saw after I phoned. Last fall he bought a one-third interest in a new twelve-story apartment house on Eighty-third Street and Park Avenue."

"Briefly, some of the items you reported yesterday."

"He's a senior member of the firm of McDowell, Frost, Hovey, and Ulrich, One-twenty Broadway. Twenty-two names on the letterhead. He was co-chairman of the Committee of New York Lawyers for Nixon. Two years ago he gave his son a house in East Sixty-eighth Street for a wedding present. He's a director in at least twenty corporations—I don't think the list I got is complete. He was Harold F. Tedder's counsel for more than ten years. He has a house on Long Island, near Great Neck, thirty rooms and eleven acres. In nineteen fifty-four President Eisenhower—"

"That's enough." Wolfe turned. "As you see, Mr. Frost, I realize that my perspicacity is not infallible. Of course some of Mr. Panzer's items invite further inquiry—for example, is the estate on Long Island unencumbered? Is there a mortgage?"

Frost was no longer frosty; he was too near boiling. "This is unbelievable," he declared. He was close to sputtering. "You have actually paid this man to collect a dossier on me? To examine the possibility that I'm a kidnaper and murderer? Me?"

Wolfe nodded. "Certainly. You're a lawyer with wide experience; you know I could exclude no one who was there. Mr. Panzer is discreet and extremely competent; I'm sure he—"

The doorbell rang. I got up and went to the hall for a look, returned to my desk, scribbled "Cramer" on the scratch pad, tore off the sheet, and handed it to Wolfe. He glanced at it, closed his eyes, opened them in three seconds, and turned to Frost.

"Inspector Cramer of the police is at the door. If you would prefer not to—"

Frost's wires snapped. He jerked forward, his eyes blazing. "Damn you! *Damn* you! You phoned him!"

"I did not," Wolfe snapped. "He is uninvited and unexpected. I don't know why he's here. He deals only with death by violence. If he has heard of my conclusion that Mr. Vail was murdered, I don't know when or from whom. Not from Mr. Goodwin or me." The doorbell rang. "Do you want him to know you are here?"

"You're a liar! You're to blame—"

"Enough!" Wolfe hit the desk. "The situation is precisely as I have described it. Archie, admit Mr. Cramer. Do you want him to see you or not? Yes or no."

"No," Frost said, and left the chair. Wolfe told Saul to take him to the front room, and when Saul had gone to the connecting door and opened it, and Frost was moving, I went to admit the law. From the expression on Cramer's face I expected him to march on by to the office, but when I turned after shutting the door, he was there facing me.

"What were you doing with Noel Tedder last night?" he demanded.

"Don't snap my head off," I said. "I'd rather tell you before a witness. Mr. Wolfe will do." I walked to the office, entered, and told Wolfe, "He wants to know what I was doing with Noel Tedder last night. He didn't say please."

Cramer was at my elbow. "The day I say please to you," he growled, and went to the red leather chair, sat, and put his hat on the stand.

"I suppose," Wolfe said, "it's futile to complain. You have been a policeman so long, and have asked so many people so many impertinent questions, and so frequently have got answers to them, that it has become spontaneous. Have you any ground at all for expecting Mr. Goodwin to answer that one?"

"We might arrange a deal," I suggested. "I'll ask an impertinent question. Why have you got a tail on Noel Tedder if Jimmy Vail's death was an accident?"

"We haven't got a tail on him."

"Then how did you know he was with me?"

"A detective happened to see you with him on the street and followed you." Cramer turned to Wolfe. "Day before yesterday you refused to tell me where you and Goodwin had been for twenty-four hours. You said you had no further commitment to Mrs. Vail and you had no client. You repeated that in your signed statement. You did not repeat it to Draper of the FBI when he asked you last night. Your answer was evasive. That's not like you.

I have never known you to hedge on a lie. Now this, Goodwin with Noel Tedder. You're not going to tell me that was just social. Are you?"

"No."

"Goodwin?"

"No."

"Then what was it?"

Wolfe shook his head. "You have a right to expect answers only to questions that are relevant to a crime. What crime are you investigating?"

"That's typical. That's you. I'm investigating the possibility that Jimmy Vail didn't die by accident."

"Then you aren't satisfied that he did."

"Satisfied, no. The District Attorney may be, I don't know, you can ask him. I say I have a right to expect Goodwin to answer that question. Or you."

Wolfe tilted his chair back, then his head, pursed his lips, and examined the ceiling. Cramer took a cigar from a pocket, rolled it between his palms, which was silly with a cigar that wasn't going to be lit, held it at an angle with his thumb and forefinger, frowning at it, and returned it to his pocket. Evidently he had asked it an impertinent question and it has refused to answer. Wolfe let his chair come forward and said, "The paper, Archie." I went to the safe and got it from the shelf and took it to him. He put it on his desk pad and turned to Cramer.

"I think you have the notion that I have withheld information from you on various occasions just to be contrary. I haven't. I have reserved details only when I wanted them, at least temporarily, for my exclusive use, or when you have been excessively offensive. Today you have been reasonably civil, though of course not affable; imparting it will not make it less useful to me; and if it furthers your investigation, though I confess I don't see how it can, it will serve a double purpose." He picked up the paper. "I'll read it. I won't hand it to you because you would probably say it may be needed as evidence, which would be absurd, and pocket it."

He read it, ending, "Signed by Noel Tedder. It isn't holograph; Mr. Goodwin wrote it. I answered that question by Mr. Draper ambiguously because if I had told him of my agreement with Mr. Tedder he would have kept me up all night, thinking that I had some knowledge, at least an inkling, of where the money might be found. I have no commitment to Mrs. Vail, but I do have a client: Noel Tedder."

"Yeah." It came out hoarse, and Cramer cleared his throat. He always gets a little hoarse when he talks with Wolfe, probably a certain word or words sticking in his throat. "And either you have some idea where the money is or this is a cover for something else. Does Mrs. Vail know about that agreement?"

"Yes."

"And that's what Goodwin and Tedder were discussing last night?"

"Yes."

"What else were they discussing?"

Wolfe turned. "Archie?"

I shook my head. "Nothing. We touched on mothers some, his and mine, but that was in connection with the agreement."

"So your question is answered," Wolfe told him. "I'm aware that you'll pass it on to Mr. Draper, but he isn't here, and if he comes he won't get in. We have given him all the information we possess about the kidnaping, with no reservations. I do have an idea where the money is, but it is based—"

"By God, you admit it."

"I state it. It's based on deductions and assumptions I have made, not on any evidence I'm withholding. That applies not only to the kidnaping and the whereabouts of the money, but also to the death of Mr. Vail. What would you say if I told you that I'm convinced that he was murdered, with premeditation, and that I think I know, I'm all but certain that I know, who killed him and why?"

"I'd say you were grandstanding. It wouldn't be the first time. I know you. God, do I know you! When you've really got something you don't say you're convinced and you're all but certain. You say you *know*. If you've got any evidence that he was murdered and that points to the murderer, I want it, and I want it now. Have you got any?"

"No."

"Then I'll leave you to your deductions and assumptions." He picked up his hat. "You're damn right I'll tell Draper." He rose. "But if he knew you as well as I do— Oh, nuts." He turned and marched out.

I stepped to the hall and saw him close the front door behind him, stepped back in, and asked Wolfe, "So you're all but certain? Do you know what 'grandstanding' means. Where did you get the idea—"

"Get Saul."

He snapped it. I went and opened the door to the front room and told Saul to come. As he entered, Wolfe spoke. "Mr. Frost has gone?"

Saul nodded. "He bent his ear for five minutes trying to hear you, found that he couldn't on account of the sound-proofing, and left."

"I want Fred. If Mr. Purcell is at home, he will of course be nearby. Bring him as soon as possible." His eyes came to me. "Archie, I want Mr. Tedder, and Orrie with him. Also as soon as possible. Don't stop to tell Fritz about the door. I'll see that it's bolted."

"You want me back," Saul said.

"Yes. Go."

We went.

12

It wouldn't do, of course, for me to ring the Vail house and get Noel and tell him Wolfe wanted to see him. One, he might not come without some fancy persuading. Two, Wolfe wanted Orrie too, and Orrie, tailing him, might possibly lose him on the way downtown. Three, Saul had to go there to get Fred, and the taxi fare is the same for two as for one. So we walked to Tenth Avenue and flagged a cab.

It was 11:23 of a sunny Sunday morning, nice and warm for the last of April, when we stopped at the curb in front of 994 Fifth Avenue, paid the hackie, and got out. When we're going on with the program, the method of getting in touch with a tail, understood by all of us, is a little complicated, but in that case it was simple. We merely raised an arm to wave at a squirrel in a tree in the park and started to stroll downtown. Before we had taken twenty steps Fred appeared from behind a parked car across the street and came over to us and said if we had come an hour sooner he could have gone to church.

"It would take more than church to square you," I told him. "Purcell hasn't shown?"

"No."

"What about Orrie?"

"His subject showed at ten fifty-one and led him away." Fred looked at Saul. "And yours came at eleven-fifteen in a cab and went in. So you got shook for once?"

"No," I said, "he got called off. Did Tedder ride or walk?"

"Walked. Turned east at Seventy-eighth Street. Orrie was keeping distance. Something happened? What's up?"

"God doesn't know but Mr. Wolfe does. Everybody in for a conference." I turned to Saul. "If you and Fred go on down, you can read the Bible until I bring Tedder and Orrie. There are five versions in four different languages on the second shelf from the top near the left end. I'm thinking where to start looking for him. I think better when I talk."

"We can't help you think," Saul said, "because you know him and we don't, but we can help you look. Of course, if he wanted a taxi, it's Sunday and he could have got one here on Fifth, or if he thought he'd get one quicker on Madison he wouldn't have gone to Seventy-eighth to turn east. But if he has a car and it's garaged on Seventy-eighth, he—"

"No," Fred said. "Four cars garaged on Eighty-second Street. I've seen three of them." As I said, Fred was a little too solid for quick reactions, but give him time and he would collect a lot of miscellaneous information that might be useful.

"Okay," I said, "thanks a lot for doing my thinking. Now I know where he is, maybe. If you've thought wrong and he's not there, we might as well go back to Thirty-fifth Street and sing hymns until Orrie phones. Come along."

It was one chance in a thousand, but it was the only chance there was. I led them south to Seventy-eighth Street and east to Madison Avenue, halted in front of Barney's, and told them, "We might as well give Orrie the high sign first and have him join us. Then when I bring—"

"There he is," Saul said.

I turned. Orrie had emerged from a doorway across the street and was crossing the sidewalk. "All I need," I said, "is someone to do my thinking," and stepped to Barney's door and entered.

There was no one at the bar, since it was Sunday morning, and there weren't many at the tables or in the booths, but the top of a head was showing in the booth at the far end and I went to it. It was Noel, with a plate of roast turkey and trimmings in front of him, untouched, and a nearly empty glass in his hand. He looked up at me, blinked, and squeaked, "Well, for God's sake!"

I gave him a friendly grin, hero to hero. "This isn't luck," I said, "it's fate. When I learned you had gone out, it wasn't that I had a hunch, I just started to walk, and there I was in front of Barney's, and I came in, and here you are. Have you—uh—spoken to your mother?"

"No." He emptied the glass and put it down. "I was going to go up to her room right after breakfast, but then I thought I'd better wait. I thought I'd better kind of work up to it. I wanted to go over everything you said. So I came here to this booth where you said it. Sit down and oil your throat."

"Thanks, but I'm on an errand. You won't have to tell your mother you're big enough to shave; she knows it. Andrew Frost came to see Mr. Wolfe this morning, and Mr. Wolfe showed him the paper you signed, and Frost went to see your mother. He's there now."

"The hell he is. Holy Christ."

"And Mr. Wolfe sent me to bring you. I think he has an idea where the money is, but if so he didn't tell me; he wants to tell you. He said as soon as possible, which means now. You haven't touched your turkey."

"To hell with the turkey. Frost is with my mother?"

"Right."

"And Wolfe wants to see me?"

"Right."

"He slid out of the booth and got erect. "Look. You see me?"

"I do."

"Am I standing on my own two feet?"

"You are."

"Check. Let's go."

The waiter was approaching, and as Noel didn't seem to see him, I asked him how much. He said four-twenty, and I gave him a finiff and followed Noel to the door.

Outside, Saul had performed as usual. There were two taxis at the curb. The one in front was empty, and the trio were in the one in the rear. He had even arranged for a signal so the hackie wouldn't take the wrong passengers; as Noel and I crossed the sidewalk the horn of the cab in the rear let out a grunt.

When we stopped in front of the old brownstone at ten minutes past noon, and I paid the hackie and climbed out after Noel, the other taxi wasn't in sight. Saul again. He didn't know whether Wolfe wanted Noel to know that the whole army was mobilized, so he was hanging back to give us time to get inside. I had to ring, since the bolt was on. Fritz let us in, and I took Noel to the office. It had been just sixty-five minutes since Wolfe had told Saul and me to fetch. If I may say so, I would call that as soon as possible.

Wolfe did something remarkable: he left his chair and took two steps to offer Noel a hand. Either he was telling me that Noel was not a murderer, or he was telling Noel that he was with friends and since he could count on us we would expect to count on him. Of course Noel didn't appreciate it; a man who will some day be in the top bracket without trying has plenty of hands offered to him. He took the red leather chair and said, "Goodwin says you know where the money is."

"Correction," I objected. "I said I think he has an idea where it is."

Wolfe grunted. He eyed Noel. "The truth is somewhere between. I'm fairly certain. Call it a presumption. To test it we need your cooperation, your active assistance. Even with it, it may be difficult—"

The doorbell rang. I told Wolfe, "Three of my friends," and stood. "I'll put them in the front room."

"No," he said, "bring them."

So it was to be a family party. I went and let them in, told them they could come and sit with the quality if they would behave themselves, and followed them to the office. Wolfe greeted them and turned to the client. "Mr. Tedder, shake hands with Mr. Panzer. Mr. Durkin. Mr. Cather."

The very best corn. I had seldom seen him sink so low. I moved chairs up, and they sat. Wolfe's eyes took them in, left to right, then back to focus on Noel. "Time may be of vital importance, so I won't waste it. The money, all of it, half a million dollars in cash, is at your house in the country. If not in the house, it's on the premises."

"Jesus," Noel said.

"It would take all afternoon to explain fully all the circumstances that have led me to that conclusion, and I don't want to take even half an hour. You think I have sagacity, or you wouldn't have come to me with your problem. You'll accept that—"

"Wait a minute. How did the money get there?"

"Mr. Vail took it there. He took the suitcase from your mother at Iron Mine Road. You'll accept—"

"But my God, why did he—"

"Mr. Tedder. You could ask a thousand questions; I said it would take all afternoon. Do you want that money?"

"You're damn right I want it."

"Then take my conclusion on my word, tentatively at least. I say the money is there. Who is at that house now?"

"No one. Only the caretaker."

"No other servants?"

"No. We don't use it before the middle of May. Usually later."

"This is Sunday. Not on weekends?"

"We did when my father was alive, but not now. My mother says it's too cold until June."

"Mr. Vail went there last weekend. Saturday morning. What for?"

"To see about the roof and some other things. The caretaker said the roof was leaking."

"What's the caretaker's name?"

"Waller. Jake Waller."

"Are you on amicable terms with him?"

"Why, I guess so. Sure."

"A leaky roof should be attended to. How likely is it that your mother or sister or uncle will go there today to see to it?"

"My mother certainly won't. It's possible that my sister or my uncle will, but they haven't said anything about it so far as I know."

"Is the house locked up?"

"I suppose the doors are locked, yes."

"Have you a key?"

"Not now I haven't. I have one in the summer."

"Would the caretaker let you in?"

"Certainly he would. Why wouldn't he?"

Wolfe turned. "Archie. Will anyone be guarding that place? County or state or federal?"

I shook my head. "What for? Not unless someone has got to the same conclusion as you, which I doubt."

Back to Noel. "Mr. Tedder. I suggest that if you want that money you go there and get it. Now. Mr. Goodwin will drive my car. Mr. Panzer, Mr. Durkin, and Mr. Cather will go with you. They are competent, reliable, and experienced. My chef has prepared a hamper of food which you can eat on the way; it will be acceptable to your palate and your stomach. I have no suggestions as to your procedure when you get there; I didn't know Mr. Vail; you did. He returned to that house Wednesday morning with the suitcase in his car, and his time was rather limited. He wanted to act naturally, and naturally he would want to come to New York, where his wife was, without undue delay. According to the caretaker, in the published reports, he arrived about half past seven, and he left for New York around nine o'clock. Meanwhile he had bathed, shaved, changed his clothes, and eaten, so he hadn't spent much time on disposal of the suitcase; but it is highly likely that he had known on Saturday that he would bring it there for concealment and he had probably made preparations. You knew him and you must have some notion of how his mind worked, so ask yourself: where on those premises would he hide the suitcase? He anticipated no intensive search for it, since he thought it would never be suspected that he had got it and brought it there; what he had to make sure of was that it would not be accidentally discovered by a member of the family or a servant. I presume you know what the suitcase looked like?"

"Sure. Who doesn't?"

Wolfe nodded. "From the published descriptions. I think you may safely expect to find *that* suitcase. There was no reason for him to transfer the money to another container, and there was good reason not to; he would have had the added problem of disposing of the suitcase." Wolfe's head turned to take us in. "There it is, gentlemen, unless you have questions. If you have, let them be to the point. I wish you luck."

Noel squeaked, "I hope to God . . ." He let it hang.

"Yes, Mr. Tedder?"

"Nothing." Noel stood up. "Hell, what can I lose that I've got? Let's go."

I went to the kitchen to get the hamper.

13

About two miles northeast of Katonah you turn off the highway, right, pass between two stone pillars, proceed up the graveled drive, an easy slope, winding, about four hundred yards, and there is the house, old gray stone with high steep roofs. At a guess, not as many rooms as Frost's on Long Island—say twenty-five, maybe less. Trees and other things with leaves, big and little, were all around, and a lot of lawn, but although I can't qualify as an expert I had the impression that they weren't getting quite enough attention. Saul eased the Heron to a stop a foot short of the bushes that bordered a surfaced rectangle at the side of the house, and we climbed out. He was at the wheel because at Hawthorne Circle I had decided that I could use some of the contents of the hamper, which they had all been working on, and I don't like one-handed driving.

Noel, in between bites of sturgeon or cheese or rhubarb tart, or swallows of wine, had briefed us on the prospect and answered questions. The house itself looked like the best bet. Not only was there no likely spot in the stable, which no longer held horses, or the kennels, which no longer held dogs, but also Jimmy would have risked being seen by the caretaker if he had lugged a suitcase to one of them in the open. Nor was there any likely spot in the garage, which was connected with the house. The only other outbuilding was a six-room stone structure in the rear, living quarters for servants, occupied now only by the caretaker. Something really fancy, like wrapping the suitcase in plastic and burying it somewhere on the grounds, was of course out, with the caretaker around. The house was the best bet, and not the cellar, since there was no part of it that the caretaker might not poke around in, or, later, if the suitcase was to stay put for a while, a servant or even a member of the family.

As we climbed out a man appeared from around a corner—a tall, lanky specimen in a red wool shirt and dungarees who hadn't shaved for at least three days. As he caught sight of Noel he spoke. "Oh, it's you, Mr. Tedder?"

"On my own two feet," Noel said, meeting him and offering a hand. Either he believed in democracy or Wolfe had made it a habit. "How are you, Jake?"

"I'll make out if they don't trip me." Jake gave us a glance. "The roof, huh? We had a shower Friday and it leaked again. I phoned your mother."

"She's been . . . not so good."

Jake nodded. "Too bad about Mr. Vail. Terrible thing. You know they've been after me, but what could I tell 'em? For nearly a week all kinds of people drivin' in. I'm takin' no chances." His hand went to his hip pocket and came out with a gun, an old black Marley .32. He patted it. "Maybe I couldn't hit a rabbit, but I can scare 'em off." He put it back. "You want to see in your mother's room where it leaked?"

"Not today, Jake." Noel's squeak wasn't so squeaky; perhaps his voice was changing. "My mother may be out this week. These men are detectives from New York and they want to look around in the house. They think there may be something—I don't know exactly what. You know how detectives are. Is there a door open?"

Jake nodded. "The back door's open, the one off the kitchen. I cook and eat in the kitchen, better tools there. Your mother knows I do. Lucky I had bacon and eggs on hand when he came Wednesday morning. Terrible thing about him. I sure do know how detectives are, I do now." He looked at us. "No offense to you fellows."

Obviously one of us ought to say something, so I said, "We don't offend easy. We know how caretakers are too."

"I bet you do." He chuckled. "I just bet you do. You want me to help with anything, Mr. Tedder?"

"No, thanks. We'll make out. This way, Goodwin." Noel headed for the corner Jake had come from, and we followed.

To prove how competent and experienced we are I could describe the next forty minutes in detail, but it wouldn't help you any more than it did us. We had learned from Noel that the possibilities were limited. Jimmy Vail had been a town man and had never got intimate with this country place. His bedroom was the only spot in the house he had had personal relations with, so we tried that first, but after we had looked in the two closets and the bottom drawer of a chest, then what? The bed was a big old walnut thing with a canopy, and there was enough room under it for an assortment of wardrobe trunks, but room was all there was.

We went all around, downstairs and up. We even spent ten minutes in the cellar, most of it in a storage room where there were some ancient pieces of luggage along with the other stuff. We looked in the garage, which was big enough for five cars, and there in a corner saw something that would have seemed promising if it hadn't been there in the open where anyone might have lifted the lid —a big old-fashioned trunk. I did lift the lid and saw something that took me back to my boyhood days in Ohio. But a couple of cardboard boxes had held my two-year collection of birds' eggs, and here were dozens of compartments, some with one egg and some with two or three. I asked Noel if they were his, and he said no, they had been his father's, and the trunk held more than three hundred different kinds of eggs. I lifted the tray out, and underneath it was another tray, not so many compartments but bigger eggs. Orrie came for a look and said, "Let's take that. It may not be worth half a million, but it's worth something." I put the top tray back in and was shutting the lid when I heard the sound of a car.

The garage doors were closed and the sound was faint, but I have good ears. The parking area where we had left the Heron was on this side of the house, but not in front of the garage. The door we had come through was standing open—the door from the garage to a back hall. I stepped to it quietly and poked my head through, and in a moment heard a voice I had heard before. Margot Tedder. She was asking Jake whose car that was. Then Jake, telling her: her brother Noel and four detectives from New York who were searching the house for something. Margot asked, searching for what? Jake didn't know. Then Margot calling her brother, a healthier yell than I thought she had in her: "Noel! *Noel!!*"

Preferring the garage to the outdoors as a place for a conference, I sang out, "We're in the garage!" and turned and told Noel, "It's your sister."

"I know it is. Damn her."

"I'll do the talking. Okay?"

"Like hell you will. She'll do the talking."

It's a pleasure to work with men who can tell time. Saul had started to move when I called out that we were in the garage, and Fred and Orrie a second later, and I had moved back from the door, taking Noel with me. So when Margot appeared and headed for Noel, with Jake right behind her, and Uncle Ralph behind Jake, all my three colleagues had to do was take another step or two and they were between the newcomers and the exit. And both Saul and Orrie were only arm's length from Jake's hip pocket. It's a real pleasure.

I was at Noel's side. As Margot approached she gave me a withering glance, then switched it to Noel, stopped in front of him, and said, "You utter idiot. Get out and take your gang with you."

I said politely, "It's as much his house as yours, Miss Tedder, and he got here first. What if he tells you to get out?"

She didn't hear me. "You heard me, Noel," she said. "Take this scum and go."

"Go yourself," Noel said. "Go to hell."

She about-faced and started for the door. I raised my voice a little. "Block it! Saul, you'd better get it."

"I have it," Saul said and raised his hand to show me

the gun he had lifted from Jake's pocket. Margot saw it and stopped. Fred and Orrie had filled the doorway. Uncle Ralph made a noise. Jake looked at Margot, then at Noel, and back at Margot. Saul was back of him, and he didn't know he had been disarmed.

"You wouldn't shoot," Margot said scornfully, and I have to admit there was no shake in her voice.

"No," I told her back, "he wouldn't shoot, but why should he? Five against three, granting that you're one and Jake is with you. As Jake told you, we're looking for something, and we haven't finished. Noel told you to go, but it would be better for you to stay here in the garage, all three of you, until we're through. One of you might use the phone, and we'd be interrupted. I don't—"

I stopped because she was moving. She went to the door, just short of Fred and Orrie, just not touching them, and said, "Get out of the way."

Orrie smiled at her. He thinks he knows how to smile at girls, and as a matter of fact he does. "We'd like to," he said, "but we're glued."

"I don't know how long we'll be," I told her, "but there's a stack of chairs there by the wall. Fred and Orrie, you—"

"Jake! Go and phone my mother!" Her voice still didn't shake, but it was a little shrill.

And by gum, Jake's hand went back to his hip pocket. I was almost sorry his gun was gone; it would have been interesting to see how he handled it. His jaw dropped, and he wheeled and saw it in Saul's hand. "It's all right," Saul said, "you'll get it back." Jake turned to Noel and said, "Fine lot you brought." He turned to Margot. "I guess I can't."

"You guess right," I told him. "Fred and Orrie, you stay here and keep the peace. Noel and Saul and I will look around some more. But it has occurred to me that I may have overlooked something. Wait till I see." I went to the corner where the big trunk was, lifted the lid, took out the top tray, and put it on the floor gently. Then I reached in and got the loops at the ends of the second tray and eased it up and out, and I damn near dropped it. There at the bottom of the trunk was an old tan leather suitcase. I took three seconds out to handle my controls, staring at it, then carefully put the tray on the floor to one side, straightened up, and said, "Come and take a look, Noel." He came and stooped over to see, then reached a hand in and heaved, and out it came. At that point I decided that he might really have two feet. I had expected him to squeak something like "Jesus Holy Christ what the hell," but he squeaked nothing. He just reached in and got it, put it on the floor, undid the clasps, and opened the lid; and there was the biggest conglomeration of engraved lettuce I had ever had the pleasure of looking at. I glanced around. Purcell was at my elbow, and Jake was at his elbow, and Saul was right behind them. Margot was approaching, hips stiff as ever. Noel, squatting, with a hand flattened out on top of the find, tilted his head back to look up at me and said, "I didn't believe him, but I thought I might as well come. How in the name of God did he know it was here?"

Orrie, still in the doorway with Fred, called over, "Damn it, have you got it?" Margot was saying something which I didn't bother to hear, and Purcell was making noises. I looked at my wrist; it's nice to know exactly what time you found half a million bucks. Eight minutes to three. I went and put the trays back in the trunk, gently and carefully, closed the lid and came back. Noel was fastening the lid of the suitcase, paying no attention to what his sister was saying.

"Okay," I said, "we'll move. Saul and Noel will take it out to the car." I put out a hand to Saul. "The gun. I'll unload it and leave it on the kitchen table. Fred and Orrie will follow Saul and Noel. I'll stay in the kitchen to guard the phone until you have the car turned around and headed out. When you tap the horn I'll come. Miss Tedder, if you came to see about the leaky roof, don't neglect it just because we got in the way. As Mr. Wolfe remarked to your brother just this afternoon, a leaky roof should be attended to."

14

When the doorbell rang at five minutes to six Monday afternoon I was in my chair in the office, leaning back, my feet up on the corner of the desk, looking at the headline on the front page of the *Gazette*:

VAIL RANSOM FOUND
$500,000 in Birds' Egg Trunk

With that second hot exclusive given to Lon Cohen in three days, our credit balance with him was colossal. The picture of the suitcase on page 3, with the lid open, had been taken by me. The article, which I had read twice, was okay. I was given a good play, and so was Wolfe, and Saul and Fred and Orrie were named. I had given Lon nothing about Margot or Uncle Ralph, but had mentioned Jake's gun. A gun improves any story.

The money was in the bank, but not the one it had come from. Noel had demonstrated that he was neither piker nor a soft touch. When I had put the suitcase on the couch in the office, and he had opened it, and we had all gathered around to admire the contents, including Wolfe, he had taken out a couple of bundles of cees, counted off two grand and handed it to Orrie, then two grand to Fred, two to Saul, and five to me. Then he had asked Wolfe, "Do you want yours now?" and Wolfe had said it would have to be counted first since his share was a percentage; and Wolfe had gone to the kitchen to tell Fritz there would be four guests for dinner. It was then five o'clock, but at seven, just two hours later, Fritz had served us the kind of meal you read about. No shad roe.

The arrangement for the night was determined by two facts: one, there wasn't room in the safe; and two, Noel didn't want to take it home, which was understandable. So when bedtime came I got pajamas for him and took him up to the south room, which is above Wolfe's, checked the towel supply and turned the bed down, and took the suitcase up another flight to my room. It wouldn't go under my pillow, so I made room for it on the bed stand right against the pillow. We hadn't counted the money.

It was counted Monday morning in a little room at the Continental Bank and Trust Company on Lexington Avenue, where Wolfe has had his account for twenty years. Present were an assistant vice-president, two tellers, and Noel and me. Of course Noel and I were merely spectators. They started on it a little after ten, and it was a quarter past twelve when they declared finally and positively that the figure was $489,000. Noel took twenty twenties for pocket money; $100,000 was deposited in Wolfe's account; and an account was opened for Noel with a balance of $388,600. There would be no service charge, the assistant vice-president told Noel, with a banker's smile at his own hearty joke. We had said nothing about where it had come from, and he had asked no questions, since Wolfe was an old and valued customer, but he must have had a guess if he ever looked at a newspaper. Of course the *Gazette* wasn't out yet.

Noel and I shook hands in parting, out on the sidewalk. He took a taxi headed uptown. I didn't hear what he said to the hackie, but I gave myself five to one that he was going straight to 994 Fifth Avenue. A nice little bank balance in his own name is very good for a man's feet. I took a little walk to call on Lon Cohen.

I rather expected some kind of communication from Mrs. Vail or Andrew Frost before the day was out, but the afternoon went by without a peep. I also rather expected that Wolfe would put on a strutting act, his own special brand of strutting, explaining how simple it had been to dope out where the money was, but he didn't, and I wasn't going to pamper him by asking for it. I got back in time to dispose of the morning mail, which was skimpy, before lunch, and after lunch he finished his book and got another one from the shelf, and I got onto the germination and blooming records. There would soon be some new cards to add to the collection, with the bank balance where it now was.

When the doorbell rang at 5:55 and I took my feet down from the desk and went to see, there was Inspector Cramer.

That broke a precedent. Knowing Wolfe's schedule as

he does, he may come at 11:01 or 6:01, but never at 5:55. Did it mean he wanted five minutes with me first? It didn't. When I let him in, all I got was a grunt as he went by, and when I joined him in the office he was in the red leather chair, his hat on the stand, his feet planted flat, and his jaw set. Not a word. I went to my chair, sat, planted my feet flat, and set my jaw. We were like that when Wolfe came in. As he passed the red leather chair he grunted, a perfect match for the grunt Cramer had given me. In his own chair, his bulk adjusted satisfactorily, he grunted again and asked, "How long have you been here?"

Cramer nodded. "So you can ride Goodwin for not telling you. Sure. You ride him, and he needles you. A damn good act. I've seen it often enough, so don't waste it on me. You lied to me yesterday morning. You said you had an idea where the money was. Nuts. You *knew* where it was. How did you know?"

Wolfe's brows were up. "Have you shifted from homicide to kidnaping?"

"No. If you knew where it was you knew who put it there. It must have been Jimmy Vail. He died Wednesday night. You told me yesterday that you had no evidence, either about the whereabouts of the money or Vail's death. That was a barefaced lie. You used the evidence about the money to get your paws on it. Now you're going to use the evidence about Vail's death to pounce on something else, probably more money. How many times have I sat here and yapped at you about withholding evidence or obstructing justice?"

"Twenty. Thirty."

"I'm not doing that now. This is different. I'm telling you that if the evidence you've got about Vail's death is evidence that he was murdered, and if you refuse to give it to me here and now, whatever it is I'll dig it up, I'll get it, and I'll hang an accomplice rap on you and Goodwin if it's the last thing I do this side of hell."

"Hhmmm," Wolfe said. He turned. "Archie. I have a good memory, but yours is incomparable. Have we any shred of evidence regarding the death of Mr. Vail that Mr. Cramer lacks?"

I shook my head. "No, sir. He probably has a good

deal, little details, that we lack." I turned to Cramer. "Look. I certainly know everything that Mr. Wolfe knows. But yesterday he not only told you that he was convinced that Vail was murdered, I'm with him on that, he also said he was all but certain that he knew who had killed him. I'm not. Certain, my eye. I'd have to pick it out of a hat."

"He didn't say that. That was a question."

Wolfe snorted. "A question only rhetorically. You said I was grandstanding—your word. Apparently you no longer think so, which isn't surprising, since I have found the money. In effect, you are now demanding that I do your interpreting for you."

"That's another lie. I am not."

"But you are." Wolfe turned a palm up. "Consider. As I told you yesterday, my conclusions about the whereabouts of the money and Mr. Vail's death were based on deductions and assumptions from the evidence at hand, and I have no evidence that you do not have. Yesterday you said you would leave me to my deductions and assumptions. Now you want them. You demand them, snarling a threat."

"You're twisting it around as usual. I didn't snarl."

"I'm clarifying it. I am under no necessity, either as a citizen or as a licensed detective, to share the product of my ratiocination with you. I am not obliged to describe the mental process by which I located the money and identified the murderer of Miss Utley and Mr. Vail. I may decide to do so, but it rests with my discretion. I shall consider it, and if and when—"

The doorbell rang. As I went to the hall I was considering whether it was Andrew Frost with a legal chip on his shoulder or some journalist after crumbs. It was neither. It was Ben Dykes of Westchester County and a stranger. It might or might not be desirable to let them join the party, so I only opened the door to the two-inch crack the chain permitted and spoke through it. "Back again?"

"With bells on," Dykes said.

"You're Archie Goodwin?" the stranger asked. He showed a buzzer, not Westchester. New York. "Open up."

"It's after office hours," I said. "Give me three good reasons why I should—"

"Take a look at the bells," Dykes said and stuck a paper through the crack.

I took it, unfolded it, and looked. Thoroughly. It was a little wordy and high-flown, but I got the idea. "Mr. Wolfe will want to see this," I said. "He's a great reader. Excuse me a minute." I went to the office, waited until Wolfe finished a sentence, and told him, "Sorry to interrupt. Ben Dykes from Westchester with a New York dick for an escort, and with this." I showed the paper. "A court order that Archie Goodwin is to be arrested and held on a charge of grand larceny. On a complaint by Mrs. Althea Vail. It's called a warrant." I turned to Cramer. "Got any more questions before I leave?"

He didn't even glance at me. His eyes were fastened on Wolfe, who had just said that he had identified a murderer. Wolfe put out a hand, and I gave him the paper, and he read it. "She's an imbecile," he declared. "Bring them in."

"We don't need Goodwin," Cramer said. "You'll have him out on bail in the morning."

"Bring them," Wolfe snapped.

I returned to the front, removed the chain, pulled the door open, invited them in, and was surprised to see that there were three of them. Presumably the third one had stayed at the foot of the steps as a reserve in case I started shooting. You've got to use tactics when you go for a gorilla. I soon discovered how wrong I was when they followed me to the office and the third one darted by me to Wolfe's desk, whipped a paper from a pocket, and shoved it at Wolfe. "For you," he said and wheeled and was going, but Ben Dykes caught his arm and demanded, "Who are you?"

"Jack Duffy, process server," he said and jerked loose and trotted out.

"A goddam paper boy," Dykes said disgustedly. I stepped to the hall, saw that he shut the door as he went, and stepped back in. Wolfe had picked up the document and was scowling at it. He read it through, let it fall to the desk, leaned back, closed his eyes, and pushed his lips out. In a moment he pulled them in, then out, in, out . . .

Dykes said, "All right, Goodwin, let's go." The New York dick had suddenly recognized Inspector Cramer and was trying to catch his eye so he could salute, but Cramer was staring at Wolfe. In a minute Wolfe opened his eyes, straightened up, and asked his expert on women, me, "Is she a lunatic?" He tapped the document. "This is a summons. She is suing me, not only for the money in the suitcase, but also to recover the fee she paid me."

"That hurts you," Cramer growled.

Wolfe regarded him. "Mr. Cramer, I have a proposal. I would prefer not to describe it for other ears, and I think you share that preference. It is within the discretion of the police to postpone service of a warrant of arrest if it is thought desirable. I suggest that you advise Mr. Dykes, who is accompanied by a member of your force, to wait until tomorrow noon to take Mr. Goodwin into custody. After they leave I'll make my proposal."

Cramer cocked his head and screwed his lips. He had to pretend to give it a hard look, but actually there was nothing to it. By now he knew darned well that Wolfe wasn't grandstanding. He spoke. "Dykes is from Westchester. He has a New York man with him for courtesy, but the arrest is up to him." His head turned. "What about it, Dykes? Would you have to phone White Plains?"

Dykes shook his head. "That wouldn't be necessary, Inspector. I'm supposed to use my head."

"All right, use it. You heard what Wolfe said. If it's just a stall, you can take Goodwin tomorrow."

Dykes hesitated. "If you don't mind, Inspector, I'd like to be able to say that you made it a request."

"Then say it. It's a request."

Dykes went to Wolfe's desk and picked up the warrant, then turned to me. "You won't leave the state, Goodwin."

I told him I wouldn't dream of it, and he headed out, followed by the dick, who never had got to salute Cramer. I got in front of them, wanting to be polite to a man who had postponed tossing me in the can, and let them out. When I returned to the office Wolfe was speaking.

". . . but I must first satisfy myself. As I told you, I

have no evidence. Mr. Goodwin has already been served with a warrant, and I have been served with a summons, and I prefer not to expose myself to an action for libel."

"Nuts. Telling me privately, libel?"

"It's conceivable. But in candor, that's not the main point. I intend to take a certain step, and it's highly likely that if I told you what I have deduced and assumed you would make it extremely difficult for me to take it, if not impossible. You wouldn't dare to take it yourself because, like me, you would have no evidence. You'll hear from me, probably tonight, and by tomorrow noon at the latest."

Cramer was anything but pleased. "This is a hell of a proposal."

"It's the best I can do." Wolfe looked at the clock. "I would like to proceed."

"Sure you would." Cramer reached for his hat and put it on. "I should have let Dykes take Goodwin. I'd sleep better if I knew he was in a cell." He rose. "You'd have had to take your certain step anyway." He moved and, halfway to the door, turned. "If you call me tomorrow and say you've decided that your deductions and assumptions were wrong, God help you." He went. That time my going to see that the hall was empty when the door closed wasn't just routine; he might really have stayed inside to get a line on the certain step. As I stepped back in Wolfe snapped, "Get Mrs. Vail."

That wasn't so simple. First I got a female, and after some insisting I got Ralph Purcell. After more insisting he told me to hold the wire, and after a wait I had him again, saying that his sister wouldn't speak with Nero Wolfe or me either. I asked if he would give her a message, and he said yes, and I told him to tell her that Wolfe wanted to tell her how he had known the money was in the house. That did it. After another wait her voice came.

"This is Althea Vail. Nero Wolfe?"

He was at his phone. "Yes. I am prepared to tell you how I knew where the money was, but it's possible that your telephone is tapped. I am also—"

"Why on earth would it be tapped?"

"The pervasive curiosity of the police. I am also prepared to tell you various other things. Examples: the name of the man to whom you gave the suitcase on Iron Mine Road; how I know that there was no Mr. Knapp; the reason why Mr. Vail had to be killed. I shall expect you at my office at nine o'clock this evening."

Silence. She hadn't hung up, but the silence lasted so long that I thought she had left the phone. So long that Wolfe finally asked, "Are you there, madam?"

"Yes." More silence, but after half a minute: "I'll come now."

"No. It will take some time and would run into the dinner hour. Nine o'clock."

"I'll be there." The connection went.

We hung up, and I turned to Wolfe. "What's all the hurry? You haven't got a single solitary scrap."

He was glaring at the phone and switched it to me. "I will not have you carted off to jail on a complaint by that silly wretch. It should be worth keeping. Is that thing in order?"

"I suppose so. It was the last time we used it."

"Test it."

I got up, slipped my hand in between my desk and the wall, and flipped a switch. Then I went and sat in the red leather chair and said in a fairly low voice, "Nero Wolfe is going to put on a charade, and let us hope he doesn't break a leg." I went to my desk and turned it off, then went to the kitchen, opened a cupboard door, did some manipulating, and flipped a switch, and in a few seconds my voice came out: "Nero Wolfe is going to put on a charade, and let us hope he doesn't break a leg." I reached in and turned it off, returned to the office, and reported, "It's okay. Anything else?"

"Yes. That idiot may have a gun or a bomb or heaven knows what. Stay near her."

"Or she may have a lawyer."

"No. No indeed. She's not that big an idiot." He picked up the summons and scowled at it.

15

She came at 8:50, ten minutes ahead of time. I was getting Wolfe's okay on a change in the program when the doorbell rang. In order to stay near her I would have had to sit in one of the yellow chairs near the red leather chair, and I prefer to be at my desk, or I would have had to put her in one of the yellow chairs near me, and Wolfe prefers to have a caller in the red leather chair because the window is then at his back.

It was a pleasant May Day evening, and she had no wrap over her tailored suit, so the only problem was her handbag—a big black leather one with a trick clasp. I learned about the clasp when I tried to open it, after I had got it from her lap and taken it to my desk. Her reaction to my snatching it, which I did as soon as she was seated and had no hand on it, showed the condition of her nerves. She made no sound and no movement, but merely stared at me as I took it to my desk, and she said nothing while I fiddled with it, finding the trick clasp and opening it, and inspected the contents. Nothing in it seemed to be menacing, and when I went and put it back on her lap she had transferred the stare to Wolfe. I might have felt a little sorry for her if it hadn't been for the warrant that Ben Dykes would be back with at noon tomorrow. When you grab a woman's bag and open it and go through it, and all she does is sit and stare, she could certainly use a little sympathy.

There was no sympathy in Wolfe's expression as he regarded her. "This isn't an inquisition, Mrs. Vail," he said. "I have no questions to ask you. It will be a monologue, not a tête-à-tête, and it will be prolonged. I advise you to say nothing whatever."

"I wouldn't answer any questions if you did ask them," she said. Her voice was good enough. "You said there was no Mr. Knapp. That's crazy."

"Not as crazy as your invention of him." Wolfe leaned back. "This will be easier to follow if I begin in the middle. Mr. Goodwin has told you how I reached the conclusion that your husband was murdered. That didn't help much unless I could identify the murderer, and as a first step I needed to see those who were at that gathering Wednesday evening. Let's take them in the order in which I saw them.

"First, your son. When he came to hire me to find the money for him I suggested the possibility that he had had a hand in the kidnaping and knew where the money was, that he couldn't very well just go and get it, and that he intended to supply hints that would lead to its discovery by me—or by Mr. Goodwin. When I made that suggestion at the beginning of our conversation, I thought it was a real possibility, but by the time our talk ended I had discarded it. For such a finesse a subtle and agile mind would be needed, and also a ready tongue. Such a witling as your son couldn't possibly have conceived it, much less execute it. So he had come to me in good faith; he hadn't been involved in the kidnaping; he didn't know where the money was; and he hadn't killed Mr. Vail."

"You said you would tell me how you knew there was no Mr. Knapp."

"That will come in its place. Second, your daughter. But you may not know even now what led Mr. Goodwin and me to suspect that Dinah Utley was a party to the kidnaping. Do you?"

"No."

"Your brother hasn't told you?"

"No."

"Nor the police?"

"No."

"The note that came in the mail. It had been typed by her. I won't elucidate that; this will take long enough without such details. When Mr. Goodwin saw that the other two notes which you had found in telephone books —I know now, of course, that they were not in the books, you had them with you and went to the books and pretended to find them—when Mr. Goodwin saw that they too had been typed by her, the suspicion became a conclusion. And ten minutes' talk with your daughter made it manifest that it was quite impossible that she had been allied with Dinah Utley in any kind of enterprise, let alone one as ambitious and hazardous as kidnaping. Your daughter is a vulgarian, a dunce, and a snob. Also she had come to demand that I find the money for her, but even without that it was plain that she, like her brother, had not been involved in the kidnaping; she didn't know where the money was; and she hadn't killed Mr. Vail.

"Third, your brother. From Mr. Goodwin's report of his behavior Wednesday afternoon, or rather, his lack of behavior, his silence, I had tentatively marked him as the one who most needed watching. After twenty minutes with him, him in the chair you are in now, I had to conclude that it was impossible. You know his habit of looking at A when B starts to speak."

"Yes."

"His explanation of that habit was enough. A man with a reaction so hopelessly out of control cannot have effective and sustained control over any of his faculties. He would never trust himself to undertake an operation that required audacity, ingenuity, and mettle. There were many other indications. His parting words were 'I guess I *am* a fool,' and he meant them. Patently he was not the man.

"Fourth, Andrew Frost. As you know, he came yesterday morning, but I learned nothing from that interview. There was nothing in his words or tone or manner to challenge the possibility that he was the culprit, and, except for you, that was the only possibility that remained. But through an assistant I had already learned enough about him to exclude him—his record, his position in his profession and in society, his financial status. That didn't exclude him as a possible murderer, but it was inconceivable that he had been involved in the kidnaping. He would have had to conspire with at least two others, Miss Utley and Mr. Knapp, and probably more, with the only objective in view a share of the loot, and therefore he would have been at their mercy, in mortal danger indefinitely. What if one of his confederates had been caught and had talked? To suppose that such a man had incurred such a risk for such a return? No."

Wolfe shook his head. "No. Therefore it was you. You had been a party to the kidnaping, you had killed Dinah Utley, and you had killed your husband. I reached that conclusion at ten o'clock Saturday evening, but I wanted to see Mr. Frost before I acted on it. It was barely possible that after talking with him I would reconsider my decision about him. I didn't. Will you have some refreshment? A drink? Coffee?"

No reply. No movement.

"Tell me if you want something. I'll have some beer." He pushed a button and leaned back again. "Also before I acted on it I had to examine it. I had to satisfy myself that no fact and no factor known to me rendered it untenable; and first came motive. What conceivable reason could you have had for getting half a million dollars in cash from your bank and going through that elaborate rigmarole to deliver it to a masked man at an isolated spot on a country road at midnight, other than your ostensible reason? Please bear in mind, Mrs. Vail, that from here on I am not reporting; I am only telling you how I satisfied myself. If in this instance or that I chose the wrong alternative you may correct me, but I still advise you to say nothing."

I never saw advice better followed. She had a good opportunity to speak, for Fritz came with beer, and Wolf poured, but she didn't take advantage of it. He waited for the foam to sink to the proper level, then lifted the glass and drank.

He leaned back. "I found only one acceptable answer. The man you delivered the suitcase to was your husband. He probably was masked, for both you and he gave meticulous attention to detail throughout the operation. Very well; why? What were you accomplishing? You were establishing the fact that you had suffered a loss of half a million dollars, and that fact would net you ninety-one per cent of the half a million, since you would deduct it as a casualty on your income-tax report. I haven't inquired as to whether such a casualty would be deductible, and I don't suppose you did, probably you merely assumed that it would be. If your income for the year would be less than half a million, no matter; you could carry the loss back for three previous years and forward for five future years. Well worth the effort, surely."

He came forward to drink, then back again. "Other facts and factors. Why did you and your husband bring Dinah Utley into it? You couldn't plan it to your satisfaction without her. Take one detail, the phone call from

Mr. Knapp. You wanted no doubt whatever in any quarter that the kidnaping was genuine, and you thought there must be a phone call. Mr. Vail couldn't make it, for even if he disguised his voice it might be recognized. It would be simpler and safer to use Miss Utley, your trusted employee, than to have some man, no matter who, make the call. Of course the call was never made. Miss Utley not only typed the notes; she also typed the transcript of the supposed conversation on the phone. I presume her reward was to be a modest share of the booty.

"Was it you or your husband who conceived the notion —No. I said I would ask you no questions. All the same, it's an interesting point, which of you thought of coming to me, since that was what led to disaster. No doubt it seemed to be an excellent stroke in your elaborate plans to achieve verisimilitude; not only coming to me but also the hocus-pocus about getting here; ten thousand dollars wasn't much to pay for establishing that you were desperately concerned for your husband's safety. You couldn't foresee that I would insist on seeing your secretary, but when I made that demand your check was already on my desk, and you didn't dare take it back merely because I wished to speak with Miss Utley. Nor could you foresee that I would propose a step that would expose me to the risk of an extended and expensive operation, and that I would demand an additional sum as insurance against possible loss. You didn't like that at all. Your teeth bit into your lip as you wrote the check, but you had to. Fifty thousand dollars makes a substantial hole in half a million, but you had made it so clear that nothing mattered but your husband's safety, certainly money didn't, that you couldn't very well refuse."

He poured beer, drank when the foam was right, and went on. "I don't know if you regretted that you had come to me when you left, but you certainly did later, when Miss Utley returned after seeing me. As I said, I'm not reporting, I'm telling you how I satisfied myself. I got an inkling of Miss Utley's temperament and character when she was here, and more than an inkling from what your brother told me about her. From questions Mr. Goodwin and I asked her, and from our taking her fingerprints, she became apprehensive. She feared that you had somehow aroused my suspicion, that I suspected her, and that I might disclose the fraud; and when she returned she tried to persuade you to give it up. You wouldn't. All the preliminaries had been performed; you had the money in the suitcase; you had given me sixty thousand dollars; all that remained was the consummation. You tried to remove Miss Utley's fears, to convince her that there was no danger of exposure, and you thought you succeeded, but you didn't.

"Shortly before eight o'clock you left in your car with the suitcase in the trunk, not knowing that, instead of subsiding, Miss Utley's alarm had grown. An hour after your departure she took the typewriter from the house, put it in her car, and drove to the country. Here there are alternatives; either is acceptable; I prefer this one: after disposing of the typewriter she intended to go to where Mr. Vail was in hiding, arriving before he left for the rendezvous with you, describe the situation, and insist that the project be abandoned. But something intervened, probably the difficulty of disposing of the typewriter unseen in a spot where it would surely never be found, and to see Mr. Vail she had to go to Iron Mine Road, which had been named in one of the notes she had typed."

Wolfe drank beer. "Some of what I have said is conjectural, but this is not. Miss Utley got to Iron Mine Road before you did. When you and your husband arrived, you in your car and he in his, she told him of her fears and insisted that the project must be abandoned. He didn't agree. He didn't stay long to debate it; he was supposed to be concealed somewhere by kidnapers, and even in that secluded spot there was a possibility that someone might come along. He put the suitcase in his car and drove off, leaving it to you to deal with her, and you tried to, but she wouldn't be persuaded. She may have demanded a large share of the half million to offset the risk, but I doubt it. From what your brother said of her it's more likely that she was filled with dismay. Either she made it plain that she would wreck the project by disclosing it, or you were convinced that she intended to. Infuriated, you assaulted her. You hit her on the head with something—a handy rock?—and as she lay unconscious you got in her car and ran it over her, nosed the car into an opening, dragged the body to the ditch and rolled it in, got in your car, and drove away. If, ignoring my advice to say nothing, you ask why I say that you, not Mr. Vail, killed her, I repeat that I had to satisfy myself. If he killed her, why was he killed the next day? There was no tenable answer.

"To satisfy myself it wasn't necessary to supply answers to all relevant questions. For example, where was your husband from Sunday to Wednesday morning? I don't know and need not bother to guess, but since other details were carefully and thoroughly planned I assume that one was too. It had to be some spot where both he and his car could be effectively concealed, especially in the daytime. Of course you had to know where it was, since something might happen that would make it necessary to alter the plan. No doubt you and he chose the spot with great care and deliberation. Wherever it was, probably it lacked the convenience of a telephone, so he had to get to one Tuesday evening in order to make the calls to Fowler's Inn and The Fatted Calf, but that was after dark, and of course that detail too was prudently contrived.

"For another example of questions that can be left open, why did you tell your son he could have the money if he found it? Why not? Knowing yourself where it was, you knew he wouldn't find it. Still another example, why did you and your husband insist on keeping silent about the kidnaping for forty-eight hours after he returned home? A good guess is that you wanted enough time to pass to make sure that no trail had been left, but it doesn't have to be verified for my satisfaction. Regarding any known fact or factor I need only establish that it doesn't contradict my deduction—my final deduction, that you killed your husband. As for his coming to see me Wednesday morning, posthaste after his return, it would have been surprising if he hadn't. He wanted to learn how much ground there was, if any, for Miss Utley's fears; what he learned, over the telephone from you, was that she was dead; and he departed, again posthaste, to go to you.

"He knew, of course, that you had killed Dinah Utley, and you were completely at his mercy. He couldn't expose you as a murderer without divulging his own complicity in preparations for a swindle, but the swindle hadn't been consummated; there would be no swindle until the deduction had been made on your income-tax return and you and he had signed it. Meanwhile he had a cogent threat, and he used it. He demanded the entire half a million for himself. You were in a pickle. After all the planning, all the exertion, all the painstaking, all the zeal, even after your desperate resort to murder, you were to get nothing. That was not to be borne. Jimmy Vail must die."

A noise came from her, but it wasn't a word; it was merely the kind of involuntary noise that is squeezed out by a blow or a sting. Wolfe went on. "You planned it with the care and foresight you had so admirably demonstrated in planning the kidnaping. You needed a drug, and since you assuredly wouldn't take the risk of procuring one in haste, you must have had one in your possession—probably chloral hydrate, since you may plausibly have had it in some mixture in your medicine cabinet, but that's another question I may leave open. Either luck was with you Wednesday evening, or you knew him so well that you could safely calculate that when drowsiness overtook him from the drug you had put in his drink he would die on the couch instead of going to his room. For the rest you needed no luck. After Mr. Frost left you went down to the library, found your husband in a coma as you had a right to expect, dragged him across to the desired spot, and toppled the statue on him. With your marked talent for detail, undoubtedly you took his feet. Shoes dragged along a floor will leave telltale marks, even on a rug, but a head and shoulders won't. Certainly you didn't leave it to luck whether the statue would land where you wanted it. You wiggled it to learn its direction of least resistance. Evidently the thump wasn't heard, because the inmates were all in upper rooms; and the statue didn't hit the floor, the main impact was on your husband's chest, and it would have been more of a crunch than a thump."

Wolfe straightened up, took in air through his nose as far down as it could do, and let it out through his mouth. His eyes narrowed at her. "Mrs. Vail," he said, "I confess that I am not without animus. I have been provoked by the suit you have served against me, and by your complaint against Mr. Goodwin, subjecting him to arrest on a criminal charge. But even so I would hesitate to upbraid you on moral grounds for the fraud you conceived and tried to execute. Millions of your fellow citizens will cheat on their income tax this year. Nor would I reproach you without qualification for killing Miss Utley; you did it in the instant heat of uncontrollable passion. But killing your husband is another matter. That was planned and premeditated and ruthlessly executed; and for a sordid end. Merely for money. You killed him in cold blood because he was going to deprive you of the fruit of your swindle. That, I submit, was execrable. That would be condemned even by—"

"That's not true," she said. It barely got out through her tight throat, and she repeated it. "That's not true!"

"I advised you to say nothing, madam. That would be condemned even—"

"But it's not true! It wasn't the money!" She was gripping the chair arms. "He could have had the money. I told him he could. He wouldn't. It was Dinah. He was going to leave me because I had—because of Dinah. That was why—it wasn't the money."

"I prefer it that he demanded the money."

"No!"

"He threatened to expose you as a murderer?"

"No. He said he wouldn't. But he was going to leave me, and I loved him." Her mouth worked, and her fingers clawed at the chair arms, scratching at the leather. "I loved him, and he was going to leave me."

"And of course that might mean your exposure." Wolfe's voice was low, down almost to a murmur. "Away from you, no longer enjoying your bounty, there was no telling what he might do. So he had to die. I offer you my apology. I concede that your end was not sordid, that you were in mortal danger. Did you try to gull him, did you deny that you had killed Dinah Utley?"

"No, he knew I had." She made fists. "I was insane, I must have been. You're right, I knew what would happen if he left me, but that wasn't it. I must have been insane.

Later that night I went down to the library again and stayed there with him until—"

She jerked up straight. "What am I saying? What did I say?"

"Enough." Not a murmur. "You said what I expected you to say when I accused you of killing your husband merely for money. That was absurd, but no more absurd than your attack on Mr. Goodwin and me after we found the money. You intended, of course, to put the onus on your deceased husband—to have it inferred that he had arranged the kidnaping to get the money for himself, with Dinah Utley as an accomplice, that he had killed her, and possibly even that he had killed himself through fear or remorse, though that would be rather farfetched—a man would hardly choose that method of committing suicide. But you should have known that you would arouse—"

He stopped because his audience was walking out on him. When she shifted her feet to get up, her bag slipped to the floor, and I went and picked it up and handed it to her and followed her out. Having circled around her in the hall to get in front, I had the door open by the time she reached it, and I went out to the stoop to watch her go down the steps. If she went home and finished up the chloral hydrate, that would be her funeral, but I didn't want her stumbling and breaking her neck on our premises. She wasn't any too steady, but she made it to the sidewalk and turned right, and I went back in.

Going to the kitchen, I got the tape and the playback from the cupboard and took them to the office. Wolfe sat and scowled at me as I got things ready, switched it on, ran it through to what might be the spot, and turned on the sound. Wolfe's voice came.

". . . in the instant heat of uncontrollable passion. But killing your husband is another matter. That was planned and premeditated and ruthlessly executed; and for a sordid end. Merely for money. You killed him in cold blood because he was going to deprive you of the fruit of your swindle. That, I submit, was execrable. That would be condemned even by—"

"That's not true. That's not true!"

"I advised you to say nothing, madam. That would be condemned even—"

"But it's not true! It wasn't the money! He could have had the money. I told him he could. He wouldn't. It was Dinah. He was going to leave me because I had—because of Dinah. That was why—it wasn't the money."

It went on to the end, good and clear, as it should have been, since that installation had cost twelve hundred smackers. As I turned it off Wolfe said, "Satisfactory. Take it to Mr. Cramer."

"Now?"

"Yes. That wretch may be dead within the hour. If he isn't at his office, have him summoned. I don't want him storming in here tomorrow to bark at me for delaying delivery of a confession of a murderer."

I reached for the tape.

16

She not only wasn't dead within the hour; she's not dead yet. That was three months ago, and last week a jury of eight men and four women stayed hung for fifty-two hours and then gave up. It stood seven for conviction of first-degree murder and five for acquittal. Whether this report gets published or not depends on the jury at the second trial. If it hangs too, or acquits, the script will have to go into a locked drawer in my room, with several others to keep it company.

If you care about whether I took another trip to White Plains, I did—Tuesday noon, escorted by Ben Dykes. By then Mrs. Vail had been taken to the District Attorney's office, but everyone was too busy to worry about me. I was out on bail by five o'clock, but I had had my fingerprints taken for the nineteenth time. It took a week before the charge was quashed, and the cost of the bail cut Wolfe's hundred grand down to $99,925. Even so, I'm having plenty of time to go for walks, getting angles on people and things. Having reached that bracket by the first of May, Wolfe relaxed and has stayed relaxed. If you offered him ten thousand bucks to detect who swiped your hat at a cocktail party yesterday he wouldn't even bother to glare at you.

praise for *The Normal One*

"An overdue and important book."

—*The Weekly Standard*

"*The Normal One* is Jeanne Safer's breakthrough book, deftly written yet full of hard-won insights about a crucial aspect of family role-playing that has gone beneath the radar. Though it deals with what we think of as extremes—the high-achieving 'perfect' sibling who compensates for the dysfunctional one—it has something to say to all of us about the parts we take on, apparently willingly, that become straitjackets in later life. In bravely facing and incorporating her own personal story, Safer has written an immensely moving and valuable book."

—Molly Haskell, author of *From Reverence to Rape: The Treatment of Women in the Movies*

"Wise and compassionate, *The Normal One* fearlessly speaks the truth about the challenges of being an 'invisible' sibling. This is a comfort book in the truest sense!"

—Laurie Fox, author of *My Sister from the Black Lagoon*

"Usually we don't think of sibling relationships as taboo—unless, of course, they are severely unequal. In this rare and honest book, psychologist Jeanne Safer looks at those of us who became the 'normal ones,' and sees who we are by what we so often fail to acknowledge: the damaged dreams of our siblings who are unable to live normal lives. I came away from this remarkable book gripped by new insight and inspired by Safer's courage both in describing her own relationship with her brother and in naming what she argues is our 'Caliban Syndrome.' If you are a normal one, this book may well change your life."

—Molly Peacock, author of *How to Read a Poem… And Start a Poetry Circle*

other books by jeanne safer

Beyond Motherhood: *Choosing a Life without Children*

Forgiving and Not Forgiving: *Why Sometimes It's Better* Not *to Forgive* for judith kaufman

Jeanne Safer, Ph.D.

Delta Trade Paperbacks

The Normal One

Life with a Difficult or Damaged Sibling

THE NORMAL ONE: LIFE WITH A DIFFICULT OR DAMAGED SIBLING
A Delta Book

PUBLISHING HISTORY
Free Press hardcover edition published September 2002
Delta trade paperback edition / October 2003

Published by
Bantam Dell
A Division of Random House, Inc.
New York, New York

Cover design by Belina Huey
Cover photo courtesy of the author

Book design by Bonni Leon-Berman

Library of Congress Catalog Card Number: 2002067529

ISBN 978-0-385-33756-4

Published simultaneously in Canada

146122990

author's note

The names and identifying characteristics of everyone interviewed in this book have been changed.

acknowledgments

I WANT TO THANK the "normal ones" I interviewed for their generosity, courage, and insight; I hope I did justice to their experience. Don Meyer, founder of Sibnet, and the siblings who participate in this invaluable Internet network welcomed me. My research assistant Marcey Needel was of immense help and relentless in her pursuit of every possible document on this elusive subject. I am indebted to my editor, Philip Rappaport, and my agent, Jennifer Rudolph Walsh, for believing in my work and for giving me the opportunity to write this book. Special gratitude goes to my dear friends Sue Grand, Leonard Schoolman, and Harriet Wald for their encouragement; to Paul Russo for assistance both technical and emotional; and to my husband Richard Brookhiser for sustaining me. Jackie Cantor, editor of this paperback edition, has been a tireless advocate, as has Edward Clark, Medical Director of Primary Children's Medical Center in Salt Lake City. *The Normal One* is dedicated to my beloved friend and colleague Judith Kaufman, whose observation years ago I never forgot: "Someday you will have to write about your brother."

I traveled around a great deal . . . I would have stopped, but I was pursued by something. It always came upon me unawares . . . Then all at once my sister touched my shoulder. I turn around and look into her eyes. Oh Laura, Laura, I tried to leave you behind me, but I am more faithful than I intended to be!

The Glass Menagerie by Tennessee Williams

contents

introduction

NOBODY KNOWS I HAVE A BROTHER. My best friends never hear his name. He has always been a source of embarrassment and discomfort for me, but I've never wondered very much about his impact on my life. Being his sister feels vaguely unreal and irrelevant; my destiny has nothing to do with his.

This is astonishing, because I am a psychotherapist who has spent years trying to understand my own and my patients' childhoods. Somehow I've managed to erase my own closest relative.

I am not alone. Beyond slogans ("all men are brothers," "sisterhood is powerful") and the occasional soft-focus picture book, shockingly little attention is paid to siblings in general, much less to troubled, difficult, or disabled ones. And although millions of people have such relatives—85 percent of Americans have siblings, so few extended families are exempt—practically nothing has been written about them. Worse, little has been *thought* about them; newspaper headlines (the Kaczynski brothers, wayward presidential siblings), literature (Dostoyevsky's *The Brothers Karamazov*, the plays of Williams and O'Neill), the Bible (Cain and Abel, Joseph and his brothers), and the dreams of their higher-functioning brothers and sisters tell their story, not psychological research.

Their influence is intensified because it is so hidden, even in a culture where people willingly expose the most intimate details of their lives.

The purpose of this book is to reveal the neglected, lonely, and lifelong trauma of growing up with an abnormal brother or sister and its effects on personality and society; the reality of the lives of the "normal ones" is far more complex than the sentimental image presented by the media and even by their own families. It examines the world all such siblings share, whether the disability is mental or physical, minor or catastrophic, ignored or overemphasized. It analyzes how and why their influence is repudiated, and offers remedies.

Normal ones suffer from a psychological condition I name "the Caliban Syndrome" after the brutal, repugnant slave of the magician Prospero in Shakespeare's *The Tempest,* the not-quite-human creature who tried to rape Prospero's flawless daughter Miranda. Caliban is the "thing of darkness" Prospero must accept at the play's end. Because a damaged sibling is always a disavowed part of self, I believe every intact sibling must come to terms with the Caliban within in order to become fully human. Understanding the influence that such a sibling inevitably has on one's destiny is an essential—and frequently avoided—task.

Whatever their relationship in the external world, damaged siblings loom large in the internal world of their normal brothers and sisters, as manifested in the four symptoms of the Caliban Syndrome that this book examines:

- Premature maturity
- Survivor guilt

- Compulsion to achieve
- Fear of contagion

The Caliban Syndrome has an impact far beyond the immediate families of the disabled and the difficult. These relationships are an exaggeration of the dynamics of every sibling relationship, which like every other human bond always has its dark side. Disconnecting internally from unacceptable aspects of a sibling is as universal as the primordial emotions these relationships evoke, and we pay a price for amputating them. Without acknowledging hate and repudiation, we can never truly love ourselves or anyone else; superficial assertions that short-circuit the full intensity of these prohibited emotions never work. Neither does professing spiritual uplift or sugarcoating the lifelong rigors and frustrations of having your closest relative never be your peer. Acknowledged or not, growing up with a difficult or damaged sibling is one of the defining experiences of a person's life.

The disabled and their parents have much-needed advocates; until now their siblings have had practically none. In their behalf, I take issue with the current politically correct euphemism "special needs" children because I believe that all children have special needs. Compassion for the extraordinary trials their families endure and admiration for their achievements should not blind us to the damage done by ignoring the toll on their normal siblings. I use the terms *normal, abnormal, intact,* and *damaged* not to make value judgments but to reflect more accurately the point of view of higher-functioning siblings, who typically live in an environment that requires them to suppress taboo emotions, judgments, and the evidence of their senses. Idealizing their lives as somehow ennobling, and concomitantly denigrating and denying that there is indeed such a thing as normality (with all its contradictions and complications), damages everybody and leads to dangerous self-estrangement in society as a whole.

No one with an abnormal sibling has a normal childhood. Consciously or unconsciously, every intact sibling is haunted by the fear of catching the disability, a fear that always has a modicum of psychological truth. Family gatherings and significant events become occasions for anxiety and suppressed shame. Cheerful caretakers, mature before their time, they are supposed to consider themselves lucky to be normal. They feel tormented by the compulsion to compensate for their parents' disappointments by having no problems and making no demands, and they are often unaware of the massive external and internal pressure to pretend that nothing is amiss. Their success is always tainted by their sibling's failure, their future clouded by an untoward sense of obligation and responsibility. Their goal is to be as different from their sibling as possible. They live forever in the shadow of the one who does not function.

It is not my intent to create a new category of victim; the Suffering Olympics already has a surfeit of contenders, and I believe passionately that defining yourself as a victim—no matter what you have endured—is the opposite of insight, and actually perpetuates the ordeal by cutting off the possibility of integrating and overcoming it. In fact, one of the most striking characteristics of these siblings is their lack of complaint and their tendency to hide from themselves the burdens that their very normality has placed on them. I want them to know and others to appreciate what they, and those like them, experience.

* * *

THE BOOK BEGINS with the story of my relationship with my own older brother, who was emotionally troubled from childhood on and also became seriously ill as an adult. It reflects the guilt, the grief, and the self-knowledge I have gained from my ongoing struggle to overcome my resistance and acknowledge his significance in my life. Sixty other "normal ones" aged seventeen to seventy-five, whose brothers and sisters range from microcephalic to highly obnoxious, tell the poignant, often secret stories of their lives. They also report their powerful and revealing dreams, which have never before been systematically studied for clues about their hidden inner world.

Having a damaged sibling marks you. No matter what you achieve, where you go, or who you love, that other's life remains your secret alternative template, the chasm into which you could plunge if you misstep. Whether you know it or not, his is the doom you dare not duplicate, the fate you contemplate with shame, guilt, secret envy, and—always—relief. You are ashamed that you are related, guilty that you have a better life, envious that nothing is expected of him, relieved that you are not the misfit to be scorned or pitied. Because a sibling is your closest relative, you are eternally enmeshed with each other. Your sanity and stability are forever suspect. You can consciously disconnect your destinies, but you cannot sever the fundamental tie because it embodies the disavowed part of your history and character with which you must come to terms or never truly know yourself. I hope this book eases and illuminates the way.

PART I

Where Have All the Siblings Gone?

chapter 1

My Brother, Myself

the stranger in the attic: steven and me

ALTHOUGH I HAVE AN OLDER BROTHER, I have always been an only child. We grew up in the same house, had the same parents and the same coloring. I spent my entire childhood with him, but I don't remember one shared moment, one heart-to-heart conversation. I never looked up to him, never mentioned him in any of the voluminous diaries I've kept or in either of the books I've written. I own no photograph of him, no keepsake. Having a sibling has been an abstract, oddly detached concept for me rather than a real experience.

How desperately I've worked to keep it that way.

My brother Steven—even now it feels strange to call him

that—was the classic problem child: obese, truculent, picked on by his peers, and troublesome to his teachers. He fought constantly with our parents, who could not conceal that he was an embarrassment and a burden; I was their darling and delight. He flunked out of college; I excelled. He barely made a living; I became Dr. Safer, like our father. His wretched marriage disintegrated; mine was profiled in *Life*. My innate superiority was as just and natural as slavery felt to slave owners. He seemed a changeling, an absence, or an inconvenience—a disruption to my family rather than a member of it. In reality he was a warning: my dark and dreaded opposite.

Only when I visited him in the hospital in 1999 after one of his legs was amputated because of advanced diabetes—he lost the other as well the following year—did I begin to reconsider our relationship or indeed realize that we had one. A man much more than seven years older than I, his eyes full of weariness, sat in a wheelchair, surprisingly glad to see me. The determination and courage in his demeanor, the urgency and undiminished joy with which he spoke of wanting to lead his dance band again (his musical ability was the one talent in which he had always clearly surpassed me), put me to shame. Although subsequent interactions proved far more problematic, and too much damage had been done for anything consistently positive to flourish, I finally knew I had a brother.

This encounter, the first after years of obliviousness broken only by occasional pro forma birthday cards and visits kept as short as decently possible by both of us, provoked what may have been my first dream about him, from which I awoke in terror: he was trying to rape me. I experienced his reappearance in my life as a violent invasion of my inner world from which I could no longer exclude him. It is the only nightmare I have ever welcomed.

* * *

In my subsequent search for any remnant of our shared history, I collected every shred of evidence of Steven's presence I could retrieve, much of it from drawers in my parents' house that had been unopened for decades. I scanned the snapshots, report cards, letters I had written, home movies, and my own minimal memories. *Recovery* is not the right word for this task; so much never registered to begin with. Seeing the paucity of images, the pitifully few mementos or even thoughts about him that I retain, shocks me now as it never did before. It used to feel so unremarkable to have nothing of him in my life; why would you have mementos of somebody who played so little part, who barely entered your consciousness? I always assumed that the gap in our ages and interests made us inhabit nonintersecting worlds, but that was the flimsiest of justifications. The lack of evidence is damning: I made my closest relative disappear. This grossly unfair, inhumane obliteration, which our parents covertly initiated and abetted, does not even qualify as disowning him—that would imply there had been a relationship, even if it were later repudiated. All my life it seemed the most natural thing in the world. Long before computers, I had a highly effective delete key in my psyche.

Steven and I grew up in a middle-class Jewish family in Cincinnati, Ohio. We were both planned and were born seven years apart; World War II intervened. Our (using that inclusive plural pronoun makes us seem more related than I ever felt) father was a shy and diligent anesthesiologist, our mother the consummate suburban "homemaker" with an artistic flair. Our parents, generous children of immigrants, had the intellectual and economic aspirations of their generation and strove to give their own children the best of everything. Consequently, we had the music lessons, the birthday parties, the summer vacations complete with annual pilgrimages to New York City and its boutiques of children's clothes that were the external trappings of successful family life.

There were minefields in this landscape that I discovered only later. My father had several bouts of serious illness—ulcerative colitis around the time of Steven's birth, cardiac symptoms when I was a year old (he was told then that a faulty heart valve would kill him within the year, although he lived thirty-one more), and nearly fatal peritonitis that kept him hospitalized three months when I was ten and Steven was finishing high school. Our parents' marriage, cozy and playful in my early years, fell apart spectacularly in my adolescence—not coincidentally, right after Steven left for college.

In examining the photographs I unearthed, I was struck by how few, other than the class pictures everybody bought, depicted Steven after age two. This is telling because my father was a skilled and prolific amateur photographer; there were plenty of shots of me. In the only portrait of us together, I am less than a year old, and it was obviously posed. He seems to have morphed from an unusually beautiful blond toddler with a winning smile and an exquisite outfit into a downcast, already overweight seven-year-old. The pictures confirm my memory: I never saw him laugh. There was but one happy Polaroid, added to the collection within the last twenty years, of Steven in middle age, decked out in a bow tie and red-striped vest, leading his band and playing his trumpet with gusto, for an audience of strangers.

Judging from the data, my brother was in trouble before I was born, but my arrival exacerbated it spectacularly. There are families where it is an advantage to be born one sex or the other, and female was definitely the right option in mine; my father could not tolerate a rival, my mother needed a mirror, and I filled the bill for both. Qualities that must have seemed defiant or difficult in him seemed fetching, even inspiring, in me.

The name I was given epitomized my role in the family, which virtually guaranteed a rift between us. My mother called me "Gene," on the theory that, since she expected me to become a writer, I should have a mannish pen name at the ready; her daughter was going to be unusual and had to make it in a man's world. My father sensibly suggested I might prefer the feminine form, "Jeanne," and as in most things, his will prevailed. The original name she chose, even with modifications, presaged my destiny. I was enshrined as the replacement son, the shiny new female version of the hopelessly inadequate boy, whom both my parents unconsciously considered damaged goods to be discarded. Here was a second chance, a child who would not—who dared not—disappoint, whose cleverness and determination were no threat but rather the compensatory source of pride and joy and promise. I was dressed for success in a masculine name, and all their dreams were transferred to me.

My mission was assigned to me along with my name, and I chose to accept it. In their eyes Steven was already a lost cause who represented their shortcomings as parents. I was to be the anti-Steven and learned early to define myself as his opposite. My becoming a star would make them stars, and my precocity was lovingly nurtured toward that end. The three of us constituted the perfect family unit, even if achieving it took editing out one member.

Steven was a convenient receptacle for all negativity and strife. We had no problems; he was the problem, and there was no solution. Using a child for this purpose, a popular strategy, is undetectable from within a family. My parents could not see that Steven was starving for their love or that he hated himself for disappointing them. To them he was primarily a hardship to be endured. They were acutely aware that he was abnormal, but they could not bear to think that they had anything to do with it; they rendered themselves as helpless and hopeless as he was. Making someone the embodiment of self-inflicted failure precludes any possibility of growth or healing, even as it absolves you of responsibility. The fault had to be his. To think otherwise would have disrupted their carefully constructed, fragile equilibrium, their sense that they were good people and good parents; it would have brought trouble squarely into paradise.

I don't know what, if anything, was really the matter with Steven, other than having the wrong parents. Although he had no intellectual deficit, the school problems apparent in even his earliest report cards—the low grades in conduct, the repeated Steven-could-try-harders—would suggest a learning disability or attention deficit disorder today. He got in no terrible trouble and tended to get beaten up rather than to beat up others, although he did fight physically with his girlfriends later. Depression, obesity, and isolation, never drugs or criminality, plagued him.

At home his misery was manifested in constant turmoil; *sullen* and *surly* best describe his predominant moods. He fought with my parents all the time, about nothing in particular, although his grades, his weight, his "laziness," and his choice of companions were reasons for dispute. At the dinner table, from childhood through adolescence, silence alternated with fits of rage, and spectacular exits were the norm. He seemed at a continual simmer and would strike out for no apparent reason. My mother counterattacked; my father withdrew or pleaded for peace that never came. On one vacation when he was a teenager (I always shared their room and he stayed alone), he became so furious—again I have no idea why—that he insisted on getting a train ticket home. There was relief all around when he left.

One of the ways my parents demonstrated that they had given up on Steven was by making no concerted or effective efforts to discipline him when he sulked or raged. They treated him as though he were a force of nature whose outbursts could only be weathered. This sent him the message that he was exempt from basic rules of conduct, which reinforced his conviction that he was unsocializable. I was expected to back them up by sitting quietly through the storms and the quiet-before-the-storms that ruined every family occasion. They felt unable to control him, so they never taught him to control himself.

Although I hated his outbursts, I secretly envied his freedom to indulge in them. He didn't have to behave, and he suffered no consequences. When you have no position, you have no position to lose.

Nobody set proper limits with Steven until five years ago when, over my mother's silent protest, I said at a dinner that I would leave the restaurant if he maintained his angry silence. It felt like a dangerous breach of etiquette. I was fifty years old.

In hindsight I realize that his obnoxiousness and the tension he created so alienated me that I could not notice, and did not wish to see, his underlying anguish and despair. I could not stand to know that Steven had no other way of calling attention to himself or fending others off. Not knowing how to please, he could only provoke.

Although undoubtedly my brother was chronically enraged at me as well, I remember no untoward violence between us; he would certainly have been blamed and punished for any fights we had, since I was so much younger and more devious. My only scary memory is his having shown me a picture in a storybook that frightened me horribly at age five—it was terrifying enough that I opened the same book with embarrassed trepidation at age thirty-five.

Why did my parents, with their medical sophistication, not intervene? My mother, at least, noticed that something was gravely amiss and begged my father to get psychiatric help for Steven; family therapy would of course have been unthinkable. My father, disdaining the profession, flatly refused; he was probably too ashamed at the prospect of exposure before his colleagues. To this day my mother has not forgiven herself for capitulating.

The most startling exclusionary act my parents ever committed, the one Steven never recovered from, was a decision they made about our living arrangements. For the better part of five years, from the age of eleven, he actually stayed by himself in the attic, separated from my parents and me by another apartment on the intervening floor.

On the surface it was a perfectly rational temporary solution, dictated by necessity. We were living in a cramped two-bedroom apartment on the ground floor of a house owned by my father's parents, who occupied the second floor. My mother frantically tried various arrangements, but a prepubescent boy and his baby sister could share a bedroom for only so long, and nobody could sleep comfortably in the living room, so Steven had to be moved to the third floor. My father concurred for reasons rooted in his past. He refused to move out of his parents' house even after he could easily have afforded his own; we constantly looked at real estate, but no place met his exacting standards. His flamboyantly handsome, far more sociable older brother, also a doctor, had been shamelessly preferred by their mother, and he must have thought he could finally get some attention from that smart, imperious, and cold woman by living downstairs from her. Though my mother agonized over this decision, she felt she had no choice. Her fears of abandonment, and memories of brutal arguments between her own parents, prevented her from taking a stand in Steven's behalf; marital harmony had to be preserved, and he was the casualty.

Both my parents were driven by buried needs that made them disregard the consequences of their plan. Only after four years did my father finally decide to build a house, but by the time it was finished and Steven had his own room, he was ready to leave home for college and for good.

Guilt prompted my mother to furnish Steven's hideaway with everything a boy could desire. His banishment was not at all strange to me—the place seemed glamorous, exotic, and blissfully private (solitude was the one commodity I had too little of), and I don't remember his objecting. But he was an outcast, the stranger in the attic. Every night, cut off from his family, he slept all by himself on the third floor in lonely luxury, while they, safely ensconced with their good child, lived in artificial happiness below.

My brother's exile to the attic simply made evident what had long been the unspoken truth: there was no place for him with us. I never imagined he was miserable up there, though my mother later lamented that he cried when he climbed the stairs at night. His snug den probably also became a retreat from the uninviting family circle two floors down. Still, he must have felt utterly abandoned, the physical barrier fortifying the psychological one that was by then impenetrable. He was to stay on a different level for the rest of his life.

Separating Steven from the family was intended—unconsciously, of course—to remove the source of all ills. Although superficially life did become more tranquil in our charmed circle when he wasn't around, exorcising him had ominous implications for me that I have never escaped. With a child's logic I figured out that he was ostracized because he was bad; this made the consequences of being anything like him dangerously real. What if I lost my temper once too often, got a less than stellar grade, gained too much weight—failed at anything? What if I relaxed my guard and my charm or my competence crashed? Could the same thing happen to me if I no longer measured up? Just to be on the safe side, I made many mental additions to the list of things I dared not be: unhappy, whiny, demanding—anything that could be thought of as childish. One false step, and I could lose everything too. I understood none of this at the time.

Failing was an all-too-real threat because my emotional life was far from ideal, even though (and also because) I was the chosen one. I never consciously connected my imperfections with Steven, but I was terribly aware of them; it must have been easier for me to feel normal because he was so visibly abnormal. I was physically awkward and prone to what I now identify as anxiety and depression, although, luckily, I loved school. And so acclimated was I to the company of adults that I never felt entirely comfortable with other children. While I was never scorned, I was never popular either; I have felt like an outsider all my life. What saved me is that I knew how to make my parents happy.

How could these people, both of whom were decent and capable of devotion, have treated their son so badly? They tried to support him later and would not have dreamed of literally disinheriting him. At critical moments they came to his aid; my mother persuaded the dean of his college to readmit Steven, and he graduated. But because they blamed him for their own inability to relate to him, the damage they did was profound. The traumas of their childhoods, the troubled relationships with their own parents and siblings, of which they were unaware, drove them to it. Their behavior, rather than malevolent, was tragically blind and misguided.

My father, such an adoring presence when I was a little girl, withdrew from Steven early on. Only once do I remember the two of them attending an activity alone together—a baseball game that neither especially enjoyed. My mother was the more engaged parent, who fought some battles for him and took care of him when he was ill, but she could never listen to him. She alternated between blaming him and blaming herself.

Steven had the misfortune to be a bad reflection, in both senses of the term, on each of his parents. In him they saw sides of themselves they shrank from rather than what all parents yearn to see—an image of their better selves. It was a terrible fit.

His mother had to have a child who emulated her, whose talents and temperament matched hers, and whose successes fulfilled her frustrated aspirations. To justify her life, she needed somebody in whose glory she could shine. Steven showed her she was a failure.

For his father, Steven represented qualities that he detested in himself and that his own mother had repudiated—shyness, depression, and emotional hunger. Though he had been slender as a young man, he had gained some weight himself by the time he had a family. He could find in his son none of the academic brilliance, discipline, and self-containment on which he prided himself and for which he was valued. He had always lived in the shadow of his own brother, and he put Steven there too. And having lost his mother's love to a rival, he would not tolerate another; he and he alone would be the masculine center of attention for his wife. He was reproducing the pattern in his own family, only this time he did the rejecting. Steven was too much like his father's own nightmare vision of himself, the awful truth that even professional success could not undo. His son was a more fitting receptacle for his self-hatred than his daughter. Steven shamed him.

That both my parents were youngest children, with older brothers, also made it easier for them to identify with me.

I had my own reasons for being their willing accomplice, and an agent in my own right, in the secret campaign to keep the Safer family Steven-free. I helped erase him to ensure that I would remain the focus of attention. Instinctively, since his life was a cautionary tale of the consequences of failing to please, I kept myself up by putting him down, calling attention to his deficits and my own assets. I had to denigrate Steven to reinforce my superiority, which otherwise would have been in doubt.

I am struck by how utterly lacking in empathy or compassion for him I was, and how I never felt the slightest twinge of guilt for being so blatantly favored over my brother. Why didn't I try to relate to him? Family dynamics kept us apart. I needed to see our parents in the same flattering light they shined on themselves, and appreciating Steven's perspective would have ruptured our bond. Any relationship between us would have upset the family and my place therein and highlighted qualities of my own that threatened to destroy everything I had.

One of my very few early-childhood memories related to Steven has always disturbed me because it exposes an unsavory effort to maintain my status at his expense: when I was probably five years old and Steven had a cold, I used his toothbrush once, hoping to catch his cold and usurp the unusual amount of attention that was being lavished on him because he was sick. There was something desperate as well as calculating in the gesture; perhaps my exalted position was not as unassailable as I thought. I did not want him taking up residence among us again, even temporarily, so unbeknownst to anyone, I took an extra precaution to make sure he stayed in his place. In a family that practices exclusion, even a station as secure as mine never feels entirely solid, because it rests on the unstable foundation of parents' favor as well as on the miseries of another.

My collusion with my parents and my efforts to reinforce my superiority continued after we had both left home. In a letter I wrote them from college, I commiserated with my mother about the most recent havoc Steven was wreaking, in the coldly self-righteous language I had so thoroughly imbibed over the years that it had become formulaic:

> What can be done with a person like this? How do you instill self-reliance and strength of character, or even raw endurance, in someone so buried in bitterness and failure on every possible level?

In many ways my strategy paid off handsomely. I brought out the best in my parents, particularly before I sought my independence as an adolescent and broke the magic circle. The cost became apparent only recently: it robbed me of my brother and of part of myself.

Despite the serious failings of his family, Steven himself is ultimately responsible for his fate; even as a child he was no martyred innocent. He overcame some of his liabilities after he left home, but he remained mired in bitterness, recriminations, and entitled victimhood. These attitudes are never confined to one's family alone. He also neglected himself physically and for years avoided any sort of therapy; in both habits he was, unfortunately, his father's son. My parents and I contributed mightily to his sorrows, but his own choices perpetuated them.

The one thing they did right was foster Steven's musical talent. Appreciation of music and the ability to make it was something the four of us genuinely had in common, even if we never enjoyed it together. They let him experiment with instruments—even a drum set—until he discovered the trumpet, and then patiently went through candidates until they found the right teacher for him—a man whose name and benign influence I still remember. He was the only one of us ever to play professionally. We attended his performances, where I had the unfamiliar experience of seeing Steven in the spotlight. He was featured in his high school show, wearing a pith helmet and playing "Tiger Rag"; I would later audition to sing in mine but never made the cut. Music has been his rampart through every hardship. This is something we share, but he does not know we do.

Unfortunately for both of them, my father, who played a mellow clarinet and saxophone, never played duets with his son, though he clearly inspired him. Steven still performs the music my father loved, big band hits of World War II vintage, along with jazz of many eras. It is the sole unambivalently positive bond they had.

Steven's pivotal position in our family became clear only when he left, and all the pathology he had contained over the years spilled out. It is no accident that our parents' marriage then imploded and my relationship with my mother exploded; the effort of keeping him at bay had united us. So well did we hide his role in plain sight that I only noticed it recently; it had worked like a charm.

During the wretched tumult of my parents' separation, I turned to Steven for help for the only time in my life, but by then it was too late. I called him at college and he rebuffed me, saying my mother was paranoid and my father above reproach.

ALTHOUGH STEVEN FOUND SATISFACTIONS and compensations in subsequent years, trials both mental and physical were added to his childhood tribulations. His marriage failed, he had limited success as an insurance agent, and diabetes struck in his thirties, a baleful paternal legacy. Steven endured bypass surgery at age forty, was too ill to work by age fifty, and by age sixty had lost all kidney function and both his legs. He ended up spending more time in the hospital than out of it. Because of our estrangement, he never turned to me for comfort.

Though beset with problems, Steven had a better time in life outside the family than he ever had within it. He longed for family connections and found them among our father's relatives. He made friends who stood by him and finally met a woman who was devoted to him and who saw him through his devastating illnesses.

He led his dance band, by now a weekly fixture in the city, through everything and started to sing in it as well. He hosted a radio show featuring the music he loved.

Far more gregarious and civic-minded than anyone else in the family, he joined community groups and rose to the top in several of them. Fraternal organizations became the center of his life; he was president of the brotherhood of his temple and a prominent member of Big Brothers, the men's organization that helps fatherless boys. He found symbolic ways to be a brother, having never been mine.

But he recently got a sickening and gratuitous reminder that his earlier exclusion from his family would never end. Two years ago our mother, at age eighty-seven, moved to a nursing home in the early stage of Alzheimer's disease. (Our father had died years before.) When Steven went for the first time to visit her there, the staff refused to admit him. According to their records, her only child was a daughter. She had not told them she had a son.

the dark mirror: steven in me

> When I was a child, I spake as a child, I understood as a child, I thought as a child: but when I became a man, I put away childish things.
>
> For now we see through a glass, darkly; but then face to face: now I know in part but then shall I know even as also I am known.
>
> *I Corinthians*

As I began to reconsider my brother and myself, all I felt—when I felt anything at all—was shame and shrinking away from him and from qualities in myself that evoked him. Fear lurked behind the shame. I was conscious of not wanting to be like him, but I had no idea how deep my repudiation went, how much it shaped my life, and how impossible a task it really was. As I understood more, the shame (at least the part about how I regarded him) turned to guilt, tempered with frustration. As my empathy for Steven grew, I felt more compassion for the ways I resemble him. Now much has melted into sorrow and a sense of irredeemable loss.

I had a long way to go. Only three years before, when I was in my brother's hospital room and the nurse addressed him as "Mr. Safer," a preposterous thought went through my head: who is this man? Of course I would have recognized "Mrs. Safer" (my mother) and "Dr. Safer" (my father, my uncle, or myself), but here was a startling and unfamiliar prefix to the family surname. So little time had I spent in Steven's company as an adult, so little did I know him or see him with other people, that I had never heard his name before. My reaction mimicked the scene in *The Bald Soprano,* Ionesco's absurdist play, in which two people upon meeting keep remarking "How bizarre! And what a strange coincidence!" as the accumulating details they trade about their lives lead inexorably to the conclusion that they are husband and wife. In the original production, my edition notes, "this dialogue was spoken and played in a style sincerely tragic," as it deserves.

* * *

I AWOKE THE DAY I started to write about Steven from a startling dream:

> I keep trying to sharpen my pencil, but I can't get the sharpener to work. I'm struggling to regain consciousness, fighting through a haze that seems almost viscous, as though I'm drugged and waking up from anesthesia. Then I hear water running ominously and rush into my office. There is evidence of a major leak in the corner, but I don't know where it's coming from. I try frantically to get someone to fix it.

This dream, which seemed compellingly real, revealed how conflicted I felt about telling our story. As much as I needed to record it, I was frightened of how I would feel; writing makes things inescapably real. I was fighting to wake up to the truth, but it was still a battle not to remain unconscious about our connection; there had to be good reasons why I had always concealed it from myself. The dream told me that the defenses I used to prevent Steven from "leaking" into my life were not impermeable. The carefully constructed identity that I had hermetically sealed off from his dangerous influence—epitomized by the room where I work as a professional psychoanalyst—was no longer secure.

I never doubted that my nonrelationship with my brother was peculiar and that it set me apart from what most other siblings feel for one another; this was just a piece of information noted in passing, nothing consciously envied or longed for. His absence in my life hardly registered; in order to miss something, you have to see its value, and it was critical for me to devalue him. For most people with brothers and sisters, being a sibling is as implicit a part of their identity as stature—not something they think about every day but a basic fact. It was never part of mine. Being Steven's sibling got relegated to the attic of my consciousness. This didn't seem odd to me, although people are always surprised to learn of his existence. I became proficient at discounting him so early that I never noticed the effort.

Thinking about our connection, or being reminded of it, has made me uncomfortable for as long as I can remember. Once when I told a therapist that I strove to be Steven's opposite and was asked to enumerate the traits I fled, I felt almost physical resistance to identifying them, as though "fat, angry, unpopular, unsuccessful" might stick to me if I said the words aloud. In my long years of psychotherapy, many issues subliminally related to him got resolved, though Steven barely surfaced again directly. Still, I was immensely relieved that he could not attend my wedding, which spared me from having to introduce him to people. Although I told myself differently, I shunned Steven because his being, not his behavior, embarrassed me; he gave the lie to my mental health.

My urgency to differentiate myself from him in mind and body (though the family resemblance has actually gotten stronger as we have aged) was based on a very real threat: every day, on the third floor, I observed the consequences of failing to fulfill the mandate. To be physically unappealing, emotionally immature, or burdensome would shame me in my parents' eyes and might exile me too forever from their favor. Efforts to excel on all fronts, begun on their behalf, continued on my own.

Not only do I drive myself to perform; I have to make it look easy. As Steven's counterweight, I embodied success as he embodied the reverse; it was what I was, not something I should, or could, work at. So proficient have I become that a patient of mine lamented that even the flowers in my vase arranged themselves effortlessly. The unglamorous source of this art is my assumption that people will abandon me if I fail to live up to their expectations.

What worried me most was always threatening to come true. Anxiety that I would turn into Steven has pursued me from childhood on, though never identified as such. I tried to shape my personality to be immune to his flaws. These exertions have been so pervasive and so underground that I can only track them by seeing how unsettled I am when they falter and I see him in my mirror.

Assaults on my body image are the worst, because Steven's body was considered so out of control, the visible reason he was rejected at home and at school. My own too-ample belly, which in middle age seems to have expanded inordinately and resists all efforts to make it contract, fills me with disproportionate humiliation and despair. Though I never developed an eating disorder, I feel as little sympathy toward myself for being moderately overweight as my parents conveyed to Steven. Every woman in America agonizes over the size of her thighs, but few have concrete cause to think that excess flesh could cause them to be exiled from their own families. In mine Steven's weight was not a symptom or even an affliction; it was the stigma of a flawed nature.

Internal dangers alarm me as much as overt ones. For a person whose health has been blessedly robust and who works to keep it so—another way not to emulate my brother—I am always afraid that I too could be prone to life-threatening illnesses or that mild ones will turn dire. Heredity is destiny, I warn myself, and I generalize its potential for harm. When anything goes wrong with my body, my moods, my work, or my social life, I search for signs of disaster. Everything seems tenuous; my footing is forever perilous. Anxiety does not rule me or paralyze me, and it has been tempered by years of therapy, but panic is still my reflexive response to uncertainty.

I now recognize that these troubling fantasies are manifestations of the guilt I escaped in childhood, my punishment for having a better life. Unconsciously I believe that my achievements intentionally caused my brother to fail. Now the one who used to feel entitled to everything does not think she deserves even the successes she has worked diligently to achieve. I prevent myself from enjoying victory too much by thinking that defeat is just around the corner.

Pessimism is the harshest, most persistent legacy of being Steven's sister. If something is even a little wrong, I assume it's rotten to the core; like a cold, a temporary setback could signal the beginning of a relentless downward spiral. This attitude doesn't interfere with my efforts, but it mars my pleasure and satisfaction and makes relaxation elusive. Curiously I reserve negativity exclusively for myself; for everybody else I am an enthusiastic proponent of the power to change through insight, work, and will. A paradoxical combination of exuberance, resilience, and catastrophic expectation coexist in my temperament.

Because I am so demanding of myself and regard my own emotional and physical imperfections with the same abhorrence that Steven evoked, I do not assume I can count on compassion from others, and I am always relieved and grateful to be proved wrong. It is hard not to expect that if I seem depressed or unproductive those I love or admire will give up on me, just as I feared my parents would turn away if I veered too close to Steven.

In my darkest moments I used to feel a nameless dread. The content of that dread is clear to me now: the image of Steven that my family created is the awful truth about me, the Caliban within, whom I fight to conceal from everyone.

STEVEN, WHO SO RECENTLY SEEMED to have nothing to do with my destiny, in fact has played an unacknowledged role in every significant choice I have made. Arranging my life to circumvent or repair the problems he caused, or to prevent a repetition, has been my unconscious agenda.

Steven is one of the reasons I chose to be childless, although other factors influenced this decision, and avoidance was not my principal motivation. My fear of having a child like him was a projection of my fear of becoming him myself, deflected onto the next generation. I was also afraid of becoming Steven's mother, mired in guilt and self-recrimination because her son felt so alien, and feeling incapable of nurturing him. I got the best of what my parents had to offer, but family life as I knew it was not an experience I was in a hurry to reproduce.

Steven was not irrelevant to my becoming a psychoanalyst, my chosen vocation since childhood. Making a difference to others as I never could to him was a form of surrogate reparation, as well as a way to transform the amorphous anxiety we lived in by understanding it. The optimistic side of my nature needed to disprove my parents' unspoken dictum that his problems could never be solved. And earning a doctorate made me even more my father's heir. No wonder that whenever I suggested to Steven that he go into therapy, he was insulted and considered my heartfelt plea condescending.

How my brother behaved affected what I sought and fled in relationships. Because of him I became unduly sensitive to the silent treatment, or even slightly raised voices, and completely intolerant of tantrums. It is essential for me to feel understood because Steven never was. I have also always sought substitute brothers and treasure the love of my male friends as the compensation for the bond I forfeited with him.

My image of my brother has never been entirely watertight. There are fragments of evidence about him that do not fit my family's gloomy perception, but I used to patch the "leaks" quickly; when the designated receptacle of negativity does something positive, the world turns upside down. He has devoted himself to causes and gets along fine with people outside his immediate family; how can the problem have been all his?

So intent have I been on making myself different from Steven that I neglected to notice the positive things we have in common; it is impossible to see someone clearly if you are always busy running in the opposite direction. I share my brother's love of music and delight in performing it. And the determination—some might even say stubbornness—on which I pride myself pales beside his valiant battle to express himself musically and give joy to others despite the physical suffering he endures every day. It is an exceptional feat of bravery that I can only hope to emulate.

I still feel shame when I think about Steven, but the focus has changed. I am no longer embarrassed to be related to him; I am ashamed of how I regarded him. The guilt I never felt has also become unavoidable. He was the family scapegoat, and I colluded to keep him so. I cannot reverse the favoritism that was undeserved, nor the ways it distorted both our lives and prevented any trust or real love from developing between us. I do not pity him as an inferior; I grieve because my closest relative was and always will be far too distant from me.

It feels impossible to be myself with Steven. I once thought about calling him to let him know I was going to be on television, but I had no idea how he would respond. Would he feel like I was rubbing his nose in my success if I told him, or be offended if I did not? No spontaneous gesture seems possible, only second-guessing and management. I, who pride myself on sensitivity and understanding, draw a blank when it comes to him.

Several months ago a bout of illness forced me to cancel a longed-for vacation. For the first time it dawned on me that my brother has never had a real one since the unhappy trips he took with our family forty years ago, while I have been all over the world. Such sickening contrasts in our fortunes, once a source of secret relief, now only pain me.

When I went back to Cincinnati two years ago to close up the house our parents had finally built, the one in which Steven briefly had a proper room of his own, I saw once more how conspicuous he was by his absence. He wanted none of their possessions, only a few trinkets he had bought on a trip we took in the early 1960s; there was nothing that bore any relation to him or that he felt attached to. He never had a real home as long as I can remember, and he now lives by himself in a cluttered apartment still furnished with the dresser and night tables that had been his consolation prize in the attic. I wept because he had so few happy moments or memories there and none of them with me.

The day I visited him in the hospital after his leg was amputated changed forever the way I experienced my brother. I saw strength of character, a passion for living, and a capacity for endurance in him that made me feel proud, and I told him so. These qualities had to have been latent in him all the time of our childhood, unappreciated by his family.

Soon afterward we had the first real conversation of our lives. He said, through tears, that he did not want us to be unreconciled, and I welcomed the opportunity with tears of my own. I told him that I had been unfairly favored and that it had not been good for me either, which seemed to surprise him. I said I was glad he had found more love in adulthood than he had gotten in childhood, that though we couldn't change history, we could still have something real together, and he seemed to want to try.

But it did not last. He retreated back into the familiar sullen shell and repulsed any efforts to coax him out; he would not, or could not, muster the energy to engage with me and let me into his life at this late date. Perhaps he did not trust my sincerity or want to open up the past again. Maybe he prefers anger to anguish and finds it easier to be alienated than grief-stricken about what we never had.

After the terrorist attack in New York on September 11, he called to make sure I was unharmed, but he didn't want to talk to me.

There will be no "closure" in this relationship, at least not between us. The only transformation I can count on has already occurred, within me. The reconciliation he said he desired may be out of reach, and I may never be much more than the chip on my brother's shoulder.

Even if we never meet again, Steven is indelible to me now. In my mind at least we both have three dimensions now and, since I finally have the capacity, the possibility of some remnant of a real relationship. And though I know the odds are against it, I hope we can have even a little time as brother and sister before we lose each other forever so soon after finding each other for the first time. We would get something precious that has been missing in our lives. The irony is almost unbearable; I hate to see that just as I acknowledge how much he is a part of me, he refuses to acknowledge me as part of him. Just when I can give something genuine of myself, he insists I still offer nothing. As soon as I discover him, he makes himself disappear, this time by his own choice.

Now that I see through the glass less darkly, I long to be face to face with him, to be known even as I know. But that is not to be. He hides from me. Turning the tables is the only power he thinks he can wield over me; to be thought inhumane when I appreciate his humanity at last is my punishment. Who can blame him? It was true for too long. I accept his rejection, though it grieves me. I will carry it to my grave. I am glad I finally know the truth. The leaks in my office will never be repaired again; I don't want them fixed. This is the achievement I'm proud of, and my consolation.

chapter 2

Everybody's an Only Child

FACING HOW I BURIED MY BROTHER'S ROLE in my life has been an ordeal; I now understand why I avoided it for fifty-four years. To broaden my perspective—both out of professional interest and because studying emotional experience has always been the way I cope with it—I surveyed psychological studies of siblings. Extensive research turned up practically nothing, even in the psychoanalytic literature, my own specialty, which focuses specifically on what is hidden and expelled from awareness. To my astonishment, I discovered that the resistance and disconnection I battled in myself also pervades my profession; psychoanalysis, the talking cure, is strangely silent about siblings.

"Siblings" does not appear in the 404-page index to the twenty-three-volume *Standard Edition* of Freud—there are a mere five citations for "brothers and sisters"—but "Siberia" does. The founder of psychoanalysis symbolically relegated his own seven siblings there and set the precedent for his followers to ignore the influence of their own and their patients' closest kin to this day. The major textbooks in the field followed suit, focusing virtually exclusively on relations between parents and children. No panel on siblings had yet been held at a scientific meeting and only a handful of articles were published in psychoanalytic journals as late as 1980, three generations after Freud first wrote about the power of the unconscious and the centrality of early family experience. Eloise Agger called attention to this omission in her 1983 paper "Psychoanalytic Perspectives on Sibling Relationships," and now another quarter-century has passed with nary a comprehensive study in print; without accumulated data, the occasional articles that do appear reinvent the wheel. Scientific literature outside the psychoanalytic tradition is similarly scant, although siblings are more conspicuous in imaginative literature and biography, where the taboo seems to have less power.

How and why have siblings escaped scrutiny? Everybody, clinicians and theorists included, wants to be an only child. This desire was compelling for Freud and had subtle but major impact on his theoretical formulations. An adored firstborn son, he never got over his guilty triumph that his unwelcome nine-month-old younger brother died when Freud was one and a half years old; later he noted that this experience had left him with "the germ of self-reproach" and had "determined what is neurotic, and also what is intense, in all my friendships." His mother had six more children, all daughters, before his tenth birthday. Hostility among siblings, he wrote, is "far more frequent in childhood than the unseeing eye of adult observers can perceive." Yet it is imperceptible in the Oedipus complex, in which a son's only rival for his mother's love is his father. All younger potential competitors (particularly dead ones of the same sex) are peremptorily disposed of. Despite his own favored position—his eldest sister's piano was given away because the noise of her playing bothered him—Freud unwittingly recapitulated sibling rivalry all his life. His tumultuous relationships with friends and colleagues were marred by his need to be the center of attention, his jealousy of potential usurpers, and his sensitivity to betrayal.

Freud's blind spot has been incorporated into the discipline he founded, and his followers, mostly siblings themselves, have been eliminating rivals ever since. As much as it has changed since the early days, psychoanalytic theory still emphasizes parent/child interactions, which leads to training and clinical practice that emphasize parent/child interactions. This vicious cycle keeps every new generation of clinicians blind and deaf to what was originally excluded; even now siblings rarely merit more than informal discussion in case presentations, and it is an unusual analysis in which they receive enough attention. Sibling conflicts of their own prevent most therapists from recognizing the omission and make them collude with their patients to avoid addressing them in depth. They consider it normal, and fail to inquire, if patients never mention a sibling by name or at all or act as though the person were an extra rather than a costar in the drama of their lives. My own treatment is typical; in fifteen years of intensive work, I spent no more than fifteen minutes discussing my brother, and my analyst, whom I later learned had a borderline sister herself, never noticed. Her own efforts to differentiate herself from this sister must have made her consider my attitude as a natural, reasonable fact of life rather than an anxiously constructed and precariously maintained compulsion. The process is insidious and almost undetectable: you find what you look for and ignore what you do not want to see, and you can only help others know what you can recognize in yourself. In professions as in families, avoidance begets avoidance. This is why the psychology of siblings remains terra incognita.

If feelings about even normal siblings are buried, feelings about abnormal ones are buried much more deeply. Therefore I believe that the disproportionate number of people with damaged siblings who become psychotherapists exacerbates the problem. An informal survey of my acquaintances in the field revealed a plethora of hitherto unmentioned dysfunctional sisters and brothers; my colleagues and I are motivated as much by the unconscious need to demonstrate how sane, intact, and different from our siblings we are as by the more conscious vocation to help others.

Personal resistance is not the only factor preventing siblings from getting proper attention. The asymmetrical nature and hierarchical structure of the classical psychoanalytic situation itself (as well as most of its therapeutic siblings), in which the analyst is the authority figure and strives to be a blank screen onto which the patient unilaterally projects internal conflicts, naturally tends to elicit more feelings about parents. As this model shifts to a more egalitarian exchange to which both participants contribute—a development gathering force in the field—siblings may return from their long Siberian sojourn.*

---

*There is some evidence of change. Vamik Volkan and Gabriele Ast, *Siblings in the Unconscious and Psychopathology* (Madison, CT: International Universities Press, 1997) is a recent contribution to the psychoanalytic literature. Salman Akhtar and Selma Kramer, editors, *Brothers and Sisters: Developmental, Dynamic, and Technical Aspects of the Sibling Relationship* (Northvale, New Jersey: Jason Aronson, 1999) is a volume of ground-breaking papers from one of the first psychoanalytic panels on siblings, held at the Twenty-ninth Annual Margaret S. Mahler Symposium on Child Development in 1998.

Now that my own experience has sensitized me to hidden sibling themes, I am struck by how frequently and unexpectedly they appear and how powerfully they affect my patients' relationships with others and with me. Jeremy Mitchell, a young English professor in therapy with me, could not forgive himself for leaving his girlfriend of five years. Though their separation was well considered and civil, he was convinced that he had ruined her prospects and destroyed her self-esteem forever. Visions of her anguished face haunted his dreams. Although she was in fact successful, charming, and independently wealthy, he imagined her living in a trailer park, destitute and alone. He felt he had forfeited his right to visit their familiar haunts, and he avoided streets where she might see him with the new woman in his life. He even contemplated ending his new relationship and returning to the old one to assuage his unbearable guilt and his tormented conviction that he did not deserve to have his own life if it came at another's expense. For months we struggled to understand the inordinate intensity of these feelings, but they did not abate. Only when I began writing this book did I suddenly realize that his crushing sense of responsibility for his girlfriend exactly mirrored his experience with his older sister, who had been anorectic, seriously depressed, and isolated throughout his childhood. His mother had constantly admonished him to keep his sister company and interpreted his natural desire to have an independent life as selfish and destructive—feelings he had internalized and applied to the other woman he felt he had abandoned.

For no apparent reason my patient Mark Monroe impulsively married and instantly conceived a child. My newly developed sibling antennae allowed me to recognize and point out that these events immediately followed the engagement of his preferred, academically successful, but socially inept younger brother whom he had once referred to as "a tough act to precede."

I also became aware that patients can feel like damaged siblings with me. On New Year's Eve Kathy Emerson, an unmarried lawyer about my age, told me how miserable she felt that once again she had no date and would be celebrating with her younger sister and her husband. She always dreaded weekends, staying home because she felt she had no right even to walk on the street alone in a world full of couples. Since she knew I was married, it occurred to me that she must feel envious of me as well. Her distress and implicit envy made me feel terribly uncomfortable, because I knew it was justified; surely she had noticed that in many ways my life was better than hers had ever been. I was luckier than she was; was it not presumptuous and hurtful of me to point this out? My hesitation, I realized, came from guilt masquerading as tact; I sidestepped the topic not because I wanted to spare her but because I wanted to spare myself from her justified wrath; here was another unseemly and undeserved triumph that I dared not enjoy or reveal—much like my earlier, seemingly effortless triumph over my own brother. Then I heard myself asking her a question that seemed almost sacrilegious and that I had never dared to put so baldly before: "How does it feel to know that I have more than you do?" She was profoundly relieved to be granted permission to admit her envy and to describe how shameful, self-hating, and unlovable it made her feel, how it corroded her relationship with her actual sister and with other women. This exchange allowed her to claim more for herself—including, ultimately, a husband of her own.

If, as Joyce's Stephen Daedalus said, "a brother is as easy to lose as an umbrella," why isn't a parent? Try as we might to eliminate them, parents are engraved on our psyches in a way that makes negating their importance far more difficult. They loom so large because they are the first and most prominent figures in every child's life, and we need them to survive. For this reason no therapist would fail to notice if a patient never mentioned a parent or would accept the explanation that a mother's or father's influence was insignificant. Siblings become essential only in extreme situations like death, divorce, or natural disaster when parents are unavailable, and then they are unlikely to be ignored.

When I began research on this book, I discovered that problem siblings are no more popular to talk about than to write about or think about; even the most forthcoming, self-aware people become disturbed, dense, and defensive. I had no trouble finding interview subjects for my two previous books, on choosing not to have children and on resolving intimate betrayal, both topics that can make people anxious and uncomfortable. This time, though, half the people I approached refused, and their explanations made no sense. "It was so long ago that I hardly think of him now. We were five years apart, so I was much more affected by my sister, because she was only a year older," said a woman who had moved three thousand miles away from her autistic brother and left his care to this sister. A man who had frankly described the devastating aftermath of his mother's suicide to me previously pronounced his relationship with his manic-depressive sister "too painful to talk about." Of those who agreed to be interviewed, there was also a dismaying 50 percent dropout rate. A California teacher had eagerly agreed to discuss her troubled, chronically unemployed brother as long as I promised not to identify her family. She sought this reassurance although I had indicated in advance that names and details would be changed. After failing to answer the phone for our interview appointment on three separate occasions, she wrote me a note:

> I realize it was presumptuous of me to be willing to label my brother "dysfunctional." His journey has simply been rich in "dreams deferred." I don't want to demean him or assume that I have prevailed and he hasn't. The last thing I want to do is cause more harm.

Labeling her brother dysfunctional is not presumptuous but objectively accurate, and asserting that she prevailed where he failed is not an assumption but a fact. How will telling the truth that both of them know all too well without naming him cause more harm to her brother? Guilt—for doing better and being glad she did—compels her to euphemize and to protest her good intentions.

"I can't talk about him because he's not here to defend himself," explained a singer whose schizophrenic brother had been missing and presumed dead since 1985. Although she had previously appeared on television to say that fear of passing on her brother's mental illness had made her decide not to have children, to discuss the details of their relationship as siblings even anonymously felt to her like a wantonly aggressive act. It was acceptable to acknowledge their shared genes but not their shared life. She too had a fantasy that to express what she actually thought of him would destroy her brother all over again.

Why are so many people convinced that to tell the story of their siblings is to betray or damage them further? Some are over-identified; sharing a paranoid view of the world is one way to maintain some connection and to avoid grasping the strangeness, sadness, and severity of a brother's or sister's pathology. Since it would be exceedingly unlikely for any sibling to recognize the disguised source in a book, the normal ones' worries also conceal their wishes; they fear that even changing names would fail to protect the guilty.

Although a small number of people welcomed an opportunity to discuss their families and felt gratified that someone was finally paying attention to them after years of invisibility, distress was a much more common reaction. Many of the brave souls who showed up confessed that the prospect of the interview had caused sleepless nights and anxiety attacks. More than one said that only their sense of responsibility, desire to be helpful, or devotion to me prevented them from canceling; their early experiences as dutiful, mature helpers made them face their fears. A fifty-year-old journalist who had spent years in therapy but had not spoken to his embittered, underachieving sister for a decade explained, "I've attained a kind of resolution and insulated myself from my family. I finally have a text for my life, but the spaces between the words are wider than they ought to be, and that's where she is. If I went in there, the text is going to get disorganized, and I would have to look at what I never let myself notice. It would involve a radical revision of my sense of self. She's the door that never gets opened. I don't dread very much, but I dreaded thinking about this." Metaphors involving perilous portals were common; a systems analyst said, "I'm afraid if I crack open that door, I'll never be able to shut it." No wonder it stays double-bolted for most of us.

A writer who had chronicled extensively her paranoid sister's devastating impact on her life and had even performed a one-woman show in which she spoke in her sister's voice ("It's so much in my head that it's easy to do," she told me) confessed that the prospect of being interviewed about their relationship was more than she could handle, although why perplexed her. She realized that she was too frightened about what might come out of her mouth and how it might make her feel, when she could not control the content in advance.

Even when reticence is conquered, insight is surprisingly hard to come by. Many people simply recite catalogs of outrageous conduct by siblings that parents had failed to control, behavior they felt subjected to but that seemed to have nothing to do with them. Trouble with their siblings was an external event, something to endure or to flee, that had little effect on their internal reality or sense of themselves. Asked whether he had anything in common with his psychopathic sister, a seventy-year-old executive said, "Absolutely nothing—it's a black and white situation." Sometimes the connections hid in plain sight; an otherwise refreshingly frank and forthcoming therapist whom I interviewed about her paranoid schizophrenic brother noted that her first husband turned out to be paranoid "just like my father." Until I pointed out the similarity, she had never connected him with the brother whose suspiciousness and hostility permeated her life; to do so would have been too close for comfort.

When a relationship deteriorates, even positive memories can be obliterated. A teacher told me that as a young girl she had admired her older half-sister who later behaved hatefully and had a disastrous marriage. Her sister's collection of cashmere sweaters was an image of success, and she used to fantasize that one day she too would own a beautiful blue sweater. She had no idea that she was wearing just such a sweater to our meeting.

* * *

NO AMOUNT OF PSYCHIC MANEUVERING can alter the fact that having siblings is one of the defining experiences of childhood, with lifelong reverberations. Children become aware of one another before they recognize their own fathers, and they spend as much time together as they do with either parent. Siblings are your first peers, the first mirror that reflects an image your own size. Their impact does not cease when you leave home. As any adult who attends a family function can attest, the old hierarchy with its familiar but inextricable rules has a dismaying way of reasserting itself. No future tie is exempt from their influence; relations with them are the prototype for friendships, romances, and professional connections with coworkers, rivals, and collaborators for the rest of your life. Ultimately they are the only surviving witnesses to your intimate history. Nobody else will remember your childhood.

PART II

The Burden of Normality

chapter 3

Prospero's Damaged Family

FREUD MAY HAVE MISSED sibling dynamics because of problems of his own, but Shakespeare, whom he esteemed as a precursor, did not. While siblings figure prominently in works from *A Comedy of Errors* to *King Lear,* he portrays relationships in a damaged family with unparalleled insight in *The Tempest*—a theme that, not surprisingly, is rarely noticed; art reveals what science conceals. The relationship between Caliban and Miranda, symbolic siblings in *The Tempest,* resonates deeply for me as an uncannily accurate poetic depiction of my relationship with my own brother. This connection led me to name the syndrome that afflicts all normal ones after Caliban, the archetypal damaged sibling.

Since the magician Prospero, the central figure in *The Tempest* and its author's spokesman, calls the play a dream ("We are such stuff as dreams are made on"), psychoanalytic dream interpretation can illuminate the sibling symbolism in Shakespeare's last work as well as the psychological condition whose name it inspired.

Boundaries of person, time, and space are fluid in the language of dreams, and symbols have multiple meanings. Nothing—words, gestures, sequences of events—is arbitrary. Actions following one another chronologically can signify cause and effect. Everything and everybody in a dream also represent aspects of the self; therefore the play simultaneously depicts the outside world and the protagonist's inner state. Similarly "Caliban" in the Caliban Syndrome is both the abnormal sibling in the normal one's life and an image in the normal one's psyche.

Shakespeare's portraits of Prospero, Caliban, and Miranda plumb the secret depths in one particular type of damaged family—the one I grew up in—and also illustrate themes common to them all. As in our psyches, the relationships among these characters are shifting and multifaceted and are not confined to their literal roles; thus a son (or daughter) is simultaneously a brother, a father, and an aspect of oneself.

The tempest of the title is a magical storm that Prospero, exiled duke of Milan, conjures to bring his treacherous brother Antonio and his entourage to the island where he was shipwrecked, so that moral order can be restored. He lives there with his flawless daughter Miranda, his servant/sprite Ariel, and his "savage and deformed slave" Caliban, who plots to murder him. Prospero creates scenarios to punish and pardon his brother, foil the plot, marry off his daughter, and recover his dukedom. Then, renouncing supernatural powers, he drowns his magic book and breaks his wand. He has brought about a new level of integration around him and within him. Redefining his relationship with Caliban ("this thing of darkness I / acknowledge mine") is the last thing he does.

Every pair of siblings in the play has both a damaged and a more intact member, and exemplifies the destructive undercurrents of these relationships at their most extreme. Twelve years before the play takes place, Antonio usurped his scholarly, inattentive brother's throne and cast him and his young child out to sea; Prospero repudiates their kinship ("to call [him] brother would even infect my mouth"), although he ultimately forgives him. During their stay on the island, Antonio encourages one of his shipmates, the king of Naples's brother, to plot another fratricide. In both cases the envy and malice of the less successful sibling cause him to wrest power from his brother and make himself the center of attention.

More subtle but no less devastating is the symbolic sibling relationship between Miranda and Caliban. By the time we meet them, there is no more possibility of rivalry; the "sister" is a princess and the "brother" is a slave. Their roles are fixed, and the barriers to mutual affection or empathy unbreachable. Prospero calls her "mine loved darling" and "a third of mine own life" but has only curses for the "demi-devil" Caliban. The radiant beauty and the vicious brute are complete opposites, even in the meaning of their names; his is a near-anagram of "cannibal," and hers means "wonderful." Prospero tells Miranda that he adopted Caliban and at first tried to educate this bastard son of a witch but repudiated the creature—it is never clear whether he is fully human—after he tried to rape her. His opinion and treatment of the repulsive and irredeemable Caliban, whom he keeps enslaved by casting spells that torture him, seem entirely justified:

Thou poisonous slave,
Got by the devil himself upon thy wicked
Dam . . .
A devil, a born devil, on whose nature
Nurture can never stick, on whom my pains
Humanely taken, all, all lost, quite lost!
And as with age his body uglier grows,
So his mind cankers.

Caliban tells a different story. He claims that the attempted rape was an act of vengeance because Prospero had exploited, rejected, and disinherited him:

When thou cam'st first,
Thou strok'st me, and made much of me . . .
and then I loved thee
And showed thee all the qualities o'th'isle . . .
Cursed be I that did so. . . .
For I am all the subjects that you have,
Which first was mine own king.

The education that Prospero so humanely (and perhaps condescendingly) bestowed only increased his frustration and despair:

You taught me language, and my profit on't
Is I know how to curse.

On the surface these two "siblings" are mirror images. But it seems inconsistent that sweet, innocent Miranda, who has compassion for every living creature, expresses nothing but loathing and contempt for Caliban ("'Tis a villain, sir, / I do not love to look on"). She witnesses Prospero torturing him and never protests; in fact, in a speech so cold that many editors believe it to be falsely attributed to her, she justifies and encourages her father's behavior:

Abhorred slave,
Which any print of goodness wilt not take,
Being capable of all ill . . .
But thy vile race (Though thou didst learn) had that in't which good natures
Could not abide to be with; therefore wast thou
Deservedly confined into this rock,
Who hadst deserved more than a prison.

Just as Miranda's character is imperfectly perfect, Caliban's is not entirely base or dull-witted. Although he certainly does behave monstrously by inciting two drunks to try to kill his master, there is also disturbing evidence that calls into question Prospero's and Miranda's assumptions about him. Caliban speaks some of the most intoxicating poetry in the play:

Be not afeard, the isle is full of noises,
Sounds, and sweet airs, that give delight and hurt not;
Sometimes a thousand twangling instruments
Will hum about mine ears; and sometime voices,
That if I then had waked after long sleep,
Will make me sleep again; and then in dreaming,
The clouds methought would open, and show riches
Ready to drop upon me, that when I waked,
I cried to dream again.

Since the island is his birthright, he has a legitimate grievance. He is a lonely and repulsive outcast whom everyone guiltlessly hurts and humiliates; his bitter hatred is not entirely unjustified. At the end he shows remorse, shame for his terrible judgment, and sincere desire to reform:

> *and I'll be wise hereafter,*
> *And seek for grace. What a thrice-double ass*
> *Was I to take this drunkard for a god*
> *and worship this dull fool!*

—thereby belying the Prospero family myth that he cannot learn and cannot respond to kindness. Caliban, condemned as inherently and willfully vicious, strives for sense and virtue. He is the only character Prospero underestimates.

Every member of this family is damaged, overtly or covertly; Ariel, the magic spirit who does Prospero's bidding, is spared only because he is not human. No one is exempt from the consequences of being related to Caliban—neither the disillusioned father who repudiates him because of his deformity and rebelliousness, nor the naïve daughter whom Prospero idealizes and makes the bearer of his destiny.

As is typical of parents in these families, Prospero unconsciously repeats with his "son" his traumatic relationship with his own brother when he usurps Caliban's "kingdom" and robs him of his freedom. His own behavior and history shape Caliban's character more than he knows. To label Caliban, whom Prospero sadistically punishes for disobedience, "my slave, who never / Yields us kind answer" is to deny that he has had any role in making his son hate him; why should a slave respond otherwise? Prospero disinherits him and blames Caliban's mother for his physical and mental defects ("This misshapen knave, / His mother was a witch"). He abandons his son, abdicates all responsibility, and then justifies this behavior as deserved and caused exclusively by his son's nature.

Since he has defined Caliban as a "beast," Prospero need *not* treat him humanely:

> *Thou most lying slave,*
> *Whom stripes [i.e., lashes] may move, not kindness*

He expresses in extreme terms the buried feelings of a father overwhelmed, as mine was, by an unmanageable disturbed child whom he experiences as alien; dissociating oneself from such a child assuages shame and guilt. Never imagining that his own pedagogic methods could be at fault, this utterly unempathic father insists that his son could not be taught: I did not fail you, you were impossible. He finds a far more appealing and tractable pupil in his daughter. As children do, Caliban lives out the role his family assigns to him. He lashes out at both Prospero and Miranda by assaulting her (as my own brother did in my dream); when one child is perniciously preferred over another—either a damaged or an intact child can be so favored—their relationship is poisoned forever.

Widowed, exiled, and dreadfully disappointed with his son and with his own situation, Prospero turns to his daughter to compensate him for his losses, lavishing all his love and learning upon her; as a woman, she is no threat to his authority. He creates her in his own image and arranges for her to fall in love with a man he chooses, who also adores and idealizes her. He sets her up for life.

Curiously Prospero fails to protect Miranda from Caliban,

despite showing the most extreme preference for her; even though Caliban has tried to rape her, her father insists over her objections that she accompany him to "visit" Caliban. Parents are compelled to expose their intact children to a damaged sibling's outrageous or frightening behavior in order to reinforce their own denial that anything is wrong with the family. Higher-functioning children frequently become embittered and estranged because their parents failed to acknowledge or protect them from a sibling's outbursts. Alternatively, they can join their parents in minimizing the severity of the impact of the exposure and blame themselves for being affected by it. Children who, like Miranda and me, are completely identified with their parents do not register the hostility latent in their parents' treatment of them.

Caliban handles the mental as well as the physical dirty work for the family, as marginalized siblings often do. Prospero recognizes his essential functions:

> *But as 'tis,*
> *We cannot miss [i.e., do without] him. He does make our fire,*
> *Fetch in our wood, and serves in offices*
> *That profit us.*

His most important "office" is to be defined as the source of all discord and to serve as the repository of all negative emotions—rage, envy, and lust. Caliban embodies the antithesis of Miranda's virtues and makes them gleam even brighter in comparison. His presence is essential because he permits father and daughter to maintain their idyllic, unambivalent bond. Miranda subtly colludes in reinforcing Caliban's role by allying herself exclusively with Prospero's point of view. Her disputed speech accurately expresses the taboo feelings of an intact child; if he is all bad, she can be all good. She validates the legitimacy of her father's actions, insuring her position as the child who is no trouble, a source only of delight, inspiration, and joy: Miranda needs Caliban in order to be Miranda.

Splitting character traits between siblings is common in damaged families, and it is only a superficial advantage for the one who is assigned the positive characteristics. A person who defines herself in opposition to another can never develop an independent identity and is always warding off the dark side the other represents. The task of every intact sibling is to recognize this split and reabsorb the qualities that she has colluded in depositing in her opposite.

Caliban symbolizes not only Miranda's damaged sibling but also Prospero's, as well as everything in his own character that he disavows. Coming to terms with him is Prospero's final and most difficult achievement. He anticipates their confrontation with more trepidation and outrage than his reunion with his brother Antonio, whose treachery had less justification. "We must prepare to meet with Caliban," he grimly tells Ariel (not wanting to face his nemesis alone), as the hour of the planned conspiracy approaches, even though he has arranged for it to fail. Miranda remarks, "Never till this day / Saw I him touched with anger, so distempered." Meeting Caliban arouses such intense emotions because it is Prospero's ultimate encounter with himself.

After Prospero gives up his magic powers and forgives his brother, he directs Ariel to catch Caliban and his confederates and to terrify and befoul them. When they appear before his entourage suitably chastised, he says:

> *this thing of darkness I*
> *Acknowledge mine . . .*
> *He is as disproportioned in his manners*
> *As in his shape. Go, sirrah, to my cell:*
> *. . . As you look*
> *To have my pardon, trim it handsomely.*

Caliban responds:

> *Ay, that I will; and I'll be wise hereafter,*
> *And seek for grace.*

In this exchange the relationship between Prospero and Caliban is transformed. Caliban is no longer Prospero's slave but his willing servant. Prospero becomes a different kind of master, one who motivates not with the threat of punishment but with the promise of forgiveness. Caliban voluntarily and remorsefully accepts the task of cleaning Prospero's quarters. They are left together at the end, their bond now based on choice rather than compulsion.

But since Shakespeare is a realist, this is not an unambivalent resolution. They accept but do not love one another; there is no sentimental embrace—although they did shake hands in one misguided production I saw. Their inequities of station do not vanish; Prospero cannot resist calling attention to Caliban's deformity and illegitimacy and continues to order him around. The servant is still sullen and uncouth, and the master has not stopped being arrogant and superior. Caliban remains a thing of darkness, but now he is an acknowledged one. There can never be "closure" in their relationship, only expanded possibilities. Yet Caliban acquires humanity, and Prospero regains it. Their rapprochement, partial yet profound, is a model of how an intact sibling can begin to integrate a damaged one.

The order of events in the play's denouement is psychologically significant; Prospero must renounce magic and pardon his brother before he can acknowledge Caliban. First he gives up the illusion of omnipotence, the self-righteous conviction that he is unrelated to Caliban and that he can keep himself separate and untainted forever. Accepting his own past and his troubled relationship with his brother Antonio is also a necessary prerequisite. Coming to terms with Caliban—who, like all siblings and sons, inhabits Prospero's internal as well as external world—is the final step in ending his isolation and reentering society as a more fully developed man.

Miranda is the only member of the "family" who does not change, because she never acknowledges her kinship with Caliban; their relationship simply ends when she leaves to marry the man her father chose for her and to become queen of Naples. She never questions her judgment of him even when she has been proved wrong. She is so intoxicated with her beloved and with the opportunity to continue her seemingly perfect life that she hardly notices the changes around her. Real Mirandas cannot go away and find unambivalent love without consequences, however hard they may try. Because coming to terms with Caliban is coming into one's own, the price of avoidance and flight is to stay a dutiful daughter/wife forever and never to evolve into a fully independent, self-aware woman; without her shadow she has no depth—and without compassion for Caliban, she can never have true compassion for herself.

What will become of Caliban? His fate and future relationship to Prospero are uncertain; reconnecting is all that matters. Such relationships have built-in conflicts that never cease and do not need to. By the end Prospero has lost Miranda, but he keeps Caliban. Will he take him back as a servant to Milan? Will he give him back the island? He does not free him as he does Ariel because Ariel is an aspect of his magic, not of his human nature. Prospero, and his audience, can never be free of Caliban. He is part of all of us. If we become wiser and recognize our humanity, we too can change our relationship with him, though we cannot sever it.

chapter 4

America's Damaged Families

IN THE REAL WORLD as in the dramatic world of *The Tempest*, nobody in a family is exempt from the chronic crisis that a damaged child creates. Though few parents respond as disastrously as Prospero does, stress permeates even the most loving household. The personalities of the parents and their own histories determine how they deal with the trauma and whether they turn their children into Calibans and Mirandas. Only the wisest and most emotionally fortunate avoid imposing massive portions of their own old conflicts upon them. Whatever the family dynamic ends up being, the normal child will be scarred, even if the scars do not show.

It is hard to imagine the level of tumult, anxiety, and sheer effort that life in a damaged family involves. The abnormal is normal; siblings who return home after a respite are shocked at the intensity of the distress they endured every day—the retarded brother's blasting radio at six A.M., the autistic sister's tantrum over a lost purple crayon—that they now realize they minimized in order to endure. They bear an inner weight of unarticulated sorrow at having missed much of the freedom and insouciance of childhood that others take for granted. "I spent summers playing in the hallways at the Mayo Clinic during my sister's surgeries when other kids thought mayo was something you spread on bread," a minister recalled wistfully. The injury need not be catastrophic for a problem sibling to loom larger than a normal one; you still have to, in the words of an anorectic woman's sister, "arrange life around it."

To discover that a child is seriously impaired in mind or body changes everything. Whether the news comes at birth or later—and even if the extent of the problem is unknown or ignored—it plunges parents into mourning and casts a pall over their lives. Overtly or covertly their initial despair gets communicated to their other children. It is shattering to realize that you will be denied forever the very satisfactions for which people have children in the first place, that your gratifications will be limited and your responsibilities and anxieties ever-expanding. You worry about providing proper care your whole life and about who will take over after your death. This is the gravest possible blow to the universal fantasy that a child will be a perfected version of oneself, that family life will be harmonious, and that siblings will unambivalently love one another.

Even when parents eventually accept their fate and find meaning in whatever relationship is possible with the child, disappointment and the loss of possibility are permanent, revived whenever they witness the rituals and achievements of ordinary life—the graduations, weddings, and professional successes—that other parents savor. Family members are forever adjusting expectations, trying to make the best of it. Healthy children notice and cannot be protected from the truth. They grieve, they feel guilty, and they struggle to compensate by achieving for two.

What families learn about a child's disability and when they learn it affects how they respond. Immediate despair that a baby has been born with cerebral palsy is different from the slowly dawning distress that a first-grader who looks normal cannot learn to read or the uncomprehending, helpless horror of watching a seemingly healthy adolescent slip into madness. No wonder parents minimize the problems when they can, hoping against hope that their child is only "different," "sensitive," or a "late bloomer." Nobody can help covertly comparing the problem child to all the perfectly healthy ones in the neighborhood; a nurse whose multiply handicapped sister was her parents' full-time project and her own after-school responsibility recalled envying the happy, normal family of ten next door.

Many siblings never even know a sibling's diagnosis, either because the condition is hard to categorize or because the parents choose not to find out. Ambiguity heightens their anxiety, and they grow up with an undercurrent of vague depression and nameless dread that must be kept to themselves. They learn to keep secrets.

Abnormal children provoke forbidden feelings that are too painful and shocking for most parents to admit; wanting to abandon one's own flesh and blood, hoping they will die, wishing they had never been born, repulsion—and even hatred—are utterly antithetical to what good people are supposed to feel. Adoptive parents are troubled by thoughts of wanting to give the child back. Every parent lives with ambivalence, but theirs is not sufficiently offset by joy. Destructive fantasies are more dangerous because they would be easier, and more tempting, to carry out against a helpless, troublesome child. A headhunter I interviewed with a cerebral palsied brother had no trouble identifying with Richard and Dawn Kelso, the philanthropic couple active in advocacy for the disabled who made headlines in December 1999 by wheeling their afflicted ten-year-old son into an emergency room once too often and leaving him there. Unless religious parents consider their fate a manifestation of God's will or a mark of divine favor, they bear the additional burden of feeling like sinners as well as victims. A sense of shame and defectiveness ("How could I produce a Caliban?") alternates with a desire to blame the child or the other parent, as Prospero does. Putting feelings aside in order to do one's duty consumes less energy than facing the full brunt of a tragic predicament.

Caretakers who cannot accept their terrible thoughts must bend over backward to prove they care; obsessive dedication to the disabled neutralizes the desire to neglect or destroy them. They throw themselves into the problem, or they throw the problem away by denying how bad it is—often at the cost of their relationships with their spouse and their other children. Problem children hold together many a bad marriage and destroy many a good one. What parents cannot allow themselves to feel, they cannot allow their normal children to feel either; any uncensored emotional outburst ("Can't we send Johnny to Mars or just not bring him home from camp?") would hold up a mirror to what they struggle to excise in themselves. The cycle of guilt, denial, and expiation, of alternating overcompensation and avoidance, inevitably draws the normal child in. Like a barely detectable sound or smell, unmentionable, unmetabolized pain pervades the atmosphere.

To recognize that guilt over violent wishes plagues all intact family members does not detract from their genuine devotion; confronting and learning to tolerate hostility makes authentic compassion for oneself as well as for the afflicted possible. Labeling and accepting taboo emotions defangs them. Insight protects the healthy from compulsion, frees them from self-torture, and enhances their efforts on behalf of their abnormal relatives; facing hatred deepens love.

Contrary to appearances, parents' emotional needs, not their children's, determine whether a Caliban (or a she-Caliban) is designated as central or peripheral in a family. What these children evoke from their parents' own family experience—particularly unresolved issues with siblings—influences how they are treated more than the type or severity of their injuries. Two families in which the damaged children have identical diagnoses can be radically different to grow up in. The memories, fantasies, ideals, and fears of the parents create the template into which a child's actual personality is fit—the more unresolved the conflicts, the more procrustean the template. Gender also matters; fathers may bury themselves in work, and mothers in overinvolvement with the difficult child. If, like Prospero, a father who had a brutal rivalry with a brother cannot bear his own sense of failure and disappointment, he will reject or ignore his impaired son and focus all his attention on his normal daughter, adoring her but also demanding perfection and obedience from her, obliterating her difficulties and failing to protect her from her brother's outbursts. Likewise, a mother who feels inferior to her sister may find a vocation in dedicating her life to a disabled daughter while simultaneously belittling, rebuking, and neglecting her normal one and pressing her into service as her auxiliary in life and her surrogate thereafter. Self-sacrifice masks retroactive revenge—she punishes her sister by favoring the daughter who reminds her of herself.

Even in wealthy families sustained contact with siblings, no matter how seriously dysfunctional, is regarded as a duty, just as it is on *The Tempest*'s desert isle; the motivation is emotional, not financial. Adults who embrace caretaking with a vengeance typically expect their unimpaired children (especially daughters) to follow suit and subtly communicate that to demur is unconscionable. Younger girls frequently baby-sit for and physically tend their older brothers and sisters at the expense of their own social lives, their roles a combination of precocious parents and unpaid practical nurses. A woman with a brain-damaged brother remembered that "Rita, help us out" was a constant refrain in her house. Healthy siblings get involuntarily elected "family vice-presidents,"* with responsibilities but no authority.

Problem children get away with murder because their parents practice a covert form of favoritism, the disciplinary double standard. They are treated with a confusing combination of authoritarianism and overindulgence, while a far stricter code of conduct applies to the healthy child, who must not have or be any problem. Rivalry between normal and handicapped children is particularly

---

*Z. Stoneman and P. Berman, eds. *The Effects of Mental Retardation, Disability and Illness on Sibling Relationships: Research Issues and Challenges* (Baltimore: Paul H. Brookes, 1993), p. 357.

hard for parents to tolerate. Discouraging competition drives animosity underground, where it festers.

A young painter torn between pursuing her art on one coast and taking up the role of her brain-damaged brother's guardian on the other described her predicament:

> It's a tremendous burden that my brother has a head injury. I'm supposed to be Mother Teresa—you're put in position and expected to make something great of it—you're always grieving that there's nothing you can do to save the situation. My parents never let themselves get upset. My father looks down on my brother and doesn't interact with him. My mother doesn't stand up to him and tell him he can't manipulate us all by having temper tantrums. I'm the receptacle of everybody's feelings.

Healthy children in damaged households get too much attention or too little but rarely enough of the right kind. If resources are concentrated on rehabilitating and managing the problem child, they become invisible; or if, like Miranda, they are chosen to repair their parents' broken dreams, they become vessels of exaggerated expectations. Some are actually conceived as replacements to compensate for their parents' disappointments or to provide what one designated sibling bitterly called "genetically engineered caretaking." Either way they are abandoned.

How can hurt feelings or a skinned knee ever take precedence over the trials of a sibling who is paraplegic or paranoid? Normal children—even preferred ones—never come first in a crisis and must stifle the impulse to object. One attention-starved little girl begged to be enrolled in the same school for the neurologically impaired that her brother attended, but her parents still did not get the message. Research shows that intact children—and also their seriously impaired siblings—thrive when the dysfunctional sibling is finally institutionalized because they are relieved of constantly having to accommodate the other's difficulties and deformities. Finally they can bring a friend or a date home without dread.

Even outside the family nobody—including researchers on disability—notices normal ones. One study examined the effects of sibling kidney transplants on recipients but ignored donors. Another analyzed how vision-impaired children fared with sighted sibling guides without considering the feelings of the guides. When it comes to sibling dynamics, psychologists are as blind as their subjects.

Problem children frequently require disproportionate amounts of attention from their parents, and normal siblings are inevitably neglected. But many parents allow the abnormal one to deplete the oxygen of family life by imagining—and communicating—that the normal one is low-maintenance. Not only do healthy children get less care; they are assumed to need less. Parental justifications and expectations—subjective interpretations rather than objective needs—do the deepest damage. When a successful lawyer whose brother had made repeated suicide attempts announced to his mother that he was getting a divorce, she said, "You were supposed to be my happy child." Another mother told her daughter by way of encouragement, "Isn't it great that you're okay, so you can take care of yourself?" Parental neglect is also fostered by envy; the normal child did not produce the "monster" and is not responsible for its problems—and one day he can escape.

Since their children's dark emotions are even more threatening than their own, parents implicitly pressure them never to express—or even to recognize—rage, terror, or resentment. Split-off feelings do more damage because they cannot be integrated, and they influence behavior in ways the person cannot see.

Love and fear cause children to don their parents' emotional straitjackets. They want to identify, show solidarity, and provide consolation; they need to avoid stigma, secure their own position in the family, and guarantee their parents' love. "My parents never admitted that they were depressed or angry, so my anger was strangled too," said the sister of a hyperactive woman who could not speak. "There are the taboo things you can never say, like 'I wish you never existed,' that you would tell a normal sister and never think twice." Thinking, acting, and feeling only what you are supposed to becomes another type of caretaking. The best way to prove to others and to reassure yourself that you are different from a damaged sibling is to have no difficulties, make no demands, and harbor no grudges; to be perfect and prematurely mature are universal signs of the Caliban Syndrome. Your mission is to become the mirror image of the damaged sibling whose likeness threatens to emerge at any time—and that always will.

Every intact sibling secretly wonders, "Why didn't it happen to me—or when will it?"—the fear of contagion that is an earmark of the Caliban Syndrome. Sharing a sibling's awful fate would be fitting punishment for the guilty triumph of being better off; survivor guilt plagues every normal one, overtly or covertly. Dreams about the damaged one dying or being cured are common; both solutions make the problem vanish.

An "invisible fence" like those used to keep dogs in yards cordons off the dangerous emotions of normal children. A dog is shocked for straying and learns to confine itself to designated boundaries. Eventually external constraints are unnecessary. Nothing shows; the dog seems miraculously tractable. In the psyches of healthy siblings, the all-too-human anxiety and hostility disappear like the natural canine impulse to chase cars.

In an ingenious study, a researcher had two small and overtly well-adjusted children improvise a "radio play" about their mute brother. Her tape recordings revealed extraordinarily intense fantasies of murder, mutilation, decapitation, and torture "not readily visible in their lives."*

The inner world of normal siblings brims with secrets, hidden from themselves as much as from others. All their lives they seek a sanctuary untouched by the other's plight, a door they can close without guilt. Everybody tells them they are the lucky ones; what right have they to complain? Their lonely sorrow is as intolerable as their sadism. Fulfilling such stringent expectations of being good, responsible, and trouble-free is a full-time job that leaves little time for living.

As adults, competent siblings may not be intimates, but at least they are equals. A damaged brother or sister will never be a peer, a companion, or a confidant. If the younger sibling is the normal one, role reversal begins at birth; a young athlete remembers painstakingly trying to teach his spastic older brother to ride a bicycle. The most tender bond with a caretaker or advocate cannot be fully reciprocal. Even when someone says, "My Down syndrome sister taught me the true meaning of love," there are unacknowledged losses in that love.

---

*Helen Featherstone, *A Difference in the Family: Living with a Disabled Child* (New York: Penguin, 1981), p. 35.

* * *

MEDIA COVERAGE of the troubled and disabled, with its relentless tone of moral uplift, sanctifies every stricture families impose on their normal siblings. The topic seems to evoke nothing but treacly sentimentality. ("My retarded sister is my hero—my love, my heart, my angel," a movie star told *Us* magazine.) The press recognizes only one role for them: members of the "starting lineup of a team deep in talent," as the usually restrained *New York Times* called the brother and sister of the first quadriplegic to graduate from Harvard. Like a Homeric epithet, "supportive" always precedes their names.

Uncritically extolling self-effacement as their natural and proper vocation undermines normal children's right to dreams of their own. Helping the mentally or physically handicapped is always presented as a family project; to participate with less than wholehearted enthusiasm is unthinkable. The Harvard graduate's "teammates" have already tolerated their mother attending classes with their paralyzed sister since she was eight and leaving the family in another state to live in her dormitory room through college—a sacrifice that was not even essential, since extensive services would have been available for her care. Now they are expected to bask in her reflected glory for the rest of their lives. They are supposed to accept altruistically that, even if they too were to graduate from Harvard, there would be no front-page photograph of their mother walking triumphantly beside them, no heartwarming TV special, no book contract or motivational speaking career; being their sister's sibling forever defines and confines them.

There is a troubling undercurrent in stories like this: that narcissism can lurk beneath the veneer of maternal devotion, and that obsessive dedication to one child, however deserving, can lead to the abandonment of others, who have no choice but to participate in their mother's herculean efforts.

Even the neurologist Oliver Sacks perpetuates the myth of the saintly sibling. In an article* about an autistic painter whose parents—both professors—devoted their lives to scrutinizing her symptomatology and wrote two books minutely detailing her development, he mentions in passing her "intellectually gifted and accomplished" brothers and sisters. The household is "one where eager interest and attention turn in all directions, and where intellectual play and fun pervade the atmosphere." Seduced by this idyllic fantasy, he does not imagine that these children could harbor any resentment of their parents' extraordinary preoccupation with their deeply troubled sister or that living with her might not have been an unalloyed delight.

The saddest consequence of the inspirational imperative is that many normal siblings buy into it. Finding no corrective in the culture to the role in which their families cast them, they embrace it with zeal. When, in a departure from the norm, *The New York Times* published a story on the tribulations of siblings of the disabled, one wrote an immediate disclaimer in a letter to the editor, insisting that growing up with a retarded sister had caused her no difficulty whatsoever.

Any account of the triumphs of the disabled that ignores the toll on their siblings—even if the siblings themselves collude in denying that toll—is naïve at best and irresponsible at worst. It is, however, an easy trap to fall into. In *My Left Foot,* the bracingly

---

*Oliver Sacks, "Leaving Nirvana," *New York Review of Books,* March 31, 2001.

uncloying film about a paralyzed Irish artist, there is a scene in which the hero's father and brood of siblings grumble that their mother has once again served them nothing but watered-down oatmeal at tea because she spends what little money there is for his rehabilitation. I never gave a thought to the impact on them until I began researching this book.

While some siblings accept, and even embrace, their destiny as members of the "team," others are (mostly privately) outraged, having experienced the obverse of the soothing stereotype in their own families. A graphic designer whose autistic brother tried to strangle her when they were children, and who struggled for years to get her parents to recognize the danger he presented, is acutely aware of the discrepancy between the illusion and the reality of damaged families:

> I'm trying to eradicate the *Hallmark Hall of Fame Special* myth—"how I learned the meaning of life by having a disabled sibling." The cover of *Newsweek* on autism had a beautiful blond good boy. People just want to look at the pretty kids on *Jerry Lewis,* the sanitized version, not the ugly cases like my brother. The severely disabled aren't telegenic. It's a crisis when elderly caregivers die—siblings should not be expected to sacrifice their lives. I would have killed myself or both of us if I'd been forced to take my brother in—it shouldn't have to be a choice between my life and his. Too bad if I don't want to go into special ed as my profession—who signed me up?

Normal siblings have two life tasks: to recognize the enormous impact a damaged sibling has on them, and to forge an identity in which that sibling is peripheral. The first makes the second possible.

chapter 5

My Sister Ate My Homework

At Home with Damaged Siblings

EIGHT-YEAR-OLD JACKIE HANSON spent hours putting the finishing touches on the cover of her very first book report—crayons, sequins, glitter, the works. But her pride was short-lived, and her teacher never saw her resplendent creation. She had to hand in her assignment the next day with no cover—and no explanation—at all. Thinking it might be tasty, her autistic sister had ripped the cover off and chewed it up when Jackie wasn't looking. "I couldn't be angry—how could I be?—when she messed up like that," Jackie recalled. "Ambivalent feelings weren't allowed, only love and strength."

Incidents like this are commonplace when you grow up with an abnormal sibling, even one whose difficulties are less catastrophic than Jackie's sister's. A far cry from the petty squabbles of the "he hit me"/ "he hit me first" variety, the onslaughts are relentless, pervasive, and extreme—and so traumatic that healthy siblings' voices quiver when recounting them years later: "A simple conversation was nails on a blackboard"; "We lived in a state of siege"; "It doesn't have the cachet, but it's just as painful as a mother dying of cancer"; "I always think that people with normal siblings seem so foreign—how could it be possible?" they say. That so many of them suppressed their true feelings at the time is part of the trauma of the Caliban Syndrome.

Unlike the usual sibling conflicts, these problems rarely diminish when you leave home, and they often escalate. And what happens when your parents die? Violations great and small disrupt childhood, complicate adolescence, cast a pall over adulthood, and loom much larger than typical troubles with brothers and sisters, even if the culprit dies. A minister developed hypertension and suffered anxiety attacks after her deformed and retarded sister died. A man in his seventies still vividly recalls his sister's scenes at age six. As a hospital administrator who was beginning to process the impact that her brother's tragic combination of explosiveness, dedicated scholarship, and ultimately fatal muscular dystrophy had on her life declared, "Once a sibling, always a sibling."

Home life is a series of little murders of privacy, pleasure, peace of mind. Beloved possessions get ruined without repercussions—the carefully constructed train display wrecked, the prom dress bought with a hard-earned paycheck hung back in the closet besmirched with pizza. Either because they could not understand or are exempted by parents, the culprits are rarely punished. Family activities get spoiled. "We never went to church or a movie together because somebody always had to stay with her," said a veterinarian whose multiply handicapped sister "could not be left alone for a second." A violent, neurologically impaired boy's sister remembered how "everything focused on him—which house we lived in, what TV shows we watched. We catered to him completely at home because his life sucked."

An actor's parents never attended any of his high school performances because they had no one to watch their reclusive daughter. A painter, on the other hand, wished her parents had not attended her piano recital; they brought along her furious brain-injured brother, who, just as she sat down to play, shouted out, "You're not my sister—you're some stranger!" for the entire audience to hear. A nurse's parents permitted her "completely nutty" learning-disabled brother to drag the whole family to twenty-six stores to find him the right pair of shoes. One teenager discovered that her brain-damaged brother was calling her friends up for dates in the middle of the night, and another that his alcoholic sister went knocking on his friends' doors. A retarded boy and a learning-disabled girl bombarded their normal sister from both directions: "You couldn't say a sentence without one or the other interrupting, and you could never have anything last." The normal ones were all expected to endure these trials with the patience and adult understanding—the premature maturity—that no child naturally possesses.

Social life suffers drastically. Many such children curtail activities to baby-sit for siblings, often much older than they, when paid caretakers are unwilling or unaffordable. And who wants to have friends over when your sister parades around in her underwear, or jumps out and rips people's clothes, or when your unwashed, belching brother punches people to say hello? An obese, peculiar, or antisocial sibling also makes you look bad in the eyes of the all-important peer group. "I could never bear to tell my friends that my sister took the 'retard bus' to school," a magazine editor recalled, fearing that her sister's deficiency would somehow reflect badly on her although she was a superb student herself. Naturally the healthy children try to flee or pretend their nemesis does not exist.

But going out is as excruciating as staying in. A minister's daughter remembers hiding under the pew at church when she was supposed to sing hymns to avoid being associated with her autistic sister. A political scientist's brother with Tourette's syndrome and autism "mortified" him, and his own "inhumane" response haunts him still:

> There was a high threshold of people I wouldn't bring home or tell. I felt such shame—it was a constant internal struggle. I just couldn't stand being seen in public with him and wanted to hide under a rock, and now I want to suppress those feelings. I want to slug people who snicker as much as I want to back away myself. Sometimes I long to put my arms around him and stare down anybody giggling, to stand between him and others to shield them or him. Every time I step outside, I'm repelled by him and repelled by my repulsion.

Defending a damaged sibling from the scorn of strangers expresses compassion while simultaneously assuaging guilt for secretly sharing their prejudices. While some people look back on their earlier embarrassment and judge it selfish, "spoiled bratty," or worse ("I feel I'm evil because I still want to run away from her and try to find ways to escape dealing with her"), for many their childhood dread of how their playmates would react evolves into adult dread of how fiancés, colleagues, and utter strangers will react. ("When people ask if you have a brother and what does he do, I try to change the subject—I'm so glad I live out of town," the political scientist said.) When a lawyer's drunken, paranoid brother came banging on her office door, her first response was not fear but relief that no clients or colleagues were around to witness it. A Caliban is a terrible reflection on you and, on the deepest level, of you as well.

Normal siblings are inundated daily with behavior that is not only noxious but also frightening, incomprehensible, and wretchedly sad. Pity and outrage intermingle, and anger implodes, when the perpetrator is also a victim. A novelist whose disturbed older brother endured both ostracism and multiple eye operations, and beat her up with impunity, described her complicated reactions: "He was such an outcast—so isolated, such an ugly, weird kid and so abysmally lonely that I knew he was hurting all the time. That he was both sick and vicious made it extremely confusing." "I was forbidden from being mean to him, and he could be mean to me—when he got taunted, I became his punching bag," said Jennifer Martin, the hospital administrator whose perpetually enraged brother had a fatal form of muscular dystrophy. "But how could you wish someone would die who was going to die?" Wrestling alone with such devastating contradictions drives some to consider suicide and others to run away from home.

The hardest thing to tolerate is the inevitable but unpredictable temper tantrums to which siblings across the entire spectrum of difficulties are prone. You know their frustrated anguish will cause an eruption, but you never know what will provoke it or when. Most parents handle this situation abysmally, permitting the abnormal child to become a tyrant and demanding forbearance from the more rational one. "My mother's line was always 'She's not well, so you should give in to her so she won't throw a tantrum,'" said a financial adviser of her explosive borderline sister. "Her agonies took precedence." "I was told as a kid 'Be nice to your poor sister,'" a boutique owner said. "There was always an excuse for her outbursts, and I had to dance around them. She used up the family quota on scenes."

Many people use the metaphor of a "time bomb" to describe the chronic, palpable tension they lived with. Anxiety hangs over the dinner table, follows you into the car on outings, and punctuates weekends; there are no respites. An artist said of her brain-damaged brother, "You didn't even have to pull the cord very hard, and there's no real reason when it goes off. I could never let my guard down. I had to be mobilized—there was such an undercurrent of anger that he could direct at you." The memories persist years afterward; "he has tantrums in my dreams—they're indelible."

Some injuries are so incapacitating that one woman described living with her afflicted sister as "like having a dog around"—but even dogs can be taught to behave. Compassion wears thin when neither the sibling nor the parents make any attempt at control. Illness or disability evokes passionate determination and self-reliance in some people and sullen self-involvement in others. A retarded brother is "selfish, not just slow—he blasts his music all night because he's angry inside," said the brother who had to listen to it. A neurologically impaired brother leaves all chores to his able-bodied sister: "I'm frustrated with him for being lazy and never helping—even if it's his brain, can't he try? If I tell him, he gets furious. Underneath I don't believe it's all the disability; I think he's mad at the world and at me," she concluded. Parents frequently do not intervene, set proper limits, or defend their normal children's rights. Self-indulgence and disregard erode sympathy when the acting out never stops. After getting the tenth call from the police, "I hold her at least partly responsible," said a manic-depressive's sister. "She's thirty-seven and has been given options, but she plays the mental illness card whenever it suits her."

Normal children also absorb an inordinate amount of their parents' stress. Seeing your mother weeping in the kitchen from exhaustion every night after striving all day to find the right placement for your multihandicapped sister who never seems to fit the treatment criteria ("the deaf schools won't accept her because she's blind, and the retarded programs say she's too high-functioning") takes a silent toll, making the witness feel simultaneously helpless and hyperresponsible. Misplaced parental anxiety has overt consequences as well; a stockbroker remembers that, after his eighteen-year-old sister was arrested for selling heroin, his father, fearing that he would be corrupted by the same bad company, precipitously moved the family to another town and sent him away to boarding school.

Parents can go to shocking lengths to shield a damaged child, irreparably harming the normal one in the process. "My sister wet her bed until age fourteen. Our mother took off her wet sheets and put them on my bed so the maid wouldn't think badly of her," the financial adviser recalled. A television producer who shared a bed with her enuretic retarded sister at times during their childhoods (although the family was not destitute) remembers the urine flowing to her side of the bed, literally immersing her in her sister's physicality. In a dream the sister of an autistic boy graphically portrayed the unacknowledged damage he inflicted:

> I realize that my brother has been missing the toilet for years, and that the eaves of the house are dripping with his urine. When I point this out to my mother, she replies nonchalantly, "It's an act of God."

"Take Susie along" is an oft-repeated refrain. Children are entreated by their frantic parents to include abnormal siblings of all sorts in their activities and to share their friends, which they are often loath to do. The distinction between loving inclusion and guilty coercion gets blurred. "I couldn't have my own life," says an architect who was pressured to invite her bizarre brother to her sweet-sixteen party. The parents may insist on taking Susie along themselves; a gifted student's mother and father made her tour of prospective colleges a family affair and brought along her hyperactive brother, who ran away and was found hours later by the police. Sometimes you have to go along with Susie against your will; a teacher was sent to the same camp as her partially blind, depressed sister. "I loved it, but she hated it because she couldn't make friends, so our parents came and took us both home." As a teenager, the veterinarian with the severely disabled sister spent her summers working as a counselor at a camp for the handicapped at her parents' behest—a job that she expected her own children, all normal, to take on. The demands parents make on a normal one are frequently passed along to posterity.

Feeling obligated to make these siblings more central than you want, and feeling resentful or wretched about not wanting to, does not stop when you no longer live together; you agonize about their role on significant occasions for the rest of your life. "I'm already worrying about having to spend Christmas with her and her horrible passive husband after my mother dies, and my mother's in perfect health," the sister of a troubled narcissist observed. A designer spent most of her own baby shower trying to coax her bulimic sister out of the bathroom where she had locked herself, and the financial adviser's borderline sister has not spoken to her for forty years because she made someone else her maid of honor. They steel themselves for their parents' funerals.

Distance lends perspective—and disenchantment—to what you endured at home and unwittingly adapted to. Every time actor Jack Morelli enters the house where his family still lives, the poignancy of his reclusive sister's life hits him afresh. "I get caught up in how sad it is, how someone can exist like this. I feel like a guest there because everything is so regimented," he said. A teacher with a retarded brother found that "it's really hard going back and seeing how they yell rather than teach him how to do things. Everybody's even more frustrated now because he's older. I forget how it was." "Gosh, I thought he was better than this," said a librarian who minimized the severity of his autistic brother's disability to assuage his own guilt for moving away. More than one normal sibling was disturbed enough by a visit to seek treatment afterward.

Some siblings, like Amy Goodman, a young publicist with a

schizophrenic brother, never dare to go home because they know what awaits them:

> The chance that the homeless person I see on the street in my town could be my own brother scares the shit out of me—this is somebody I grew up with. I don't want to be presented with his illness at its height; if I can avoid that I will.

Despite your best efforts, however, impossible siblings have a way of showing up at your door—or, on one memorable occasion, in the river in front of your door, as happened to Janice Becker:

> My crazy sister went AWOL from the hospital. She came to my apartment, ran down to the Ohio River in her underwear, raving that I was the devil, and jumped in. I got helicopters and police boats, but she's so strong that it took hours to fish her out. The story was on the first page of the local paper—without a picture, thank God.

Lots of people have less than Grandma Moses–perfect holiday family gatherings, but few are as dramatically awful as the one that boutique owner Mimi Newhouse's mother and borderline sister ruined:

> I'd cooked a full Thanksgiving dinner, everybody's there. My sister picks up the tablecloth and proceeds to throw everything off the table, screaming "You're so selfish." Dishes go crashing, the meal's destroyed. The rest of the evening is spent

> cleaning up and trying to put something together. Then my mother comes over to me and whispers, "You know she's not all there. She's very sensitive."

The fallout can continue into the next generation. The lawyer's schizophrenic brother not only appeared at her office but made a nutcracker shaped like a penis and insisted on displaying it to her young daughters at her home. "He had no idea it was disturbing, offensive, and appalling," she said, as she struggled to decide whether to bar him from visiting in the future. Not only does the destructive behavior persist, but the parental attitudes that failed to contain it do also. The perverse pattern of preference is repeated, as parents, who are now grandparents, cannot attend their grandchildren's graduations because their multihandicapped daughter is home from the institution for the weekend. A real estate broker said, "I told my mother that I wouldn't bring my son to see her if my sister the drug-addicted prostitute was there, and she said, 'Then I guess you're not coming around anymore.'" When a seriously learning-disabled woman finally married, her sister said, "I hope she doesn't get pregnant right away, because her baby will monopolize our mother's attention just as my sister always did." Their tone is primarily one of resignation, not complaint.

In the midst of adult pursuits—college, child-rearing, making a living—healthy siblings are forced to deal with brothers and sisters in crises ranging from bouncing checks to hijacking jets, from drunken stupors to homicides. The role of rescuer is thrust upon them by siblings, parents, or their own heightened sense of duty. Their feeling of responsibility can be uncompromising; while she was recuperating from chemotherapy, a woman's depressed brother shot himself through the head in their parents' home, and she blamed herself that she did not have the stamina to stop him.

Even a sibling's happiness provokes anxiety. "What if he meets someone in the day care program and gets married?" fretted a retarded man's sister, picturing herself trapped forever taking care of his prospective progeny. She felt she would be forced to choose between his fulfillment and her own all over again.

Nobody simply grows apart from a damaged brother or sister, as do people with functioning siblings whose lives diverge; obligation, guilt, or the need to repudiate are too great. Whether they rebel or comply, their parents' admonition to take care of the troubled one makes them maintain at least minimal contact; an involuntary bond binds them together.

A sibling does not have to be massively incapacitated to weigh you down. You may keep your distance physically, but psychically the clingy, whiny sister on her fourth marriage, and the obnoxious, parasitic brother on his fourth job, lurk in the background, disturbing your peace of mind. "I rarely see her though she lives a few blocks away," advertising executive Dana Thompson said of the fragile older sister she never got along with. "Everything is always about her, even when my son was born and our father was dying. Our mother keeps encouraging us to have a relationship, but I can't stand to spend time with her. She becomes overwrought at the smallest thing and starts screaming at every family occasion. I know she's had a harder life than I have, but she makes no effort, and we have nothing in common. No matter what I give, it's never enough." As we spoke about this troubled and troubling woman, Dana realized how deep her repulsion actually went and how intertwined their destinies continued to be despite her attempts to extricate herself: "She's like a little worm that invades everywhere, a thread that's another color—purple thread in a pink fabric, subtle but there—a nut I can't crack."

SOMETIMES THE "LOVE AND STRENGTH" that Jackie Hanson summoned at age eight when her sister ate her book report cover are bound to fail, and the taboo feelings so carefully suppressed come tumbling out. It happens to most siblings, and it haunts them for the rest of their lives. They never forget these scenes and never forgive themselves for being so human.

Randy Lane looks like a winner in life's lottery. Boyish, athletic, with all-American good looks, he is one of the country's most prominent young political scientists, a tenured professor at age thirty-five. His affability and laid-back charm make it hard to imagine the hidden anguish he still feels because of a night twenty years ago when, provoked beyond endurance by his autistic, Tourette's-afflicted older brother, he lost control:

> I was at my parents' beach house with a bunch of friends from college. He insisted I play a game of Sorry with him—we used to play board games and I'd always let him win—and threw a tantrum when I refused. I couldn't take it anymore, and we started physically fighting in front of everybody. I had my hands on his throat, holding him down, and he screamed at me, "I wish you'd never been born." "Shut up, you fucking faggot," I yelled back. Then I said, "Don't blame me, it's God's

> fault." My mother started weeping and promised "we'll never let him embarrass you again," and then drove home with him in the middle of the night. I was devastated by the unfairness and the tragedy, and she thought it was just embarrassment I was feeling. We never discussed it. What I did was disloyal, dishonorable, and unchristian.

Even in his rage the insult Randy hurled at his brother was generic; to have actually repeated back what his brother had said to him would have been unutterable because it was too true. And while he deflected the blame for his brother's miserable condition onto God, he himself still bears the guilt for his momentary lapse of compassion. Like so many normal siblings, the person for whom he really has too little compassion is himself.

chapter 6

My Sister Spoke to Me

Dreams of Normal Siblings

AT NIGHT normal ones tell themselves truths about their predicament that no one—themselves included—listens to during the day. Their dreams, which have never been systematically studied before, provide a unique glimpse of a secret world, expressed in poignant and poetic personal language.

The purpose of dreams is to expose the unacknowledged dimensions of experience. Since normal siblings must conceal a salient part of their inner lives from themselves, their dreams are especially telling and are the most unvarnished source of information about the emotions their damaged siblings evoke. During sleep, when their guard is down and the consequences of self-disclosure are less dangerous, normal siblings' forbidden thoughts, feelings, and fantasies emerge. To understand these nocturnal messages is to know what it really feels like to live with the Caliban Syndrome and where to begin to reverse its effects.

Damaged siblings figure prominently in the dreams of their normal brothers and sisters, often overtly. Although some of these dreams are populated by murderous maniacs and amorphous monsters that symbolize siblings who are frightening or overwhelming, most siblings appear recognizably as their daylight selves. Dreams specific to normal ones fall into three categories, all indicative of the unique, often unspoken burdens they shoulder, and some of which may overlap. Their predominant themes are the Magical Solution, the Awful Truth (my rape dream was of this type), and the Real Resolution (fortunately, my leaky office dream falls in this category).

the magical solution

The most common sibling theme in dreams is the intact sibling's desire to normalize the family by making the sibling's problem (or the problem sibling) go away. There are two ways to accomplish this—to repair damaged siblings by "arranging" for them to be magically healed, or to remove them by killing them off. Very rarely do normal siblings actually murder damaged relatives in cold blood in their dreams; more frequently they safely discharge their hidden hatred by "discovering" that the person has died.

Since dreamers are the authors and directors of their productions, they are responsible for everything that happens therein; nobody ever dies of natural causes in a dream. Rendering yourself the witness or the innocent bystander to fratricide is one way of disavowing the wish to commit it, while simultaneously expressing that very impulse. Susan Kim, the devoted caretaker of her retarded brother, reported occasional daydreams in which he died, always in an explosion of gore:

> Every once in a while I imagine something hideous happening to him—he's so vulnerable and totally trusting. I worry that he has high blood pressure, so his head blows up.

In reality she treats her brother with great gentleness, but she always feels she is not doing enough for him. All her violent thoughts find a safe outlet in her fantasy life or are directed against herself.

Amy Goodman, the young publicist who never went home so she could avoid seeing her schizophrenic brother wandering the streets, wants to have it both ways. Her dream expresses a longing to repair his destroyed life and another to rid her own of the havoc he wreaks:

> I can't remember if he became sicker and was institutionalized, or if he was curiously all better.

Most sibling dreamers opt for the unambivalent fantasy of the miraculous transformation that cures the sufferer, improves the siblings' relationship, and—because everything in a dream also reflects the dreamer—heals the self. Rebecca Ashford feels dreadful that she cannot tolerate any contact with her miserable, schizoid brother, so she fixes him up in her dreams:

> He's completely normal. I walk in the room and say, "Danny, you look so good!"

"This is rare for me," she added sadly.

Physical and mental deformities alike disappear in dreams. Dancer Ashley King has two dysfunctional sisters—one borderline, the other bulimic—and is filled with shame and fear that she could turn into either one. "In my dreams," she says, "they are both really skinny and sane," so she can be too. Gloria Miller's relationship with a sister afflicted with Elephant Man's disease has been marred by mutual envy and hostility mixed with regret and sorrow. "I dream she's perfect and we have a wonderful time together," the healthy one says. In an unusual variation on the theme, Frank Gardiner makes his seriously retarded brother devious rather than damaged:

> I used to dream all the time that there was nothing wrong with him and that he was just faking.

Fixing the unfixable, or saving the irredeemable, is a frequent occurrence in sibling dreams. Marilyn Daniels, whose brother is serving a protracted sentence in the penitentiary for murdering a police officer, dreamed he saved her from rape; she made him prevent, rather than commit, a heinous crime. Marilyn converted her criminal brother into a hero, so she could look up to him rather than see him behind prison bars for the rest of their lives, at least while she slept.

Dreams in which a sibling no longer has the disability that prevents real contact or love between equals give a brief respite that is both painful and pleasing to recollect. Sarah Lattimer, whose sister

Mary is an ineducable, aggressive deaf-mute, had a recurring dream "like the Helen Keller movie. We had a wonderful afternoon together—I was her teacher, and we bonded." "To this day, I'm sensitive about Helen Keller jokes," she noted, wishing that her sister could resemble that extraordinary woman and that she herself could be "the miracle worker."

The fantasy of magical repair has multiple functions. It can be a dream come true, but it can also put a sibling on notice about the psychological work ahead. Jackie Hanson always longed for her mute, almost-twin sister to talk to her, although she knew it could never happen in waking life:

> Joan and I were assigned to separate groups. . . . Then all of a sudden she said one sentence: "I want to stay with you." I woke and remembered, "Oh my God, she spoke." It left me with a twinge of sadness.

Jackie understood that the dream announced the theme that would preoccupy her for years: creating her own autonomy by disentangling her identity from her sister's.

Normal ones often dream that a suffering sibling has died, or they discover to their astonishment that one who actually has died is still alive. In either version grief is strikingly absent. These dreams are an opportunity for "good" siblings to express death wishes too shocking or sinful to be stated outright; clergy and children of clergy are especially prone to them. A woman from a devout family, awaiting her fatally ill brother's demise with profoundly mixed emotions, dreamed:

> I was home for Christmas, and he was there. We were sitting in the living room talking. All of a sudden I thought, "You're not supposed to be here, you're dead." Then I started to feel awful; I wanted somebody dead who's going to die.

A rabbi whose youth was marred by the inordinate attention his parents gave a quadriplegic brother who needed constant surgeries dreamed about the man's unwelcome resurrection:

> Right after the funeral I dreamed that I saw him alive and well. I said, "Why are you here—aren't you supposed to be dead?"

The brother who had inadvertently robbed him of his childhood, a deprivation he had overtly borne without complaint, had not died for him psychologically, though he himself had officiated at the funeral. In the rabbi's unconscious his brother was still a lively presence who continued to affect him. Even posthumously Caliban will take up residence within you.

the awful truth

Dreams can remind normal siblings of the dark side of their relationship with an abnormal sibling. The purpose of these often terrifying nightmares is to prevent denial and call people's attention to anxiety-provoking information that it would be perilous to ignore.

Often the emotions rather than any specific content carry the message the dreamer needs to hear. Samantha Greenberg, who lived with amorphous fears about her retarded brother's potential for violence, regularly awoke in a cold sweat when he appeared in dreams that were too vague to pin down and too easy to discount. The only thing she recalled was "a feeling of panic that I don't know what he's going to do." Nobody in Samantha's family had considered him dangerous; her dream—especially because it recurred, as if to make her pay attention—warned her that it was true.

Unsavory facts about the sibling dreamer are highlighted in their dreams as well. Jane London felt too guilty and inhibited ever to raise her voice to the incompetent sister who was her lifelong burden; in the privacy of her own bedroom she said and did everything she publicly suppressed:

> I was shaking her and screaming at the top of my lungs. I felt bad afterward, but I've always been so frustrated and enraged with her.

Compassionate caretakers in waking life became furies in their dreams. Ellen O'Brian, the illustrator whose family expected her to attend far too much to her dull and demanding, severely learning-disabled sister, dreamed that her sister had a baby—a distinct possibility that Ellen dreaded in advance. "I was so angry that I was yelling at the whole family," she said, allowing herself to dream the reaction she would feel honor-bound to suppress when the blessed event actually occurred.

Images of witches are not confined to children's fairy tales or horror movies; they populate the dreams of normal siblings whose abnormal brothers and sisters are malevolent, frightening, or destructive. After her sister, who took good care of her when she was younger, turned vicious when she grew into an attractive rival, Jessica Kaplan repeatedly envisioned her as a witch. Candy Fine, the pregnant copywriter whose neurologically impaired brother threatened her security enough that she is leaving the country, found herself reliving scenes from the frightening film *The Blair Witch Project*, starring him:

> There's a feeling of supernatural doom, being in the woods. Babies and little children are in danger.

"Growing up, I always had the feeling that something weird would happen in my family, something irreparable," she said. She is taking drastic measures to protect her own future family.

Anxiety dreams are ubiquitous among pregnant women, but when a woman grows up with a sibling who has birth defects, the content is specific and literal. Candy also dreamed that "a friend is pregnant. The baby she's carrying is probably dead, but she would have to deliver it anyway."

This dream has layers of meanings beyond the universal ambivalence that maternity evokes. Candy is actually not sure whether her disturbed brother is psychically alive, and she wishes he were dead physically as well. The situation she dreams about also expresses her fear of contagion, deflected onto the ever-popular "friend" who stands in for herself; she is terrified that the child she carries could be emotionally dead like her brother and that she could do irreparable damage like her mother. She must "deliver" the dead baby to deal with her feelings about it; otherwise it will fester inside her and force her to run from the past forever.

Sometimes an anxiety dream expresses an internal as well as an external reality that is hard for the normal sibling to accept. Lisa Masterson, the "genetically engineered caretaker" of her drug-addicted brother and his progeny, washed her hands of the problem in a frequently repeated dream:

> My brother's in trouble, and I'm scared because I don't think I can help him.

Lisa is telling herself two truths—that reforming her brother is hopeless, and that she does not want to work at it anymore. She had the most recent rendition of this dream after spending a holiday weekend at the city jail trying, for what she swears is the last time, to get her brother released on bail.

real resolutions

Dreams that give a normal sibling clues to the way out of the Caliban Syndrome are not always enjoyable or easily comprehensible, but they are precious and memorable. They tend to occur when a normal one is struggling to understand the relationship with a damaged sibling. Such dreams are steadfast inner allies, offering advice and encouragement, and pointing out the path.

When advertising executive Barbara Green finally decided to begin psychotherapy after years of avoiding addressing the grievous multiple traumas of her childhood, her dreams cheered her on. In one she "went underwater and was still able to breathe." She was telling herself that if she goes into the depths of her unconscious, she will survive and neither drown nor be flooded with anxiety or sorrow. In another she "discovered a new experience"—confronting the past rather than running from it, as she did after her brother's suicide. In a third she told herself in symbolic terms about the task ahead of her:

> I'm a prisoner in a lovely suburban home—it's gorgeous, but if I step outside, I'm dead. My mother was guarding the door. I was trying to open a window, finding clever ways to escape.

Barbara is making efforts to "open a window," to let in the light and air of the present. She can indeed find a way to escape the deadly confinement of a life, like her mother's, that looked good on the surface—but she must first be clever enough to realize that she is imprisoning herself in it.

Carrie Grainger was puzzled that she was repeatedly "freaked out" by what she should have easily dismissed as just another "I'm back in school again" dream:

> I'm supposed to graduate from high school, but I've forgotten to show up in history class.

Carrie's beloved younger brother had a psychotic breakdown during her last year of high school. Her dream shows her that, like every normal sibling, she needs to study the past, to master the subject of her own history, before she can "graduate" from the Caliban Syndrome.

chapter 7

Invisibility and Perverse Preeminence

A TELEVISION ANCHORWOMAN RECOUNTED an image from her past that affected her profoundly, but that she knew would never be shown on the nightly news:

> My best friend in high school had a brother with cerebral palsy. I remember going to her house, and the first thing you saw when you walked in was a floor-to-ceiling blown-up photograph of him in his wheelchair—he'd been the CP poster child the year before he died. There wasn't a single picture of my friend, who had nothing wrong with her, anywhere in sight—and she was alive! It made me cry every time I went over there.

The reporter's friend was in an impossible position. How could she compete with a martyr, and how could she complain about favoritism when she alone was alive and well? Her friend shed the tears that she herself could only suppress with shame.

Invisible is the word normal children most often use to describe their place in the family, whether their damaged siblings are dead or alive. Their everyday trials and tribulations pale beside the catastrophe of their siblings' predicaments, so it seems natural that they should never come first; what is a parent to do when one child is throwing a fit of hysterics or having a seizure and the other wants help with her homework? The chronic overlooking is rarely intentional. Rather, it is what happens when desperate, overwhelmed adults with problems of their own try to cope with situations that no parent bargains for and few have the emotional resources to balance. As a result, many healthy siblings grow up with a hunger for attention that is never satisfied and that seems wrong to feel. Their needs, so consistently ignored, become invisible to themselves.

The alternative to being invisible is being all too visible, having a position of perverse preeminence in the family. Normal children who become the focus of their parents' dreams live anxiously in the spotlight and feel compelled to compensate for their damaged siblings; when you are "all I have left," as one father told his healthy daughter, everything depends on you. The obligation is crushing, and failing to live up to it is as devastating as having no right to attention; in fact, they are mirror images. Just as the invisible ones are expected to be mature and self-sufficient, the preeminent ones must excise their weaknesses, doubts, and contrary aspirations. In both cases part of the personality is lost.

To stay conscious of a normal child's requirements while coping with an abnormal one is a daunting task for even the most diligent of parents. The day my patient Peter Lehman's infant daughter was diagnosed with a severe spinal abnormality, he helplessly watched his healthy three-year-old son fade into the background as the retinue of neurologists, nurses, therapists, and anguished relatives descended upon the house. He felt himself being sucked into the maelstrom of caring for her and struggling to determine the proper treatment while trying to comfort his wife and handle his own anger, exhaustion, and depression. Because he had to detach from his feelings to conserve psychic energy, he knew that he could do little more than go through the motions with the boy. For years he was pursued by dreams that his son was in danger and that he was unable to rescue him. Fortunately his ability to empathize with his healthy child eventually limited the damage, but it cost years of anxiety and tension. A more typical and more pernicious scenario is for parents to manage stress and simplify their lives by eliminating awareness of the normal child's separate existence. If they think normal children need them less, they are not forced to make solomonic choices in allotting attention, or to be tormented by guilt about abandoning them, as Peter was.

There are several ways to make a normal child disappear: by focusing exclusively on the problem child, by permitting the problem child to violate the other child's rights, by assigning the normal one excessive responsibility, and by failing to acknowledge doing any of these things.

Ill children are squeaky wheels whom no parent should ignore, and tending them can indeed be all-consuming. The real problem, however, is not the time and effort spent but the parents' expectation that healthy children tolerate neglect for extensive periods without complaint—or agree that they are not being neglected at all.

"Everything was focused on the one who was sick," said Linda Simon, who lost track of how many operations her younger sister's intestinal abnormalities required. "I cried when she would go to the hospital because I wanted to go too—why couldn't I be ill?" She was so desperate to get her parents' attention that she took a drug overdose as a teenager. "It was my way of saying, 'I'm here too, don't forget me.' The family went into counseling as a result." Linda eventually found a constructive way to realize her childhood wish: she became a nurse. Attention given and received is clearly still a matter of great concern for her, since she went out of her way to assure me that if I called at a particular time for our interview, I would be guaranteed her "undivided attention."

These children go to various lengths to get noticed, from dying their hair purple to trying to kill themselves. One woman remembered announcing to her mother at age three that she wanted to be a butterfly; that way she would be recognized for her beauty, and she could also escape. But few are able to overcome their parents' powerful need to ignore them.

Normality is a liability in some families. A deformity (and its meaning to a parent) can be the reason to prefer a damaged child, or it can legitimize a preference actually based on other factors. Cindy Goodman's mother made her feel that she never measured up to her brother, whom she favored because he was a boy. His cleft palate—for which his classmates labeled him "Mushmouth"—was a way to rationalize the inordinate attention she paid him, an additional reason he was special. "He had the obvious problem, yet I felt I had one," this retired guidance counselor said. "My mother constantly asked me, 'Why can't you be more like him?' and I always felt handicapped by being normal, as well as female. He was picked on as a child, so she had a sense of pity and compassion for him that she didn't have for me. He got all kinds of special attention—she gave him a present every time he had an operation. I didn't understand it, but I remember accepting that I'd never deserve as much. He grew up to be extremely successful, the best and the brightest. When I finally graduated from college at the age of thirty, my shining hour, my mother called to ask if she could give me the same present that she had gotten him for his last birthday."

Cindy's mother, like many parents, was entirely unaware of her behavior and its impact on her daughter. "I told my mother recently what she had done, and she had no idea. She insisted that she had treated us exactly alike," Cindy said. Her childhood experience had one positive effect; it made Cindy sensitive to justice and inclusion in her professional as well as her personal life.

Parents are often tempted to make compensatory gestures to problem children or to treat them with a spurious equality that diminishes the uniqueness of the normal one. They buy the unmarriageable sister the same dishes and linens as the bride, and they reflexively offer the crippled brother "the best seat in the house." But even forever sharing or ceding the limelight is not as damaging as forfeiting the right to object.

Patterns of preference can outlast the disability. Marcey Gibson's elder sister wore a brace to correct scoliosis when she was a child, which made her the object of their mother's solicitude. Thirty years later the mother still calls Marcey by her sister's name.

Gloria Miller's sister, deformed by Elephant Man's disease, was labeled "Duck-Ass" by her classmates. To spare the girl further torment, Gloria's mother forbade Gloria to invite friends to the house; hypersensitivity to one child's feelings made her insensitive to the other's. Gloria had a recurrent dream common among healthy siblings: that she had a room of her own—an inviolate space that was hers alone. The symbols normal children use to depict their siblings can be even more explicit and less benign; in her dreams financial adviser Maggie Payne's uncontrollable sister, who never forgave her for refusing to ask her to be her maid of honor ("I wanted my wedding to be the one thing in my life she didn't spoil," said Maggie), became an amorphous monster crawling up the sidewalk and taking up all the room on the street where their family lived.

The automatic sympathy that parents extend to problem children in an effort to mitigate their pain often becomes a license for those children to misbehave. When Ben Ramsey's brother, jealous of his academic success, stabbed him in a fight, their parents exhorted them both not to "play so rough." "He had carte blanche in the family," said Ben. "Because they couldn't get angry at him, they got angry at me."

Siblings of the handicapped are given far more onerous responsibilities than other children. The issue is not the tasks themselves but being taken for granted. Since she was a little girl, nineteen-year-old Jamie Walters has been diapering her microcephalic elder sister and curtailing her own after-school activities to stay with her. "I never minded taking care of her," she said. "I resented that my mother didn't acknowledge that I was helping." They long for the very recognition and appreciation of their sacrifices that, paradoxically, their parents are incapable of providing.

Some children have to be mute as well as invisible—neither seen nor heard. Hospital administrator Jennifer Martin was designated the bearer of the unspeakable truth about her brother's fate, and it almost destroyed her. Throughout her childhood she saw him became progressively incapacitated by muscular dystrophy ("I stared raw powerlessness in the face") and had to uncomplainingly accept when his frustration turned to violence directed against her. Then, as a seventh-grader, reading about the illness for a science project, she discovered to her horror that his condition was fatal—a fact that her parents had concealed from her. Unable to contain this awful information alone, she confided in a school counselor, who mentioned it without her permission in a family therapy session. "My parents felt that I had betrayed them. They wept and said they didn't know how he would live through knowing it—I'm feeling suicidal from guilt, and this is what they're worried about. I felt bound and gagged by the situation." Jennifer looked fruitlessly for books to help her cope with the combination of grief, rage, self-hatred, and helplessness she felt as a sibling of a seriously ill brother, and she finally found some insights in the literature on families of alcoholics. "I share the disability of our family," she concluded. "Our family *was* a disability. Not only did they treat me as not important, but I treat myself this way. Therapy has helped me honor myself even if they could not."

TO BE CHOSEN is more insidious than to be invisible, as I know from my own experience; specialness, though overtly preferable, extracts its own price. "I had to be perfect," said a woman whose life goal was to make up to her parents for her brother's fecklessness. "They put all their hopes on me. It didn't matter who I was; I had to be more. I carried the weight of having to be normal and functioning and achieving—I never had the right to be immature in any way, to act out or stamp my foot. I was the Rock of Gibraltar. Even if you're successful, you never really feel lucky." Preeminence, which requires children to mold their personalities to their parents' specifications, is perverse because it distorts the self.

Children with damaged siblings who are designated the bearers of their parents' destinies experience more pressure than other children because the demands placed on them are double—they must simultaneously fulfill parental aspirations and compensate for their sibling's failure to do so. Everything depends on them. Living with the concrete example of what not to be intensifies the chosen one's anxiety and urgency to succeed at this impossible task. Their compulsion to achieve is a crushing symptom of the Caliban Syndrome.

The fallout from being invisible is to become self-effacing; perverse preeminence breeds perfectionism, morbid self-criticism, and fear of failure. Internalizing parents' exacting standards, chosen children become compulsive compensators who cannot tolerate any aspect of themselves reminiscent of their siblings. For them, excelling is not an ideal; it is an emotional life preserver.

The perfections they are required to attain can take the form of actions, achievements, or feelings; a normal child in the spotlight must be unfailingly good, successful, or happy in order not to forfeit the precarious position as the one who is favored and who does not disappoint.

For Christine White, a minister's daughter with hyperactive twin brothers, not only her parents but the entire congregation dictated how she should act: "Our family had to be a shining example of godliness and perfect behavior—and I had to double my perfect behavior so the parishioners wouldn't think less of my parents because they couldn't control my brothers."

Compensating for a sibling by succeeding academically is usually a conscious project and tends to become an obsession early on. A young chemist, frantic with tension about falling down on the job, recalled that even in grade school she was "the only child who used to cry over workbook exercises." She bore this responsibility in silence; "I never was willing or able to ask for any help because I didn't want them to know I had any problems."

As teenagers, such children inhibit their natural rambunctiousness and rebelliousness. "I never let myself be reckless," said the sister of a boy who was always in trouble. "In high school I never stayed out late or got drunk. I made sure to spend weekends at home and never violated a curfew because I didn't want my parents to worry." Having to be exemplary constricts their self-expression and makes them wistful for the wildness other children consider their birthright.

Katie Clark, a web page designer, was acutely aware that she had to achieve for three. "My older autistic brother had a difficult time finding and keeping a job even with help, and my younger depressed sister had even more of a struggle. My parents couldn't expect as much from them as they do from me, so I felt immense pressure to succeed because the others wouldn't. I had to be the normal one—the high achiever who got good grades and became well established in my career. I've never been able to drop the shackles of responsibility for a moment." To be what she defined as irresponsible—traveling cross-country instead of working without a break—would seem perilously close to her siblings in her own as well as in her parents' eyes.

Like invisible children, preeminent ones keep their struggles out of sight, though one young man was so crushed by expectations that he dared to confess to his father. "He wanted me to be a doctor, but I finally told him, 'I'm just average, and it's not going to get any better.' I just want to be like everybody else and not have to try so hard all the time." To relax and be himself is to fail.

For Jackie Hanson, who was eight years old when her autistic sister ate her book report cover, the demands were emotional. "My perfection was in my feelings," she said. "I spent my childhood making up for my sister who couldn't function. I would not let on that I was upset. I was always tuned in to what others were feeling and not tuned in to myself, so I became the agreeable, quiet kid. I was so restrained because she was so much the opposite." Vigilance to her parents' needs required her to suppress her own personality and force herself into the mold of "not my sister" that she later spent years trying to break.

The role that one woman (who later became a comedienne) called the "little sunbeam" is especially popular in damaged families. To have at least one child who is cheerful—and therefore not hopeless, furious, or tyrannical—eases demoralized parents; to be that special child is to have the power to make your parents smile, no matter what the cost in self-estrangement.

Bringing his parents joy has always been Jeff Myer's job. The mission assigned to him, and that he embraced, was to be the anodyne for the anguish caused by his suicidally depressed older brother. His naturally buoyant and resilient disposition suited him for the task of dispelling the pall that his brother's moodiness, antagonism, and despair cast over the family. "He never had friends, and you had to walk on eggshells around him," Jeff said, "so my job was to neutralize that. My parents coddled me in some ways and set impossible goals in others. I was expected to approach life with ease—to be carefree, easygoing, light rather than heavy, sociable rather than sullen. I had an explanation ready for everything that could be perceived as a problem, and they were eager to buy it; they couldn't bear another child crippled by unhappiness."

Having to be happy all the time because a sibling is always wretched is hard work. To accomplish this feat, Jeff trained himself early on to eliminate any untoward reaction automatically. Without being fully aware of his motives, he ceaselessly cultivated good moods because he risked turning into his brother if he ever lapsed into a bad one; with practice he became so adept that dark thoughts barely registered. This skill had the paradoxical effect of causing him to feel disconnected from all his emotions and intensely anxious lest a negative one slip past his early warning system. Enforced, artificial positive thinking made him intensely miserable.

Jeff was unable to remove the smiley face when he left home; the obligation to be happy had become a habit. As an adult, he constantly monitors his contentment quotient, lest he fall short of his own lofty standard; despite his considerable achievements, everyone else seems more successful and more satisfied than he.

The breakup of his marriage when he turned thirty-five put Jeff into a tailspin that even his best efforts could not completely reverse; here was a failure that partook of his brother's. When, for the first time in his life, he told his mother how upset he was, she said only partly in jest, "You were supposed to be my happy child." Her statement showed him the source of his self-imposed vocation; he understood how much the need to be cheerful had originally been external and had cut him off from experiencing or processing even normal grief. "My life as I've constructed it has always been fragile, and my ability to love or even know myself has been precarious," he said, almost welcoming the authentic painful emotion.

What happens when, after spending your childhood molding your personality to fit others' specifications, you grow up and suddenly have nobody to please but yourself? Illustrator Ellen O'Brian faced this common predicament of the preeminent child when she felt at a complete loss on her first unsupervised job: "I'm the only functioning sibling of three in my family, so I got a heavy dose of 'you can do anything.' My parents pushed me ahead in school. I thought, 'I'll be the best artist'—it was important to do really well, and I did. Then I had to prove myself to my teachers—even though I was aware of it, I couldn't stop it. I thought I was perfect."

As long as she had some authority figure in loco parentis, Ellen could recapitulate the role of the high-achieving special child that had been her lifeline. But entering the world of independent professional work required different skills: "I do well when I get feedback, when someone's noticing, but it's hard to carry things out on my own." With nobody to praise her and none of the obvious yardsticks of success by which she had formerly measured her achievement now available, she "floundered around." There were days, she discovered to her distress, when she found it impossible to motivate herself, when she felt uninterested in her work, and when she resented having to cater to her clients' whims. These normal reactions, so foreign to her and so threatening to her persona, paralyzed her with insecurity and self-doubt. "All my life I had responsibilities I didn't want," she told me, "even if they were just emotional—I had to do well to support my parents and make them feel good. This career is the first thing I've pursued just for myself, and I feel like a wreck. Part of me runs away from that responsibility and can't take the freedom. I feel really shaky now that nobody is seeing or hearing about my work, and I'm having trouble gauging if I'm on the right track." Ellen recognizes that with no higher authority to conform to, she must finally learn to answer to herself.

INVISIBILITY AND PERVERSE PREEMINENCE are obverses, complementary yet intersecting roles thrust upon the normal sibling by traumatized and unconscious parents. Both are types of abandonment; the requirements of the invisible and of the preeminent are lost in the shadow of their "special needs" siblings—a euphemism that excuses ignoring the healthy or making impossible demands on them. This concept, which has gained wide acceptance in the contemporary world, is in fact a form of affirmative action in the family that has the unintended effect of denigrating the concept of normality. It is a covert form of discrimination against normal children; the sibling of the child with special needs is not supposed to have any needs.

Jackie Hanson, who experienced firsthand the damage this mentality wreaked in her own family and grew up to become a professional advocate for the disabled, believes that no child is well served by defining abnormality away:

> I don't make apologies for using the word *normal*. To be afraid to say that someone like my sister is not normal is denying reality—normal is defined in the dictionary as "like the majority." I don't use the term *child with special needs* either

> because normal children like me have special needs too—ours are very special, unique, and neglected. This way of thinking does a disservice to the nondisabled and connotes that their needs don't count. Society needs to deny the consequences of differences, and it sugarcoats them for parents. This doesn't really help at all, but most don't go down the insight road.

The "special needs" mentality automatically enlists normal children in a crusade on behalf of damaged siblings. The loneliness, anxiety, perfectionism, and loss of emotional freedom that result from being forced into either of these impossible positions are exacerbated by the corollary assumption that normal children should be relieved and grateful not to have special needs. They are thereby denied what ought to be a universal birthright—to be recognized, appreciated, and nurtured as unique individuals, whether handicapped or healthy.

chapter 8

Dark Victories

IT IS A SCENE OUT OF A NORMAN ROCKWELL illustration. A teenage girl sits at her dressing table putting the final touches on her hair and makeup for the prom. Nervous but excited, she gazes at herself in the mirror. Behind her, watching the preparations with rapt attention, sits her little sister. Someday, we know and they know, her turn will come.

But a damaged sibling's turn never comes. The sister who watches so wistfully may even be older. She will spend that evening, and most subsequent evenings, in front of the television. Eventually you will move out and create an independent life full of possibilities she cannot imagine. She may (perhaps at your mother's insistence) be a bridesmaid, but never a bride. She may not go to college. While you mature, pursue a career, and find a husband, she will stay home, or have a marginal existence with a menial job, or spend years in an institution or in and out of the hospital. How can you deserve your bounty when she is doomed?

Under normal circumstances sibling rivalry is an inevitable, if highly charged, part of growing up. Competition between equals, as ferocious and wounding as it can be, rarely provokes paralyzing guilt because the victory is not a unilateral, uncontested triumph over an adversary whose defeat is a foregone conclusion. But the success of a normal child is forever tarnished by seeming to come at the abnormal child's expense; natural joy at winning feels unseemly, even immoral. Rivalry distorted by disability cannot simply fade, evolve, or be accepted; the implicit contrast with the sibling's fate always lurks accusingly in the shadows.

Intact children find their siblings' envy of their social and professional success and their physical health as disturbing as their own pleasure in beating the competition so decisively. Fear that they have no right to their ill-gotten gains drives them to conceal or sabotage their achievements or to spend their lives attempting to compensate their "victims." Even when they suffer no apparent remorse, as I never did, a nameless anxiety haunts them and makes everything they have seems tenuous or undeserved. Survivor guilt is a major component of the Caliban Syndrome.

JANE LONDON'S STRANGE, partially blind, and inept younger sister was her "assistant" when she got ready for dates in high school. "I used to feel bad about her watching me, but it didn't stop me because kids are also into themselves," she recalled. "In school I was outgoing and a high achiever—she always quit everything. After she didn't get into the sorority I was in, I tried to help her find activities she'd like. Then she quit college and tried to throw herself down the stairs." Jane was so troubled by her sister's defeats—and the implicit comparison to her own social and academic success—that she visited her sister's psychiatrist to ask if she could do anything to help. Guilt prevented her from following his excellent advice: "Let her come to you."

While her sister continued to live at home and work sporadically as a Kmart cashier, Jane, by then a happily married guidance counselor, became pregnant with her first child. Dreading the impact of her twin triumphs, Jane was seized with a compulsive need to mend her sister's unremediable plight; only by filling the void in her sister's life could she deserve to enjoy the fullness of her own. She had a dream that combined her worst conscious—and entirely realistic—fear with her most unconscious, unacceptable wish:

> I dreamed that my sister was never going to get married and that she'd commit suicide. This put me into a huge depression. It was like a strong premonition, almost a prophecy, so I tried to fix her up with every single male I knew, in a frantic effort to get her to connect. I thought I had to rescue her; it was up to me to save her from her fate. I felt despair about her empty life but never told anybody about it—I just carried it around because I thought nobody would understand, and I was also afraid that if I talked too much about her, people would think maybe I was crazy too.

In addition to their unrealistic expectations that they can alter their sibling's destinies, normal siblings are prey to malignant grandiosity, the fantasy that they have the power to destroy their rivals by succeeding. They irrationally believe that they can cause or exacerbate a sibling's failure. Both convictions are based on the fallacy that their fates and their siblings' are interlocked. Jane thought that seeing the glaring discrepancy between them would kill her sister; not being able to save her meant forfeiting her own right to happiness, and becoming depressed like her was her punishment. She had to keep her despair secret to shore up the crumbling boundary between them in her own mind.

The nightmare came true only partially. Jane's sister never did marry, but she is still eking out a life thirty years later. Jane is still trying to find ways to compensate—paying her insurance, taking her on trips—that never fully eradicate the guilt.

There is a critical difference between assisting a damaged sibling and trying to undo accidents of fate and fortune that you cannot help and did not cause. The former is brotherly or sisterly love and mature, if circumscribed, responsibility. The latter is compulsive self-sacrifice driven by the belief that you do not deserve your advantages. The one is sadly finite; the other never lets you go.

Jane's childhood attempt to "find activities" for her dysfunctional sister is a common undertaking, born of compassion, the desire for companionship, and the need to salve a troubled conscience. Ellen O'Brian, the illustrator who struggled to become self-directed as an adult, also remembers trying "to engage and entertain" her learning-disabled sister by "creating games we could play together" even as a little girl. Men in particular report having to rein in their physical competitiveness with their less able brothers, often at their parents' urging. Paul Morrison, a thirty-five-year-old systems analyst whose older brother is neurologically impaired, said with a nervous laugh, "Boys wrestle, and so did we, until I realized I shouldn't do it because he couldn't fight back—I would have whipped him too badly." Since young children make no distinctions between thoughts and actions, he believed that his desire to beat his brother literally as well as symbolically could be deadly and must be suppressed. Viewing all natural competitiveness as destructive leads to an unrealistic sense of responsibility for a sibling's life.

It is human nature to want to be the star, but nobody who is related to a friendless outcast enjoys her popularity unambivalently. Carolyn Johnson's older brother is a "high-functioning autistic—intelligent but geeky, with no concept of politeness. I sense how jealous he is that I have a social life, and he doesn't know how to go about having one himself. I feel awful when he asks me 'How do you make friends?' because I know I can't tell him things he can use." She may be a social success, but as an adviser to her lonely brother, she is worthless.

At significant moments—making the honor roll when your brother is brain-damaged, dancing in a recital when your sister is paralyzed—it is excruciating to know how much better off you are and always will be. Paul's friend helped him temporarily finesse such a moment on his wedding day:

> Right before the ceremony my brother got emotional. He said, "I'm older, I should be getting married before you." My best man calmed him down by saying his younger brother got married first too.

It took some prodding to get Paul to admit that the situations were not really comparable and that his best man's reassurance provided a comforting pretense that only smoothed over a yawning gap in their fortunes, providing fleeting solace for them both. Failing to acknowledge that his own life is so much better through no virtue of his own has trapped Paul in a cycle of appeasing his brother and then resenting the imposition, of which his behavior at the wedding was only a symptom.

To offer their less fortunate siblings at least a momentary experience of prevailing, normal siblings try to level the playing field. Paul used to throw board games to let his brother win. Manny Resnick went much farther; he threw away a brilliant career for the sake of his obsessive-compulsive brother Marc.

Marc's disadvantages weighed heavily on Manny, who had always been their physician father's favorite. "His purity mania, belching, and odd/even compulsions made life miserable," Manny said. "He feels my father never respected him, that I got all the positive vibes and he got the negative. There's some truth to that, because he does things that upset everybody, but it still made me feel bad—the only thing you can think is that you're responsible." Manny's victory over Marc for their father's affections—a competition every sibling wants to win—was too crushing for him to enjoy; he is spending his life trying to expiate retroactively by making this victory pyrrhic.

The fear of contagion that intact siblings battle caused Manny to "shut Marc out" in adolescence, a time when self-definition is particularly tenuous. Although Manny knew he "had the same tendencies" toward the disorder, he felt both guilty and relieved that he was not incapacitated by it. To further safeguard his sanity, Manny "cut the tether" binding the brothers together when he left for college and rarely called or visited Marc. "I felt terrible but happy to get out," Manny admitted, "but he fell apart when I left. I was struggling for emotional equilibrium, and he pulled me down—it was the only way I could survive."

What could have been a natural parting of the ways in another family became charged and ominous because one brother lost his way. Manny failed to realize that Marc would have floundered whether he had been there or not.

Manny was right, however, that severing the fraternal tie freed him. He had a stellar undergraduate academic career and got accepted to the top two medical schools in the country, while Marc flunked out of college and told nobody but him. With Manny's encouragement, Marc found psychiatric help, finished school—and decided that he too wanted to become a physician.

The elder brother faced a terrible choice: "Medical school was my brother's bid for my father's approval. I didn't want to take away his only chance, the last thing that was his own, so I withdrew my applications at the last minute. I didn't go, so as not to compete with him; my goal was clearing space for my brother to be okay." To do otherwise would have been to seek the favoritism he had always passively enjoyed. Often, as in Manny's case, the guilt the higher-functioning person feels is deflected from pleasure at his own advantages to distress at the other's hardships. Manny had to sacrifice his ambitions to save not only his brother but his image of himself as a brother.

But clearing space so radically was not punishment enough for a lifetime of prevailing; in graduate school Manny unwittingly took on his brother's depression and the full brunt of his symptoms: "It finally got to me. I had the same problems he had had as an undergraduate but that were unusual for me—writer's block, hopelessness, the same repetitive thoughts—I hit a wall. I felt stupid and angry for painting myself into a corner." He understood his problems not as self-inflicted punishment and identification with Marc but as evidence that he was doomed to share his brother's fate.

Like Jane's nightmare, Manny's fears came true only partially, and his solution worked only partially. Manny recovered psychologically, married, and made a name for himself as director of a major cultural organization, a profession that suited him better than medicine because it was independent of obligations. ("I was headed toward psychiatry, with some unconscious idea that I was going to cure my family, so in that sense it was freeing not to become a doctor.") Mark did attend medical school, but his life has continued to be problematic even with the M.D.; "he ended up crusting over his earlier wounds—he manages to keep going professionally, but his private life's a mess."

Highly successful siblings like Manny are especially prone to feelings of omnipotence; as people of action, they cannot bear to know that they can do nothing to erase the discrepancies between them and their siblings. Despite the enormity of his sacrifice, Manny still does not believe that he has done enough for Marc: "I'm not a good brother, I'm a failure as an older brother. I still distance myself from him; I don't call him as much as I should. I'm not the friend and counselor I should be to him. I'm still afraid—afraid of social embarrassment—and on a deeper level I worry I still could be dragged down into depression and mental illness like him." Assuming that Marc would appreciate being "counseled" is a form of subtle condescension. Manny's obsessive fears that he mistreats his brother by separating from him and that he resembles Marc more than he does are the only ways their lives are actually alike. Marc is obsessed with everything; Manny is still obsessed with Marc. Manny clings to the notion that his intercession could improve Marc's life; guilt is often preferable to helplessness.

A brother who steps aside to promote a sibling professionally can consider himself a good samaritan even if his efforts yield mixed results, but a brother who steps into the only arena where his problem sibling excels feels like a usurper and a spoiler. Normal children assume they must automatically defer and squelch any striving that may detract from the other's constricted sphere of competence; to aspire is to supplant, and to compete is to steal. The implied comparison to their sibling's lesser achievements is a whispered accusation, never far from consciousness.

The one unassailable talent that Ben Ramsey's older brother David possessed was his beautiful singing voice. David, who had attacked Ben with a knife when they were children, had "lots of different start-and-stop careers" and even managed to get himself thrown out of the Peace Corps in his twenties. Aside from occasional gigs with bands and solo performances with church choirs, David, now sixty years old, has been supported by his parents, while Ben—a fine amateur singer himself—worked his way up to a job as a buyer in a department store. The brothers had finally reached an uneasy truce, when a thrilling and unexpected invitation came Ben's way at age forty-five. "A friend's daughter was getting married and asked me to sing at her wedding. I was excited and honored but very worried about performing, since David is a professional musician," said Ben. The night before his debut, he had a liberating nightmare:

> I dreamed I was wandering through a maze and couldn't find the wedding. I was tremendously anxious that I was going to be late. When I finally got there, David was already sitting at the back of the stage. Then I forgot what I was supposed to sing. He began to cue me, but when I tried to do it, I totally

> choked. I had no voice—I couldn't squeeze out the first note. I woke up horrified that I wasn't going to be able to do it.

Fortunately, Ben's fears were groundless: "When I stood up and sang in reality, all my fears vanished—this dream was a real turning point. It revealed my inhibition to supplant my brother, so it is interesting that he did not steal the show. That was a big deal." Ben must have felt punished enough for his ambition by the dream (and relieved that his dream-brother gave him permission by assisting) to feel entitled to find his voice. Having a brother's blessing—even if it is self-generated—legitimizes competitive feelings that might otherwise seem far too dangerous to act on.

What happens if a brother is so disabled that he will never have any area of expertise and feels nothing but impotent envy and anguish at his sister's superior abilities? Twenty-seven-year-old Sandy Wilson tries to manage her brain-damaged older brother Michael's jealousy and her own guilt by preempting even the possibility of achievement. "If I succeed, it takes away from what he has," Sandy reasons, so this hardworking and talented young woman subtly thwarts herself at every turn. That Michael suffered his injuries at birth and still shows vestiges of the intellect that would have been his exacerbates her extreme self-effacement. "I haven't been able to commit to anything or anybody because I know he would resent me even more bitterly than he does already," she says, as though she could regulate her brother's emotional state by lying low.

Sandy struggles to meet two contradictory and equally urgent demands: compensating her parents for their disappointment in her brother by being a perfect, self-sufficient and successful daughter, driven by the compulsion to achieve, and simultaneously protecting her brother from knowing about these accomplishments. Her own desire for self-expression gets buried somewhere in between. She tries to compromise by never letting herself do anything—at least overtly—that Michael cannot; ambition and compassion battle within her.

Sandy has found some ingenious ways around her dilemma: "I chose a women's college because he couldn't have gone there even if he could have attended college, so it was my own space." The campus had the additional advantage of being thousands of miles away, so she could conceal her achievements more successfully. After failing her driving test twice at home because she "felt so bad that he could never drive," she allowed herself to pass on the third try by taking the test far from Michael.

Geographic solutions like Sandy's are common; having the sibling out of sight puts him at least temporarily out of mind, and the person can feel freer to find herself without having to witness his resentment. Of course, since the sibling's image is still carried within, real and lasting separation occurs only when the control that the image exerts diminishes.

Sibling-related guilt is so compelling that normal children tend to attribute more of their conflicts to it than is actually the case and ignore other issues in their lives. Much of Sandy's anxiety is self-generated, so that even though she is now living in her "own space," she continues to restrict herself emotionally and intellectually for reasons that have little to do with Michael. She has yet to select a career and avoids getting seriously involved with any man—"I'm afraid to date because he can't," she explains; her brother's distress, while real, is also a convenient excuse. Like many healthy siblings, she is so obsessed with dealing with her afflicted brother that she has not paid sufficient attention to problems that are only superficially related to him; many young women with successful brothers—or no brothers—have paralyzing fears of intimacy and trouble defining their professional identities. The problems with Michael are serious and real, but they are not the only problems Sandy faces.

Sandy's anxiety increases as her desires for a relationship and for creative outlets get stronger and harder to resist. If she is to fulfill herself, she must accept a painful but ultimately comforting fact that every normal sibling must face: even if she accomplishes nothing, she has already surpassed her brother because she has a fully functioning brain and he never will—the "damage" is done. One manifestation of grandiosity is to imagine that you are more central to a brother's self-esteem than you really are; another is to believe that you would be problem-free without him. Sandy's brother probably has a greater influence on her feelings than she has on his. Since he will feel bereft and envious whatever she does—and probably not as much as she projects onto him—in the words of Dorothy Parker, she might as well live.

Internalized guilt about success can last a lifetime, long after a sibling could be directly affected. Once a sense of nonentitlement becomes part of a person's identity and set of assumptions about the world, it is extraordinarily hard to shake. Fifty years after Maggie Payne's embittered, enraged sister stopped talking to her for refusing to make her maid of honor, Maggie still hides her light under a barrel. As if to protect herself retroactively from her sister's envy, Maggie never feels pride in anything she accomplishes. "I made a killing in the stock market, but I couldn't enjoy it or even acknowledge it," Maggie confessed, as if her "killing" had actually killed someone. "I didn't tell anybody. It's as if nothing of mine has any importance. I need to see myself as a person who doesn't have anything, and if I do achieve something, it's got nothing to do with me—all the good things about my kids I attribute to them. My mother told me I was responsible for my sister's misery and I believed her, but I think I would have felt it anyway—my sister was paranoid, friendless, and depressed and extraordinarily envious of everything I did."

Not only what siblings say but what parents convey makes people like Maggie feel undeserving of a good life. They must watch their self-defeating attitude and work constantly to counteract the deep-rooted convictions that interfere with their appreciation of what they create, in difficult circumstances.

Many healthy siblings imagine that they can help a sibling succeed or at least prevent a failure by holding themselves back, but this is clearly impossible when the person has committed a terrible crime. Law-abiding brothers and sisters can feel compelled to self-destruct, as if to repent for crimes they should have been able to prevent. Kinship makes them involuntary participants.

Marilyn Daniels was the only stable influence on her younger brother Sam; their parents were violent alcoholics who virtually abandoned both children. Marilyn, like Manny, was lucky in her personality and labored to make the best of her natural advantages; "I always had an easier time in life than he did—I don't know why," she said. She remembers constantly getting Sam, an intelligent but wretchedly lonely, hyperactive child, out of scrapes that became more frightening as he got older: "I always had him in tow, and he was angry all the time." The only member of her extended family who was not a felon, she was the stable, hardworking, reliable one; he was a drug addict by the time he was fourteen. When she could no longer cope with Sam's escalating violence and criminality, Marilyn left town and worked her way through college. She had had only minimal contact with her wayward brother for several years when she heard a chilling report on the radio:

> The announcer said a policeman had been killed in a drug bust downtown, by a guy carrying a .38. For some reason I knew it was Sam—he was twenty-three at the time. I took all my clothes off, took two showers, dressed again, and drove around aimlessly for hours.

Just as Manny preferred to feel guilty over his brother's woes rather than accept his inability to reverse them, Marilyn's actual inability to prevent the murder was less tolerable to her than a fantasized culpability for it. She felt her destiny was linked to Sam's, that somehow she shared responsibility for his crime—and that she too had to pay:

> Part of my DNA did that. I felt I was implicated—even though I understand I couldn't have stopped him, I still feel somehow I should have—if only I'd stuck around a little bit longer.

Marilyn had been on her way to class when she heard the news, but she never made it back. "I skipped out of my finals—I tried not to drop out of school, but I couldn't. I drank and smoked for two years." She could not bear to succeed when her brother had failed so disastrously. As if to prove their resemblance, she punished herself by unleashing on herself a less lethal form of the destructiveness he had turned on another. She not only hid her light, as Maggie did; she almost extinguished it. The more disastrous the failure, the more extreme is a sibling's reaction.

For the first three years of his fifty-five-years-to-life sentence, Marilyn sentenced herself to rehabilitate Sam. To atone for the "crime" of abandoning him, she sent Sam money and books about "religion, psychology, and success" and went into debt to pay his appeal lawyer's retainer; "I still believed I could be his savior," she said. Then she had a dream that granted her permission to take care of herself once again:

> I dreamed that he decided to change careers, that he'd get another job in jail—that there would be some change, that he'd actually have some choices. It made me cry. Afterward I started to allow myself to do things.

Prior to this dream, Marilyn had seen her brother as the prisoner of his fate; now she understood that he had choices, even in jail. Because she believed that their fates were linked, this was her way to relieve herself from annihilating guilt; she could return to college and feel she had a right to prosper. Even profoundly damaged siblings are responsible for their actions and can exercise their wills; recognizing this reality gives their relatives permission to exercise their own wills.

To finally have your home, your parents, or your life to yourself when a sibling is institutionalized or dies is another dreadful victory—one that almost cost Jennifer Martin her life. Jennifer, who had accidentally discovered that her violent but talented brother's degenerative disease would eventually kill him, once screamed at him, "I wish you would hurry up and die," when he beat her and seriously considered suicide afterward. "I must be a monster for hating him," she remembers feeling. "How could I want him to die when he was going to die? Therapy helped me realize that anybody in my position feels like that, and I just voiced it." Jennifer and her brother were partially reconciled by the time he died, after great suffering. "His death was a relief to the whole family, even though they were shocked when I admitted it out loud," she said, finally accepting the excruciating mixture of relief, pity, and guilt that anyone would feel, without hating either her brother or herself.

As trying as it was to live with the sister who ate her homework, it was devastating to lose her. Jackie Hanson recalled the awful moment when her mute, hyperactive almost-twin left for the group home where Jackie knew she would spend the rest of her life. "I had promised her she would never have to go," Jackie said, "and here I was going back on my word, although it couldn't be helped and she ended up much happier there." A woman whose retarded brother blasted the radio at dawn daily wept when she saw the expression on his face as he signed the papers that would send him away for good, even though she greedily anticipated the quiet. However much havoc a deeply damaged sibling wreaks, it is hard not to believe that the freedom and comfort you enjoy when he departs are bought by an innocent person's imprisonment.

Normal siblings face a formidable task from which others are exempt: to succeed when their closest relative fails. They must embrace the fortunate yet tragic accident that no action of theirs can alter: that they were born with the undeserved advantage of a sounder mind or body—that they are the normal ones, fated to live a normal life. Simply being whole is the darkest victory of all.

They need to learn that, despite their competitive urges, they have not intentionally built their good fortune on the ruins of another's. They have to understand that self-expression and fulfillment are inalienable rights that having a dysfunctional sibling does not require them to forfeit. Feeling this freedom involves learning to tolerate guilt, accept limitations, and recognize that their victories, however dark, defeat no one. They are hard-won, legitimate achievements worth celebrating.

chapter 9

Passing Caliban On: Normal Siblings as Parents

PEOPLE ALWAYS TRY to make different mistakes than their parents, and they always fail. As parents, normal children are especially prone to repeating sibling experiences; their reactions to their own children combine how their parents behaved and how they felt as siblings themselves. Like all parents, normal siblings pick particular offspring to be new editions of their own brothers and sisters—the more troubled the tie to the originals, the more involuntary and arbitrary the projection. Despite their best efforts, they perpetuate past family patterns in unexpected ways; the actors change, but the script remains the same.

Anxiety that their new family will recapitulate their old one can be quite conscious; one woman said, "My brother represents all the fears I would have if I had children." It is no accident that a disproportionate number of normal siblings choose not to reproduce.

Although your children do not have to be disabled to evoke painful feelings about damaged siblings, having a troubled child of your own after you grew up with one feels like déjà vu all over again. It is impossible to avoid reliving the original emotions—especially the ones you carefully erased the first time around.

Barbara Green fled the scene after her beloved brother, only one year her senior, committed suicide at twenty-two. She doesn't even remember the date he asphyxiated himself in the very car in which he had taught her to drive. "I never asked about the details," Barbara admitted with barely detectable distress twenty years later. "I'd bailed several years earlier as his mental illness became serious. The night he died I took the car and drove away into my own life—I became the wild child, doing drugs and going to clubs to blot it out." Her behavior, so seemingly callous, was actually an attempt to keep herself from following him into despair or death, a protective shield of disconnection common in victims of trauma.

But Barbara can flee her past no longer because her children are forcing her to relive it; she has not only a son who resembles her brother but also a daughter, one year younger, who reminds her of herself. She pointed to their picture on her desk at the advertising agency she runs—a serious-looking boy of eight and his far brasher little sister, who has her mother's keen eyes and energetic stance. "I see how reserved he is, and it scares me," she said. "His teacher says he seems depressed and sad. He was so quiet when I took them on vacation recently. My daughter is more like me—I see her repeating the pattern with my son." History seems to be recycling, and she cannot stop the process.

Barbara is terrified of failing her son as she thinks she failed her brother—a universal fear among surviving siblings who become parents. Engulfed in her own tragedy, she cannot distinguish between the responsible parent she now is and the helpless younger sister (with irresponsible parents) she used to be. She does not realize that she has resources as a mature adult that she lacked as an overwhelmed twenty-one-year-old—the power of insight, and the will and courage to explore the horror she has buried for so long. Although she cannot prevent herself from reliving with visceral immediacy what was once unbearable, her relationship with her children offers her an opportunity finally to work through these emotions and lay them to rest.

Like every normal sibling, Barbara must reexperience her own anguish—as well as her guilt, anger and feelings of impotence—to protect her children from the fallout. Then she can discover that a depressed son, with an attuned mother, need not relive the tragedy of a suicidal brother. She needs to identify her compulsion to save her brother retroactively through her son. This could take a variety of forms; she may compensate by overprotecting him or by trying to force her daughter to be more involved with her brother than Barbara was with her own. She should also prepare to experience a wrenching anniversary reaction when her children reach the same ages that she and her brother were when he took his life.

"I don't have a model for how to be a good sibling or parent," Barbara lamented. Fortunately self-knowledge can teach her what she needs to know to be the latter and help her see that her concept of what the former entails was impossible to achieve. The best way to keep her son alive and her daughter sane is to explore her own feelings as fully as possible; the more a normal sibling exposes her hidden past, the less she will act it out.

Having a traumatic sibling relationship is not only a tragedy; it is also an opportunity for insight that can profit the next generation; knowing your vulnerabilities can help you manage them. Maggie Payne, the financial adviser whose refusal to make her hostile sister her maid of honor provoked a fifty-year feud, was determined that her children have a different experience. "The most important thing to me was that my three children be friends and love each other—something I missed all my life," she said, holding back tears. "This still is a tremendous area of sadness for me." She knows that bending over backward to provide a healthier atmosphere in the home she created caused its own problems: "I wasn't allowed to show anger as a child since my sister always did, and it wreaked havoc with my kids—I didn't like them being angry because the hostility was just overwhelming in my house." In her zeal to keep her children from behaving like her sister (and herself), she squelched even their normal aggression. Knowing what she did and why did not entirely prevent Maggie from making mistakes, but it helped her lessen their impact. Her sorrow about the failure of her own sibling relationship is diminished by the pride she takes in helping her children feel love rather than hate for one another.

Just as awareness limits the psychological damage an abnormal sibling causes, obliviousness perpetuates it. Normal siblings who excise all negative feelings toward their own parents tend to treat their children as they themselves were treated; maintaining an air-brushed version of their own family life causes them to oppress their normal children by requiring sacrifices never recognized as such. They demand the same premature maturity that was expected of them and so perpetuate the Caliban Syndrome. Intact siblings who get the subliminal message that they must copy their parents' mode of caretaking in order to be loved pass this attitude on. Becoming their parents' posthumous surrogates vis-à-vis a sibling is a foregone conclusion rather than a considered, difficult decision. A lack of ambivalence about the huge sacrifice that lifelong caring for a seriously debilitated relative entails is always suspect and has repercussions in the next generation.

Paul Morrison is oddly free of resentment toward parents who never figured out what was wrong with his seriously disturbed and disruptive brother, nor got proper treatment or investigated placement for him, let alone considered the impact their abdication had on their healthy son. "My dad assumed that kids were taken away if you pursued aid, and that frightened him, so he didn't do it to avoid a heart-wrenching separation," Paul explained. He discovered only last month, at age thirty-eight, that his brother was actually autistic rather than retarded as he had always thought. "As a kid I just knew he was different, and I never tried to find out why—I took my cue from my parents," he said. He considers his father a model of noble self-sacrifice, ignoring the fact that his behavior irreparably harmed the child he was ostensibly trying to protect.

Paul is still taking his cues from his parents. "I told them at an early age that I'd look after my brother. They put no pressure on me—I was a very responsible little tyke. My life was programmed for this from the beginning," he says matter-of-factly, never wondering who wrote the "program." "I told my wife that he'd always live with me."

A son who feels required to carry out his parents' unexpressed commands to devote his life to his brother's care must deny the severity of the disability and the sacrifice it entails. Even though Paul confessed that his reaction, every time he visits his parents' home, is "Gosh, I thought he was better than this," he feels compelled to recreate the circumstances he grew up in; when informed that good group homes exist for people like his brother, he said, "I don't care to know that." Asked whether spending their childhood with a massively dysfunctional uncle could harm his children, his response was a combination of moral uplift and death wish: "It would broaden them, and maybe I'll outlive him so they won't have to endure it." Like his father, he blinds himself to the toll his resolution will take on everyone involved; being a brother counts more than being a father. Having been made a martyr himself, he intends to make his own children martyrs too.

The problem with Paul's decision is that it is no decision at all but a compulsion that amputates all negative feelings. Had he researched alternatives, consulted his family, and acknowledged the problems they all faced, he could have chosen to have his disabled relative share his home—if he could also afford to make provisions for his brother's care. This would have been a difficult but tolerable situation as long as other members of the family were not coerced into being responsible for his brother at the expense of their own lives and emotions.

Parents need their children to see the world through their eyes; the more disturbing and precariously held the view, the more threatening a contrary perspective can be. Sarah Lattimer is surprised and dismayed that her own three children, all normal, have a more negative attitude toward her deaf-mute, hyperactive, violent sister than she does. She cannot understand why they refused to be counselors at the same camp for the severely handicapped where her parents arranged for her and her two able-bodied siblings to spend every summer as teenagers, or why they are less than enthusiastic about visiting their aunt or taking her out in public. "My parents always encouraged us to take her out, because that's what we're fighting for," Sarah said. "I'd boldly walk her through the grocery store—this was my cause. It's funny that my kids don't have the same attitude; it upsets me."

Sarah's parents were missionaries, whose belief that "God has selected our family as a special place for Mary" helped them cope with the tragedy of their eldest child's massive disabilities. Although Sarah insists she "didn't miss out on childhood," she described scenes that would try a saint—hours of daily caretaking that took her away from extracurricular activities, never being allowed to have friends over, forgoing all family outings and celebrations, having no claim on her parents' attention. "They were advocates for accepting that this was your lot in life," Sarah explained uncomplainingly. The Lattimers' attitude sanctified their sacrifices, but also made it inconceivable—even sinful—for their daughter to object to being saturated in a culture of disability. A daughter who is emmeshed in her parents' view of the world expects nothing less of her own children.

Sarah thinks of her own family as a continuation of her childhood experience; "We're a family of five, just as my family was," she noted. She too is deeply religious and, like her parents, considers herself an advocate of "this is your lot in life." When her children express what she was forbidden even to feel, she becomes anxious and uncomfortable and is likely to communicate more displeasure than she realizes. Although she insists—and truly believes—that she "puts the children first," she is also convinced that carrying on the Lattimer family mission to put her sister first is a fundamental and universal moral duty.

Sarah embraces her family's attitude unquestioningly and wants to recapitulate it; ironically, a pattern can repeat itself even when a healthy sibling bends over backward to repudiate a parent's behavior, often in ways that the sibling fails to recognize. When Jane London discovered that one of her daughters had a serious stuttering problem, she was determined never to turn the child into a helpless invalid as her mother had done with her socially awkward sister; she also resolved that her normal daughter would never be saddled with a troublesome sister as she herself had been. She is keenly aware that her own mother—an unhappy and isolated woman—had always identified with and preferred her sister. "My impaired daughter has the same coloring as her aunt, whom my parents treated as a frail, damaged kid," Jane said. "So I never let her say, 'This is hard for me,' because I didn't want her to feel entitled to whine or be a weakling. I didn't want her to be a cripple like my parents made my sister."

These motives seem rational and in the child's interest, but there is another, less conscious, and more harmful side; in her fervor to protect her healthy daughter from being "shortchanged," Jane shows as clear a preference for one child over the other as her own mother did, rejecting and criticizing her struggling daughter in favor of the one who, like herself, "does well." It is embarrassing for her to admit that she prefers the child who resembles her; she would be shocked to realize that she is behaving much more like her mother than she ever intended.

Relationships with damaged siblings reverberate through many generations, including those not yet born. When normal children become parents, they may find to their dismay that by trying to avoid one kind of trouble, they have caused another.

Issues provoked by damaged siblings have affected at least three generations of women in the Goodman family. Cindy Goodman was the invisible sister whose older brother was not only physically deformed by a cleft palate but was also brilliant and was preferred by her mother for both reasons. All her life she felt that her claims to attention "never measured up" to either his abilities or his disabilities. When Cindy became the mother of a schizophrenic son and a younger unimpaired daughter—replicating her own family constellation—she was determined that her daughter not suffer the same fate. "I paid lots of attention because with me none was paid," Cindy said. "My parents were so lacking in compassion for me. I have to make sure that just because my daughter's not handicapped her life is as important as my son's." She showed empathy and concern to preserve her daughter Amy's autonomy, repeating several times that she "must pay attention" to her. The attention included shielding Amy from the worst details of her brother's psychotic episodes. "I keep her appraised of what's happening with him, but I don't go into specifics so as not to diminish her own experience—I turn to friends instead," she explained, demonstrating rare sensitivity and self-control in dreadful circumstances. Cindy is proud of the independence and self-esteem that she has fostered in Amy. "She is so much different from me—and I like that," she said.

I got a dizzyingly different picture from Amy, who is thirty-five and pregnant with her third child. According to her, Cindy had indeed avoided making her invisible—and had made her feel perversely preeminent instead. Her guilt, her resentment, and her oppressive sense that she is responsible for her mother's emotional stability is intense and utterly unsuspected by Cindy. Amy agreed that attention was paid, but only so that she could focus on Cindy, who, having been ignored by her own mother, needed to be the real center of attention for her daughter. Their mothers' demands may have diverged, but Amy, like Cindy before her, feels she never measures up to them. Though the mother and daughter do differ, some of their underlying issues are identical.

Amy knows how crushing Cindy's centrality in her life—and how conditional her love—has felt. "I always thought it was my responsibility to take care of her emotionally, to make up for my brother," she said, "and I was always afraid she'd cut off contact if I didn't please her. I worry about how every decision I make will affect her, like I have no right to do anything independently."

Recently Cindy has been making a particularly onerous demand on Amy—one she never mentioned to me. "She's putting blatant pressure on me to move back home, constantly sending my husband job announcements," Amy said. Since she already visits home more frequently than she wants to and has no desire to live there, opposing her mother's wishes is trying her sorely: "I've needed to be physically present, to make up for what he can't provide—who else does she have? I have her only grandchildren. I've felt like an only child."

Amy is still struggling to separate from Cindy, but meanwhile she too is determined to pay attention to her own children's needs as hers were not; bearing the burden of her mother's happiness without the support of her only sibling makes her want to guarantee that her children do not suffer the same fate—so she has conceived a spare sibling for them. "It would really have been nice to have had another brother or sister and not feel as isolated as I did when he got sick," she explained. "There seems to be lots of support among siblings. Having three will be better for them because they'll feel less pressure—I want that for my kids." So intent is she to retroactively remedy her own life that she cannot imagine that even her idyllic solution could create other problems. Her children, despite her efforts, may never be as close as she desires. She could unduly favor the "insurance policy" baby who represents the perfect sibling she herself wanted to rely on, or reject it if it fails to meet her expectations; assigning a role to a child in utero, irrelevant to its actual qualities and realities that are always different from yours, is a tricky business. And Cindy may have more of a sense of how her own history is getting played out than she realizes; despite her sincere desire to "protect the next generation," she confessed to me, "I tried not to recreate my own family, but in some ways I did it anyway."

Some normal siblings, like Maggie and Cindy, go to any lengths not to repeat their parents' errors; others, like Paul and Sarah, think their parents made none. Like Barbara, all of them dread seeing their damaged siblings' faces reflected in the faces of their own children—and they always will. Their fear is a deflected manifestation of the fear of contagion, a symptom of the Caliban Syndrome. How can they limit the extent to which they pass Caliban on?

Accepting that to some degree you are inexorably bound to reproduce at least part of the essence if not the form of your original family relationships, and not only in ways you consciously choose (or wish), is a crucial step. This involves giving up the grandiose notion that you can change history. No human being can control everything—the unconscious is particularly recalcitrant to such efforts—but self-knowledge gives you a huge advantage. Question your own agenda, inquire into your own motivation, and do not expect your children to fix your past. Above all, listen to your children and be aware of the universal tendency to fit them into molds and roles that meet your needs rather than theirs. Think about the impact your sibling has on you and how your parents dealt with each of you, including hidden dimensions; pay special attention to what you do not want to know. The deeper your knowledge of your own past relationships with Caliban, as the secret repository of your hopes and fears, the less you and future generations will be condemned to repeat them.

PART III

A Life of One's Own

chapter 10

My Brother's Keeper

"WHO WILL TAKE CARE of my brother when my parents are dead?" is the question, literal or metaphoric, that haunts every normal sibling. From the able-bodied brother who refuses to work to the mentally impaired sister who neither sees nor speaks, abnormal siblings provoke soul-searching in their kin. If her disability is incapacitating, should you institutionalize her, pay for her care, or let her move in with you? If your relationship with him has been aversive since childhood, must you maintain at least minimal contact simply because he is your closest relative or because your mother asked you to? What degree of involvement does conscience require and convenience permit? Try as you may, you can never simply forget about such a sibling. Must you be your brother's keeper, however *keeping* is defined? Even asking the question makes you suspect; after all, Cain had already murdered his brother Abel when he asked it of God.

Guilt is rarely absent from the thoughts of healthy adults about their damaged siblings because no amount of devotion or care can make the damaged whole or blot out the dark victory of their own normality. Expectations of parents and a sense of duty, as well as love, compassion, and ignorance of humane alternatives, cause some to assume excessive responsibility for siblings in dire need; the "blood is thicker than water" mentality binds others even to those they dislike and do not have to care for directly.

Whether they embrace caretaking as a mission or categorically refuse it; whether they struggle with the conflict between theirs and the other's needs or make an uneasy truce, siblings of the abnormal are forced by accidents of fate to deal with a dilemma that nobody else has to think about. Contact with them can run the gamut from the occasional check or strained phone call to around-the-clock tending. Intact siblings are never free from worry or self-recrimination no matter what they do; those who insist that they were "programmed for this [total responsibility] from the beginning" doubt themselves as much as those who assert that "I would kill myself or him if I had to take him in." These concerns rarely get discussed because they seem so shameful.

Years before they are likely to be called on to take over caring for their seriously disabled siblings as their parents expect them to do, Jack Morelli and Sandy Wilson are losing sleep over their anticipated burden. How will they recreate the carefully constructed environments in which their misguided but dedicated parents have cocooned their fragile children? How could they refuse to try?

When I asked Jack, a thirty-four-year-old actor, about his reclusive older sister Margaret's fate after his parents' death, his voice trembled with anxiety. "Oh my God, that's all I think about," he told me. "I've lain awake nights starting at age thirteen worrying—what is she going to do?" Worrying about what he is going to do with her causes Jack even more insomnia; Margaret, whose condition has never been diagnosed, dropped out of high school and has lived with her parents ever since: her only short stint working—in a fast-food restaurant—came to a devastating end when the other employees locked her in the basement as a practical joke. "She spends her life in isolation, watching TV and collecting artifacts from 1963," Jack said, equally cognizant of the pity and annoyance she evokes in him. "She ruins everything at home. My parents tolerate this—that's the way they cope. Only in my twenties did I realize that they're part of it, that her situation is their fault; she gives my mother a sense of purpose, and my parents think that by spoiling her, they're providing for her. When I try to talk to them about her future, they say, 'God will take care of her.' How can they say that? Everything is so regimented—how can I reproduce it? I worry that this fragile house of cards will topple."

Instead of resenting his parents for designating him God's factotum, Jack worries about recreating a protected atmosphere for Margaret. But by refusing to discuss or to plan for their daughter's future beyond naïve assertions of faith, they abdicate their responsibilities toward both their children—an all-too-common scenario.

Although Jack admitted that this plan might be "too hopeful," he thought he might be able to install Margaret in an apartment down the street and pay her bills. Like many intact siblings, he intermittently denies the full extent of his sister's disability and minimizes the amount of care she requires because he cannot stand the implications for his own life; to know the truth would make him feel even more guilty, anxious, and angry. It is also hard for him to take a stand against his parents' implicit wishes and refuse to take over for them. "I feel inextricably bound to them all, and I wish I didn't," he says. "We'll probably have to live together someday, so I wouldn't want to have a child—it would be another person to be responsible for. Other people don't have to worry about this as young adults." There was, though, a glimmer of possibility beyond resigning himself to a life as constricted as his sister's: "I have to learn to realize that even if I move to South America they won't combust." Jack also has to learn that they won't combust if he lives in this country either.

"I saw an article in the paper about the three issues we normal siblings face," said twenty-seven-year-old Sandy, whose brain-damaged, paranoid older brother Michael cannot hold a job and refused to move into an apartment his parents found for him because the Disney Channel was not available there. "First it's making friends and bringing them home, then it's romance, and then it's aging parents. I feel like a statistic—my course is plotted till I'm sixty!" The course Sandy claustrophobically foresees leaves no room for her own wishes; she already stifles them, ostensibly to avoid Michael's jealousy. "My parents won't consider an institution, and they don't plan for the future," she told me. "My mother constantly asks me to reassure her—'You'll take care of him, won't you?' It's definitely expected. I'm forced to accept their agenda, or I'd be letting everyone down." The tension in Sandy's voice, in her slight body and prematurely serious expression, is palpable as she speaks, stifling sobs; she seems almost physically weighted down by a fate that is as unbearable as it is inescapable.

Most normal children are so caught up in their own guilt and their parents' blinkered expectations that they never question what is actually in the best interest of the disabled; to consider other options besides providing care themselves seems selfish and cruel.

Sandy, however, charges that devoting her life to her brother would not only oppress her but isolate him. Unlike Jack, she recognizes the severity of her sibling's problems. "My parents have an image of him and an image of me, both of which are actually their projection. I've suggested for years that he should be with other brain-injured people, and they refuse, but when he went to a group on his own, he enjoyed it. They are denying him his peers; he's more social than they are, and less functional than they think he is. Why is our culture so group home–phobic?"

Other intact siblings express little of the ambivalence or angst that oppresses Sandy and Jack. Religious faith, moral codes, filial or fraternal devotion—as well as less lofty motives like self-punishment or avoiding other relationships—prompt them to regard caretaking as their mission in life. They are guardians and proud of it.

Sarah Lattimer's attitude toward directing her massively handicapped sister Mary's care is so low-key that she wondered if her story was relevant to this book. "I'm a matter-of-fact person," she explained, "so when it fell in my lap, I surprised myself by rising to the occasion." With a combination of denial and calm acceptance, this daughter of missionaries says, "I don't feel it's had a tremendous impact on my life because it's just another thing—other people have fathers who travel all the time. My approach comes from my faith; I have to step up to it." Her religious convictions, as well as her identification with her own parents and her ability to suppress the natural ambivalence of anyone facing this burden, contribute to Sarah's "oh well, that's the way it is" mode of coping with Mary.

Compassion, culturally defined responsibilities, and unresolved emotional conflicts have caused Susan Kim to take up the role as her retarded brother's live-in guardian with a vengeance. "I'm the eldest daughter in a Korean family," said this successful but sorrowful businesswoman. "It's shameful to think you wouldn't want that responsibility, and I don't believe in doing anything half-assed." More than duty or perfectionism binds her to her brother: "My relationship with him is the best of everybody in the family. I'm not a patient person, but with him I am more so than with my normal siblings. It's a conscious effort on my part to be, and to work at being, understanding, open, and tolerant. You have to be thoughtful and respectful; check your ego at the door." Being self-effacing and steadfast for her brother is an important source of Susan's self-esteem; she prides herself on taking better care of Sam than their mother ever did. "I hired a teacher to help him, something she never thought to do," she said.

Susan does acknowledge, as Sarah does not, that her exertions take a toll: "My weight goes up and down, and the stress is physically manifested in rashes. I go home exhausted from always trying to do the right thing. It's the curse of being who you are—otherwise I wouldn't be proud of myself." She assumes that her herculean efforts are required because her brother would not flourish without them. In a group home, she is convinced, "he'd be miserable, locked up like an animal and drugged." There is something both grim and gallant in her uncompromising stance.

Many people assume that the only alternative to sacrificing their lives to care for damaged siblings is imprisoning them in a place like the Willowbrook Developmental Center, the huge, notorious institution for the retarded in Staten Island where, a 1972 exposé revealed, incontinent children were kept in pens like animals. In fact, most people I spoke to whose handicapped siblings live in the smaller group homes that now predominate praised their warm environments and caring staffs. "My brother has never been happier," they said. Finding the right setting is still not easy, but at least now it is often possible.

Concern for her brother's welfare and misinformation about community resources are not the only reasons Susan tends him at huge personal cost; her role as his protector provides her with an unassailably noble rationale for avoiding an intimate relationship with a peer. "Whomever I would choose would also have to be unusually patient and understanding to be involved with my brother," she insists, "and I haven't met anybody compassionate enough to even ask them the question." Caring for him serves her needs as much as his.

Living with a relative who needs constant attention is an engrossing and onerous responsibility that should never be undertaken without serious consideration of the consequences for your life and for those you love; no one should agree to it automatically. The motives of those who do take it on are never purely altruistic. Guardians usually have a hidden agenda—pleasing (or not disappointing) parents, deflecting intimacy, expiating guilt and hostility, structuring their own lives. Recognizing these normal feelings makes you a better caretaker, one less likely to inappropriately enlist others in the effort and more able to take care of yourself.

"I don't envy people whose parents don't plan," said Jackie Hanson, whose parents finally placed her homework-eating autistic sister Joan in a group home where she is "not unhappy." Jackie chose to become Joan's guardian after working through her intense feelings about her sister, with whom she had been psychically merged throughout childhood. "I visit once a month," she told me, "and it feels fine and voluntary, whereas before it felt like an obligation. Dealing with our relationship changed that; we're very close now." With luck and hard emotional work, it is possible to become a loving caretaker who is neither oblivious nor a martyr.

Sometimes, however, the only way to care for yourself is to refuse to care for someone else; working through intense feelings about the person does not necessarily make a good relationship possible. Not everyone can be, or should be, a brother's keeper. When siblings are overwhelming, abusive, relentlessly irresponsible, or simply unbearable, disengagement is the only prudent course of action—though rarely a conflict-free one for a brother or sister. "I can't ruin the family that I'm building," said a woman whose crushing guilt about her choice caused her to flee the country with her husband and child. Nonetheless, repudiating your responsibility for such a sibling can be self-affirming and in the interest of the impaired person.

Katie Clark's relationship with her volatile autistic brother was so aversive that she went to college three thousand miles away—a common ploy to create emotional distance from a problem sibling through geographic distance. "Staying home and having to deal with him made me panic," she said. When she returned, she reconsidered the foregone conclusion that she would take over his care—a role she had always dreaded but felt compelled to accept. Four years of separation gave her another perspective and altered how she defined both her duty and her brother's welfare. "I've distanced myself from my family even though I now live only an hour from them," Katie said. "Being away at college and talking to people there made me realize that support doesn't have to come from relatives. I can't maintain my own sanity and be his caretaker, although acting on this conviction induces a lot of guilt. People know what they can handle—if you know you can't and you do it anyway, you're doing a disservice to the other person. I wonder whether my parents are wrong to have my brother live at home—he might be better off if they found a residence. Since I've been back, I've talked to other people in my situation, and it's been a revelation how much happier a sibling can be there. This hadn't occurred to me before."

Charlotte MacDonald's very life depended on her declining guardianship for the violent, epileptic brother who had tried to strangle her when she was six. "At age nine," she said, "I made a pact with myself that if they made me come back and take care of him, I would kill myself." After her mother died several years later—her life shortened, Charlotte is certain, by the rigors of caring for her son—Charlotte prevailed on her father to find placement for him. This move, necessitated by tragic circumstances, proved the salvation of both siblings. "He's more functional than he's ever been," Charlotte said with palpable relief. "The staff at the home is very good, and we don't have to worry about what's going to happen when my father dies." Guardianship should never be an option when it would imperil the designated guardian's physical or psychological survival. It is no crime for your own life to come first.

In addition to yielding to family pressure or working out their own psychic conflicts, many siblings maintain masochistic relationships with impossible relatives because they confuse setting boundaries with abandoning the desperate. Even when they manage to cut off contact, they take the blame if the person self-destructs; guilt is always waiting in the wings.

After Nathan Kingsley's unsocialized borderline sister died of a drug overdose, he never forgave himself for setting limits with her. "Ten years ago I told her not to visit any more," said Nathan, displaying the portfolio of pictures of his sister that he carried everywhere. "She was so surly, nasty, and mean. I said, 'Stay away if you're not going to be decent.' I'd set her up in college, but she never could make a go of it—she fancied herself a radio star or a beauty queen. She was so different from everyone else in the family. My parents turned over their entire lives to her." Like his parents, Nathan made every effort to help his miserable and provocative sister, whose life was a revolving door of treatment programs, prostitution, and drug addiction, until he banished her because of her effect on his own children. "Dee Dee—she made up this name for herself—used to spend every New Year's with us, but being around her became too uncomfortable." Despite his sensible course of action, Nathan torments himself for letting his sister down. "I cut myself off from her—I could have done more," he said wretchedly. "I gave her refuge and never let her come back to it. I think I could have turned her around, and I ignored her." In his anguish Nathan fails to realize that his fantasy of saving Dee Dee makes him as grandiose as she was. Instead of punishing himself from being a heartless brother, he should commend himself for being a responsible father.

Children are not only the beneficiaries but frequently the agents who liberate their parents from sibling bondage; ironically, they most often serve this function for parents who promised their own parents that they would be caretakers for life. The "be nice to your poor sister" refrain does not stop in adulthood or even when the supplicants are dead. Since children suffer the consequences of chronic exposure to noxious aunts or uncles, they have legitimate grievances that parents can sometimes recognize more easily than their own travails. Children provide a jolt of reality, a fresh perspective, and a justification for a course of action that their elders would feel too guilty to pursue for themselves alone.

"My mother's biggest fear was that I wouldn't take care of my sister," said boutique owner Mimi Newhouse. "But why should I take care of a grown woman?" Mimi's sister—who had returned clothes she borrowed to Mimi's closet covered with pizza and overturned Mimi's fully set table at Thanksgiving—has not improved with age. Despite resentment that "she never got it together and can't keep a job," Mimi's sense of obligation (and residual discomfort about her own prosperity) made her periodically bail her sister out. "When I let her work in my store, she answered the phone with an edge in her voice and alienated my customers and employees." She also alienated Mimi's daughter, the manager. "My daughter said, 'It's her or me,' and then I finally fired her," said Mimi, with a combination of guilt and gratitude. "My mother left me my sister—and she reminds me of my mother. She makes me feel responsible. Why is this so hard?"

Disconnecting from taking care of an impossible sibling is so hard because it feels like you are betraying the parental trust that differentiated you from that sibling in the first place. Though parents may think otherwise, siblings have less responsibility for damaged siblings than their parents do—and parents would make arrangements if they had no normal offspring to rely on. From within a family it can be difficult to see that a sibling should not automatically come first, before your children, your spouse, your profession, or yourself.

Norman Albee calculates that he has given his wayward sister

$100,000 over the years, to no avail. He paid for her divorce, for her mortgage to prevent the bank from foreclosing on her house, and for a lawyer to keep her out of jail when she helped her daughter kidnap her own daughter, and he did it all without ever being thanked, at his mother's behest. "Everything was for my mother's peace of mind, because she asked me to look out for my sister after she died," said the dutiful son, now seventy years old. "We used to dread the phone calls. She's like a millstone trying to drag me under—you sink, but she'll survive." His own daughter saved his peace of mind by insisting he stop intervening; it took her thirty years to convince him. "She realized we'd had enough of my sister, and eventually I stopped taking her calls," he said, relieved that his daughter gave him permission to disobey his long-dead mother.

Recognizing that you have no control over a sibling's behavior, when that behavior has disastrous consequences, is horrendously difficult even if no parent is expecting you to remain involved. Janice Becker, who had fished her mentally ill sister out of the river, gravely accepted the truth. "There's nothing I can do. I can't bring her home and let the cycle start all over again with her stopping her medication. I feel anger because she is where she is and I am where I am, but no guilt, because everything I've got I've worked for—I tried to help above and beyond." Though Janice was rational and resolute, she still had tears in her eyes when she described seeing her sister, obese and in rags, begging for food in front of the church they had attended together as children. Even when guilt is gone, grief remains.

Lisa Masterson stopped "soup to nuts caretaking," including paying for her cocaine-addicted brother's rent and countless drug treatment programs, when his therapist instructed her to do so.

"It's the hardest thing to see him in pain, but no matter what I did, he was still in pain," she concluded. Fortunately, she found a way to fulfill her destiny as a "genetically engineered caretaker" by assisting those who could profit from her intervention: she helps raise the three children he fathered with three different mothers.

A sibling does not have to be flamboyantly or publicly dysfunctional to try the patience of his brothers and sisters and provoke them to sever the tie out of self-protection. Set designer Jim Brown's younger brother Dan started bouncing checks in college. In the subsequent thirty years Jim loaned Dan money, found him employment ("His attitude and ethics were such that they let him go—I felt bad for him and that I'd recommended him"), and encouraged him to go on interviews ("When I suggest anything, he screams at me"), but he never kept a job. Dan finally moved back into their mother's apartment, content to let her support him. "He doesn't want to work," Jim said bitterly. "It would take away from his time on the computer. He uses diabetes as an excuse now, but I have it too. Why should he depend on an elderly woman?"

Jim has come to realize that it is pointless or worse to try to assist his brother. "There's nothing I can do to make the situation better, and nothing I should do. You have to be able to talk and for the person to see there's a problem. I'd like to feel there's some way to help my brother and my mother, but I've given up trying. If I had to pay my rent, I'd dig a ditch, but he's guaranteed food and a roof, so why should he bother? My mother hasn't the strength to kick him out."

Once again an unresolved sibling issue in a parent's past reappears: "It's psychological backlash. My mother feels guilty for her own brother's actions—he abandoned his pregnant wife and never saw their son, so she has to bend over backward to be the antithesis of what he was."

Jim has dealt with his disappointment by distancing himself from his brother and mother's unhealthy relationship. "I used to care for him," he told me, "but I've stopped. I told both of them I would not support him after her death." He calls this technique "pain management": "I've lived with physical pain, and I work not to let it affect me. I compartmentalize that part of my life. This is psychological pain. It's really upsetting, so I try not to think about it, but I wouldn't be surprised if I'd put it somewhere where it's another color, another pressure. If I dwelled on it, I'd get depressed."

Jim's approach, while it takes considerable energy and is only moderately effective, is preferable to the harm he would do by implicitly condoning his brother's sponging. When coping with a troubled and troubling sibling, damage control is often the best you can do.

One way normal siblings deal with their often hopeless desire to make a difference to their damaged sibling is to generalize it by joining a helping profession; they are overrepresented in the ranks of therapists, doctors, nurses, and advocates and educators of the disabled. The pull to pursue these careers is so strong that one woman protested that she resented the assumption that she would "sign up" as a special ed teacher, as though she naturally fit the hereditary job description. Even then she could not entirely escape; she ended up writing books about therapy rather than conducting it herself.

"Ninety percent of my career choice was Johnny," said social work student Samantha Greenberg. Life with her oppositional, "extremely low IQ" brother had sensitized her to the plight of the disabled, and she decided to dedicate her professional life to helping people like him. But Samantha also expected to devote her private life to helping her brother; she is another dutiful sibling to whom it never occurred that there was any other option. "I always assumed his place should be with me and that whoever I'd marry would have to understand," she said, "until the other students in my class said, 'You're going to take this on?' They made me realize it's not something you automatically have to do."

Samantha's fellow students enlightened her both personally and professionally. "Before they questioned me, I thought, 'Who else is going to do it?' I felt a real family sense of duty; in a helping profession you don't do much asking about your own feelings. But now I'm considering the impact on my own family—and what if he wants to get married too?" The "revelation" she came to with her colleagues' assistance will be in the interest of Samantha's future family, as well as in the interest of the families she will counsel from a newly broadened perspective.

Although a career as a symbolic caretaker meets the needs of many normal siblings, it can also represent an oppressive continuation of the role forced upon them as too-responsible, prematurely mature children. Coming into your own may require leaving the profession as well as rejecting that role in private life.

Rebecca Ashford left social work and simultaneously cut off contact with her unmanageable learning-disabled brother when she realized that both "jobs" were making her miserable. "My profession was entirely determined by my position in my family," said Rebecca, who is now an illustrator. "My family was such a burden to me and always came to me as a mediator; I was in charge of my brother since I was sixteen years old, when my mother got cancer. I fought all his battles. He was an albatross around my neck. Social work was a continuation of that role in the rest of my life; helping is what I do—and I choose not to do it twenty-four hours a day anymore."

Rebecca had never questioned her life's work until recently. "It was all just obligation, and I didn't know it," she said. Nonetheless, even though Rebecca knows that she is making healthy choices, she plagues herself with recriminations on both fronts: "I no longer want the responsibility, but leaving social work was guilt-provoking; I couldn't shake the depression. I feel terrible that I can take care of everyone else but can't be there for my own brother. But I put in my years, and I'm paroled." Though she set herself free, Rebecca still feels like a criminal.

The most common reason siblings assume responsibility for abnormal relatives is to carry on what they believe is a family tradition of caring. In a surprisingly large number of cases, however, healthy children feel that they must remain involved with a brother or sister at no matter what personal cost precisely because their parents did not care.

"I couldn't live with myself if I abandoned my brother like our parents abandoned us," said Pam Lewis, a lawyer whose paranoid schizophrenic brother broke down her office door and presented a penis-shaped nutcracker to her young daughters. "I said to him, 'Our parents didn't do right by us, so let's make a pledge that we'll always be there for each other.'" Pam is frightened and repelled by her brother, who has been arrested for stalking, but she forces herself to maintain contact as an act of "fraternal obligation." "If I never saw him again as long as I live, I wouldn't care," she admitted. "I have no particular love for him and I don't even like him, but I have a responsibility to do all that's possible simply because he's my brother. I feel sorry for him—to reject him would make me a bad person. We were both rejected all our lives, so I'm sensitive to this; I've got to help him." But fraternal duty is not the only obligation in life: "Recently I've felt less anxious to be the good sister because he's becoming increasingly violent. I can't endanger and sacrifice myself or my children. In what degree am I my brother's keeper?"

Pam's question is inescapable, even for those who did not face the wrenching decision about whether to provide direct care. Siblings berate themselves relentlessly for what they feel as much as for how they behave; no matter how much they are provoked, they cannot forgive themselves for lacking proper brotherly or sisterly love. Shame and guilt about neglecting or rejecting a damaged sibling pursue them like furies.

Guilt-assuaging outings are a popular way to make restitution. Susan Kim steels herself for the week-long fishing trip with her retarded brother that she schedules annually. Political scientist Randy Lane was sickened by the intense relief he felt when he moved to a distant city and could no longer take his Tourette's-afflicted brother to the local amusement park "Every year, onerously, we used to go for the whole day, but it got too mortifying," he admitted. Randy can hardly bear his dual feelings of contempt and revulsion for his brother and for himself: "I blame myself for not doing more for him, especially since my father won't even go to fucking dinner with him." He feels like a failure as a human being because he lacks "the wonderful ability that some people, like the group home staff, have to not let it affect them at all." When I point out that compassion can be far easier to feel for someone who is not your brother, Randy says shamefacedly, "I should feel more because he is."

Those who cannot tolerate direct contact substitute the guilt-assuaging check. "I give gifts of money to all four of my brothers," said the only one who is not in jail; "it's empowering." In addition to providing occasional financial relief for his family members, this gesture reaffirms his superiority to them, which is always in doubt. But even hearing a sibling's voice is too much for some people; however obligated she feels, Diana Lamm cannot bring herself to return her psychopathic brother's birthday messages on her answering machine. "I know I should call him back," Diana says, "but I think of five million things I have to do including scrubbing the basement floor, so I can't. I ask myself if I should be taking care of him. Even if I wanted to, I don't know if I could. I'm so dissociated from him, he's like a stranger. It's almost like my brother's gone already." Like virtually everyone I interviewed, Diana never told her therapist—or anyone but her husband—about these feelings.

"I could pick up the phone, but he's so irritating," Rebecca Ashford said. "My brother has a way of grating on your nerves—a simple conversation is nails on a blackboard. I can't handle the frustration; I have no patience." Despite everything Rebecca did to assist him, she continues to blame herself for how he makes her feel. "The big unresolved issue I'll take to my grave is my failure as a sister. If only I could stand to make him feel like he has somebody, that he could talk to me once a week—he wasn't loved by my father. I used to wonder how I could stand to invite him if I got married, so I've decided I won't have a wedding."

Candy Fine, the pregnant copywriter who is so horrified at the prospect of dealing with her paranoid brother for the rest of her life that she is moving her family to France, despises herself for what she believes is cold cowardice. "When he was in the hospital, I went every single day. It was only twenty minutes away—I felt so guilty if I didn't that I couldn't live with myself."

Candy voiced a secret worry that afflicts the majority of normal siblings: "Do I love him because he's my brother, because he's a good person, or because I'm supposed to? I can't tell because I'm afraid it's the latter—and I don't want to think about it too much. If it were true, I'd be sorry for him—he needs people to love him, and he's not that lovable. This question comes to mind when it shouldn't—I feel so guilty that I can't sleep with my husband."

As in the biblical story, the normal ones are marked like Cain, doomed by sibling thought-murders to roam the world without respite. Their punishment is never to be permitted unadulterated joy.

chapter 11

The Caliban Syndrome I: Repudiation and Identification

THE CALIBAN SYNDROME AFFECTS every normal child—the invisible and the preeminent, the caretaker and the estranged, the insistent denier and the painfully conscious are all equally prone to it. Damaged siblings lodge deeply in the psyche, where they leave indelible marks on intimate relationships, even with the unborn.

Caliban is the sibling image that normal ones carry within, a potent fantasy derived from actual experiences, parental attitudes, and personal interpretations, that silently shapes the self.

The four symptoms of this syndrome affect everyone differently, but no one escapes:

premature maturity

Normal children grow up too fast. They are expected to shoulder too much responsibility for their siblings and themselves without complaint. As a result, they substitute spurious autonomy for "childish" dependency. If they internalize their parents' standards, they become masochistic and strangers to their own needs.

survivor guilt

Normal children are tormented by being (as well as relieved to be) forever better off than their siblings. They never feel fully entitled to happiness or power. Every achievement is tainted because it occurs in the shadow of one who can never compete. Knowledge of their undeserved advantages makes them prone to anxiety, self-sabotage, and the excruciating grandiose notion that any success of theirs exacerbates their sibling's failure.

compulsion to achieve

Normal children must succeed for two, both to compensate their parents for having a child who cannot fulfill their dreams, and to prove their own superiority and worthiness to themselves—qualities that are always in doubt. The pressure they feel breeds perfectionism, inordinate fear of failure, and the inability to relax and enjoy life.

fear of contagion

Dread of magically catching the disability plagues normal siblings. This fantasy originates in guilt that they were spared and shame that they have more in common with the damaged one than they want to admit. It leads to hypervigilance for signs of damage within the self and the secret conviction that normality is tenuous or a sham.

FEAR OF CONTAGION, the most insidious symptom of the Caliban Syndrome, has paradoxical manifestations: either repudiation or identification with the damaged sibling. The former—the course I chose—is a phobic attempt to excise the other's presence from your life or psyche; the latter is merger with the damaged one. Either you think you have nothing in common with the sibling, or everything.

In contrast, acknowledgment—the insight Prospero attains at the end of *The Tempest* when he says of Caliban, "this thing of darkness I/acknowledge mine"—integrates both repudiation and identification into the self. Normal siblings must feel the power of the Caliban Syndrome in order to transform it.

repudiation

"My sister is my model of what not to be" is a common, and frequently conscious, refrain for normal ones. Many devote their lives to what one called "setting myself in opposition." Striving to become, and to maintain yourself, as "not my sibling"—not fat, not friendless, not lazy, not crazy—is motivated by dread that the undesirable traits will "rub off" on you. Fear of contagion is so compelling that it even affects those whose siblings have genetic defects that they do not share; plenty of intellectuals worry about "waking up retarded like my brother." Whether contagion is impossible (no one acquires attention deficit disorder), unlikely (few sighted people go blind), or inevitable (everyone feels depressed on occasion), the source of the anxiety is being related biologically and psychologically to a damaged sibling.

In the dynamics that underlie *The Tempest,* Miranda needs to make sure everything Caliban-like within her stays in Caliban. Therefore she suppresses her lust, her hostility, and her yearning for independence—everything that is not what her father needs her to be. In the play she simply feels none of these things; in real life Mirandas have to work at it.

Molding yourself into the opposite of a problem sibling, the most common form of repudiation, creates a cordon sanitaire around the too-close-for-comfort catastrophe of the other's life. Externalizing the damage keeps the defects safely deposited in the sibling. But walls of psychic separation are hard to build and require constant maintenance. They are also never entirely impregnable.

Art historian Bob Mansfield is riveted by the numbers on his bathroom scale. Despite his striking presence, dashing wardrobe, and fine physique—which he spends three hours a day at the gym perfecting—he insists he has "no concept of how I look. It's a blind spot, even after thirty years of therapy." In an attempt to "always appear exactly the same at any given moment in public," Bob, a gourmet who also managed restaurants, has maintained his weight at precisely 168 pounds for years, "never deviating or fluctuating"; "I don't eat a lot," he said. A three-hundred-pound sister who is only one year younger ("we were sort of like twins") is the negative inspiration for this exacting regimen. "She's a constant reminder of what to not let happen—I say, 'I have none of that,' he explained. "I'm afraid of not being attractive and the limitation that that would present; I'm self-conscious about my weight to this very minute."

Although Bob is clearly aware that his single-minded pursuit of svelteness is a reaction to his sister's obesity, he does not link his compulsive exactitude with her; only when I pursued the topic did he remark that his sister was not only hugely fat but that her weight "fluctuated wildly." Nor did he relate his need to be a "model of self-discipline who feels pressure never to fail at anything" to his sister's abdication of self-control. Most importantly, this otherwise insightful man missed the common element in their characters: food rules them both. Obsession with embodying the opposite of a sibling always has its unconscious side.

A brother who is immobilized by despair is the cautionary example for publicist Karen James. "I don't like to be depressed," she said. "I want to get past it as quickly as possible. When I'm upset, I try to distract myself." Karen works so hard not to be paralyzed that she throws herself into activity; she forced herself to go out dancing the night she broke up with her boyfriend. "I realize how much my behavior has been defined by my brother," she says. Karen's technique, which in moderation would be a sensible antidote to inertia, is excessive and desperate. Any feeling that must be automatically neutralized because of sibling resonances can never be worked through.

"I'm in charge," asserts Dana Thompson. "I've worked so hard to become competent because I'm the only sane one in the family." Dana's whiny, self-involved, barely functional older sister—whom she already dreads having to spend holidays with after their mother dies—is her negative model. When her sister suggested that they were alike, Dana recoiled in horror: "I wanted to shout, 'I'm nothing like you, don't mistake this'"—a judgment she would not have had to deny so vociferously if she did not fear it was correct. Dana finds herself inordinately disturbed by any intimation of incompetence, however trivial. "I felt surprisingly defensive when the baby-sitter criticized my housekeeping," she said. "I know how hard I've worked to be different, but I never talked about this in therapy. There's much more here than I think about."

Those who insist that they are the absolute antithesis of a damaged brother or sister are always suspect; they behave as though admitting the slightest commonality would contaminate them. When asked what he had in common with the psychopathic sister he had bailed out financially for years, Norman Albee categorically dismissed the notion. "It's a night-and-day situation—we're two completely different personalities," he said huffily. "There is no emotional connection at all." He claimed that filial duty alone had prompted his largesse, which had stopped only when his daughter intervened; in fact, his need to demonstrate his superiority and underscore the differences had also prevented him from extricating himself from this oppressive obligation sooner.

"Do I see my brother in myself? Not in the least," Jim Brown responded to my inquiry. Jim, who had finally given up trying to find this shiftless man jobs after decades of frustration, was at pains to emphasize the contrast between them, even when the effort was costly. "I avoided applying for disability although I really needed it after my accident," he said. Earlier in their lives the distinction had been less clear. "We shared a room growing up," Jim said, "and it made me want to get away from home. I thought, 'That could be me—I want to make sure it's never me.' There are things you don't want to know." That his difference from his brother is tenuous was one of them.

Normal siblings anxiously scan their feelings and behavior—and even their appearance—for signs of the repudiated other. "I'm always afraid," said Mimi Newhouse, whose borderline sister had ruined her Thanksgiving. "Do I have this in my package? Is this why I've never been in a long-term relationship?" The very qualities they dread sharing have a way of showing up, like the siblings themselves, at the worst possible moment. When the connection can no longer be denied, a person's equilibrium can be seriously disrupted.

Jane London regularly reassured herself that she had nothing in common with the peculiar sister who had thrown herself down the stairs and whom she had frantically and unsuccessfully tried to introduce to men. "I used to think one of us was adopted," she said. "We just don't belong in the same family." Like a mantra, Jane repeated, "We look nothing alike." She made sure that they acted nothing alike either. "It's scary to have a sister who's just not making it. I pushed myself socially and professionally because I want to see myself as healthy and not debilitated like her." When Jane's husband deserted her and their three children, however, the carefully nurtured distinctions seemed to vanish. "I wondered why my marriage didn't work. This was very subterranean, but I thought, 'Here we are, two sisters, and neither of us is married.'"

Since Jane had reported dreaming that her pregnancy had caused her sister to commit suicide, I asked whether the divorce had made her consider taking her own life. "I did take an overdose then," she admitted with shame. Why had she omitted mentioning this obvious resemblance until pressed? "I probably wanted to keep it separate," she answered. "I'm so afraid of being like her that I was blind to the connection. I keep looking for differences because I don't want to see similarities. I tell myself that I've got it together. It's like a curse on our family that I could end up as lonely, lost, and empty as she is."

Fear of contagion causes a person to overgeneralize, to confuse having a character trait in common with being identical to a sibling, as though any drop of the other's pathology polluted the entire personality. The context of Jane's despair was far more circumscribed than her sister's and its impact far less serious; Jane regained her resilience, but her sister had none to recover.

Repudiators believe that their health and sanity are precarious and contingent on having nothing in common with the damaged sibling. They assume that their problems are not really their own, that their doom is borrowed from an external source. The fear of contagion is a failure to differentiate; the sibling's flaws feel like a malignant magnet that can suck you in (one man called it a "gravitational pull") rather than an aspect of shared history and personality that must be negotiated.

It is realistic not to want to be too closely associated with a sibling who does not function; being able to distance oneself is part of being the normal one. But feeling horror and self-loathing at any shared characteristic indicates major unfinished business with the sibling and the self; to hate or fear the one is to hate or fear the other.

As a young child, Sharon Bergman was sexually molested by her deeply disturbed older sister. Although Sharon has had no contact with her tormentor for years, she still feels invaded by her. Even seemingly benign traits in common seem ominous. "If I ever see that my handwriting resembles hers or hear something similar in my voice, it gives me a tiny 'oh my God' feeling," she said. "She had a hand tremor, and sometimes my hands shake. I don't want to see that in myself. I picture myself as being so distinct from her, making such different choices." Sharon fears that all her efforts at differentiating herself are in vain, and what she sees makes her physically ill. "I'm practiced in being streamlined, in creating a nice, sleek shell, a sense of polish, but when my hand shakes, I think, 'This is a crack; nasty stuff might seep out.' At the edge of my brain I have a feeling that something in my core is damaged or stinking or repellent. I don't want to have any of her characteristics—it would mean I have some piece of me that's crazy like her."

Sharon still feels like her sister's victim. To free herself, she must recognize that the "nasty stuff"—her own perversity and her desire to exploit the helpless—is her own, no matter what the original source. She also needs to add the category "different but with things in common" to her emotional vocabulary.

Carrie Grainger is a lovely young woman with a glamorous career in the fashion industry, but she lives in terror that she will become schizophrenic—or that she already has the telltale signs. "I worry that somebody will turn me a certain way and spot my defect," she confessed. "For example, I'm shy on the phone, so I make it very quick. I'm seen as cold, but really I need to hang up so I don't screw up. It's not wanting to be found out." Carrie's adored brother, who was only a year younger than she and with whom she had shared a bedroom for twelve years, had a breakdown at seventeen from which he never recovered. She does not trust her reprieve. "I get heebed out if I'm not doing enough or I have quiet lazy days," she said. "I live in fear that like him I'll be fine, and then I'll get sick suddenly. There's a general feeling that things will fall apart any minute."

Carrie's emotional and physical closeness to her brother, as well as her guilt about distancing herself from him, exacerbate her fantasy that she must share his fate. Like many siblings of the mentally ill, she wonders whether she has really been spared and whether she deserves to be. "I didn't help him enough," she frets. "I went on with my life. I stopped missing him." Going mad herself would be a fitting punishment for repudiating him.

Boundaries with damaged siblings are disturbingly permeable. Their faces stare back at you from your mirror or from your child's face, and you see a nightmare version of your fate reflected in their ruined lives.

Jessica Kaplan's older sister Ricky had tenderly nurtured her when she was a baby, but envy later turned Ricky's love to hate. "I can't hold on to my good memories of my sister even though I have them because she turned on me so chillingly," Jessica said. "She terrifies me." It is not only the way Ricky treated her that chills Jessica; Ricky's treatment of her own child feels like a monstrous premonition. "She let her husband beat her daughter, and her son is a suicidal male prostitute. This is horrible—could I become as bad a mother as she? There are dangerous similarities between us. I could destroy my better life. Maybe that's why I want to stay away," she concluded. Understanding the purpose repudiation serves can diminish its power.

"I look at my sister Martha, and I see this total mirror of myself in her face, and I get embarrassed because I sound just like my sister Denise," said Ashley King, a dancer who is the only functioning member of her large and disreputable family. "It makes me feel so weird, like I've left my body. I get sick to my stomach. All I want to do is to show them that I'm not like them because they are such losers. It's difficult to realize they don't reflect who I am." Despite her siblings' visceral effect on her, Ashley struggles to disentangle her identity from theirs by talking rationally to herself and making efforts in her own behalf. "I'm such a hard worker—I take my profession very seriously," she said with justified pride. "I tell myself you can't choose your family, that I'm like them, but that I make different decisions."

Sibling contagion feels hereditary even if the disability is not congenital; believing oneself to be the bearer of bad genes is one form of repudiation. Diana Lamm is threatened by her brother's malign influence not only on her own sanity but on her son's. "When my son was born and people said he looked like Ron, it sent shivers down my spine," she said, as though her son were predestined to reproduce his uncle's life. Although Diana, a political speechwriter with a stable marriage and family, keeps her brother, a much-divorced alcoholic dentist accused of raping his patients, at arm's length, a creepy pronouncement of his reverberates in her brain. "He once told me, 'You're just like me—whatever I have, you have,'" she said. "So my every self-destructive streak or impulse makes me think, 'Am I playing out the family dynamic?' It haunts me." Her brother is trying to drag her down to his level by asserting a spurious identity between them, but Diana cannot see this because it jibes with her own worst fears.

Normal abnormal moments, the lapses of rationality that everybody experiences, are portentous for Diana as they are not for people without a sibling Mr. Hyde lurking in their psyche. "I'm so terrified of mental illness that I misinterpret the normal peaks and valleys people have. My husband doesn't feel it the way I do, it doesn't touch him," she said enviously. Hypervigilant normal siblings need to recognize the irrational origin of their fears for their children and themselves. It helps to have a mate who validates your sanity—even if he or she cannot empathize with your dread—and who neutralizes the malign influence of a brother's hateful wishes.

The greater the trauma, and the more successful the surviving sibling, the more she suffers from shame and fear of exposure. Barbara Green, the high-powered CEO of an advertising agency, had a wretched family history to hide. Her sister was severely retarded, and her older brother had committed suicide when she was a teenager. "My closets are so full," she commented. Her anxiety surfaced in a dream:

> I'm in Saks Fifth Ave, but I don't have my shoes on, and I don't want anybody to see. The floor is disgusting. I say to myself, "I'll just go and buy a pair"—but people will still know that I came in without them.

Even though she is now living a put-together life of Saks Fifth Avenue elegance and can afford to buy fancy shoes, there is no concealing that she came into the "store" barefoot. She can never effectively remove the evidence of her "filthy" past, the floor on which she walks. Covering up is not the answer for Barbara; she has to clean out her closets.

It is impossible to be fully aware of the power that repudiation exerts on your life choices; even women who make conscious efforts to remove themselves from pathological brothers end up inadvertently marrying men just like them.

Lawyer Pam Lewis, whose paranoid schizophrenic brother broke down her office door and gave her daughters the penis-shaped nutcracker, knew she was "attracted to the dark side" because of him. "I've always had friends who were mentally unbalanced or extremely weird," she admitted. Did the "bizarre man" she recently divorced remind her of her brother? Pam seemed taken aback at this question. "I always thought he resembled my crazy father, but gee, my husband's a lot like my brother, now that you mention it," she said. "I never made the connection."

I asked Lisa Masterson, the "genetically engineered caretaker" of her psychopathic, drug-addicted brother, if he reminded her of her psychopathic, drug-addicted former husband. She too "didn't connect" the two men. "I never saw any of James's tendencies because I have this heartbreaking problem with my brother John. I viewed him as more like me, somebody else who took care of everybody. He was my helpmate to help John. "Psychological thinking was never part of my world—awareness is so fabulously lacking in our society."

Although Lisa failed to see the similarity between her brother and her husband, she dwelled so anxiously on the potential similarity between her brother and any child of hers that she decided not to have any. "I'm deathly afraid to have a kid with a problem," she said.

Like Diana and many other normal siblings, she projected fears about sharing her brother's pathology onto the next generation.

REPUDIATION IS AN INTERNAL PSYCHOLOGICAL MANEUVER, a defense provoked by anxiety that the damage will infiltrate your personality. It is possible to repudiate a sibling you see every day, as I did. Estrangement and disengagement, in contrast, are the realistic responses of a normal sibling who recognizes that no healthy relationship with the damaged one is possible. Biology, even coupled with compassion and insight, may not be enough to sustain it.

Some siblings feel like changelings, beings from an alien universe. Their parents imagine that they took the wrong child home from the hospital. An unhappy combination of character traits, subtle disabilities of unknown origin, and family dynamics makes any common ground there ever was irretrievable; these siblings are too disturbed or too disturbing to have in your world. When efforts to reach them fail, normal ones are left with a void where a brother or sister ought to be.

"He has a different vocabulary for life" is the way Candace Peters describes her peculiar brother, who was one of those boys who relates more to electronic gadgets (and later to computers) than to people. "He never wanted to be part of the family," she said. "He was never there in the first place—he had nothing to do with our lifestyle. Everything about him was strange. I can't imagine it any other way. My mother says, 'I don't know where he came from—and you're just like me,' and my father tried to tolerate what he couldn't make sense of." Candace, a hard-driving investment banker, is "completely estranged" from this "shut-down, dyslexic oddball" who barely supports himself and continues to sow dissension, as he did when he was an assaultive, alienated child.

Candace "attempted to rectify" the family feud that her brother provoked years ago, but to no avail. "Every year I used to send him a birthday card telling him the news, which he never answered. He never acknowledged my daughter's birth." Now she is not indifferent to him, but she accepts that there can be no rapprochement. "Why would I go back to get something I'm never going to get?" she said. "My disconnection from him is so powerful that I've disconnected from it. I imagine it's all about pain. He doesn't have the means to work through his problems. I'm sad that he's paralyzed in his fear and that that is all he can do. I feel he isn't in my family anymore."

Candace was struck by how many women of her acquaintance have similar situations with their brothers. "In my investment group, everyone has a difficult brother, everyone is the biggest money maker in the family, and nobody talks about it," she observed. "Why is this so closed off?" Residual guilt, sorrow, and shame keep nonfunctioning siblings safely sealed away.

Maggie Payne, whose borderline sister has fought with her for decades, had a similar experience when she asked members of her book club to volunteer to be interviewed on this topic. "They all shrank back," she said, "and I know that several of them have brothers who are a disaster. Why is this so hard to discuss? You have to admit the isolation of it, that you are embarrassed and upset." Maggie herself understands this reaction from the inside. "Only people who know me extremely well know I have a sister; she's not part of my life." Until recently Maggie never mentioned her sister's name because "it would have made her too real." Although she wants nothing more to do with the woman with whom she "never remember[s] a happy moment," she spoke about their shattered relationship with obvious distress. "She's had a profound effect on every area of my life," she said. "I wish she would have tried to understand; I would have been receptive. I've worked so hard on it." Although it grieves Maggie that they never will have a happy moment together, speaking her sister's name aloud permits her to work through their relationship within herself.

"Five years into therapy my therapist asked me why I never called my sister by name," said Jacob Wilde. "I got defensive, but he was correct. She is the door that never gets opened." Jacob and his embittered, isolated sister have not spoken for fifteen years. "Even thinking about her, let alone making contact with her, unsettles my image of my self, my life, and my family," he said. "I have my crazy core too, my own place where I don't want to reach out or be bothered with anybody. I'm not so different. Even though I molded myself into her opposite, I recognize there is another half to me—the shadow me that is 'not her,' the self I'm not supposed to be." You can never integrate what you amputate, and nobody without a shadow is real.

identification

Repudiators flee their shadows; overidentified siblings are enveloped in theirs. While they too strive to be different, they fear they are doomed to fail. They think they share more pathology than they actually do because they are psychically merged with their damaged brother or sister.

Marilyn Daniels, whose brother murdered a policeman, practically feels she committed the crime herself because she and her brother share DNA. "Just because I got a few more IQ points doesn't mean I don't have the same tendency," insisted this kind, highly responsible woman, who felt so guilty that she dropped out of college to punish herself at the time. "He's big and strong like me. Part of me longs for constant stimulation just like him. We're so connected it's amazing—he got the matter, and I got the antimatter. I know I'm the kind of person who could kill. Put me in a dark room with a baseball bat, and you want to be on my team, not the opposition. If this hadn't happened to him, who knows what I would have done?"

Convinced that her brother's act was a monstrous reflection on her own character, Marilyn isolated herself for years afterward. "It became harder to connect," she said. "What would people think of me?" Although she is now more forgiving of herself—and has never committed an aggressive act—she still does not trust her ability to control her hostility. "I continually question myself. I have to be on point to be sure I'm doing things right, because my standards are really low." Physiological kinship blinds her to her moral superiority.

Gentle people fear that they could be violent, and lively ones worry that they are dull. Ellen O'Brian, the thoughtful and intensely emotional illustrator, imagines that she is as tedious and flat as her seriously learning-disabled sister. "My identification with her is huge," said Ellen. "She's like some part of me—the worst part. She talks in a monotone about boring details, so when I ramble, I get concerned. She's definitely the source of my insecurity—'Will people like me? Am I strange like her?'"

Ellen believes she is indelibly tarred with the same brush as her unappealing sister because she was "clumped with her" by parents who prevented her from expressing anger and by classmates who picked on them both. Even though she overstates the case, she correctly identifies one damaging attitude they have in common: "the forced cheerfulness that covers an icky, painful sense of being defective." Years of reflection have helped the high-functioning sister overcome this unwelcome evidence of kinship. "I broke out of my shyness, although I still worry that no one will want me," she says, "and I'm trying not to be cut off from feelings." Developing herself in ways her sister cannot is teaching her that to share tendencies with another is not to share destinies.

Identifying too closely with a mentally ill sibling can be hazardous to your health. Psychiatrist Laura Russo's manic-depressive younger brother Tom, whom she had always admired for his daring and independence, once took her for a walk over slippery boulders on an ocean jetty in a storm. "The waves were crashing over the rocks," she remembered, "and he kept trying to edge me out. He wouldn't have minded if one or both of us had gone under—and I thought I was chicken for not doing what he wanted."

Laura was so merged with her beloved brother—and so invested in denying Tom's insanity—that she saw herself as a coward rather than him as a would-be fratricide. "Here I am in the profession," she said, "and I refused to believe Tom was ill until later, when he tried to hijack an airplane. Then I was stunned that I'd been confusing destructiveness with strength. I'd idealized him; I needed a healthy member of the family."

Twenty years after this horrifying incident, the toll Tom's illness has taken is unmistakable. "He was like a terrified animal when he had the breakdown," said his stylish, artistic sister with quiet anguish. "Now he looks like a weird homeless man. He's stabilized on medication, but hollowed out; it's like he's not there—I can't find the brother I love." With guilt and grief-stricken relief, she sees how alien he has become: "To see that Tom's the one suffering so greatly is unfathomable. It's a place I don't understand or make sense of. On one hand there's torment, and on the other secret gratitude that it's not me, that I never had to go to that degree, that I could always pull myself out. I'm very adept at protecting myself, but I have a deep resonance with his agony."

Laura never forgets how much the sophisticated physician and the sedated madman have in common; in fact, she is so acutely aware of her own potential for psychosis that she blurs the distinction between them. "He came out of the womb worried, but I was terribly shy as a child and didn't have any fun in my soul," she told me. "You might just as easily have thought I would be the one to have problems. There's a genetic component to this, so there but for the grace of God go I. We share a depressive core. I've gotten off easy—I just got the core; he got the whole ball of wax. I identify with him as being lost in the world; I have visited the shell he can't crawl out of. I never feel I'm all that far away from it; none of us are. My wearing black is not a fashion statement."

Laura still admires her brother's will and denigrates her own. "I wouldn't have the courage that Tom has to go on because I know the torture he's been through—I would have suicided long ago." She also knows how she has restricted her life and what she has lost to ensure her sanity: "I think, as he does, that people are not comforting, so I didn't marry—to care so much and hate so much would have made me more vulnerable, and that's not unlike him. In some ways he is my twin brother."

Although she knew it would be helpful to her to discuss Tom

("naming a disability makes it real"), Laura dreaded it; she still sees the world too much from her brother's paranoid perspective. "I'm terrified he'll read this," she told me, "and recognize himself, that he'll see how I have exposed him. It would reinforce the fact that he does not deserve to live because he's so crazy. To diagnose him or talk about him, even anonymously, feels like a betrayal."

When Laura calls Tom's delusion that his madness deserves the death penalty a "fact," and discussing her own feelings about their relationship a "betrayal," she shows how much her identity is still fused with his. Mental illness is not a capital offense, and she should not forfeit the right to her professional or personal judgments. To consider them intentional humiliations is her projection.

Disentangling one's own identity from a once-intimate sibling's is a lifelong process that is never watertight. Nonetheless Laura no longer denies major ways in which her world diverges from Tom's. "His safest state is to have nothing asked of him," she said. "That's not me; I want a lot asked. I am astonished at how much I've shaken loose from the brother I so adored, and how much our connection was based on my not recognizing who he was."

The distance separating the normal sibling from the abnormal one may still not feel very great at moments, but it is the difference between a vibrant if poignant life and a living death. The metaphor Laura used for this difference unconsciously recalls the fateful moment on the jetty when she began to define the boundary between them by refusing to be edged out to madness and returning to the shore: "he slipped through the cracks."

chapter 12

The Caliban Syndrome II: Acknowledgment

COMING TO TERMS with Caliban means that the "thing of darkness"—now not so dark and not so much of a thing—feels fully "mine." In my case, and for many normal siblings, acknowledgment meant recognizing that I made my closest relative into a "thing," that his image was indeed a dark force in my life, and that I denied ownership of the intimate, indelible connection between us. Affirming this truth required me to grieve for the pain I inflicted and the pain I suffered. It forced me to see through my myth of the happy family and the fantasy that I escaped unscathed or blameless. I had to face every feeling, no matter how shocking: that I hated, envied, and despised my own brother and wanted to get rid of him; that I took pleasure in his damaged state and wanted to call attention to it to elevate my own status in my family; that I did not want him to get better; and that I enjoyed my special place and its privileges. It also meant recognizing that my own childhood was amputated and that I was deprived of a precious bond that sustains other siblings and enriches their lives.

Acknowledging and owning the Caliban within does not change reality; it changes perspective. Coming to terms with a relationship does not necessarily improve the relationship or, as I found to my sorrow, bring about a lasting reconciliation. It does, however, increase compassion for Caliban and for yourself.

Acknowledgment takes a lifetime. It begins with recognizing that there is something to acknowledge in the first place, and it consists of equal parts mourning and appreciating, forgiving (at least yourself) and allotting responsibility. Many people use the metaphor of reluctantly opening doors ("my sister is the door I never open"; "I'm afraid that if I open that door, I'll never be able to close it")—usually ones that have been heavily padlocked and then concealed. Calling your brother or sister by name, and no longer excluding them from your thoughts, is an indication that the process has begun. Memories may resurface. Powerful, unexpected new emotions emerge; when siblings have been erased, increased anxiety about them should be welcomed. You may find yourself not crying as much, or as in my case, the tears may start.

My relationship with my brother, which so closely mirrors Miranda's with Caliban in *The Tempest*, exemplified the Caliban Syndrome. Survivor guilt, the only symptom I ostensibly lacked, proved the most telling, and the key to lessening its hold on me.

The four symptoms of the Caliban Syndrome diminish as acknowledgment proceeds:

premature maturity

Premature maturity becomes maturity—usually manifested as increased tolerance for immaturity. People feel that their lives no longer depend on being the good, undemanding, unflinchingly responsible, or self-sufficient miniadults their parents needed them to be, which also allows them to allow their own children to be children.

survivor guilt

Gratitude for good fortune replaces self-blame that it is undeserved, and accomplishments can be celebrated free of concern that they harm siblings.

compulsion to achieve

Success is no longer seen as an urgent necessity to compensate parents; people learn to relax.

fear of contagion

Repudiation and identification give way to acknowledgment—the compassionate recognition of partial kinship.

* * *

IN MIDDLE AGE two women with different family dynamics have come to similar conclusions about their situations. Each has mature understanding and acceptance coupled with self-knowledge that illuminates how she has overcome the Caliban Syndrome.

Janice Becker, the screenwriter who endured the double nightmares of fishing her psychotic sister out of the river and losing her depressed brother to suicide, is philosophical about her experiences. "Maybe I'm just a superficial person," this amiable, considerate woman suggested lightly but not unseriously. "I was guilty for a while, but then I realized that's stupid—what's the point of feeling guilty for your health?"

Both tragedies affect Janice deeply. She is not above weeping when she describes either her sister's degradation or her brother's death, and she "always has flowers at church for his birthday," but she knows her sanity distances her from both of them forever, and she is grateful for it. "I used to feel terrible that I wasn't understanding enough, because I knew things affected them in ways they didn't affect me," she said. "I could never understand the depth of despair he felt or comprehend her self-destructiveness. You do things if you love the person, so how come I can't make the extra leap to concentrate? I can't do it, and thank God I can't. I have a happy fulfilling life by refusing to be an active participant in pathological family behavior. What separates us is, I know I'm not mentally ill; I'm part of them, but I'm not."

Janice has come to feel responsible only for her own efforts and achievements, not for accidents of fate. "Years ago I wondered, 'Why is it them and not me? What made the roll of the dice go one way for me?' Now I realize that that's the nature of dice." Despite a lifetime of trauma, no one is less a victim than she. "Nobody has a normal family; it's a sliding scale. It's up to you to make what you can of what you have. It takes work—and," she adds with a knowing laugh, "superficiality."

Nina Parsons' envious, fragile, perpetually unemployed sister causes her aggravation and distress rather than anguish, but she too has learned to count her blessings. "I've made a decision not to be bitter," says this thoughtful playwright who has to work as a drama teacher to make a living. "I understand depression from the inside, but I've always been able to edge myself out of it." One way she does this is to discharge her hostility through art: she wrote a play about an envious sister who kills herself. Like therapists and special educators, artists are overrepresented among normal siblings. Fear of contagion has dissipated over the years and turned to relief. Nina does not apologize for her advantages. "When a sister's deformed, you're afraid it's catching, but when you grow up, you realize you're fortunate. You appreciate your luck compared to the other's misfortune, but you don't gloat because you're a decent person. The juxtaposition of weakness makes you appreciate your strengths and take more risks." Nina has also accepted the limitations of her relationship with her sister and found more functional, more generous replacements. "I've substituted close relationships with friends," she said. "They're like my older sisters now."

Once the rage that so many suppress surfaces and diminishes, sorrow comes to the fore; to know what you have gained, you must face what you have lost. Therefore mourning for the past, for what one woman called "my lost childhood," is a critical step in the integration process and one that is often neglected. As Jackie Hanson said, "Once I dealt with my intense guilt and anger about her, next came mourning and sadness; I saw what holes there were in my life.

People say you can't miss something you never had, but I definitely feel I missed out." Normal ones grieve for the loss of their childhood, their innocence, their possibilities for a unique kind of companionship, and for a feeling of optimism and order in the world that may not be realistic but keeps most people going. Their sorrow is not only about the past but about a future that can never be. "I think of all the adult rituals that other siblings have," said Jackie, "and I suddenly realize somebody's absent. My sister will never help me plan my wedding. A random law of nature that went awry caused this; it makes no sense then and now."

Though the grief can seem unsupportable, it is the most authentic emotion many siblings feel and one that was too threatening to express growing up. "I always seem more connected to myself when I'm really, really sad," said Carrie Grainger, whose schizophrenic brother disappeared into a mental hospital when he was seventeen. Before she cut off her feelings radically to protect herself, she remembered missing him so much that she would lie on the floor in his room and smell the carpet to remind herself of him. "I saw a movie trailer about two siblings where one breaks down, and I left the theater," she told me. If Carrie follows her grief wherever it leads, which is possible now that she has maturity, experience, and support, she will be able to remain in the theater in the future and perhaps regain some of her tie with her beloved, doomed brother.

Candy Fine, who is so afraid of her brother's bizarre violence that she is moving to France, is also oppressed by the tragedy of his life. "My brother's situation gives me an underlying sense of sadness, particularly after he lost his memory, for reasons no doctor can explain," she said. "What is it all for? Why are people born to live in this prison? He's had such a lonely, misunderstood life; when he dies, it will be the end of his sentence." This grief may never completely leave her, but she needs to realize and accept—as shocking as it sounds—that his death will end her sentence too.

Since coping with an abnormal child consumes massive amounts of a family's energy, normal ones are forced to shortchange their own experiences and feelings. "There are large gaps in my childhood," said Manny Resnick, who forfeited his acceptance to medical school so his obsessive-compulsive brother could attend. "I have only the outlines. When you grow up in a household with this going on, you shove everything under the rug, so my memories are attenuated." One of the things that is lost is your natural place and even your gender role in the family hierarchy. "I had to be the big brother," said the sister who was five years younger than her retarded brother. Normal ones know that the tumult of healthy family life—confidences, squabbles, moments of solidarity—is forever alien. A woman who always felt alone and estranged from her troubled sister said, "I always think growing up with regular siblings seems so foreign—how could it be possible?"

While mourning is necessary so there will be an end to mourning, many siblings are stuck in relentless, self-punitive remorse that makes closure impossible. In contrast, those whose brothers and sisters are functional hardly even remember childhood spats. At age fifty Pam Lewis still berates herself that she dressed her brother, who later became a paranoid schizophrenic, as a girl when he was three, as though she contributed to his pathology thereby. "I felt so bad looking back," she said. Carrie Grainger is sick with regret about her response as a typically clueless teenager to her soon-to-be-psychotic brother: "On my brother's sixteenth birthday, he wasn't sick yet, but he wasn't okay either. I got really furious with him and demanded, 'What's wrong with you for not being with friends?' I made him cry. It was the saddest moment of my life." More consistent lack of sympathy or empathy—let alone feeling repulsed, cold, or ashamed—provokes even more damning internal indictments. "My one regret in life is how I failed as a sister, that I couldn't feel compassion for my own brother," said Rebecca Ashford. Randy Lane condemned himself as "dishonorable and unchristian" for calling his brother names in a fight. Demanding saintliness of oneself is a symptom of unresolved premature maturity, and coming to realize that these untoward reactions are natural, inevitable, and no reflection on one's moral character is an essential part of self-acceptance. Embracing the abnormal sibling always involves embracing the flawed self as well.

Compensations for being the normal one emerge as grief and emotional perfectionism recede. Sober appreciation of what you have gained at so great a cost helps you feel consoled and proud. This recognition differs from the saccharine and self-obliterating exhortation to "count your blessings" forced on many normal ones in childhood, because it is based on having enumerated your curses first.

Many women with damaged brothers create intact surrogates through close friendships with men, as I have always done. "I seek brothers," Rebecca Ashford observed, "I treasure my male friends"—and she effortlessly feels the compassion for them that she lacks for her biological brother. Cindy Fine has a delicious, teasing camaraderie with a male coworker, complete with the practical jokes and nonsexual tussling that she would have longed to share with her actual brother if he had been robust enough. "I look for the sort of person who can take it," she said. Those whose sisters never functioned delight in their "wonderful women friends." Finding replacement siblings reaffirms their ability to feel fraternal love and assuages their grief for what will never be possible with their actual relatives. Adult satisfactions lessen the brunt of childhood sacrifices.

Women like Rebecca who were forced to assume inordinate responsibility for an unmanageable sibling are relieved not only to choose relationships as adults but also to be able to leave them guiltlessly. "I have a second chance of doing it right with my friends," Rebecca said. "I'll always be the reliable one, but I can change who I'm doing it for and not waste my time; inappropriate neediness, and I'm out of there."

Most normal siblings have no illusions about the difficulties of their childhoods, but they know that they also have more understanding as a result. Their self-knowledge is often deeper, their sensitivity to suffering heightened, and their appreciation of the human condition more profound than people who have had easier lives. Being a murderer's sister cost Marilyn Daniels years of anguish, but, she says, "it helped me to understand and embrace my own darkness. I really comprehend violence, rage, and drug addiction; we humans are all alike and so alone." Jennifer Martin's brother, afflicted with fatal muscular dystrophy, beat her when they were children and went on to become a scholar and spokesman for his illness before it killed him. "There's no scenario I can imagine that I couldn't handle because I've faced the worst already," she said. Her fury at her brother's brutality and her sorrow for his agony are now tempered with "immeasurable pride that he discovered a way to make a difference—that this man who would never be kissed found hope and love through his work." Anger at her own suffering commingles with appreciation for the courage that both siblings eventually showed.

Actor Jack Morelli feels that his reclusive sister is the source of his quirky humor, as well as the empathic solidarity with outsiders that informs his work. "I notice outcasts," said Jack. "My eyes are open in the margins because of Margaret; she's one of them. My impulse to be an artist comes out of some damage of my own and also from my sensitivity to her state, from thinking about it and watching it consciously." Jack no longer simply recoils from Margaret's strange personality, because he sees it as part of himself and as not without virtues: "We both have eccentric senses of humor based on strange repetitions—I've turned it into a successful style."

Jack is touched by the power of his parents' devotion to Margaret, misguided as it is. He also marvels at his sister's ability to enjoy the simple pleasures that are all she will ever have. "It's miraculous that she's never depressed. She's so thrilled and excited about the smallest things, like the first warm day. Margaret is now a source of pride," he said with admiration, even tinged with envy.

ALTHOUGH THE ESSENTIAL WORK of acknowledgment is integrating the subjective image of Caliban within the self, reconciliation—or a least a changed relationship—with the actual sibling frequently follows. The damaged one does not have to be capable of participating for this to occur and need not even be alive. But on rare and fortunate occasions a genuine rapprochement takes place—sometimes initiated by the newly insightful abnormal sibling himself.

Ben Ramsey never forgave his older brother David, the chronically unemployed singer whom he had dreamed coached him through his own first concert, for encouraging their father to disown him and kick him out of the house. "He had carte blanche in the family. His attitude was that I got what I deserved because I was provocative, so I had nothing more to do with him," said Ben, still smarting at age fifty-eight. "He's always been like a shape or an unpleasant presence that I try to stay away from as much as I can. There are lots of closed doors."

Ben was not exactly enthusiastic ten years ago, when David contacted him. "He was turning fifty and said he was setting goals and wanted to try to resolve the problems between us," Ben recalled. The meetings began shakily, "with lots of old hurts" on both sides. "In one of our first dinners," Ben recalled, "I told him he talks at me and doesn't have conversations. 'You're so self-centered,' he answered, 'that I feel I'm disappearing when you start to talk.' I realized that that's exactly how I feel with him—I experience another voluble presence making me disappear; there's no room for our two egos. As we continued talking, I found we both imagined each other as our father. I identified with him completely."

To their mutual astonishment, once they started communicating and listening to one another as adults outside their authoritarian father's sphere of influence, they found far more common ground than either could have imagined. Ben saw that neither of them had been spared, that each was both damaged and intact. He also started to appreciate David's virtues and to notice similarities that his own outrage had obscured. "He's more like me than my other siblings," Ben said. "The others rewrite, but he doesn't deny or make nice about how awful our father was. I had imagined he had the same vices as my father, but in fact he's a very good father himself. His two children are wonderful kids, and they're thriving. I really thought they'd be all fucked up, and they're great. It became more and more clear that the worst of him came out in relating to me."

The brothers now meet twice a year. David's grasping, devious wife, whom Ben detests, is a greater impediment to increased intimacy than David himself. While unconditional fraternal love will always elude them, much has been repaired. "He and I get along pretty well now and have gained more time—we talk about things besides personal history. We've put a lot to rest, and I can see he's a kind person. He's interesting—I like him now." The door that seemed barricaded forever has opened for good, and behind it Ben found a human being more genuinely related to him than he dreamed.

Only his death permitted my patient Nancy Solomon to convert her repudiation of and resignation to her brother into acknowledgment. With pained empathy I had been hearing about Nancy's wayward younger brother Joseph for years—how she tried repeatedly to make contact with him only to be rebuffed, how every conversation was strained and subtly accusatory, how she was unable to comprehend his life as a mostly unemployed technician living with a desperate welfare mother while she herself had long held a responsible job. I knew about her efforts to reconnect him with their parents, who had always preferred her and her middle-class life—her one success on his behalf. She had told me about Joseph's wild and lonely boyhood and how he had later turned to addiction and petty crime. Although her own childhood was full of pain and fear, she had been the dutiful daughter and the gifted student and had tried to be her brother's advocate far more than I had been for mine. But Joseph's sudden death at age forty-five, and the self-directed brutality with which he declined to fight his illness, was still a ghastly shock: though suffering from peritonitis and in extreme pain—the physician who performed the autopsy told her he had never seen anyone choose to endure such agony—he had refused to go to the hospital and had stayed silently in bed until the end.

Nancy was virtually motionless and mute for the next three months. She was overwhelmed not so much by the loss of her brother as by the circumstances of his death and what they revealed about his life, her life, and their relationship. The only way she could comprehend him, or assuage her guilt, was to mimic his self-destructive behavior.

Then one day she announced that she had finally said Kaddish for Joseph. Intoning the Jewish prayer for the dead laid many conflicting emotions to rest and allowed her to voice others that had previously been unspeakable. "I accept that he let himself die," she told me. "I so much understand what his despair felt like, because I've felt it too—the horrible longing and the floundering, the dread of falling into a black hole and being the black hole. You're the endlessly needy, empty vessel, and you're really angry at the same time—an empty vessel full of anger. When it comes down to brass tacks, you're out there alone and there is nobody to help."

Nancy understood that neither she nor anyone else could reach her brother, because no relationship can be sustained unilaterally; despite their shared despair, their paths no longer intersected. "At a certain point I just couldn't try anymore," she admitted. "What did I have in common with this man? I was the good child, and he was the bad one. I was not the best of sisters. We were opposites, and we were set in opposition by our parents, so we couldn't have each other for support or be a united source of strength. My relationship with my parents is much easier without him."

Three things changed as a result of Nancy's admission: she accepted her parents' offer to transfer Joseph's inheritance to her, she made them dinner and served the dishes that the three of them preferred but had avoided at family occasions because her brother disliked them, and she married the man she had been afraid to commit to for five years. She chose life.

TALKING IS A FUNDAMENTAL FORM of self-expression. Learning to speak their minds, to voice taboo thoughts and feelings, is critical for normal ones, who are so often nonpersons in their families and strangers to themselves. But for Jackie Hanson, whose sister Joan—the one who ate her homework—was mute as well as autistic, learning to speak for herself changed her life. It also made a genuine if forever wordless relationship with her sister possible.

Jackie's childhood mission was to provide her sister with a mouthpiece, and she had to silence herself to accomplish it. "She didn't have a voice, so I became her voice," she explained. "I'd make up what she was saying; it was as if I were actually speaking for her." For her part, Joan performed the role of the nonverbal pseudoconfidante: "I confided in her, but not in a meaningful, two-way way." So much of Jackie's energy was "directed to tuning into Joan and being perfect" that she tuned herself out. She never "revealed"—or even entered—her own inner world.

In Jackie's consciousness and in everyone else's eyes, the sisters were fused physically as well as vocally. "We look a lot alike, so people joke that we're twins. So much of how I understood myself was in relation to her—I defined myself not as an individual but as a conjoined [i.e., Siamese] twin." But since Joan was "destructive and embarrassing—she looks so normal, though her behavior is so abnormal," Jackie made sure that her own behavior was always constructive and a source of pride. "I couldn't be aggressive in public," she said. "I was so restrained because she was so much the opposite."

Maintaining this artificial state of merger kept Jackie ignorant of the parts of herself that were disturbingly like her sister. By depositing all rage and impulsiveness safely in Joan, and by assuming the role of Joan's devoted spokeswoman, she could remain Miranda-like; she was selfless in both senses of the word.

Two dreams revealed Jackie's predicament and how she resolved it. In the first she told herself why she became Jackie/Joan despite the liabilities:

> The newest camper in my bunk at summer camp was a frail, deformed child who barely looked like a person. Nobody wanted anything to do with her because she had sharp bony spikes; if you touched her she'd break, but it would also be very painful. I decided I had to be connected with her—this was the only person I could relate to—so I picked her up. I felt instant rapport, intense love, and an immense sense of fulfillment and gratitude.

"The spikes were her illness," Jackie said, "but her fragility was an illusion. We had this intense nonverbal bond where everything that needed to be said was spoken through contact, like a mind-meld. Nobody else paid attention to us."

Jackie's interpretation of her dream expresses her insights into the meaning of her merger with her actual sister and explains why she perpetuated a bond that was actually bondage. But the dream has an additional level of symbolic significance: her dream-sister is also herself, the part of her that feels fragile and repulsive, that is harmful and frightening to others, that retreats into a wordless, infantile, symbiotic world with Joan. Their idealized blissful union allowed Jackie to avoid the real world, real relationships, and threatening feelings. But in the dream Jackie was telling herself that the spiky camper is also the she-Caliban within who must be acknowledged and distinguished if the real Jackie is to speak.

Jackie's second dream, which she had after her sister was institutionalized, indicated that the separation was proceeding. Although it fulfilled a lifelong fantasy, she felt sad when she awoke:

> People were being split up into groups, and Joan and I were assigned to separate groups. She suddenly became much smaller—I was my adult size and I was holding her like a child. The adult me (I was an adult and a child at the same time) agreed that it would be okay, that she should go with them. Then all of a sudden she said one sentence: "I want to stay with you."

Since this dream was Jackie's creation, she was responsible for all its events. She separated her sister from herself, and she also put her own wish into her sister's mouth. These contradictory dream-actions reveal how conflicted she is about being "grouped" with Joan. The sadness she felt was her sense of loss as she chose to grow up and away from Joan. Accepting that she wanted to "split" from her sister allowed her to see herself as an adult, for to stay merged would have doomed her to be a speechless, dependent child forever.

The distinction between them had now become unmistakable. "She's not my peer," Jackie said. "We've not developed the same. We've diverged—she's immature and always will be."

Jackie now faced another hurdle. Once she discovered her own voice and learned to listen to it, the things she heard were shocking; she had to revise her self-image to include the Joan-parts and the buried feelings. "I felt intense guilt and anger at her that I never knew were there before," she said. "I had never let myself recognize I hated her because I would have hated myself; now I can't stop experiencing it." Jackie wisely credits recognizing her negative emotions with transforming her merger with Joan into genuine sisterhood; she recently decided to become Joan's guardian. "It feels fine and voluntary," she said. "I used to define connection as obligation—dealing with all my feelings about her changed that. Because I can be ambivalent, because I'm not denying, I can really relate to her now." Jackie knows that her merger with Joan also allowed her to avoid her true peers, who could speak. "I have to face this void and not fill it artificially," she said.

Separating from Joan not only permitted Jackie's individuality to develop; it inspired her vocation as a professional advocate for the disabled who frequently speaks out on the plight of normal siblings. This career is not a reflexive continuation of her earlier merger but expresses the mature desire to better the lot of Joan and others like her, as well as sympathy for others like herself. She has achieved what every normal one must strive for: to speak in a voice that is genuine and truly your own.

When you fully acknowledge Caliban, you are no longer the normal one, the person who either repudiates or identifies with your damaged sibling more than you know; you are yourself.

bibliography

The following works most influenced my understanding of siblings, especially those with abnormal brothers and sisters.

FICTION

William Shakespeare, *The Tempest*

Tennessee Williams, *The Glass Menagerie*

PSYCHOANALYTIC BOOKS AND PAPERS

Virtually all psychoanalytic texts, including every one I consulted, refer to *The Standard Edition of the Complete Psychological Works of Sigmund Freud* (London: Hogarth Press, 1966). Of Freud's works, *The Interpretation of Dreams* had the most direct influence on *The Normal One.*

Abrams, Jules, and Florence Kaslow, "Learning Disability and Family Dynamics: A Mutual Interaction," *Journal of Clinical Child Psychology* (Spring 1976): 35–40.

Describes the impact of a particular and subtle disability on families from a psychodynamic perspective.

Agger, Eloise, "Psychoanalytic Perspectives on Sibling Relationships," *Psychoanalytic Inquiry* 8 (1983): 3–30.

A seminal paper calling attention to this neglected area of study.

bibliography

Akhtar, Salman, and Selma Kramer, ed., *Brothers and Sisters: Developmental, Dynamic, and Technical Aspects of the Sibling Relationship* (Northvale, NJ: Jason Aronson, 1999).

This book, written for professional psychoanalysts, consists of eight papers. Rosemary Balsam's brilliant (and accessibly written) contribution, "Sisters and Their Disappointing Brothers" was a revelation of my own buried psychology. Harold Blum's discussion of Balsam's paper, "The Legacy of the Defective and Dead Sibling," was also useful. Other papers in this book that informed my thinking included Salman Akhtar and Selma Kramer's "Beyond the Parental Orbit: Brothers, Sisters, and Others" and Vamik Volkan's "Childhood Sibling Rivalry and Unconscious Womb Fantasies in Adults."

Balsam, Rosemary, "On Being Good: The Internalized Sibling with Examples from Late Adolescent Analyses," *Psychoanalytic Inquiry* 8 (1988): 66–87.

Insightful and helpful in understanding my own sibling experience.

Bank, Stephen, and Michael Kahn, *The Sibling Bond* (New York: Basic Books, 1982).

Chapter 9, "The Embroiled Family: 'Well' and 'Disturbed' Siblings," clarified my understanding of how families (including my own) assign roles to siblings, and how these roles become part of each sibling's identity.

Bergmann, Thesi, and Sidney Wolfe, "Observations of the Reactions of Healthy Children to their Chronically Ill Siblings," *Bulletin of the Philadelphia Association of Psychoanalysis* 21(1971): 145–61.

One of the earliest psychoanalytic attempts to understand the experience of normal ones via case studies.

Charles, Marilyn, "Sibling Mysteries: Enactments of Unconscious Fears and Fantasies," *Psychoanalytic Review* 86, no. 6 (1999): 877–900.

This recent article was instrumental in clarifying how their own unresolved traumas cause parents to pass Caliban on.

Graham, Ian, "The Sibling Object and Its Transferences: Alternate Organizer of the Middle Field," *Psychoanalytic Inquiry* 8 (1988): 88–107.

This paper helps explain and remedy the neglect of siblings in the psychoanalytic literature.

Lidz, Theodore, Stephen Fleck, Yrjo Alanen, and Alice Cornelison, "Schizophrenic Patients and Their Siblings," *Psychiatry* 26 (1963): 1–18.

In a study based on one of the most extensive, in-depth studies of the families of schizophrenics, the authors specifically address how and why the siblings of catastrophically disturbed people escape mental illness.

Solnit, Albert, Ruth Eissler, and Peter Neubauer, eds., *The Psychoanalytic Study of the Child* 38 (New Haven: Yale University Press, 1983).

One section of this annual volume is devoted to "The Sibling Experience." Of the six papers therein, Alice Colonna and Lottie Newman's "The Psychoanalytic Literature on Siblings"—which revealed the astonishing paucity of information about them—was eye-opening. "Parents and Siblings: Their Mutual Influences" by Marianne Kris and Samuel Ritvo, and Janice Abarbanel's "The Revival of the Sibling Experience During the Mother's Second Pregnancy," provided valuable insights into the hidden aspects of family dynamics. Hansi Kennedy's "Growing Up with a Handicapped Sibling," in volume 40 (1985) of the same publication, includes case studies that specifically address the unconscious aspects of being a normal one.

Titelman, David, "Grief, Guilt and Identification in Siblings of Schizophrenic Individuals," *Bulletin of the Menninger Clinic* 55 (1991): 72–85.

Case studies of anguished normal ones, written with great empathy.

Volkan, Vamik, and Gabriele Ast, *Siblings in the Unconscious and Psychopathology* (Madison, CT: International Universities Press, 1997).

Waugaman, Richard, "On Patients' Disclosure of Parents' and Siblings' Names During Treatment," *Journal of the American Psychoanalytic Association* 38 (1990): 167–94.

This paper makes the important point that calling siblings by their names makes them real.

OTHER (NONPSYCHOANALYTIC) PSYCHOLOGICAL PUBLICATIONS

Seligman, Martin, *The Family with a Handicapped Child: Understanding and Treatment* (New York: Grune and Stratton, 1983).

Dr. Seligman's paper "Siblings of Handicapped Persons" describes the inner world and family experience of normal ones and surveys extant studies.

Stoneman, Zolinda, and Phyllis Berman, eds., *The Effects of Mental Retardation, Disability and Illness on Sibling Relationships: Research Issues and Challenges* (Baltimore: Paul H. Brookes, 1993).

An overview of research methodologies and findings.

Vadasy, Patricia, Rebecca Fewell, Donald Meyer, and Greg Schell, "Siblings of Handicapped Children: A Developmental Perspective on Family Interactions," *Family Relations* 33 (1984): 155–67.

A survey of studies on the effect of seriously disabled children on families.

BOOKS FOR THE GENERAL READER

Featherstone, Helen, *A Difference in the Family: Living with a Disabled Child* (New York: Penguin, 1981).

A moving and insightful work written by a psychologist about her own experience; it also includes research findings.

index

about the author

Jeanne Safer, Ph.D., has been practicing psychotherapy for twenty-eight years. A supervisor and faculty member at the Postgraduate Center for Mental Health and the National Institute for the Psychotherapies, Dr. Safer is the author of *Beyond Motherhood: Choosing a Life Without Children,* and *Forgiving and Not Forgiving: Why Sometimes It's Better* Not *to Forgive. Beyond Motherhood* and *The Normal One* were finalists for the Books for a Better Life Award. Dr. Safer lives in New York City.

Printed in the United States
by Baker & Taylor Publisher Services